Promiscuous Gir
Wale

MW00416956

Nicole Jackson

COPYRIGHT© 2016 Promiscuous Girl: Keyasia and Wale by Nicole Jackson Published by Nicole Jackson Presents. Unless otherwise indicated, all materials on these pages are copyrighted by the Nicole Jackson. All rights reserved. No part of these pages, either text or image may be used for any purpose other than personal use. Therefore, reproduction, modification, in any form or by any means, electronic, mechanical or otherwise, for reasons other than personal use, is strictly prohibited without prior written permission.

Nicole Jackson

Contact Info:

Author Nicole Jackson | **Facebook**

nicole3317@gmail.com

This book is dedicated to a few people closest to me. I wrote this book, while several things were happening in my life. Serious situations. So, this goes to my cousin LaTonya, and then Corinthian. (I stole his name) And to my business partner/ex/whatever I want him to be Super Man aka Keith (free him) With them sweaty ass hands. But yall aint heard that from me. LOL. Here's another one.

Nicole Jackson

Chapter 1

Holding her cell in her hand, she contemplated. At this point there was really nothing more to say. It was what it was, but he wouldn't give up. Amir Junior could be quite convincing, but Keyasia was no longer under his spell.

Still, there were some remnants of the feeling he once provided, which urged her to answer.

"Whaaat?" she huffed into her cell.

"Man, why you playing with me, Key?" Amir Junior fumed.

She sucked her teeth, and rolled her eyes. Due to their facetiming he could see her disdain for him, clearly. "Nigga, please. Why are you playing with *me*, is the better fuckin' question?"

"So, busting out my windows and slashing my tires is cool, right?"

She grimaced, as she pointed directly at the camera. "That should tell you to stop playing with me. I kept telling you that I'm not the one. You had to learn the hard way, though."

Licking his lips, he fought to keep his composure. "Look, Key, I didn't call to argue. You fucked up the Beamer. You did that. But Ion care about that shit. That car can be replaced. I'm concerned about the fact that you won't talk to me. It's been weeks, and I miss the hell out of you."

She pursed her lips, unwilling to fall for his bullshit. "As you should. I haven't talked to you for a reason. Let's not forget."

He squinted his eyes. "And what reason is that?"

Nicole Jackson

She tossed her head back. "God, this boy. Always playing crazy."

Amir sat studying her. She was always with the dramatics, but in a weird way he loved that about her. There was definitely never a dull moment. "You done yet?" he questioned the moment she focused on the camera again.

"That's the point *I'm* trying to make." She bucked her eyes. "I'm done. Finished. Through, nigga. So, why the fuck are you on my line?"

"But why are you through?" he pressed.

"Huuuh," he huffed in frustration. "Because you're a liar. A cheater. A manipulator. A fucking coward. Do I need to continue?"

He grimaced, as he licked his lips. "But where did all this come from? We were just chilling. Doing us, and then you just went left."

"Okay." She nodded, as she slid her tongue across her teeth. "I see that I have to break it down for you. First off, I should've left your ass alone for good when this whole baby situation popped up. I'm really not in the step-mama kind of spirit. But nooo, I let you talk me into giving us another shot. I thought that you would be appreciative of how forgiving I was, but I was mistaken. You took my kindness for weakness, and every time something goes wrong between us I see online that you're having family day with ya BM. How fuckin' convenient. And this is after you swore up and down that it was nothing between you and Ugmo but that baby. But now the bitch is my sometimes competition, and nobody has time for that. The bitch aint on my level, and if you wanna flex your muscle, and show me that you have options…then I can't deal. I'll become a non-factor, and let you do you. The shit is too much, and I didn't ask for this."

"Man, what are you talking about? We took our daughter to Chuck E Cheese. What's wrong with that? I aint fucking with that girl beyond our daughter. The fuck are you talking about?"

Keyasia scowled. "Boy, miss me with that. Aint no fuckin' family days if you're my man. You pick your child up, do yall, and bring her back home. That's it. But that's beside the point. You think that bitch Val doesn't want me out of the picture? She wants her fuckin' family, and is willing to do anything for me to leave the equation. So, that's why she had no shame in sending me a video of yall fucking on the comforter I bought your dog ass!"

Amir's heart dropped down to his stomach. Val, the so-called good girl, had stooped to a new low. He'd been adamantly clear about where his heart belonged, which was rightly with Key. But Val had fallen helplessly in love, and wanted them to give their child a fair shot at a complete family. Therefore, she'd respected no boundaries, and Amir had been thinking with the wrong head. He was blinded by Val's beauty, and Keyasia's difficulty at times propelled him to take the easier route. And he was now paying for his infractions.

"Alright, baby, I admit it. I fucked up. But Ion want her. On my daughter, Ion want her. Tell me what I gotta do. Please. I'm begging. Just meet me somewhere, and let's talk about this," he pleaded desperately.

"Talk about what? About how you'll change? Or how you won't do it again? Negro please. You've shown me your true colors. Out here fucking unprotected, making babies. That shit alone is really unforgivable, and then you have the nerve to play on my insecurities. Dangle that bitch in my face whenever you claim I aint acting right. Hell, nah. She can have that headache. So, get off my line, and go make some more light skinned babies with the high yellow bitch. Fuck you, *and* her. Now, good-bye." She ended the call.

For a few seconds she sat there in silence. There was a huge part of her that wanted to bawl her eyes out. After giving him over two years of her young life, she and Amir were done. He was the boy she'd known forever, and her parents loved him. He was a junior in college, had stellar grades, and had a bubbling career as a music producer. He'd been good to her in several ways, and she'd bought into the dream of them being forever. Then he throws it all away for a drunken night out with the boys. This was the night he gave into his lustful desires, bedding the prissy, smart, and beautiful Val. The chick Keyasia couldn't stand.

In Key's eyes, Val was the sneaky type who thought her shit didn't stink. She was highly intelligent, and her parents were well off. The signature good girl. But she had a thing for the very unavailable Amir Junior, and Key had always known it. They all attended TSU together, and the only reason she hadn't beaten the brakes off Val was because she was rather cool with Val's girl, Sye. Sye had been adamant about keeping the peace between the two, and Key had given her a pass. Only for Val to succeed in fucking her man. That fact wasn't revealed, until Val came up pregnant. That was when Amir was outed, and had to confess his sin to Keyasia. Still, he swore that he wore a condom, and there was no way that the child was his. So, nine months later, a DNA test was administered, and he was determined to be the father. Needless to say, Key was devastated, and ended her and Amir's relationship. But months later she found herself giving him another chance, after realizing that she still loved him. He'd sworn to never hurt her again, and now here they were.

She was single, and losing faith in finding a guy at her age that was true. No, she wouldn't stop believing in love, because she'd witnessed it firsthand with her parents. Her father loved her mother to death, and it showed. Therefore, Key knew that true love existed, but history had also shown her that guys typically took forever to get their shit together. She wasn't sure if she wanted to love a man past his flaws and all. She hadn't learned to be that accepting, and didn't know if she ever would be. Therefore, she felt this overwhelming sense of needing to be selfish, and put her needs first. Basically, do exactly what those niggas do. Whatever the hell she wanted.

The tapping on her window snapped her back to reality. "Baby, you ready?"

Keyasia shifted in the driver's seat of her Range Rover. Tucking away her phone into her Tom Ford icon clutch, she squared her shoulders, before pushing her door open. "Yeah, I'm ready."

Cane greedily rubbed his hands together, as he watched her ease out of her whip. It was hard to believe that he'd gotten her number at a gas station just a week prior, and now he was taking her out for the world to see. Keyasia was a thick, 5'7, honey complexion, beauty. In fact, she was one of the hottest chicks he'd ever snagged, and he was definitely going to capitalize on the opportunity with her.

The white Tom Ford strapless fitted dress Key wore hugged her curves, causing Cane to grab his hard-on through his jeans, as she sauntered over to the Benz he'd pulled up in. Briefly, checking out the CLS she nodded in approval. The car was official.

"Oh, okay. I see you. I like the car," she complimented, remembering she'd met him in a Cadillac.

"It's nothing, lil' mama," he offered smoothly, as he opened the passenger's door for her.

Like a true gentleman, he watched her ease into the vehicle, before closing the door for her. She gently smiled, appreciating the gesture. He then raced around the front of the car, and hopped in on the driver's side.

"Let's get the shit started, main," he expressed gleefully. "Expose you to this real nigga right here. And maybe next time you'll let me scoop you up from your crib."

Key grinned. "Wishful thinking, huh?"

He shook his head. She wouldn't bend on the issue. For whatever reason, she didn't want him to know where she lived, and had him meet her in a shopping center out in the burbs. He figured she was just being precautious, and respected her decision. That within itself told him that she was different from most broads he'd dated.

"Okay, okay." He nodded. "I hear you. But I bet your mind is changed by the end of the night."

She glanced over at him. Cane was a handsome medium brown complexioned guy. He had a few tattoos, and a bottom grill in his mouth. Per the fly guy uniform, he rocked a Robin's ensemble. He smelled nice, and seemed to possess quite a bit of swagger, so she was a little intrigued. And that night she was going to see what he was all about, and at the most have a little fun. But nothing too heavy.

"And how are you going to change my mind?" she arched a brow.

"By showing you that you're in good hands. We're hitting up Pure tonight. Popping a few bottles, and turning up in the only fashion we should."

"Is that right?"

"Hell, yeah," he insisted. "I got a section, and everything. It's whatever you like tonight."

She nodded with her bottom lip poked out. "Well, aint nothing wrong with that. Let the turn up begin."

******

"The alarm is disabled, nigga."

Wale slowly nodded, before speaking into his burner phone. "Alright, bet. Stay on the lookout." Ending the call, he placed the cell in his pocket. Securing the ski mask over his face, his two comrades took that as their signal to get to work. With glove covered hands, swinging their sledge hammers, they plowed into the rooftop of the building. Relentlessly, the three men worked, until there was a gaping hole in the roof. "Drop down," he instructed his boy Big Block.

Fearlessly, Big Block dropped to his knees, before lowering his body into the hole. He then released the ledge of the roof, dropping down into the store. Shortly after, Wale and his cousin Meeko followed suit. With precision, Wale landed directly on his feet, while his cousin stumbled to the ground. Shaking his head, he proceeded on his mission, whipping out a heavy duty trash bag. With full confidence, he knew that his boy Drake had disabled the alarming system, as he smashed the glass casing which held the luxurious jewelry. Swiftly, he snatched up every piece of jewelry in sight, tossing the items into the bag, as Meeko and Big Block did the same. In less than sixty seconds, they'd cleaned out the entire shop. They then scurried to the back door, bypassing all the security cameras. Unlocking the door, they raced out of the building, jogging down the parking lot, before practically diving into the awaiting minivan.

Giving a head nod to his big homie Bee, who was sitting at the corner of the block in a tow truck, they casually drove off the block.

"Was it like taking candy from a baaa-by?" Drake questioned with a grin.

"You already know," Wale breathed, as he removed his black hoodie, and sweats. He would never get caught wearing the same thing seen on camera. "Pull over, Trace."

Doing as he was told, the driver, Trace, pulled over to the side of the road, where a black Escalade was waiting.

"Put the license plate back on here, man. And park this bitch," Wale ordered, as he exited the vehicle.

"I got you. I'ma link up in a few," Trace said, as all the other men filed out of the van, as well.

"Alright," Wale nodded, before jumping into the passenger's seat of the Escalade. While the other men got situated in the truck, and Trace pulled off, he picked up the burner to call Bee.

"Yall good?" Bee questioned the moment he picked up.

"You already know," Wale responded, as his cousin Craven, the driver of the Escalade, pulled away from the curb.

"That's straight. I haven't picked up on a police dispatch yet, so it looks like clean green money."

"Clean, huh?" Wale grinned in a celebratory fashion.

"Hell, yeah," Bee clarified.

"Aye, sounds good to my ears, ya feel me? But we're headed to the spot. Come through."

"Shit, I'll probably beat you niggas there."

He chuckled. "Shit, I wouldn't be surprised. See you there." He ended the call.

"So, who's buying this shit, man?" Meeko questioned.

Wale shrugged him off, as he gazed out of the window. "You let me worry about that. For tonight, we're about to divide this shit up so it won't be no issues. If any of you niggas decide to do something different with your pieces, then that's on you. But I'm meeting with the people tomorrow, getting rid of all my shit. But I aint bringing nobody with me. I can tell you a price for all your shit, and bring your money back. But this aint a dictatorship, and niggas can do what they want. So, take the prices or leave 'em. It's on yall. But personally I aint holding on to this hot shit."

"Aye, as long as I can get fifty racks or better, I'm good. I know your bitch ass is gonna clutch," Big Block chuckled, but was being blunt, as usual. Anyone with the connections was going to eat a little more than the rest. It was a part of the game, and he wasn't mad. There'd been several jobs where he had the buyers in the pocket, and ate a little more. It was what it was, and if somebody didn't like it, they were free to find their own buyers, but no one ever did.

Wale laughed. "I aint even gonna speak on it." He lowered the window, tossing out the burner phone, as Craven drove down the freeway.

Twenty minutes later, they pulled up to Trace's house. Once there, they all piled out of the car, and ambled into his home. Having to ditch the van first, Trace himself hadn't made it there, yet, but his baby mother, Monkey, had let everyone else inside. One by one, they all flopped down onto his couch. Wasting no time, they emptied their bags of jewels.

At an earlier time, the Jared's jewelry store had been cased, therefore they'd priced most pieces. So, they sat there, sorting through it all, distributing the gains accordingly. After collecting his share of the win, Wale powered on his personal cell. The iPhone buzzed continuously from all the notifications he was receiving.

"Man, them hoes act like you got gold at the tip of your dick," Big Block chuckled, after hearing Wale's cell go off.

"Shit," Wale stroked his goatee. "I might do, nigga. Just ask your baby mama or your sister. But then again, if it is you better be trying to be a nigga friend," he rapped the Fifth Ward Boyz's hood anthem, playfully.

"If you did fuck my BM you didn't do a good job. That bitch still won't get a fuckin' life, and move the fuck around," Big Block grumbled.

Wale cheesed, as he stood up with his bag in tow. "That sounds like a personal problem. That's why I leave them kids where they at. Aint no hoe about to drive me crazy…especially one as ugly as Tam," he referred to Big Block's baby's mama.

All Big Block could do was chuckle.

"You gone?" Meeko glanced up, while attempting to gather his pieces of jewelry.

"Hell, yeah." Wale stretched, and yawned. "I gotta run by the house, and change."

Craven nodded. "You still trying to make it to Pure I see."

"You already know. I'ma slide through, and see what I can take home. You know. Get a little head up out a bopper."

"I bet any kind of money you gon end up with that crazy bitch, Mona," Big Block predicted.

Wale shrugged. "If that's how the wind blows. But I'm out. I'll see whoever falls through at the club."

"A'ight, boi," all the other men said simultaneously.

Tucking his phone into his pocket, he sauntered out of the house. Speedily, he stepped to his Audi, and hopped in. With a push of a button on the side of his steering wheel, a hidden panel behind his navigation system extended out, and he grabbed his nine millimeter within the compartment, replacing it with the bundled up bag of jewels.

After cautiously checking the perimeter, he started his car, and backed out of the yard with his nine in his lap. No matter how easy a job seemed, he'd always stay on his P's and Q's. Not only did he have to look out for the jackers, but also the very people he ate with. The thought of a co-conspirator becoming greedy, and knowing exactly what he had on him never left his mind. Money was the root of all evil, and no one could be fully trusted. Therefore, regardless of being a convicted felon carrying,

Wale was willing to take a pistol case over a body bag any day. His Nina never left his side.

Sometimes he had to ask himself if he was crazy. The money he made with his hustle was beautiful, and afforded him a luxurious lifestyle. But there were so many hazards. There was never a time where he could fully relax. As long as he was getting it, he'd be a target. Then the alternative was being broke, which in his eyes was the equivalence of being dead. To live freely in this world, a man needed money, and Wale was going to live it up to the fullest. He knew no other way.

Pulling up to his two-story townhouse, he parked his car. After carefully surveying his surroundings, he removed the trash bag from the hidden panel, before easing out of his ride. Within a flash he was in his crib, racing up the stairs. As soon as he stepped into his room, he rushed to conceal his wins for the night. He then proceeded to get dressed.

On the nightstand, his cell was vibrating like crazy, and reluctantly he picked up. "Say?"

"So, you good. You straight? Cause you aint call and tell me shit. Got me over here worried out of my damn mind," Mona complained.

"Aye," he drawled, while he pulled two chains over his head, as he stood in front of the built-in mirror on his wall. "Don't start that. You know I'm straight as always, but I really don't wanna hear all that bullshit." He held the phone to his ear, while stroking his waves, as he checked himself out.

"I'm just saying, Wale," she softened her tone. "You could've called and let me know what's up with you. I can't help that I'm concerned."

"A'ight. I get that, but still," he responded, as he casually strolled into his closet. There he grabbed an iron, removed the bottom, grabbed a bundle of cash out of it, stuffed it in his jeans, before putting the iron back where he'd found it. "Quit that nagging shit. It drives me crazy. And on the cool, I just got in, so it wasn't like I didn't give you a call. I haven't been given the chance."

"Okay," she sighed. "Am I seeing you tonight?"

A flash of her riding his dick ran across his mind. "I don't know. The night is young like a muthafucka."

"Well, when you decide to retire in, make *this* your final stop. Those bitches out there aint gon do you right."

He grinned. "How you know?"

"Shit, call me crazy, but you don't find yourself in my bed most mornings for nothing."

He bit his bottom lip. "Can't argue with that. But I gotta go. I'ma call you later."

"No don't call. Cum," she purred into the phone.

He chuckled. "Only if it's in your mouth."

"Ooh," she shivered. "Can I swallow?"

He grabbed his dick, knowing at that exact moment that she'd be the final stop at the end of the night for sure, now. "Damn. I'll be there around five."

Chapter 2

"We don't wait in lines, baby," Cane whispered in Keyasia's ear, as they stepped into Pure.

"I feel you," she nodded, letting him get his shine on. Knowing when a man was sticking his chest out, she didn't think it was the appropriate time to tell him that she never waited in any lines, regardless of who she'd step into the club with. But he could have the moment.

"I don't know who you're referring to, who is this nigga you heard about? Someone just talking that bullshit, someone just gave you a run around. Niggas downplaying the money, but that's what you do when the money's down…" Drake's voice blared from the speakers.

After navigating through the throngs of clubbers, they stepped to a sizable section. She discreetly nodded her head in approval. It was definitely something she'd have if she'd chosen to come there on her own. The thing was, there were already several dudes there turning up, and he'd never mentioned the fact that they'd be partying with an entourage. A very rough looking entourage at that. Although, all the men were dressed in expensive threads, she recognized street cats a mile away, and it was stamped all over every individual's face within the section.

"Come on, baby," he grabbed her hand, tugging her up the steps that led to the sectioned off area. "What's popping, niggas?" he asked, as all his boys' eyes landed on him and his guest.

"What's up?" several men greeted him, simultaneously with the usual hood handshake.

"Aint shit," Cane coolly responded, before reaching down, snatching up one of several Cîroc bottles sitting on a table. Tossing his head back, he lifted the bottle, pouring the premium vodka into his mouth, before guzzling it down.

Keyasia noticed one dude who'd quickly approached Cane. Immediately, she was struck by his attractiveness. He was at least 6'3 in height, had a peanut butter complexion, a bowlegged stance, thick wavy hair, and absolutely gorgeous hazel green eyes. He stood with two heavy chains dangling from his neck that was flooded with diamonds. On his wrist there was a diamond incrusted watch that was nearly blinding. The Versace unit he sported was rather stylish, and appeared almost tailored to his immaculate physique.

"What happened to you picking up Bubble Gum?" the dude questioned Cane over the loud music.

"Aww, man, I got tied up. After I picked up my lil' mama, there wasn't much time left. I thought she'd get another ride," Cane explained.

Keyasia studied the exchange closely. Why would Cane have to explain himself to another man was beyond her.

The man grimaced. "So, you came here without my cousin? That was the whole fuckin' reason I let you use my car, nigga. The fuck? You shouldn't have come, if you wasn't picking her up."

Keyasia pursed her lips, realizing that she'd been duped. All that bragging Cane had been doing since she'd been in his presence, all the while he was fronting, driving the next man's vehicle.

"My bad, man. I really thought that she would've came, regardless. That's what she usually do."

The dude narrowed his eyes. "Then why the fuck would I bother telling you to go get her?"

Cane scratched the side of his neck, hoping that Keyasia wasn't fully hearing their conversation. "I don't know, dog. I mean, if you want, I can still run to go get her."

"Fuck all that," the guy waved him off. "She's already on the way."

"Good," Cane nodded, taking the bottle to the head again.

In mid-guzzle, the man snatched the bottle out of Cane's grasp. "You aint getting fucked up off me, nigga. Buy your own shit. Can't even do simple shit I ask you to do. And find a way back to your own fuckin' car."

"Wale, my nigga, you know I aint mean to leave her stranded. Come on, dog. I got my lil' friend with me." he cut his eyes at Key.

The man by the name of Wale deepened his scowl. "What that got to do with me?"

Sucking his teeth, Cane shook his head in disbelief. He'd been played in front of a broad who he wanted desperately to impress. Now, he couldn't even look at her in the eyes. "Come on, let's sit down," he instructed, pulling her over to the couches.

Sitting down, Keyasia felt out of place. She was obviously kicking it with an underling, and it was seeming that he'd gotten into the section by the skin of his teeth. Very unwelcoming. With all the talk of them partying in *his* section, and drinking *his* bottles, his lies had been exposed. Nothing was his. But that wasn't the issue as far as Key was concerned. She couldn't get with the fact that he'd lied.

She shook her head, having half the mind to leave Cane sitting there alone, looking stupid. But the club was too live, and she honestly wanted to party. Therefore, as soon as the waitress stepped over to refill their bucket of ice, Key reached forward, tapping her.

"What's up?" the thick waitress questioned, glowering down at her.

"Let me get a bottle of Cîroc," Keyasia shouted over the music.

With Wale standing so closely to the waitress, he'd heard Cane's little friend loud and clear. Taking the time to really check ole girl out, he couldn't help but wonder what the hell she was doing there with the likes of Cane. The man was a screw-up that Wale had grown up with. He'd tried his best to help Cane, but the dude was his own worst enemy. So, although, his whole crew was getting to the money, he was at the bottom of the totem pole, and could sometimes barely afford to buy a bottle, less along pay for an entire section. And ole girl was bad. It just didn't make sense.

After careful observation Wale recognized the fact that everything about the chick kicking it with his boy screamed upper echelon. In fact, she looked like one of those chicks that would be on some rapper's arms. Baby girl, had a pretty face that was made up to perfection. Without the support of a bra, her breasts were saluting. Her dark caramel complexion seemed smooth, and there wasn't a hair out of place, although the club was jammed packed, and becoming quite humid. And with shopping all the time, he recognized that Tom Ford emblem on her clutch a mile away. As far as Cane knew, Tom Ford was a new version of trucks. So, lil' mama was definitely out of his league.

"The bottles are right here on the table," Wale pointed, as he spoke up.

Not being able to fully hear him from her sitting position, Key stood. "What did you say?"

"I heard you telling her to bring you a bottle. And I was letting you know that the bottles are right here. No need to pay for something that's free right in front of you," he clarified.

"Ooh," she nodded. "I didn't know. Do yall have pineapple juice?"

"Yeah." He nodded. "Here. Let me fix you a cup," he offered, as the waitress sauntered off.

Cane grimaced, as he watched his boy. As long as he'd known Wale, he'd never been this nice, especially with a broad his boys were pursuing. Keyasia seemed more than happy to allow him to make her a drink. And Wale made the drink effortlessly, although the man had never done such a thing in his entire life. Usually, people broke their necks to do things for him to get in his good graces.

"Here you go." He handed her the drink.

"Thanks," she smiled, before taking a sip.

Leaning forward, he spoke into her ear. "I didn't catch your name."

"Keyasia."

He grinned. "I like that."

Her clit involuntarily thumped, as she was turned on with his flirtatious mannerisms. "Okay."

Still perched at her ear, he said, "You can have all the drinks you want. Just help yourself, and if there's anything you need just let me know."

She nodded.

"Aye, come here," Cane interrupted, grabbing her forearm. Wale stepped back a few inches, giving them a little space.

"What's up?" she asked, while remaining planted in the same spot.

"I want your fine ass to sit down, and rap with me for a second."

Looking him up and down, as her eyes were hooded by her false, natural looking eye lashes, she said, "I don't come to clubs to sit down." She brought the cup to her lips.

"Okay." He nodded, before leaning in to speak in her ear. "But I really aint feeling you standing here, kicking it with my boy. It don't look right."

She arched a brow. "How does it look?"

"It looks like yall was flirting," he frowned.

She poked out her bottom lip, as she nodded. "Is that a crime?"

"What?" his scowl deepened. "It's like that?"

"I mean, don't you have to find a ride back to your car? I figured I'd give you a pass tonight, and let you get your shit together. Maybe we'll link up on a rebound."

His face flushed with embarrassment. "It's like that?"

"Yeah, it is. I'll get a ride home. Don't worry." She leaned in, unexpectedly kissing him on the cheek. "But I can keep this between me and you." She winked.

She was indeed letting him down, but he appreciated her not attempting to embarrass him. "Alright, man," he sucked his teeth, reluctantly. From the moment he'd met her, he'd half assed expected her to holler back when he'd approached her. Then after speaking to her over the phone, he'd felt that she was a little more than what he was used to, hence the reason he'd laid it on pretty thick in regards to his status. And now he'd blown it.

For the next few minutes, Keyasia gulped down several drinks. She'd gone from simply swaying to the music to full out performing, shamelessly. Everyone was partying, so she fit right in, but her illicit moves were hard to ignore.

"Driver roll up the partition please. I don't need you seeing Yonce on her knees. Took forty-five minutes to get all dressed up. We aint even gon make it to this club. Now my mascara running, red lipstick smudged. Aw, he so horny, yeah he want to fuck. He popped all my buttons, and he ripped my blouse. He Monica Lewinski all on my gown…" Beyoncé's voice belted through the club.

Key was feeling it, as she tossed her hair around, as if she was Bey herself. She popped her back fluently, twerking her ass in her high fashion dress.

Wale stood frozen, as Craven elbowed him. "Man, where the fuck did Cane's bullshit ass find her? I'd drink that bitch's bath water."

Wale cracked a smile. Craven was a ladies' man, and it was rare to hear him speak of a broad in such a manner. The nonchalant swag was tossed out of the window, as he ogled Keyasia.

"She's finer than a muthafucka. I can't even lie. Cane sitting there looking crazy, while she's in her own little world, and I'm fighting myself not to say fuck it, and holler."

"Shit, *if* I don't beat you to it. She aint feeling that nigga. I can see it. I'm 'bout to see what it do."

Refusing to let his cousin beat him to the punch, he stepped to her. "Who you supposed to be? Beyoncé?"

She grinned sneakily. "Nah, I'm just Key, daddy. The only somebody I wanna be."

He licked his lips. "So, what if I said that I wanted to get to know you? Would that be a problem?"

She bit her bottom lip. "But I came here with your boy."

He furrowed his brows. "Are you leaving here with him?"

She scrunched her face. "Aint that nigga rollerblading out of here, or some shit?"

Wale chuckled heartily, not expecting the quick wit. "You funnier than a muthafucka."

"Why are you laughing?" she attempted to keep a straight face.

"Fuck being on some chill shit. We go zero to one hundred, nigga, real quick. They be on that rap to pay bill shit. And I don't feel that shit. Not even a lil' bit..." Drake rapped.

"Aw shit!" Key boasted, rolling her hips. "This my shit." She rapped. "My actions been louder than my words, nigga. How you sold? I been so down to earth, nigga. Niggas wanna do it. We can do it on their turf, nigga."

Wale stood there with a grin. You'd swear that she was amongst family the way she was carrying on without a care in the world. There were a few other chicks in the section, but none were going as hard as her.

Soon, some of the other women were noticing that all the men seemed to be eyeing the unknown chick, who'd come in with Cane's broke ass, and there were two who were there specifically to push up on Wale. Therefore, they turned the heat up a notch.

"I'm 'bout to make it rain. As soon as I get change. So you can…show me what that pussy made for. I'm here to spend this money. Take it all from me. Girl, show me what that pussy made for. Headed to the stage. I see it in your face. Girl, you wanna…show me what that pussy made for…" Lil' Keke's club smash floated through the air, enthusing the boppers.

Erica, clad in stripper heels and booty shorts, stepped right in front of Wale, and bent over, wobbling her ass. Staying true to his colors, he pulled out a knot. Boisterously, he rained bills over her back, as he smacked her ass. Keyasia found the scene amusing, as she snickered. She could appreciate a man who didn't put up a front. She wanted to see exactly what she was dealing with. Obviously, Wale was a young carefree nigga, getting it. She wasn't mad at that. Hell, you only live once.

Noticing that his cousin had been distracted, Craven seized the opportunity. He approached Key, and whispered in her ear. "Something is telling me that you can move better than her."

Stepping out of his reach, she swirled her hips, letting him know that he could look, but not touch. Like a seasoned stripper, she had full booty control as she moved her ass cheeks, simultaneously. Instinctively, Wale whirled around, catching her entrance his boys. Forgetting about Erica, he waltzed over to her, attempting to shower her with the bills. She allowed maybe two bills to fall, before she shook her head, as she reached up, clutching his bundle of cash. Smoothly, she removed the knot from his hand, and placed it in her bosom.

He knelt over with laughter. Just when he'd thought he'd seen it all. Boldly, she placed a finger under his chin, lifting his head. Their eyes locked. "I aint her."

"But you got my money," he sniggled, as he pulled her into his arms.

As the deejay switched the music, she rotated in his arms, tooting her ass on him.

"Bet if I suck on that pussy that'll get you wet. And rub my hand on that clit. That'll get you wet. And run my tongue down your neck. That'll get you wet. Bet if I suck on them titties. That'll get you wet…I wanna lick you up. Baby. I wanna lick you down. Baby…" Plies and Pleasure P was now in rotation.

Keyasia vibrated her ass to the raunchy music. Wale wrapped his arms around her waist, totally forgetting that she'd come through with his boy. "I gotta get my money's worth," he lowered his head, speaking into her ear, as everyone else looked on.

Cane sat gritting his teeth. So much for being spared embarrassment.

"How could that happen?" Key asked.

"I bet if I suck on that pussy we could call it even," he offered brazenly.

Surprising the hell out of him, she promptly removed the cash from her breasts, and placed it in his hand. "This pussy aint for sale." She attempted to twist off.

"Nah, nah, where you going?" he pulled her back. "Ion want this," he insisted, putting the money right back where she had it. "It's yours. Regardless."

"But I really don't need your money." She twisted her neck.

He nodded. "I hear you, lil' mama. No disrespect at all. But that's yours. No strings attached. But don't go nowhere. Kick it with me. I like your energy."

Caught off guard, they both glanced up when the lights slowly became brighter, indicating that it was time for the club to close.

"Damn, already?" Key pouted, truly enjoying herself.

Grabbing her hand, Wale smiled. "Don't you need a ride?"

Looking down at his hand, her heart fluttered. So not typical for a reaction to a nigga she'd met in the middle of the club. "Yeah, I do, but Ion know you like that."

He furrowed his brows. "But you knew my nigga Cane, though?"

She giggled. "You have a point there."

"Alright, then. Let me take you home."

She narrowed her eyes. "Are you talking about yours or mine?"

He winked. "Come find out." he tugged her along, leading her out of the club.

Although it was two in the morning, downtown Houston was buzzing with pedestrians, as they took their time getting to their vehicles. The night seemed so lively. It took Keyasia a few seconds of standing there to realize that Wale was still holding her hand. And he did it so naturally, seemingly without much thought.

She laughed to herself, knowing that her current actions were so unlike her usual self. Although flirtatious, she was normally in a relationship, and had never entertained the notion of leaving the club with an unknown dude. But thinking about declaring her independence, she decided that she'd do something outside of the norm. Even if it only lasted one night.

"There goes my car," Wale announced.

Key curiously scanned the streets, wondering which vehicle he was speaking of. Immediately, she spotted a few slabs, and assumed that one of them was his. "Are you a part of the red line?" she questioned, referring to the fleet of cars that all shared the exact same candy red paint job.

"Nah. That's me right there." He pointed.

Her brows shot up in surprise, as he gestured at the mirror painted Lambo. The average d-boy hustling wasn't coming down like this. She personally knew a few cats with cars of that caliber, but none were as young, and edgy as Wale. "Okay."

"Come on." He pulled her along. As they approached the vehicle, a tall thick dude emerged from the driver's seat. "Appreciate ya, my nigga." Wale clasped hands with the man, before he stepped away from the car.

Keyasia's mind was hard at work, as she realized that the dude who'd pulled the car around, was in the section with them earlier, therefore it seemed as if Mr. Wale was some sort of shot caller.

With the suicide doors already extended up, he walked her to the passenger's side. "Get in." She silently obliged his request.

Seconds later, he joined her in the car, before lowering the doors. That within itself was an attention grabber, as several spectators glanced their way. Revving up the engine, he skirted off the block.

Combing her fingers through her hair, she faced him. "You know I love this car," she offered in the most non-dick-riding manner she could muster. "Me and my girls rented the Aventador 700 when we went to Miami last week."

He glanced her way. "What you know about that?"

"A little." She shrugged. "It just sort of went with the whole South Beach vibe, you know?"

He smirked, as he focused on the road. In that very moment, he knew that he hadn't just ran across a well-dressed hood rat. She spoke with sincerity without a hint of boastfulness. Something told him that she was used to the finer things in life. "Ms. Keyasia, what suburban area do your parents reside in?"

She giggled. "You spotted me a mile away, huh? A sheltered chick from the burbs. Yeah, that's me." she gave him sarcasm. "But yeah, my mama and daddy lives in Katy, right up the street from my aunt and uncle."

"In a gated community, right?" he asked, knowingly.

"Yes. And we have seven bedrooms, and eight baths. Anything else?"

He cut his eyes at her. "Are you just bullshitting me, now?"

She casually shrugged. "Maybe."

"So, you trusted Cane to pick you up from this supposed seven-bedroom mansion?"

"I never said it was a mansion." She wagged a finger. "And I parked my car, after he met me in a shopping center."

"Okay, so, your daddy's a lawyer?"

"No, my mama," she revealed with an undeniable sense of pride.

He licked his lips. "Aw, shit. She comes from a family of prestige and shit."

She snickered. "If you only knew, nigga."

He squinted. "I detect a smart mouth."

She patted her hair. "One of the best."

He lifted his chin. "Bet you aint got shit on me."

She leaned her head sideways. "I don't think that's something we want to prove, huh?"

He looked her up and down. "Maybe. You seem like the type that has to be brought back down to reality a time of two."

She crinkled her nose. "You too."

He smiled. "So, tell me, Keyasia. What are we getting into tonight?"

She seductively licked her luscious lips. "Is that your way of asking me if we're fucking tonight?"

His dick stiffened. "Would that be a problem, if I said yes?"

She batted her lashes. "I'd respect your honesty."

"Okay, then. I'ma be honest. The moment I laid eyes on you, I kept imagining you on top, riding my dick."

She palmed the side of her neck, as she listened to him talk dirty. She was no stranger to sex, but never this quickly, especially with someone unknown. Still, the way her clitoris throbbed, she knew that she was going to let her freak flag fly that night.

"Look, this aint usually my steez. I just got out of something heavy, and I'm down for whatever…tonight. Just make it worth my while."

He chuckled. "Says the girl with all my money stuffed in her breasts."

She grinned. "I tried to give it back."

"Okay." He reached over the consul, and grabbed her thigh. "Is it here, or up higher?"

She studied his hand. "Higher."

He wiggled his hand between her thighs. "You sure?"

"Yeah." She nodded, as he eased his hand up her dress.

"But I thought I saw you put it down here?" he asked, gripping her panties.

"No, you thought wrong," she gasped, as she felt him pull her panties aside, and find his way to her clit.

"That pussy's wet, though. Let me see how it smells." He brought his finger up to his nose, before she could offer any objections. "It smell sweet." He dipped the finger in his mouth. "And it tastes sweet too."

She marveled at him sampling her nectar. "So, you's a nasty nigga, huh?"

He glanced at her. "As fine as you are…I will be tonight." He eased his hand back between her thighs. He was speeding down the freeway, as he toyed with her pussy.

Deciding that she was all in for the night, she gapped her legs open, granting him full access. Propping her feet on the dashboard, she allowed him to have his way, as she rolled her hips. He swerved a bit when he glanced her way, noticing how much she was into the pleasure he gave. Feeling completely turned on, and free, she boldly reached over, cuffing his stiffness.

"You keep your eyes on the road," she instructed, as she unbuckled his belt. Reaching into his jeans, she freed his hard-on. For a few seconds she just stared at it, as his erection stood tall. His long thick rod was beautiful, and she could really see herself riding him into the sunset. "I didn't think pretty niggas were packing like this," she claimed, as she wrapped her hand around him. Rotating her wrist, she stroked him.

"Damn," his mouth fell open, as he continuously rubbed her pearl. With the pedal to the metal, he hightailed it back to his spot.

Pulling into his driveway, he quickly killed the ignition, while Keyasia continued to jerk him off.

"Come on, baby. Let's go in the spot." He pushed a button, ascending the doors up into the night's sky.

Removing her feet off the dash, she planted them outside on the ground. Standing up, she decided to leave her dress hiked above her ass. Swiftly, Wale slid out of his car, closed the doors with the electrical key, and stepped around to her side. "Why you fucking with me like this?" he questioned, wrapping his arms around her waist, as his belt buckle dangled between them.

"Like what?" she grinned deviously.

"Act like you don't know." He reached into his pants, grasped his dick, whipped it out, and slapped her bare ass with it.

Nudging her forward, they stepped up to his townhouse together. While still planted on her backside they darkened his doorstep.

"So, this is the crib, huh?" she giggled, as he nibbled on her neck.

"Hell, yeah. I want you so bad that I don't think I can pull myself away to open this door."

"Well, give me the keys," she suggested with her hand out.

He stared at her palm, before grumbling. "Fuck it." he pulled his jeans and boxers down to his knees, fully exposing his dick.

"What are you doing?" she asked, voice filled with panic.

"I gotta feel this pussy," he whispered, as he gripped the back of her neck, slightly bending her over, causing her ass to meet his hips. With his free hand, he guided himself inside of her. Even if she seemed a tad thrown off by his actions, she'd arched her back, assisting him with the penetration.

"Ughhh," she gasped, as she felt his thickness stretch her walls.

"Damn, this pussy juicing up," he grumbled, as he pumped into her.

"Oh, damn," she purred, as she threw it back at him. Her round ass bounced against him, as they moved in sync.

Biting his bottom lip, he kept a strong grip on her hips, as he went buck wild. He was beating the pussy out the frame, giving no regard to the fact that if his neighbors were to open their door they'd see the entire show. Even then he wasn't sure if he'd stop. Keyasia definitely had grade A pussy.

Key found herself clawing at the door, as he hit her with thunderous strokes. She'd never done anything this risqué, and it felt exhilarating. Letting go of all inhibitions, she lifted a leg, propping it up on the frame of the door. Nimbly, she worked her back, popping that pussy all over his dick.

"Got damn." His mouth dropped, as he pumped into her.

"Who's out there?" a voice questioned, as his next-door neighbor's door cracked open.

"Oh shit," Keyasia panicked, dropping her leg, standing up straight.

"Shhh," Wale hushed her, as he calmly reached around her, and used his key to unlock the front door. "Go ahead."

Hurriedly, she twisted the doorknob, letting them into the home. Immediately, she noticed that the posh townhouse was rather empty with very few pieces of furniture. "Did you just move in?" she asked, before he hemmed her up against the nearest wall.

"We'll get to that shit later," he breathed, as he gripped her thighs. Following his lead, she wrapped her legs around him, as he picked her up. Leaning her against the wall, he entered her once again.

"Damn," she sighed, as he hit her spot. "What the fuck are you doing to me, nigga?"

"I'ma murder this pussy," he huffed, as he hammered away. "And then bring it back to life. Only to murder it again."

Being a man of his word, Wale did just as he'd promised. He gave it to Key over and over. They'd fucked up a frenzy before collapsing onto his hardwood floor.

Chapter 3

Groggily, Keyasia lifted up. She glanced down realizing that there was a soft blanket covering her naked body. Still, she was on a hard ass floor alone, and couldn't believe she'd slept there. Peering around, she took in the living room area. She could tell that the townhouse was expensive to live in, but there'd been absolutely no effort in furnishing the place.

"This nigga don't give a damn about furniture," she grumbled, as she realized that there was only one chair, and a large television in the room.

As she considered going to search for clothing, her cell rang. Reaching over, she grabbed the iPhone, examining the screen. Accepting the video call, she stared into the camera. "Sneaky ass. What's up?"

Keyasia's longtime friend Josairah scowled. "Uh, what happened to you? I thought we were going to the mall today?"

Keyasia scratched her forehead. "That was today, huh?"

"No shit, Sherlock," Josairah uttered, as she squinted her eyes. "And where the hell are you?"

Key bit the corner of her bottom lip.

"Aw, shit. Are you with Amir?"

"Girl, please." Key pursed her lips. "I talked to that nigga last night. I finally told him that I knew that he was still fucking Val's fake ass. Then he begged, and pleaded, but I'm over it. I don't want to be step-mama of the year, anyway."

Josairah giggled. "You're stupid, man. But seriously, who are you with?"

"I shouldn't tell ya ass, cause I know you'll never let me hear the end of it. But I'm here with this dude I just met at the club."

"Keyasia!" Josairah blurted.

"See, there you go. So, I guess I'll give you the kicker now. I met this dude through his boy, after I'd shown up to the club with him."

"Wait, wait, wait. You went to the club with one guy, and left with his friend?" Josairah asked in disbelief.

"Yeah, but in fairness, that was my first time hanging with the man. We've never done more than talk on the phone, and he'd done so much lying. You know, one of those boastful niggas, always talking about the boss shit he's on. Only for it all to be bullshit, and he's stunting in the next man's shit. So, when I saw that he was full of shit, I let him down easy in the club. But I stayed to hang, and just so happen to connect with his boy."

"So, you let him smash on the first night, Key?"

Keyasia diverted her eyes. "Yeah."

"What the hell got into you?"

She focused on the camera again. "I…I guess after talking to Amir I wanted to forget about him, and the entire situation. I wanted to do me, and say fuck the rest. So, I did something outside of the norm. Even if I never see ole boy again, I enjoyed myself last night. It's a first time for everything, and it aint the end of the world. Even if I go back into keeping the kitty on lock from these niggas, I can say I got my rocks off…a few times."

"I bet you did, freak," Josairah tittered.

"Aye, you know what Jay said, right? When a good girl goes bad, she's gone forever."

"Yeah, and that nigga gotta deal with the fact that he did you wrong forever."

Wale stood in the hallway outside of the living room, hearing the complete conversation between Keyasia and her girl. He'd been reckless the night before, fucking her without protection, which wasn't something he usually did. Therefore, he was relieved to hear that she wasn't some thot, who fucked everything moving.

"You finally up, huh?" he questioned, as he stepped fully into the living room shirtless with basketball shorts on.

Keyasia eyed his chiseled chest, assuming that he worked out religiously. Although slim, he was super-cut, and his six-pack was well defined. His upper body was covered in tats, and the sight had never been sexier.

"Yeah," she sighed, as she focused on her phone. "Jah-Jah, let me call you back."

"Alright. Call me when you leave there."

"I will," Key promised, before ending the call. She then pushed the blanket aside, and stood up. "Where's my clothes?" she asked, standing before him in all her naked glory.

"Damn," he gulped. Her body was pure perfection, and the impeccably shaven snatch was calling his name.

"Damn, what?" she arched a brow.

"I hate to tell you, but I accidentally spilled my drink on your dress, while you were sleep. My bad."

"So, what am I supposed to wear?" she placed her hands on her hips.

Before he could answer, his doorbell sounded. "Fuck, that nigga's here already."

She frowned. "And I'm standing here naked."

"Okay, I'ma go grab you a t-shirt," he announced, before jogging upstairs.

"Did this nigga really just say he spilled his drink on my damn thousand-dollar dress?" she grumbled to herself.

Seconds later, Wale returned with a shirt in tow. "Here, put this on."

She grabbed the shirt, and quickly pulled it over her head. It was super long on her and draped to her knees. By the time she looked up, Wale had already ventured to his door, and had let his awaiting guest inside.

"Nigga, you got me standing out there, and them mosquitos are biting the shit out of me," Bee complained, as he stepped into the living room.

Seeing him caused Keyasia's heart to plummet down to her stomach.

Bee narrowed his eyes. "Key, what you doing here?"

Wale squinted. "How you know her, Bee?" He was hoping that she wasn't one of Bee's young tenders.

"She's my little cousin, nigga. The fuck is she doing here with you?"

Keyasia squirmed, nervously. "Bee, please don't tell my daddy that you saw me like this."

Bee scratched the top of his head. "Man," he drawled. "I aint gon do you like that. I already know how Kevin is."

Wale swallowed hard. As far as he knew, Bee only had one cousin by that name, and this Kevin was a straight hood nigga that had been known to have a quick trigger finger. "Wait a minute. The Kevin I know is her daddy, Bee?"

Bee nodded.

"Aww fuck," Wale vented. "Of all the broads to run across."

"And what is that supposed to mean?" Key sassed.

"Key, you know your daddy don't want you dealing with niggas in the streets," Bee reminded her.

"Well, I didn't know about somebody being from the streets, and I'm grown. My daddy can't tell me who to talk to."

Wale stood there, seeing Keyasia in a completely different light. He'd assumed that she was some good girl, oblivious to life in the ghetto. But with her father being Kevin, he'd grossly underestimated her. He'd known Kevin and Bee for years, and had even put in work with the two. Kevin had also talked to him in depth about his oldest daughter, and how she'd seen the most out of all his kids, due to him going to the penitentiary, and his baby mama running the streets recklessly for a few years. So, ole Keyasia was right out of the hood herself, much to his surprise.

"But your daddy is my big homie, though. I know exactly how he'll feel about me fucking with his little girl."

"But you wasn't worried about that last night, though," she squawked, calling him out.

He glared at her. "So, that's how you playing it?"

"Hell, yeah," she twisted her neck, as she folded her arms across her chest.

"Alright." He nodded.

"Yeah, alright," she murmured, as she stomped over to her clutch lying on the floor, snatching it up. With an attitude, she sifted through her bag, until she located her blunt, and lighter. Lifting the lighter up, she realized that she'd run out of lighter fluid. Looking up at him, she asked, "Uh, where is your kitchen?"

"To the left, man." He pointed, eyeing her as she switched through his home without permission.

"You just don't know, lil' nigga. Lil' cuz is a live wire. She might be too much, even for your wild ass," Bee chuckled.

"Too much for me?" Wale grimaced. "I aint met a broad yet."

"Cause you just did. She's just like her mama, and that muthafucka is a plum fool. Kevin's ass can barely keep up."

"Yeah, okay." Wale waved him off. "But yeah, you ready to get rid of this shit?" he asked, referring to the jewelry from the heist from the night before.

"Hell, yeah." Bee greedily rubbed his hands together.

"Alright, let me go tell ole girl what's up," Wale said, as he strolled to his kitchen. There he found Key sitting on his granite kitchen counter top, swinging her legs, and she puffed on her blunt. She was still as stunning as she was the night before, as his t-shirt swallowed her shapely figure. "What's that you smoking?"

"I swiped some of my daddy's Chronic from Cali," she revealed, as smoke seeped from her nostrils. "Here, take a hit." She handed him the blunt.

He stood, taking a few tokes off the blunt, before nodding. "This shit is fire."

"Is that Chronic I smell?" Bee questioned, as he entered the room.

"Yep." Key continued to swing her legs.

Bee grinned knowingly. "You clipped it from your daddy?"

"What today is?" Key played crazy.

"Well, shit, let me hit it."

After taking a few more drags, Wale handed the blunt to Bee. He then focused on Keyasia. "Who told you that you could sit on my counter?"

"Me." she rolled her eyes. "And what do you have to eat in this empty ass house? I'm hungry." She rubbed her stomach.

"Nothing. But I'ma make a run with Bee, right quick. And then I'll be back."

Key scowled. "Are you trying to leave me in this empty ass house with no furniture or food?"

"Where's the Range, Key?" Bee inquired, knowing she had her own vehicle.

"I parked it."

Wale studied her face.

She grimaced. "Why do you keep looking at me like that?"

"Like what?" he furrowed his brows.

"Like I'm some kind of damn puzzle you gotta figure out. I aint that hard to understand, nigga. Go get me some damn food, while you're out. And don't have me waiting around all day, before I fuck around and burn off, leaving your house open."

He chuckled. "That mouth is gonna get you in trouble, fucking with me."

"Kinfolk, you hear this nigga? He acting like my daddy won't light his ass up like the fucking Fourth of July."

Bee laughed.

Wale was amused by her playfulness. She didn't take herself too serious, and seemed to be a chick that knew how to go with the flow. "Alright. Keep thinking it's a game. But for real, give me about a hour or two. But I got you on the food blast."

"Okay." She nodded. "Don't take too long, before you come back and find that I stole the light bulbs out of this muthafucka," she jested, as she glanced around. "That's about the only thing I see in here."

He smiled, looking forward to handling his business, and getting right back to her.

Chapter 4

After taking a long bath in Wale's huge whirlpool tub, and helping herself to his Hennessey, Keyasia was feeling nice. It had been well over three hours, and his ass still wasn't back. The longer he took, the more she snooped through his empty residence. There may have been relatively no furniture, but his closet was filled to the brim with clothing, and most still had the tags on them.

She'd even stumbled upon a few bills addressed to Corinthian Lay, and a letter addressed to "Wild-Lay" from some girl named Mona. Supposedly, she was madly in love with him. According to the letter, anyway.

"So, that's why they call this nigga *Wale*. I guess," she mumbled to herself, as she invaded his privacy. "That nigga better come the fuck on." She dialed up the number he'd left her with, before leaving out of the door.

After a few rings, he picked up. "Yeah, what's up?"

"Hi, I'm Keyasia," she uttered, as she sat on his rock hard, uncomfortable bed. "I'm this crazy, impatient broad you left at your house almost *four* damn hours ago."

He chuckled into his phone. "My bad, main. I got caught up, but I was just about to call you. What do you want to eat?"

"Since you got me waiting like this, I think I'm in the mood for some lobster."

"Lobster?"

"Hell, yeah. There's several restaurants in the area that sell it, including Pappadeaux's, but I'll let you decide. Just call me when you get there, and I'll let you know exactly what I want."

He removed the phone from his ear for a second, staring at it. Women didn't typically come around with such demands. Usually, they'd beg to come to his home, but he'd always end up at theirs, instead, and they'd wake up cooking *him* breakfast. Then if they had no food they'd go out and buy it. This girl seemed to be from a completely different planet.

"You serious, huh?" he asked, as he placed the phone back to his ear.

"Yeah."

"Alright, I guess I can accommodate you."

"Good." She smiled to herself, as she ended the call. As soon as she hung up with Wale, her phone rang. "What's up, mama?" she answered the video call.

Raquel, her mother, squinted her eyes. "Where the hell are you, little girl?"

"I'm at a friend's."

"And who is this friend?"

She thought about it for a second. Although her mother had a degree in law, she was still a chick from the hood, and knew anybody making a few moves in the streets. Keyasia wasn't prepared to defend why she was at some criminal's house, kicking it, half naked. "His name is Corinthian," she offered, figuring no one knew Wale by his government name.

"Corinthian?" Raquel asked, full of skepticism.

"Yeah."

"And who is he? What happened to Amir?"

"Mama," she sighed. "I told you that I was done with him. I can't deal with him and that baby mama drama."

"If you say so. This isn't the first time I heard you say it, and probably won't be the last. But who is this nigga you're kicking it with? And where the hell is his furniture?"

Keyasia giggled. "Mama, stop it. I'm wondering the same thing."

"I guess. And you look mighty cozy over there. How long have you been knowing this Corinthian character?"

"For a few." Key bit her bottom lip.

"A few what? Minutes or days?"

"Mama," she huffed out.

"Mama, what? I'm asking, because you were just in love with Amir last week, and now you're somewhere with a nigga named Corinthian who aint got furniture is his damn house."

"Why you gotta be a comedian, lady?" Keyasia tittered.

"Whatever. You know we can GPS you in case shit gets hot. Tell that nigga that you have a crazy mama, and a flat out *stupid* daddy. He'on want none, and it won't be none."

"I know, mama. I told him. He aint gon play."

"He better not." Raquel lifted her chin. "And what time are you coming home? I miss my bookey."

Keyasia blushed. Her mama had a habit of babying her, but it was all in love. There were some really dark nights in her youth where all she craved was love and affection from her mama, and no one seemed to hear her silent cries. Eventually, her mama was able to get her shit together, and had since then been there unconditionally. And being the receptive parent Raquel was, she made sure to make up for her earlier absence by now showering her daughter with an abundance of love.

"I'll be there whenever ole boy gets back. He had an unexpected run to make, and left me here in his house."

Raquel narrowed her eyes. "And where's your car?"

"Umm," Key hesitated. "I…I parked it at a shopping center. I really had no intentions of being out this long."

"Really, Keyasia? What if they tow your shit?"

"Mama, you know I'm cool with all the guards in the lot, and have their numbers. So, the truck is safe."

"Whatever. That's your ass if they take ya shit."

"I know," she sighed, just as her line clicked. "Hey mama, let me call you back. That's him on the other line."

"Alright."

"Cool." Key clicked over. "Hello."

"Aye, I'm here at Pappadeaux's. What do you want?" Wale questioned.

"Bring me the lobster and shrimp salad with two Maryland crab cakes. I want honey mustard dressing."

"That's it?"

"Yeah, I can't get any wine to go, so that'll be it."

He shook his head. "Alright, man. I'll be there in a few."

"Okay." She ended the call.

Sitting there on his bed, she checked her emails, and social media notifications. In the past few days she'd gained thousands of followers on Instagram. Her father had recently launched a record company, and she'd been able to star in two of his artists' videos. Initially, her daddy had been against the idea of her being the eye candy in the videos, but after the director promised to depict her in a tasteful fashion, he'd reluctantly given her the green light. After starring in the videos, she'd begun booking club appearances, and was now a socialite on the rise. The jobs were coming in so frequently that her aunt Raven had stepped in as her manager, making sure she received the proper coins. To a young girl with virtually no real responsibilities this was a dream job, and she'd been enjoying the entire experience.

Peeping into her direct messages she noticed that she had several messages, and quite a few of them were from rappers. Them hollering at her had been quite flattering, but her parents had schooled her on the game, thoroughly. Therefore, she knew that most of those dudes just saw her as a new pretty face, and conquest. She wasn't biting the bullet.

After quietly entering his home, Wale slowly stepped to his room. He took note of how Keyasia seemingly had no qualms about making herself at home. He'd never personally taken her to his room, but there she was, kicking it. Taking the time to observe her, as she studied her phone, he noticed that even after fucking her for hours before the crack of dawn she was still beautiful. Her make-up had been completely swiped off, and she now seemed younger but also more attractive. Her long hair was still pretty much intact, as she sat in his oversized t-shirt. As she tucked her lips into her mouth, her huge dimples sunk into her cheeks, leaving him mesmerized for a few seconds. He then quickly shook it off, not liking the feeling.

"Here you go, Ms. Fancy," he sputtered, as he finally stomped into the room.

"'Bout time," she smiled.

"Is that right?" he lifted a brow, as he placed the bag of food on the bed.

"Yep," she popped her lips, as he sifted through the bag. "I see you can follow directions."

"Is that your way of saying thank you?" he questioned.

"Oh, my bad." she looked up. "Thank you for leaving me stranded at your house for hours."

"Damn, you got a smart ass mouth."

"I know. It's a gift." She winked, before removing a container filled with salad from the bag. "I'm 'bout to tear this shit up."

"Honestly, I thought you would've asked for something heavier, considering you haven't ate all day."

"Those crab cakes will put me over the edge. And don't get it twisted. I can eat your ass under the table, but I've been craving this particular salad."

"Yeah?" he grinned. "I aint gon lie, when you said that you wanted wine, I kept telling myself, 'with her ole bougie ass'. I still can't believe Kevin is your daddy."

"Ion know why not. My mama has his ass drinking wine too," she revealed, as she rummaged through the bag, before pulling out a container filled with fried seafood. "I should've known. This is the typical nigga platter. All this fried shit. I mean, it's good and all, but have you ever tried anything else on the menu?"

"Not really." He shrugged, as he sat next to her, removing his food from her hands.

"Well, you should," she offered, before cracking open her salad.

Wale sat there enthralled with Keyasia, and it wasn't because of her outlandish beauty. Beautiful she definitely was, but there was more. Usually, chicks were uneasy around him, trying to feel him out, but not her. She was being unapologetically herself, and was rather comfortable with it. That was a rarity within itself.

"So, since you left with Bee, I'm assuming that you're the new Robin Hood."

He smirked, as he bit into a stuffed shrimp. "Where did that come from?"

She shrugged. "Bee gon take some' off the rip. That's him, and I know that most people around him are doing the same thing. It's no secret."

"Well, you got all the answers," he quipped sarcastically.

"Yeah, I do."

"Okay." He licked his lips.

"But whatever you do is really none of my business. I was just asking. But I aint the FEDS or some shit."

"I hear you," he sighed, as his cell rang. Lifting the phone, he saw that it was Mona calling. He cut his eyes at Keyasia. "Aye, let me take this, right quick." He stood up, leaving the room. "Hello," he answered, as he jogged downstairs.

"Hey, what happened to you coming through last night?" Mona questioned.

"What you talkin' 'bout, main," he groaned, as he stepped through his home.

"Wale, don't play stupid with me. You told me that you was coming over last night. Please don't tell me that you decided to go lay up in the motel with some hoe from the club, instead."

Unlocking his sliding door, he stepped out into his backyard. "Mona, I really don't appreciate you calling me like you checking somethin'."

Mona steadied her breathing, fighting against herself, wanting to explode. "Wale, look, I'm not trying to check nobody. I'm just saying. You had me waiting up all night long, and then you turned your phone off. I just wish you would've told me something."

"Alright, I can accept that. My bad," he gave her a half-hearted apology.

"Okay," she drawled. "Is there a reason why you didn't come?"

"Your backyard is big," Keyasia acknowledged, as she stepped outside.

"Yeah, I got tied up," he responded, as he cautiously eyed Key.

Boldly, Key stepped in front of him. "Did you leave me upstairs to come out here, and talk to another chick?"

"You got company?!" Mona raged.

He gave her a devious grin. "What you doing out here?"

"I came to see what's poppin'." She opened her arms for emphasis. "You got me over here on some sucker shit, babysitting your house. I could be somewhere making my time work for me, getting paid, but I'm posted up in this empty ass spot, while you're everywhere but kicking it with me. And honestly, you could continue right on with your day, after you take me back to my car. No hard feelings."

"You got the bitch at your house?! But I thought bitches couldn't come to your crib, Wale?!"

Locking eyes with her, calmly, he spoke into his cell. "Say, Mona, let me call you back." He ended the call, giving her his undivided attention. "You impatient, I see. I thought that I was polite when I told you that I was taking the call."

She placed her hands on her hips. "That sounded like code for 'be quiet while my lil' bitch is on the phone'. I'm not of the 'quiet while a nigga bullshits' variety. Please come take me to my car."

He squinted his eyes. "You aint the jealous type, are you?"

"Nah, I'm the no bullshit type. If I aint the only bitch in the picture, at least make me feel like I am. A nigga with no consideration for my feelings is a nigga that I don't need to be around."

"Say," he rubbed his chin. "Ion claim to be the best gentlemen, but I left the room. I mean, what more do you want?"

She rolled her eyes. "Ion want too much of nothing, but to get back to my car. I've wasted half my day, sitting in that empty ass townhouse, on that hard ass bed. I don't care to see this muthafucka ever again."

"Well, since you put it like that…I aint leaving this bitch, until I get a few hours' worth of sleep. So, you'll be waiting, until *I* decide to make a move."

She growled. "Nigga, you got me fucked up. A bitch like me would never need a nigga like you. My people will gladly come through and scoop me up." She attempted to stomp pass him, but he grabbed her forearm.

"Wait. Where you going?"

She wiggled, attempting to break his grasp. "To get my phone. I gotta get away from your disrespectful ass."

"But how you know I want people knowing where I stay?"

She bucked her eyes. "Does it look like I give a fuck?"

"Why the fuck is your mouth so smart? You want a nigga to put his dick in it?"

"What?!" she shouted, shoving him hard. "You got me fucked up!"

"Okay, okay," he chuckled, as he pulled her into his arms. "I was just bullshitting with you. You can't take a joke?"

"Hell no!" she viciously punched his chest.

"Oww," his jaw dropped, as he grinned harder. "Your daddy taught you how to punch like that? That shit hurt."

"Good," she seethed, attempting to pry his hands off her. "Get off me."

"But what if Ion wanna do that? Huh?" he wrapped his arms tightly around her.

"I don't care what the fuck you want."

"But I apologize," he claimed, as he backed her up against his hardwood picnic table. Slowly, she sat on top of the table. "You forgive me?"

"Nope," she answered defiantly.

"You see how you keep ending on top of counters and tables? I think you're subliminally trying to tell me something. That's where I eat."

She frowned. "You aint eating shit over here."

"You sure about that?" he queried, while smoothly laying her down. In one swoop, he'd lifted the t-shirt, and was between her thighs.

"Hell, no!" she blurted, lifting her head. "Have you forgotten that we're outside?"

He shrugged, as he lowered his head. "In my backyard," he breathed, inches away from her kitty. "Who's gonna see us?" he questioned, just before going in. Using his hands, he'd spread her second lips, and zeroed in on her clit.

"Ugh!" she gasped, as he felt him rapidly flicking her center with the tip of his tongue.

Getting off on driving her crazy, he pushed her knees up to her shoulders, while keeping his tongue in continuous motion. Her eyes rolled into the back of her head, as she held her own legs in place for him. He had her leaking, as he lapped up her overflowing juices. Multitasking, he also managed to undo his jeans, before dropping them along with his boxers down to the ground, stepping out of them. Grabbing his colossal hard-on, he lifted his head. Before she ever knew what hit her, he'd swiftly slid inside of her. Releasing her legs, she propped them on top of the table, along with her hands, lifting her body, before springing her pussy up and down his length. Their skins clapped loudly, as they fucked feverishly.

Soon, the t-shirt she once wore was on the ground, and Keyasia was sitting completely up on the table with her arms wrapped around his neck, as she snaked her midsection, meeting every thrust he threw. They were fucking hard, as they both sweated profusely.

"Uh, uh, uh," she panted, as she smashed against him. "Pick...pick me up," she commanded.

With no hesitation, he wrapped his arms around her, lifting her up. Still, he eased in and out of her.

"Now, you sit down," she further instructed.

Doing as she requested, he sat down, landing her on top. Aggressively, she pushed him back, before then squatting on him. With her hands on her knees, she bounced on his dick, causing her ass to slap his balls. Effortlessly, she wiggled her hips. The way she was rolling on him, he swore she was actually dancing, as her pussy seemed to perform tricks.

"Fuck," he gritted, as he gripped her hips, watching his dick disappear inside of her, and then reappear. "Huuuh," his jaw dropped, as she opened her legs, unnaturally into a somewhat Chinese split. Her feet were dangling on each side of the table, as she leaned forward, bouncing on his dick. This allowed very deep penetration, and Wale was about to lose his mind. "Ughhhhh, where the fuck you learn how to do that at?"

"Shut up," she clenched her teeth, as she lifted off his erection, and slickly brought her lower region above his shoulders. "Put this pussy in your mouth." She literally sat on his face. Eagerly, he licked her clitoris.

Paying him back for his smart-ass remarks, she gripped his head, as she fucked his face. He could definitely hang. He was moving his tongue at lightning speed, and before she knew it her hips were bucking, as her clit thumped. Her heart was racing, as he gave her an earthshattering orgasm. Surprising her with his strength, he lifted her off his face, and back onto his dick.

"No, wait," she struggled to breathe.

"Hell, nah. It aint no wait." He shook his head, as he gripped her ass cheeks, before hammering into her.

"Ooh, wait, Corinthian," she huffed off, forgetting that he hadn't told her his real name, yet.

"Corinthian?" he repeated, never missing a stroke. "You been digging in my shit, being nosy? Huh?"

"I'm sorrrrrrryyyyyy," she got out.

"Nah, Ion believe you," he gritted, as he began to punish the pussy.

Keyasia's mouth was wide open, as he pounded into her, causing her breasts to bounce. "Ahhhhh!" she belted.

"Oh, you wanna scream? Huh? You want my neighbors to think I'm over here killing you? Huh?" he asked, as he sat up with her still wrapped around him. Gradually, he scooted off the table, before standing up, while remaining deeply rooted within her. Taking slow steps, he walked them back into his house.

Keyasia giggled to herself, realizing that she barely knew this dude as he became very acquainted with the most intimate parts of her. Feeling his tongue lather her neck, brought her back to their moment, as he now had her pinned against his stairs, pumping inside of her.

"Hhhh, uuuhh, uh," she moaned, as he repeatedly hit her spot. "I'ma, I'ma cum."

"Then cum," he urged, licking her lips, before shoving his tongue into her mouth. They kissed deeply, and she rolled her hips, throwing it at him.

"Ughhhhh," she released, but the sound was muffled as he sucked on her tongue.

He broke their kiss. "Hope you don't think this is over. I don't get tired," he breathed, as he lifted them both up, and proceeded upstairs.

Keyasia felt like Wale had worked some kind of voodoo on her, as she found her face buried on the tiled wall of his standup shower. He gripped her hair, as he hit it from the back. The warm water from the shower splattered over their bodies, as he pounded into her.

"Bend over and touch your toes," he demanded.

Completely under his spell, she followed his commands, kneeling over, grabbing her ankles, allowing him to have his way with her.

Three hours later, Wale was loudly snoring as Keyasia stood over him. "Corinthian." She shook his shoulder.

"Huh?" his head shot up, as his eyes popped open.

"I'm ready to go."

He rubbed his eyes. "I thought you was gonna get a little sleep first?"

"I was, until I realized that I can't sleep in that hard ass bed."

"Hard ass bed?" he grabbed her, pulling her on top of him. "It aint that bad, is it?"

She smiled, as their lips grazed. "This is cool, but I can't lay on this bed. It's hurting my back."

"Well, lay right here," he yawned.

"What?" she frowned.

"Lay your tired head on my chest." He gently pushed her head down, until she could hear the beating of his heart. "Now you can rest."

She snickered. "Okay, Tupac."

"Nah, just call me daddy," he uttered, as he grabbed the back of her thighs, scooting them up, assuring that her midsection was aligned with his dick. Pulling her hips up a tad, he slid inside of her.

"No, I…I can't take no more. Not right now," she whined.

"That's cool," he whispered. "I'm sleepy too. I just wanna sleep in it, if that's alright with you."

An involuntary chill shot up her spine. "Hey, what can I say? It's your world."

Chapter 5

Keyasia stepped into her house, realizing they had a house-full. Her younger cousins Ramell and Aaron were visiting, which was always a cause for celebration. They lived with their father Erick, and he lived clear across the city in Alief.

"Keeeeeeey!" Aaron shouted, as she rushed her, wrapping her arms around Keyasia. "I missed you." She rained kisses all over her face.

"I missed you too. Were yall here for the whole weekend?" Key questioned.

"Yep," Aaron beamed.

"Good," she smiled, glancing to her left. "What's up, Mel?"

"Nothing," he grinned.

Taking a few seconds, she studied her cousin. He'd grown so much since the last time she'd seen him. He was now sixteen, at least six feet tall, and had a medium build just like his late biological father, Jamel. In fact, he was the spitting image of his father, and Key could still vividly remember her big cousin's smile, as if she'd seen it yesterday. Sometimes it hurt to even think about him, or Ramell's mother Tae.

"That's good. I heard those colleges have really been coming after you. I can't believe you're a sophomore and already ranked number two in the nation," she acknowledged, referring to his high school football career.

"Aye, you know." He bounced his shoulders, boastfully. "I does my thing, cousin."

"I feel you." She nodded.

"Where you been, loud mouth?" Key's brother, Kevin Junior aka Scooter, questioned.

"Minding my business, nigga," she offered, as she twisted through the house in her stained dress.

"Keyasia, why are you all dirty? Ewe," Kevia, her nine year old sister, cringed.

"The same reason your little musty ass forgets to put on deodorant," Key scoffed.

"So," Kevia snapped with her thumb in her mouth. "That's why Amir got another girlfriend, and she's gonna beat you up."

"Yeah, just like Jermany beat your lil' ass."

"No-uh, she didn't beat me up. It was a tie!" Kevia yelled, getting riled up.

Keyasia giggled at her dramatic sister. Everyone said that Kevia looked exactly like her, and they both shared the same fiery personalities. Key couldn't deny their resemblances in either department, and often found herself arguing with her sibling who was merely a little less than half her age.

"If you say so, little girl. Don't worry about my dress." Key strutted towards their staircase.

"Keyasia, where are you going?" a deep voice startled her, causing her to come to a complete halt.

"Huh?" she slowly twirled around.

Kevin, her father, frowned. "You heard me, girl."

"I'm going to my room, daddy," she said in a whiny voice, demeanor doing a one eighty.

Nicole Jackson

"But where have you been?"

"With a friend."

"With a friend? Who is this friend?"

She took a deep breath, preparing her white lie in her mind. "His name is Corinthian, and I've been talking to him for a while."

"So, what about you and Amir?"

"I'm done with him, daddy. And I'm serious this time," she claimed.

He gave her a skeptical look. "Well, look, if you gonna keep kickin' it with this Corinthian nigga, then I'ma need to meet him, way sooner than later." He eyed her cautiously. "You got me?"

"Yes," she offered very childlike.

"And next time call us if you're gonna be gone for damn near two days."

"Daddy," she pouted. "That's why I think about getting my own place sometimes. Yall wanna act like I'm a baby. I'm about to be twenty years old."

"You *are* my baby," he clarified. "And we don't want you to move out. Not yet. You got all the time in the world to have responsibilities, but right now we want you to finish school, and allow us to take care of you. And I definitely aint ready for you to call yourself living with some nigga, even though you swear otherwise, I know you."

"Aw, daddy there you go with that. I just broke up with somebody, so you know I won't be taking that kind of leap, any time soon."

"Yeah, okay. Ya mama keeps saying that she's been having dreams about you getting pregnant for some nigga, and she said that he reminded her of me. I don't know where that shit came from, but you let these niggas know that aint nothing happening."

"Daddy, I aint having that, so no worries."

"Better not," he grumbled, as he strolled off.

"Finally," she mumbled, as she headed upstairs. Stepping into her room, she stripped down to nothing. Since she'd taken a bath right before leaving Wale's, she simply threw on some shorts and a camisole. From there, she headed back downstairs to interact with her family, which included five siblings; the youngest being just six.

Her family was loud and crazy, but she loved every second. They'd sit around, having some of the wildest conversations, as her mother was completely open with them. Raquel had no problem with discussing her past, making sure that her children would be prepared for the real world. And she was also quite the comedian.

"Aaron, your daddy still talking to that entertainer?" Raquel questioned, as they all sat in the living room on their sectional.

Aaron frowned in confusion. "Who Re-Re? She's no entertainer. She works at the bank."

"Oh, I thought she performed at little kids' parties and stuff."

"Why you say that?" Ramell questioned.

"Cause she be wearing that clown ass make-up. Hell, I thought she worked for the circus on the side."

Keyasia along with everyone else erupted with laughter. "Mama, would you please stop? I'm 'bout to pee on myself," she giggled uncontrollably.

"Key, don't blame them pissy panties on me, shit," Raquel jested.

Before Key could come up with a witty comeback her cell rang. Checking the screen, she smiled. "Hello," she answered the video call.

"What's up with ya?" he asked, looking into the camera, while wearing a blank expression.

"What's up with you?" she shot back, squinting.

He licked his lips. "Nothing much, man."

Keyasia studied his background, as she stood up. Leaving her family behind, she headed to her room.

He hooded his eyes. "Damn, where you at? Some type of party?"

"No, I'm at home," she revealed, as she traveled upstairs.

He silently sat for a while, observing her background. She indeed lived in a huge ass home, indicating that she was truly used to the finer things. He watched as she entered her bedroom, and sat on her bed.

Finally, she spoke again. "Why does it look like you're at a cemetery?"

He sighed, as he briefly lowered his head, rubbing his red eyes. "Because I am."

She batted her lashes. "So, are you there alone?"

He lifted his head, and stared into the camera. "Yeah."

She swallowed. "Who died?"

He hesitated, before diverting his eyes. He licked his lips again, seemingly attempting to keep his composure. Finally, he looked into the phone. "My mama."

Her heart skipped a beat. "I'm sorry to hear that, Corinthian."

Hearing her speak his name with such comfort stirred something within him. "There you go with that Corinthian shit. How do you know that's my real name?"

"I just do." She shrugged. "But anyway. Is there a reason you're there today? I mean, I know its Sunday, but I thought you'd be with your boys or something."

He cleared his throat. "It's her birthday today."

"Wow," she stressed. "There should be people there with you, celebrating her."

"Uh-uh. I usually come here alone."

"I hear you," she sighed. "If I'm not prying, did she die of natural causes?"

"Nah," he shook his head. "Unless you call a bullet to her skull natural."

"Damn, that's fucked up. I know how that shit is, and how you must feel."

"Lil' mama, I doubt you can really comprehend how I feel. Your mama and daddy are still breathing."

"That's true, but that doesn't mean that I don't know how you feel."

"Looking in from the outside aint gon cut it, though."

"Corinthian," she called his name, wanting his undivided attention. "Listen to me. *I* know from experience."

He furrowed his brows. "How is that, Keyasia?"

"I might not have lost my parents, but I lost someone like a mother to me."

"Like a mother, huh?"

"Yeah. My mama's best friend named Taerah was like a mama to me."

"Taerah? I think I know who you talking about. Is she kin to be Big Dee 'nem?"

"Yeah."

"Oh, okay. I remember when she was killed. Them Fifth Ward niggas were in a uproar over her dying. I aint know she was your people."

"She was more than my people. She was the only person who kept me going back then," Keyasia recalled solemnly.

"The only person? What you mean?"

She sighed heavily. "You know my daddy went to prison, right?"

"Yeah." He nodded.

"Do you know why?"

He grimaced. "I heard he killed a nigga."

"He did," she readily admitted. "But do you know why?"

"I've heard stories, but I aint for sure."

"Well," she licked her lips. "It was the dude who'd raped my mama a few weeks before. My daddy shot him in Tuffley Park."

"Damn, I aint know that. I thought that it was over dope or something."

"Nah, but in the end my daddy was pretty much defending himself, and that was how his case was eventually overturned. But that didn't happen immediately. My mama had been raped, and left scarred. My daddy got her pregnant with my little brother days before he was arrested. So, she went through that whole pregnancy alone. And then they gave him twenty-five to life. That broke my mama down, and it was like she gave up on everything. She went from being a straight A student to a street runner, and would always leave me and Scooter with one of our grannies. My grannies were too young to really step completely into their roles, so it was like I had a lot of grown-ups around me that were still trying to live out their lives, and couldn't focus on our needs. Me...I just wanted my mama and daddy back. I'd lost my daddy to the prison system, and my mama was emotionally unavailable. And nobody understood the situation better than Tae. She saw where my mama was falling short, and stepped in. She gave me the love and nourishment that I needed, and made sure that I understood that my mama's absence had nothing to do with me. If it wasn't for her doing that I don't know if me and my mama's relationship would be the same today."

Wale sat and listened intently. He thought about how he was attempting to put her in a box, thinking that she was Kevin's spoiled little girl, but was now realizing that he'd been mistaken. In his mind, he'd thought about Kevin being a hood nigga that had left his family straight, while doing his time. But it was the exact opposite. His family had been left in shambles, and Wale could undeniably detect the pain in Keyasia's voice as she spoke about Tae.

"You know when Tae died I was so scared. I thought that I was really in this world alone. Like there was nobody to really look after me. My mama would sometimes go weeks without coming around. My grannies had other little kids, and was still doing them, therefore we'd always kind of be on our own with them, even when they were around. And it was all so crazy. Somebody blew Tae's head off, while she was pregnant, not thinking twice about what they were taking from people. My mama was actually shot too, but of course, she made it. And I was like nine, feeling like I had the world on my shoulders. I mean, I was a little girl, but I had seen too much, and was really going through it. I would scratch myself, all kinds of self-inflicting bullshit. And it was like God knew that at that point he had to push through, before shit took a deeper downward spiral. My daddy came home, and Tae's death brought my mama back to life. She stepped up, and took care of me and my brother without leaving us on other people. But Tae still remains a aching wound for us all. I avoid looking at old pictures, or even going to certain places, if it triggers a memory about her. It still hurts. I used to cry myself to sleep every night, and so would my mama. But then one night she crawled into the bed with me, catching me crying for the first time. She wrapped her arms around me, and told me how much she loved me, she was sorry for not being there, and that Tae loved us. We cried together, but she would never leave me alone. For months we slept in the same bed, comforting each other. And it helps us cope, so I really hate to hear that you deal with your mother's death, seemingly alone," her voice cracked.

Nicole Jackson

He slid a palm down his mouth. "I'm alright. I been doing this on my own from the beginning."

"But you shouldn't have to," she persisted. "I don't think being alone on a day like this is good. You should be surrounded with people who love you."

"Yeah?" he licked his lips, as he contemplated. He really couldn't believe what course their conversation had taken. He usually never discussed such matters with women. Everything was superficial and light. Keyasia transitioned things effortlessly, providing comfortableness he'd never experienced before. "So, you trying to come kick it? Make sure that I aint alone?"

She blushed, honored that he wanted to be in her presence at such a vulnerable time, not to mention that they'd just parted ways hours earlier. "Yeah, that's cool. I can come over there, and let you cry on my shoulder if you need to." She smiled.

"You got jokes."

"I'm serious. But where do you want me to meet you?"

"I'm in Acres Homes right now. Come out here."

"Okay," she agreed. "Don't fall apart before I get there, now," she playfully teased.

"I'll try not to," he offered a weak smile.

"Alright, let me get dressed. I'll be out there within the hour."

"Bet," he answered, ending the call.

For a few seconds, Wale stared at his cell, as he sat next to his mother's gravestone. Nothing would ever completely remove the feel of the profound loss her felt, but ole Keyasia had definitely lifted his spirits, which rarely happened on a day like today. She was unmistakably different, but he was fully open to accepting that, hoping that she lived up to her full potential.

Chapter 6

Keyasia pulled into Garden City projects, after getting instructions from Wale to meet him there. He'd described the area in the projects he was hanging in, and she was driving through slowly, hoping to spot him. After cruising past a group of chicks congregating on the sidewalk, she spotted him standing next to a Benz, shirtless.

Wale was rocking distressed Balmain jeans with a Ferragamo belt wrapped around his waist. She also didn't miss the blue flag hanging out of his back pocket. Just with these elements alone, she knew that her father wouldn't be pleased with her choice of company, but she couldn't resist. No one had ever been able to distract her, and keep her from running back to Amir, until now. Her interest was piqued, and Amir didn't exist in this realm with Mr. Corinthian.

All eyes were on Key as she pulled up in a Range Rover. The men were trying to catch a glance, and the women were wondering where did the obviously sadity broad come from. Easing out her vehicle, she was totally comfortable with the attention. She smiled confidently, as she sauntered up to Wale. He beamed as he took in her appearance. She wore a forest green super short spandex cropped top, a matching mini skirt, along with all gold wedged Giuseppe sneakers. He was truly amazed at how the array of wand-produced curls were still intact in her hair. Baby girl was bad on another level, and wasn't typically someone you'd stumble upon in the middle of the projects. But there she was…to see him.

"You're hanging tough out here, huh?" she commented, as she stood before him. "Got your shirt off, kickin' it."

"Yeah, I'm just chilling," he answered coolly.

"You can't be chilling too hard." Her eyes landed on the pistol tucked into his jeans.

"Aye," he bucked his eyes. "To be alive is to be aware. It's a dangerous world out here, and I was the predator for way too long to now become the prey."

"Is that right?" she licked her lips.

Mona stood with a hard face. She and Wale had never been exclusive, but everybody in the hood knew that they fucked around, and was watching her closely, as he blatantly entertained another girl in her presence.

Keyasia was ever receptive in ways that Wale wasn't quite familiar with, yet. "So, is ole girl over there in the Bebe dress Mona or Dricka?"

"Who?" he furrowed his brows in mock confusion.

"Her in the yellow Bebe dress." Key boldly pointed. The girl had an even brown complexion, a pretty face, resembling Gabrielle Union, with body for days.

He chuckled. "Why you being messy? You can't tell she's the type to answer that call-out?"

She smiled delightfully. "I was hoping she would."

As if on cue, Mona swayed her sharp, childbearing hips their way. "Uh, is there something I can help you with? I seen you pointing."

"I was just asking him if you were Mona," Key offered easily.

"The one and only," Mona scoffed, as she folded her arms.

"Oh, okay." Key nodded.

"Is there a reason you asking?"

"Your name had come up before. And something just told me that it was you standing on the sidewalk," Key lied. She'd found several indecent photos of the girl in Wale's closet. She assumed that he'd been to jail before, because most of the pictures and letters were addressed to him in a correctional facility.

"Why would my name come up? Why would yall be discussing me?"

Keyasia deviously smirked. "He told me you were his cousin."

Wale couldn't help himself, as he knelt over with laughter. Keyasia was a jerk, and he was loving every second of it. Antagonizing Mona for the hell of it.

"His cousin?!" Mona blurted.

"Yeah, his cousin. And I heard you be boosting. Shit, I wanna put my order in. Do you ever hit up Neiman's?"

"Bitch, a order?!" Mona raged. "You got me fucked up! I'll sleep yo ass out here!"

"Sleep me for what?" Key played crazy. "Did I say something to offend you?"

"Lil' bitch, yo whole demeanor is offensive. Coming over here on that bullshit. You know damn well this nigga be knocking the lining out of this pussy. So, this playing stupid shit is looking crazy on you!"

"Really?" Key narrowed her eyes, causing Wale to cease the laughs. He figured she'd be in her feelings now.

"Does he strap up?" she asked, throwing him completely off.

"Hell, yeah!" Mona answered without thinking.

"Okay," she slid her tongue across her teeth, as she focused on him. "Are we gonna kick it out here, or are you ready to go? I think I wanna go sit on your face again."

His boys had been standing nearby, eavesdropping, and fell out with laughter as they listened to Keyasia. Craven was leading the pack, howling with laughter, but Wale arrogantly shrugged them all off. His cousin was the main one swearing he'd drink Key's bath water, so he'd surely allow her fine ass to sit on his face, if he was ever afforded the opportunity.

"You trying to put me out there, huh?" he questioned with a grin.

"Nah," Key denied with a hint of laughter in her voice.

"You and this bitch take me for a joke?!" Mona belted, wanting so badly to lay into Wale, but was too afraid of the consequences. After knowing him for several years, it was obvious that the boy clearly had a few screws missing.

"Ion take you for nothing. You getting yourself worked up," Wale replied casually. "If I was you, I'd take my ass back to that sidewalk, and chill. You know I'll eventually get around to calling you."

"It's like that?" Mona asked, trying her hardest to conceal the hurt laced in her voice. "You gon handle me like this out here?"

"What you want me to say?" he opened his arms. "I said I'd call you."

His boys were still roaring with laughter.

"You ready?" Key posed, completely ignoring a ranting Mona.

"Yeah, man. I'ma ride with you. My cousin Craven is gonna drop the whip off later."

"Well, come on." She possessively grabbed his hand.

"Okay, wait." He halted her, before pulling out of her grasp and swaggering over to his Benz. He then reached into the car, grabbing his shirt. "Alright, let's ride."

Mona stood with a pounding heart, as Wale stepped to Keyasia's Range Rover, and eased inside. She swallowed hard, as he and Key backed out of the spot, before cruising down the street. She was frustrated as hell, and was attempting to devise a plan in her head, because she definitely wasn't done fucking with him. This new bitch was just another hurdle. Mona vowed to be the last woman standing. Keyasia surely wouldn't last, just like all the rest.

Chapter 7

Keyasia knew that she needed to get herself together. There she was late Monday evening, receiving a proper dick-down, while she was supposed to be in class. After hanging together all night, laughing and drinking, she and Wale capped the night off with a long fuck session. And Key had kept telling herself that she would leave within the next few minutes, which ultimately translated into her staying another day. Still, she had time to attend classes, since the first one didn't begin until noon. But he wouldn't let up, hitting it back to back, giving her absolutely no room to get up and leave.

"Nigga, you're putting too many miles on this," she panted, as he pumped inside of her.

"When it's brand new I can take it for long spins," he uttered, delivering the death stroke.

They were lying on a pallet on the floor of his bedroom, since Key refused to lie in the bed. Wale had spent hours inside of her, and never wanted to depart. His phone had been turned off, as he decided to dig into her peacefully.

He was going into overdrive, drilling into her, when the doorbell rang.

"Fuck!" he grunted, hating to be interrupted.

"Oh, thank God," Key breathed. She had never been with someone who goes as hard as Wale. He'd spent so much time inside of her that she was shocked that they weren't now permanently infused together.

"Thank God, huh?" he pulled out of her, and gripped her thighs. Swiftly, he lowered his body, tossing her legs over his shoulders. While someone continuously rang his doorbell, he devoured her pussy.

"Corinthian," she gasped, as he made her legs shake. "Stooooop," she whined.

He lifted his head, after making sure that she'd reached her peak. "Look at you. You can't handle it, but was just announcing that I eat your pussy, yesterday."

"Fuck you," she grumbled, as she lied on the floor, limp.

"I was, and I will again. Just give me a minute," he promised, as he stood up, and slipped into a pair of boxers. Leaving her alone, he traveled downstairs to see who'd popped up at his home unannounced. Glancing through the peephole, he realized that it was his cousins. "The fuck are yall doing here?" he asked, opening the door.

"Shit, Bubble Gum called us, saying that you wasn't answering phones, and shit. So, we decided to come by and see if you was still breathing."

Wale shook his head, as his people stepped into his home uninvited. "Black Reign, why you listen to her crazy ass?"

"Shit, she had me thinking something happened to your ass too," Kaydoa, his first cousin, spoke up.

"Yeah, I told them that we needed to come by here. Since when you don't answer your phone?" Bubble Gum questioned.

Wale chuckled at his cousin. He and Bubble Gum were extra tight. She was tall, was considered a BBW, and had ass for days. They'd grown up together and hung like the best of friends. She was very loud, and dramatic, but it kept him in stitches. He hated dull moments.

"Man," he stressed. "I could've sworn that I was a grown ass man."

"Yeah, but you usually answer the phone when a nigga calling you, man. We know how the streets is, and you going MIA aint what's up," Kaydoa offered.

"Yeah, what's up with you? You was in here knocked out? What took you so long to answer the door?" Bubble Gum pried.

"Shit, it looks like he might got company," Black Reign acknowledged, recognizing the fact that Wale was standing there in his boxers.

"Nah," Bubble Gum disagreed. "That nigga don't bring any hoes here."

As if on cue, Keyasia stepped into the room, clad in his Rocket's jersey.

Kaydoa glanced up with a grin.

Black Reign giggled. "What the fuck is really good? Keyasia, what you doing here?"

"Yeah, I thought you and Lil' Amir had yall little thing going," Kaydoa added.

"That's over," Key claimed.

Bubble Gum stood quietly observing this unknown chick in her favorite cousin's presence. She was overprotective of him, and vice versa. And there had never been a time where he'd had a broad at his personal domain, but she couldn't deny that ole girl was beautiful.

Wale studied Key's face, searching for any signs of a lie. They'd both ended up turning their cells off, after she'd received several calls from some dude, and now he had a clue on who the dude was.

"Keyasia, Kevin know you kicking it with this nigga?" Kaydoa wanted to know.

Bubble Gum grimaced. "Kevin who?"

"Brewster Park Kevin. Bee's cousin," Kaydoa answered.

"And who is he to her?"

"My daddy," Key responded.

"No shit?" Bubble Gum grinned. "That's my nigga there. I knew they said that he had a grown daughter, but damn. My kinfolk pulled a live one."

Wale focused on Kaydoa. "Nigga, what you saying? I can't fuck with Kevin's daughter?"

Kaydoa shrugged. "If I was the next nigga most of the killers I know would never get next to my daughter."

Keyasia cut her eyes at Wale, thinking if he was a little too deep in the streets for her liking.

"Key, yall been doing some strange thangs in here, huh?" Black Reign tittered. "That nigga done left at least five love bites on ya neck."

"Did he?" she grabbed her neck.

"You'll be alright," Wale claimed. He'd gone overboard with the passion marks after that nigga kept calling her phone. He figured if she did have a boyfriend somewhere that he'd send her back to him marked up, leaving no doubt in his mind that someone else had had her.

"So," Keyasia twirled a few strands of hair around her finger. "How do yall know Corinthian, Black Reign?"

"Corinthian?" Bubble Gum blurted. "Since when do girls call you by your government?"

Wale smirked. "She's just nosy like that, and won't stop calling me that no matter how many times I tell her not to."

Bubble Gum grimaced. "Bitch, you burn candles or know hoodoo?" she asked Keyasia.

Keyasia giggled at the way Bubble Gum addressed her without really knowing her. It was definitely something she'd do herself.

"Watch out, Bubble Gum. What you trying to say?" Wale inquired.

"I'm saying. She throwing her weight around here, already. I know the rest of those hoes are feeling some type of way."

"And they can keep on feeling like that," Keyasia twisted her neck.

"Aye, I think I like you." Bubble Gum high-fived Key.

"Don't be pumping her head up." Wale sucked his teeth. "And how you know Black Reign 'nem?" he asked Keyasia.

"Nigga, she's from Brewster Park. How could we not know each other?" Black Reign asked.

"Yeah, I've been knowing Black Reign. Even though, she's like three years older than me, we used to go to the skating rink together. That's my bitch. We don whupped plenty of bitches together."

"Oh, God," Kaydoa sighed. "Why every girl from Fifth Ward think they can whup everybody's ass?"

"Cause we can," both Black Reign and Keyasia said in unison.

"Let yall tell it," Kaydoa waved them off. Black Reign was his wife, and he knew her like the back of his hand, and also knew that she could scrap with the best of them, but he just had to mess with them.

Wale narrowed his eyes. "Key, you didn't tell me you was a hood rat."

"What?" she laughed. "You got me fucked up, nigga."

"Anyway, since we came all the way over here, we might as well roll up one," Bubble Gum suggested.

"Hell yeah," Black Reign agreed.

"Not until this nigga go put on some clothes. I can't smoke with another grown ass man just wearing drawls," Kaydoa quipped.

"Fuck you," Wale chuckled, as he grabbed Key's hand. "Come on." He guided her upstairs.

"Why I gotta come too?" she asked.

"To change. I can see all your breasts in this jersey. And I know your ass aint got on no panties."

"Whatever," she smiled.

Together they went back into his room where he threw on a pair of basketball shorts, and he found her a t-shirt and shorts for her to change into as well. From there they rejoined their company, and blew a few. They all shared several laughs, enjoying each other. It was definitely something they could both get used to.

******

Nicole Jackson

Promiscuous Girl: Keyasia and Wale

"Damn, I'm sleepy," Keyasia yawned, as she eased into her truck. It was just Wednesday, and Friday couldn't come soon enough. School was cool, but a week like this she'd rather be somewhere sleeping.

So much of her school work had piled up that she'd been spending the last two days catching us, giving her little time for anything else. Daily she'd talk to Wale, but hadn't seen him since she'd left his home Tuesday morning.

He crossed her mind, as she ignited the engine of her vehicle. Just as she was backing out of the parking spot, her cell vibrated. Picking it up, she saw that it was him.

"Hey," she answered with a smile.

"What's up with ya?" he questioned.

"Nothing. Just getting out of class."

"Yeah? So, where you going now?"

"Umm." She bit her bottom lip. "I guess, home."

"Home? So, I'm seeing you when, then?"

"Corinthian, don't say it like that," she whined. "I gotta get this work done. That's the only way I won't have my daddy on my back about all the other stuff I do, like the club appearances and whatnot."

"Fuck all that club shit. I aint talkin' 'bout that. I'm talkin' about me and you. You fucking with me or you aint?"

"You know I'm fuckin' with you."

"So, what's the problem?"

She sighed. "You really trying to get me over there to sleep in that hard ass bed, huh?"

"I'm worth it, huh?" he posed the question.

"I guess," she breathed into the phone. "I'ma go grab some clothes, and come over there."

"Alright. See you in a few."

"Okay," she agreed, as she ended the call. "Shit. This nigga here. And I thought that I was fuckin' needy."

Two hours later, she pulled up in Wale's driveway. She eased out of the car wearing distressed booty shorts with a Chanel t-shirt and sneakers. Her hair was pulled into a long pony tail, putting her exquisite facial features on display. Before she reached the porch, the front door cracked open, and he peeked his head out.

"Took you long enough," Wale uttered.

Her heart skipped a beat, as he didn't even pretend that he wasn't anxiously anticipating her arrival. "You know I live clear across town," she explained.

"You should've already had some clothes with you," he rebutted, as he studied her attire, while she stepped to the door. "What you wearing, man? You aint wear that to school, did you?"

"Yeah." She glanced down at her shorts. "Why, is something wrong with this?"

"Hell, yeah. Yo' ass is practically out."

"You're exaggerating." She switched into his home with her Burberry tote bag in tow.

"Nah, that shit is too short." He closed the door, and locked it. "You aint some little slim broad, and that ass is hanging from them shorts. It aint a good look."

"Alright, Corinthian," she sighed, hoping he'd drop the subject.

"I'm just letting you know. Ion like the shit, so don't do it again," he voiced sternly.

She squinted. "Are you serious?"

"Hell, yeah."

"Oh, okay. You one of them bossy niggas, huh? Want everything your way."

"Yeah, pretty much. That's how it's gonna go between us, too. Respect my mind, and we're cool."

"I've never been good at taking orders."

"Well, you better be a quick learner. Now come on. Let's go upstairs."

She rolled her eyes, but said nothing, as she followed him. When she stepped into his room, she immediately noticed that there was a different bed. "What's this?" she questioned.

"A smart sleep number bed. I know you said the other bed was hurting your back."

She smiled brightly. "And you went and bought this expensive ass bed?"

"It was nothing, really." He shrugged. "I just figured it would help you sleep better, since you was acting like you wanted to run home. I know my shit wasn't helping the situation, so I did something about it."

She placed her hands on her hips. "Corinthian, you real sweet on me, huh?"

He attempted to hide his blushing. "I mean, you alright."

"I'm alright, huh?"

"Hell, yeah," he licked his lips, while rubbing his hands together.

"Well, I'ma take my *alright* ass home, then." She attempted to leave the room.

He grabbed her forearm. "Stop playing with me, man." Slowly, he wrapped his arms around her waist. "Why you always playing?" he kissed her neck.

Chills shot up and down her spine. "I'm saying, I never gave it to a nigga who just felt that I was *alright*."

"So, what you want me to tell you, huh?" he questioned, easing a hand up her shirt. "You want me to tell you how I shitted on my boy to get next to you? Or how that ass was so fine that I threw caution to the wind, and ran up in you naked headed? Or how I let you continue to sit on my face, even after you put me out there in the middle of the hood?" he lifted her bra, and gripped a breast.

"Umm." Her eyes rolled into the back of her head, as he toyed with a nipple.

"Now you aint got nothing to say, huh?" he whispered, as he pulled her shorts down. "I'ma throw these muthafuckas away."

"I don't think so," she protested, as he removed her panties.

"Oh, I know so," he gritted, as he spun her around, gripped her thighs, wrapped them around his waist, and lifted her off the floor. Hurriedly, he carried her over to the bed, and tossed her onto it.

"Ooh, this feels so much better," she purred, as he lied on top of her. "But you know you wrong for not getting furniture for the whole house."

"I'ma let you do that," he kissed her lips.

"Oh, yeah? I can do whatever I want with it?"

"Whatever you want," he claimed, before easing his tongue into her mouth.

Gently, he caressed her body, as she undressed him. Soon after, they were both rolling around the bed naked, as Keyasia worked her hips. She snaked her body, as he moved inside of her. Somehow she ended up on top, and she rested her breasts on his chest, as she wobbled her ass. He gripped both cheeks with his hands, as she popped her back on him.

"Damn," he grumbled, as she sat up on his dick. Her body was a sight to see, as she played in her own hair. Her breasts bounced up and down, drawing attention to the cursive written tattoos right underneath her bust line, reading *Can't hate the fighter within me. Embrace it.*

Sitting up with her, he pounded into her. They both sweated profusely, as they both reached a climax.

"Whew," Keyasia sighed, as she collapsed into the bed.

"I know," Wale breathed, as he pulled her into his arms.

She gazed up at the ceiling, as he rested his head on her bosom. A smile slowly crept onto her face. This was nice. And really weird for her. Although, she wasn't a fan of Alicia Keys, her lyrics entered her head. *You give me a feeling that I never felt before. And I deserve it. I think I deserve it. It's becoming something that's impossible to ignore, and I can't take it. I was wondering maybe, could I make you my baby? If we do the unthinkable would it make us look crazy? If you ask me, I'm ready...*

This was undoubtedly transforming into a blossoming love, and she was completely with it. And ready.

Chapter 8

"Key, did you hear me?"

"Huh?" Keyasia glanced up.

Taraj pursed her lips together. "Who are you texting?"

"Corinthian." Key finally looked up from her phone.

"Damn, that nigga gets all the attention. You wasn't listening to anything I said," Taraj complained.

Keyasia studied her girl. She and Taraj had known each other for a minute. They'd met when Taraj began spending a lot of time at Shay's, who was one of her mother's close friends. Initially, the two would hang occasionally, but had become tighter since Taraj had begun attending TSU with her. They'd been hanging daily, and she'd recently turned Taraj on to a few video gigs, which had them doing business together. But Taraj had a boo and a child at home in which she dedicated most of her free time to, so Key couldn't believe that she pointed out how somebody had all *her* attention. If that wasn't the kettle calling the pot black.

"Bitch, please. Nobody says anything when you sit on the phone with Taz all day, even though you go home to his ass every night," Keyasia spewed. The two were sitting in the school's center café at a small table, going back and forth.

Taraj studied her friend. "Why do you have all those passion marks on your neck?"

Key gripped her neck, attempting to hide the marks. "Why are you so nosy?"

Taraj narrowed her eyes. "Why are you spending all this time with this nigga, but nobody knows who he is? Is he a old ass man or something?"

"Hell no," Key scrunched her face. "What the fuck I look like?"

"Then who is this nigga stealing my friend?"

Key rolled her eyes. "He aint stealing nobody. He's my boo, and all, but I'm the same ole Key. You know?"

"Yeah, Ion know about all that. And when did you go to the beauty shop? How you know I didn't want my hair fixed too?"

Keyasia patted her thick, neat, underhanded braids. They'd been freshly done, and her fine baby hair was in full effect, amplifying her baby faced features. "Corinthian's cousin, Bubble Gum did my hair last night. I needed something done, because he'd really messed my shit up."

"Bubble Gum?" Taraj grimaced. "What kind of damn name is that?"

Key giggled. "A name, bitch. You gonna get off my cousin like that."

"*Your* cousin?" Taraj lifted a brow. "You sure are getting cozy with this nigga."

Key laughed harder. "Bitch, you should see your tight ass eyes when you're skeptical about something. Don't make those faces. You're too cute to be looking so ugly."

"Fuck you," Taraj tittered.

That was one thing Key loved about Taraj. She was pretty, but never uptight. They could crack jokes, and it never became personal. Key knew that it stemmed from them both being pleasant on the eyes, and secure enough to not compete with a friend. They were both considered people persons, but didn't call too many females their friends. For Keyasia she really just saw Taraj and Josairah as real friends, and she was truly down for them both.

"But yeah, his cousin is real cool. The bitch was a little leery at first, but once she warmed up to me it's been all love."

Taraj nodded. "Okay, but what's going on between you and him? I mean, are yall together?"

"I don't know, Taraj." She shrugged. "I'm just going with the flow."

"Going with the flow, huh?" a deep voice interrupted, as he approached them.

Keyasia rolled her eyes, immediately recognizing the voice.

"Key, what's up with you ignoring my calls?" Amir questioned, copping a seat at their table.

"I ignored your calls cause I aint feel like talking. Anything else? You need me to spell it out to you?" she snarled.

"Why you acting like you hate me? Where the love at? If it was real there's no way that it could be gone this fast."

She batted her lashes. "Amir, you know damn well that I don't hate you. But at the same time...I don't like your ass, neither."

"Okay, you don't like me, huh? But how would you feel if I was screaming the same shit? You think I don't know about you fucking with some nigga from Acres Homes? And he's a fucking burglar."

She twisted her neck. "I don't know where you're getting your information from, but you don't know what the fuck you're talking about."

"Oh, I know plenty," he contended. "I see he's marking your neck up for me to see."

"What?" she narrowed her eyes.

"Yeah, you heard me. You got all them fuckin' marks on ya neck. You lucky that I don't snatch your ass up in here. You running to hop on the next nigga's dick already. But you loved me, right? Got that nigga answering your phone. Yall lucky I didn't know where he lives. I'd come through with my people and see him. Tell that nigga that whatever yall got is temporary."

"What are you talking about, Amir?" she asked in confusion.

"That nigga you been fucking with answered your phone last night. In fact, he answered a video call, and showed me that yall was laying up, and you looked to be fuckin' naked," Amir Junior seethed.

"What?"

"You fuckin' heard me," he fumed. "I should knock your fuckin' head off."

"Do it, nigga," Key snapped. "My daddy will gobble your ass up."

"You think I give a fuck?!" Amir shot to his feet, hovering above Keyasia.

"Okay, okay." Taraj stood up, grabbing his shoulder. "Lil' Amir, chill out. This is getting out of hand."

"It's gonna get even uglier if that nigga answer another call, Keyasia. So, whatever you got going with that nigga better get under control."

"Nigga, get the fuck outta my face. I don't better do shit, but stay Black, and die!"

"You fuckin' heard what I said," he gritted, as he poked her temple with an index finger.

"Fuck you!" she shoved his hand away.

"Just remember what the fuck I said," he barked, before storming off.

"I can't stand his bitch ass," Keyasia sniffed.

Taraj tittered. "Well, that nigga is in his feelings. And you better tread softly, because it sounds like that Corinthian is king petty."

"Really, Taraj?"

"What?" Taraj opened her arms. "Don't *Taraj* me. You better go holler at your lil' boo, while he's channeling Usher on that ass. Having confessions and shit."

******

Mona opened her door, allowing him to step inside.

"What's up, man?" he asked casually, as he swaggered over to her couch.

"I'm surprised you still remembered where I live." She placed her hands on her hips.

"Say, don't start." He flopped down onto her couch. "Where my little nigga at?"

She rolled her eyes, before shouting. "Kash!"

Seconds later, the pitter patter of small feet could be heard running across the floor. "Huh, mama?" he asked upon entering the room.

She glanced down at her son. "Wale is here, baby."

Kash glanced over at the couch. "Wale!" he screamed, as he rushed him. The two quickly embraced, before going into their usual wrestling routine.

"What's up, lil' nigga? Huh?" Wale tickled the little boy.

"Stoooop!" Kash giggled his chocolate little head off.

Mona stood back, letting them do their thing. Every time she'd witnessed those moments it'd warmed her heart. Kash's biological father was a classic deadbeat, and Wale had been there for her son, since they'd first begun messing around. Even during their off periods, he'd come through and look out for Kash, buying his shoes, clothes, and taking him to the barber shop every week. And for that Wale had garnered her unwavering loyalty, and no broad walking this green earth was going to change that.

"Okay, okay," Wale breathed, placing Kash onto the couch. "That's enough. Where did all this energy come from?"

"I guess it's the candy," Kash laughed.

Wale grinned. "Boy, they don't make seven year olds like they used to, huh? When did you get so smart?"

"I been smart," Kash stated with conviction.

"Oh, yeah?" Wale brightened his eyes. "So, what you been doing?"

"Nothing. Just going to school." He squirmed around in his seat. "Where you been? It's been boring without you. Mama said that you got a new girlfriend, and that's why you haven't been coming to see us."

Wale cut his eyes at Mona. "Really? The fuck you telling him that for?"

Mona twisted her neck. "Well, it's the truth. You haven't been over here none this month, and he asks for you every day. What do you want me to tell him?"

"How about that I was busy. Anything else is bullshit, and you know it."

"But I see you didn't deny having a little girlfriend. Let's not forget that part."

"Mona, chill out, man. That's exactly why I haven't been over here. You be on that bullshit. By now you should know that I'ma be here for Kash regardless, so stop filling his head up with bullshit."

"Whatever, nigga." She frowned. "I guess I'm supposed to just ignore the fact that some new bitch just entered the picture, and you treat her better than you ever treated me. I'm not supposed to be salty, when I been holding it down? Nigga, jail time, and all."

Wale grimaced. "Why do you talk like I owe you something? Me and you been having what we have. There's been plenty of other chicks, but now you wanna kick up dust? And the jail time…thanks for the letters every few months, but if that's your version of holding it down, then my head is truly fucked up. You act like you put your life on hold for a nigga. I could've sworn you had his daddy living here, and shit. Or was you hoping I forgot that part?"

"But didn't I put him out the minute you touched down?" she folded her arms.

"But did I ask you to do that?"

She snarled. "Shit, you wasn't tripping when you came and lived here! But as soon as the money got good you jump up and get your own shit. And I had no choice but to watch you thot around. You think I wanted you doing that shit?!"

"Man," he grabbed the bridge of his nose. "Have some respect for ya son. Stop all that screaming in front of him. And you always had a choice. You could've moved on. Nobody told you to deal with it."

"What the fuck ever, nigga. And nobody put a gun to your head, and made you lay in my bed every other night, neither. And from the way you talking, you getting serious with this lil' bitch. And if that's the case, you can leave me and my son the fuck alone."

He sucked his teeth. "Look how fuckin' stupid, and selfish you sound. What me and Kash got going has nothing to do with you. And the only person you'll be hurting is him. Everything aint always about you."

"Whatever," she pouted, but deep down she was elated to hear that he wasn't allowing his new bitch to interfere with his and Kash's relationship.

"Wale, can we go to Chuck E Cheese's?" Kash questioned, anxiously.

"Not today, man. I got something to handle, but we can go this weekend, alright?"

Mona twisted over to the couch, and sat next to Wale. "Don't be sitting here lying to my son, Wale."

He curled his lips. "When have I ever been known to do that, Mona?"

"You aint been known to have hoes at your house, but that has changed, so what that mean?" she snapped. "Like I fuckin' said. Regardless of what's going on between you and this new bopper, make sure that my fuckin' son remains a priority. Or I promise that this shit will get ugly."

******

Stepping into the townhouse, Keyasia hated the quietness it offered. Before traveling there Wale had informed her that he had business to handle, and would be in later. She'd briefly mentioned her simply going home for the evening, but the way he snapped at her made her think twice about that. Frankly, it caused a few jolts of electricity to shoot up her spine. She loved how he constantly wanted to be in her presence, and wasn't shy about it.

Making herself comfortable, she tossed her Louie backpack onto his newly purchased couch. She smiled to herself, appreciating her handy work. Staying true to his word, Wale had taken her furniture shopping with him, and allowed her to handpick every single item. And being the smart-ass she was, she'd purposely tailored the townhouse to her style, which was ultra-feminine. From the bedazzled throw-pillows to posh drapery, any sane woman would notice the female's touch immediately, and it was Key's way of marking her territory. Wale had caught on to her gimmick almost immediately, but had allowed her to have her way. He was never the one to argue over the simple things in life, and if decorating the townhouse made her happy, then he was all for it. It wasn't that serious.

At moments alone like this, Key would really take the time to digest what the hell was going on in her life.

She'd literally drifted from one relationship to the next, and had practically been living with a man for nearly two months. The pressure was now on for everyone to meet Wale, and she'd been stalling them out. She was actually nervous about how her parents would react to her seeing someone so heavily in the streets, and she didn't want that to become a thing between her and Wale. Therefore, she was keeping them under wraps for as long as possible.

Deciding that she needed a soothing bath, she headed upstairs to the master bath. After plugging her phone into his high tech speakers, she stripped down to nothing, while Beyoncé serenaded her.

"No matter what you hear it's all in the past. No matter what you feelin' this love is gone last. The heart of his soul, it breathes inside of me. My man, he makes me feel so special…"

She sang along with the song, as she dipped into the Jacuzzi style tub, while the water was running. "You say you don't trust him, because he's been locked up. You say that he's trouble, because he's out in the strip club…"

Sinking into the water, she closed her eyes, thinking about Corinthian. She loved the way he had her feeling, because it had been a while since she'd owned happiness like this. And that was why she hadn't come to him with questions about titles and whatnot. That wasn't to say that she was afraid to ask, but after Amir Junior disappointing her the way that he had, she was cool on laying technical claim to someone. That was when the worries, and concerns of cheating invaded her thoughts, and she could really do without it. But she would be lying if she didn't admit that she felt that Corinthian already belonged to her.

Two hours later, she'd relaxed enough, and decided to get out of the tub. Taking her time, she dried off, before heading to his handcrafted mirror dressers, grabbing one of his tees. She then unplugged her cell, before easing into bed. She frowned when she realized that it was after midnight, and she hadn't heard from him.

"Where the fuck is he?" she grumbled to herself, as she called his phone.

She sat and listened to his cell ring, until the call rolled over to voicemail.

"Really, nigga?" she grimaced, as she scrolled to her Instagram. As usual it was popping, and there were several guys in her DM. "This nigga better appreciate what the fuck he got," she spat, knowing that she had several other options, but chose to spend all her time with him.

Fighting boredom, she took several selfies, as the grey bedazzled upholstered headboard served as her background. Anyone checking out the photos would naturally assume that she'd taken the photos from her own bedroom, as she'd gone all out with the décor of the room, even opting to have a crystal chandelier installed above the bed. As soon as she posted the pictures her notifications lit up, and she placed her phone down with a satisfied grin.

Although, she'd recently made Corinthian order every cable channel, and get Wi-Fi, she still found herself staring at the cutely decorated walls. She couldn't focus on TV as the time ticked away, and he hadn't returned her call. Soon, her mind was venturing to other places, thinking of the things he could be doing.

"Uh-uh, he got me fucked up," she clamored, as she called him again. Still no answer. "Ugh!" she vented. "See, that's why I got ta start going home, and leave these bitch ass niggas alone for a little while."

Soon, her eyes lowered, before falling asleep, alone. Still, she was restless, tossing and turning, until her phone vibrated on the nightstand. She sat up immediately, as her heart pounded. She snatched up her cell, and saw that it was him. She also noticed that it was now four in the morning.

"Yeah?" she answered with an attitude.

"You sleep?" he inquired with loud music in the background, infuriating her. It definitely sounded like he was off somewhere turning up, while she sat her ass at his house.

"The fuck you think?" she snapped.

He chuckled. "So, you got a attitude?"

"Man," she stressed. "I'm this close to cussing your ass out. The fuck you tripping on me going home, if you're just gonna have me sitting here by my muthafuckin' self?"

He sucked his teeth. "You act like I been gone for fuckin' days. Cool out. I had some shit to handle, but I already told you that."

"Yeah, right," she muttered. "Probably was somewhere laid up with a bitch, and wanna play me like I'm crazy."

"Keyasia, what the fuck are you talking about?"

"You heard me, nigga."

"Alright, man. Keep talking that shit. I'ma see what's poppin' in a second," he warned her, ending the call.

She stared at the screen of her phone with her mouth open. "I know this nigga didn't hang up on me."

Nicole Jackson

Hurriedly, she called him back, but he refused to pick up. Therefore, she dialed him again and again to no avail.

"I aint gotta put up with this," she sputtered, as she climbed out of bed, and slid her feet into her slippers. Turning on the room's light, she searched for her keys. She was so consumed with making a dramatic exit, that she never heard the heavy footsteps approaching her.

"So, what the fuck are you doing now, Keyasia?" he questioned, standing in the doorway, startling her.

"Boy," she gasped, spinning around, grabbing her chest. "Don't do that shit."

He gave her a hard face. "I asked you what are you doing."

"I'm looking for my fuckin' keys," she scoffed.

"For what?" he tilted his head.

"To go home."

"At damn near five in the morning?" he squinted.

"Yep."

He shook his head, as he stepped fully into the room. She noticed then that he was dressed in all black and was rocking a hoodie. Those were clearly his "work" clothing. "Come lay down, Keyasia. I'm sleepier than a muthafucka," he yawned.

Key snarled. "Nigga, don't think, because you came through dressed like that I'm falling for the bullshit. Those clothes don't mean shit. I done seen a lot of shit, and I aint convinced. For all I know you could've just came from laying up with some bitch. And I aint about to lay up with a nigga I don't trust."

He sucked his teeth. "Keyasia, miss me with the bullshit. You talking real crazy right now. You go to fuckin' school, so I would have plenty of time to do me throughout the day. I aint gotta wait 'til damn near five in the morning."

She folded her arms across her chest. "Well, I guess you got it all figured out, huh? You know exactly when to do you."

He shook his head once again. "You didn't hear me say shit like that. And you really need to realize that I aint that last chump you was with. If I wanna fuck another bitch, I'll just let you know. And then either you fucking with me or you aint."

She screwed up her face. "If you wanna fuck another bitch?! Nigga, who the fuck do you think I am? I aint the one. You can fuck all the bitches you want, but I bet you *I* won't be around."

Wale grabbed his head in frustration. He'd never had to argue like this. Usually, he was at the chick's home, and the moment she'd get to yapping he'd burn off. But he was in his own home, and couldn't see himself allowing Key to walk out of that door. "Look, you wanna know where the fuck I was?" he gritted, lifting his hoodie, reaching into his jeans. Angrily, he yanked out bundled stacks of cash, and tossed it onto his bed. "That's where the fuck I was." He grabbed more racks out of his jeans, and threw them onto the comforter. "Getting money."

Keyasia stood with a dumb look plastered onto her face. He easily had well over a hundred thousand dollars laid out before her. "Uh." She scratched the back of her neck. "I…I was just saying…you didn't answer my calls, and I didn't know what to think."

"But you aint jealous, though?" he furrowed his brows.

"Well," she hesitated, feeling crazy. She'd definitely made an ass out of herself by making silly assumptions.

"See, now your ass aint got shit to say," he lectured. "Like I said, I aint that nigga…what's his name? Amir? I gotta get it. My daddy aint funding my living expenses."

"Amir?" she frowned. "What does this have to do with him?"

He smirked. "There aint shit that I don't know, or can't find out about. You remember that. And didn't yall have a little dispute at school today?"

Key wore a look of confusion, really baffled as to how he knew that. Hell, Taraj didn't even know who he was, and she was the only other party present, outside of unknown spectators. "Where…where did this come from?"

"Don't worry about all that." He waved her off, as he flopped onto the bed, sitting on his money. "What was you and him talking about?"

Keyasia placed her hands on her hips. "A bunch a bullshit, really. But why did you video chat with that boy, Corinthian? That's was real petty of you."

Wale chuckled. "That bitch ass nigga ran up on you behind that?"

"Well, we both know that. Obviously."

"Fuck that nigga. Shit, if he got a problem, tell him to come see me, cause you aint got no control over what I do."

She narrowed her eyes. "What you mean by that? You were on my phone, and that is something I have complete control over."

Picking up one of the bundles of money wrapped up in rubber bands, he snapped off the band, and began counting. "What you say?" he absently questioned, as he focused on his bread.

"Ooh so, you're just gonna start counting money, while I'm talking to you?"

"Yeah," he licked his lips. "Especially when you talking rubbish. Miss me with that." He glanced up at her. "I'ma answer that phone anytime I want to. I aint letting you sit on my fuckin' face, and running up in you unprotected for you to let the next nigga do the same shit."

Her scowl deepened. "You really got me fucked up. That aint in my fuckin' character."

He continued to thumb through the cash. "If I thought that it was, you wouldn't be standing here…but a nigga can never be too careful. So, I got both eyes on that ass. Aint no need in me bullshitting you."

She lifted a brow, as she hovered above him. "And you aint jealous, right?"

"I never claimed anything of the sort. I'm very forthright with what I feel, and I believe you know that, Keyasia."

She giggled. She was always amused when he'd turn on his intellectual tone. Over time, she'd come to realize that although well-versed in the streets, he was also highly intelligent, which only made him a better criminal. He'd outwitted her several times, because he constantly thought on his feet. It was something she unmistakably loved and loathed all at the same time.

"What's so funny? Do I amuse you?" he teased.

She shook her head. "Why do you have to talk so much shit?"

"Because that's the only language you seem to understand." He tucked his lips into his mouth.

"Fuck you."

"Don't worry. I will." He winked. "But here." He gripped a knot of cash, and handed it to her. "Go buy yourself something."

Key examined the money, before grimacing. She focused on his face. "I don't need this."

He gazed up at her. "I didn't ask you what you need. It's yours. If you fuckin' with me, then there should never be a *need* for anything. You feel me?"

Her clit thumped, as he spoke. In that moment he reminded her of her father in the sense that he was willing to take care of her. Her mama had always stressed that a real man would provide for her without her ever asking for a dime. His actions were speaking loud and clear.

"Why do you spoil me like this?" she questioned, as she straddled him. "In between you and the appearance money, I'ma fuck around and be in a whole new tax bracket."

Wale exhaled through his nostrils. "Those appearances, huh? Fuck that shit," he spat.

She grinded on his dick. "Why does it have to be like that?"

"Cause," he licked his lips. "You be acting like going to the club is a job. Them niggas aint respecting that shit. They all just wanna fuck, and your job is to give the illusion that if they party at the club with you, then there's a possibility. You think I'm cool with that? Ion even like that nigga Lil' 5th's video no more. Fuck that bullshit ass video, and fuck him."

She rolled her eyes to the ceiling. "Corinthian, don't start that. It's a hustle for now." She looked down at him. "And it's quite lucrative, right now."

"Well, does it pay more than I just put in your hand?"

"Not in one job, no. But you know that. And when you think about the risks you take to get this money, it makes it all pretty even, if not less for you. The money I make is perfectly legal."

"Yeah, any fuckin' way," he snorted. "I'm done talking about that shit."

She knelt over, kissing his lips. "Stop tripping."

"I aint trippin'," he denied.

"Yes you are. But I'ma get your head right," she promised, as she unbuckled his jeans.

He continued to lie on his back, as she removed his jeans, and then boxers. Watching her was becoming sort of a pastime for him. She was incredibly stunning to him, and they both knew that she knew this as well. She was confident in a sexy way.

It wasn't long before she was riding his dick, and all arguments were placed on the back burner…for now.

Chapter 9

Outside of club Carrington's, the lot was jumping. It was a little past two in the morning, and the crowd was showing no signs of dispersing. Slabs were prowling the lot, as people made last minute hook-ups.

Wale was chilling with his boys, while boppers flocked to them, as usual. His team was smashing all the competition with top dollar exotic whips, and expensive threads on their bodies. Women were losing religion for the night, if it meant leaving with anyone a part of the crew.

"Wale!" a female shouted.

He lifted his head, trying to figure out who was calling his name across the parking lot.

"Where you going?!" Mona shouted, as she stepped closer.

Wale scowled, as he leaned against the Lambo. "The fuck this bitch screaming my name for?"

"You heard me?" she stepped up to him.

Wale's eyes swept over the lot, scoping everything around him. "Everybody from the damn club to the lot heard you."

"Whatever," she chided. "You got my text?"

He eyed her. Mona had been putting extra effort in her appearance, although she'd been attractive from the beginning. But now with the spirit of competition, she'd increased her once a month sew-ins to every two weeks, and was now wearing a waist shaper to conceal any imperfections within her figure. As a man, Wale didn't quite know what she'd been doing differently, but it was working. She looked good as fuck to him.

"Yeah, I got it," he answered her.

"So, what's up? You coming through tonight or nah?"

He adjusted his sagging Gucci jeans. "I don't know, Mona. I gotta see."

She frowned. "That's the same shit you been singing for the past three months. I mean, tell me what it is. I'm a big girl. You aint fucking with me no more?"

Propping a foot up against his car, he licked his lips. "I'm chilling right now. I been on a paper chase, and that's my focus."

"But you make time for that hoe from the burbs, though. Aint that right?"

He furrowed his brows. "What hoe from the burbs?"

"You know who the fuck I'm talking about," she scolded.

He shook his head, as he continued to watch the lot. "I really don't."

"That Instagram hoe, Keyasia!" Mona blurted.

He grinned, as he gazed down at her face. "You did your homework, huh? But that *Instagram hoe* aint from the burbs. So, whatever story you got written in that little head of yours is gonna have to be revised. Cause I guess you was thinking I went and got a good girl on you. But now, you don't know what to think," he taunted.

"Well, whatever the bitch is." Mona waved him off. "You letting her come between what we have, and I don't like it."

"Say, let's fall off in V-Live after this," Craven suggested, gripping Wale's shoulder.

He gipped the bridge of his nose. "I don't know if that's the play, main."

"Yeah, you need to be heading to my house," Mona pouted, hoping to sway him.

"Nigga, you know something I don't?" Craven asked. "Any other night it's cool."

He took a deep breath. "Mona, go'on home. I'ma catch up with you."

She nodded. "How long will you be?"

Not being the one to intentionally lie to a broad, Wale grew frustrated. "Look, Mona, I really don't know. If I even come at all. Just go to the crib, though."

Feeling played for the umpteenth time, Mona exhaled. "Whatever. I aint got time for this shit." She stomped off.

"You doing my girl wrong, man," Meeko chuckled, as he watched Mona's sexy ass disappear into the crowd.

"Yeah, she gon cry when she make it to the car," Big Block added with a chuckle.

"You niggas messy," Craven snickered, before focusing on his cousin. "But why you aint feeling V-Live tonight, Wale?"

"Cause," he tucked his lips into his mouth. "Keyasia's hosting there tonight."

Craven squinted. "Okay, so what's the problem?"

"Man, it's supposed to be quite a few bullshit rappers there tonight, trying to stunt. Ion think I wanna be there when they trying to pull her. I know its work, and shit…I don't know." He shrugged.

Craven gave him the side eye. "If I aint know no better, I'd swear that you was jealous. What, you think that you aint gon be able to control yourself if another nigga grab that ass, or some shit?"

"Nigga, however it is, I aint feeing going there," Wale snapped.

"My nigga, I hear you, but I was planning on seeing some exotic asses, before I retire in. So, that's where I'm going," Big Block spoke up.

"Me too," Meeko added.

Craven smiled. "Then that's the play. So, I take it you aint coming?"

"Fuck," Wale grumbled. "Man," he stressed. "Fuck it. I'ma fall through too."

******

"Bitch, I am so ready to get the fuck outta here," Keyasia spoke in her girl's, Jas, ear. They'd gotten to club V-Live at midnight, and now at three in the morning the strip club was packed. The two were guests of honor, and had their own section.

Jas frowned in confusion. "Why?"

Keyasia rolled her eyes. "These lil' rappers don't know how to keep their fuckin' hands to their selves."

"Shit, as much as I'm getting paid tonight, they can cop a few feels. Fawk you mean," Jas tittered.

Key crinkled her nose. "You's a thot, Jas. Ole thirsty ass."

"So," Jas stuck out her tongue.

Key simply shook her head. It was becoming evident that the whole club appearances shit was changing her friend. Jas was a pretty mocha complexion, kept a tight sew-in, and had a nice, sexy, thick, physique. No doubt, the girl was a looker, but the money and attention, was going to her head, and nothing was off limits if the price was right. Key was positively losing respect by the second, because it was crystal clear that Jas could be bought. Therefore, she couldn't be trusted.

"These hoes wanna hold me back. These hoes wanna hold me back. First I got me a Taurus, then I copped me a Lexus. I took over Florida. My connect out of Texas. Then I started sipping purple, got my shit screwed. When you feeding your circle, watch your shipments improve..." Rick Ross blared from the speakers.

"That's my shit," Key boasted, as she waved a bottle in the air.

"Why you teasing us like that?" someone whispered into her ear, as they wrapped their arms around her waist.

Immediately, she stepped out of his clutches, and spun around. "Can I help you?"

The pale, light skinned, tatted, grilled out, rapper by the name of Mucci stood there with a stupid grin on his face. "Hell, yeah. You can start by coming to sit over there with me and my boys. Let a nigga get to know you."

Keyasia gave him a forced smile. Her Aunt Raven had stressed the importance of not going in on rappers, burning bridges. In the industry, you never knew who you would need later. "Alright, give me a second. I'll be over there." She winked.

"Bet," he smiled, as he coolly stepped off.

Keyasia twirled around, and her heart skipped a beat, as her eyes locked with his. "The fuck?" she grumbled, as Wale and his boys moved through the club with arrogance. Stunting as usual, the whole crew rocked Gucci everything, from their jeans to their shades.

She arched a brow, when he continued to walk on by, although it was clear that he'd seen her. Her stomach became queasy as she wondered how much of the scene with Mucci had he witnessed.

"Damn, who are them niggas?" Jas chirped, in full lust mode.

"In the Gucci?"

"Yessss," Jas hissed. "That's where we need to be. They just grabbed a section. But I call dibs on the tall one with the red pants on."

"Bitch, please. In your fuckin' dreams. That nigga aint finna give you the time of day. Not if he values his life."

Jas's eyes roamed around the room. "Why not?"

"Take your ass over there, and find out."

Before another word could be uttered, Jas was in motion. "I will."

Keyasia gritted her teeth, as Jas sauntered her way over to Wale's section, and was infuriated when she was allowed to sit down. She was sitting awfully close to Wale, as she spoke in his ear.

"Okay." Key nodded. "He wanna play, huh?" she smoothly twisted over to Mucci's section, which was right next to Wale's.

Mucci greedily rubbed his hands together. "That's what I'm talkin' 'bout. Fuck with your boy. Sit down, baby."

Key willingly took the invitation, sitting next to him. "So, what's up?"

"I'm trying to take you home tonight," he confessed, wasting no time with formalities.

Keyasia was about to turn him down, before his boy interrupted them. "Aye, ole girl aint came back with the bottles yet," Mucci's minion pointed out.

Mucci frowned, as he glanced around, realizing that there were three waitresses alone in Wale's section. Keyasia reluctantly glanced that way, as well, realizing that Wale and the crew were being served several bottles of Cristal. Her eyes then fell down to the table in Mucci's section, and seen that they were sipping Moet. Yep, the waitresses were clearly catering to the bigger spenders, which definitely weren't Mucci and his people.

"Them crook ass niggas always trying to stunt," Mucci openly hated. "I wonder what they gonna do when them licks stop rolling in. Always trying to upstage and shit."

Keyasia giggled, as Mucci assumed she was laughing with him, when she was actually laughing at him. His name was bubbling on the scene, but it was obvious that he hadn't gotten to the point where he was really raking in the dough. He was sitting there, hating on street niggas. She also noticed how the rapper also seemed to know exactly who Wale and his boys were, which told her that Wale's rep was huge in the city.

It wasn't long before she was tuning Mucci out, as Wale's section became the liveliest part of the club, as several of the strippers flocked to the section. Every man in the section was making it rain, and Wale was the ringleader. One girl was doing a handstand, as she vibrated her ass directly in front of him.

Keyasia was waiting on him to simply lay a finger on the girl, and she was going over to him, and slapping the fuck out of him. But it never happened. He tossed some serious cash, but he never touched. For about an hour Wale partied hard, and Jas remained in his section the entire time. She was seemingly interacting with all the men, probably seeing who showed the most interest in her.

Wale was dry throwing away money, as he studied Keyasia. She'd been sitting there, talking to Mucci's bitch ass for over an hour. It was taking everything in him to not go over there, and snatch her ass up. She'd violated by even coming out in those little ripped denim booty shorts. The inside pockets were longer than the actual shorts, as they extended outside of the shorts. Her ass was dangerously spilling out of the clothing, running him hot. Admittedly, she looked great in the shorts, along with the off the shoulders long sleeved cropped top, and Giuseppe stilettos. The abundance of curls in her hair aided in her glamorous/risqué look. But he'd specifically told her that he didn't like her shorts at that length. Still, she'd done what the fuck she wanted.

"Where you going after this?" Mucci questioned Key. At five in the morning, the crowd in the club was thinning out, and he was ready to go.

"Home," she sighed, standing up.

"Damn, man," he stood as well. "Well, shit, let me walk you to your car," he offered, thinking he could try once more to convince her to chill with him.

She shrugged, as she switched off. At this time everyone was filing out of the club. Key possessed a mean walk that captured all the attention, as she stepped out into the lot.

"Got damn, fuck them hoes in there. I'm trying to see what's up with her fine ass. She the baddest thang out here," some dude announced, as he walked behind her. "Lil' mama, where that nigga at, cause he done fucked up, letting you out the house like that."

"My nigga, you too late. I'm already trying to see what's up," Mucci spoke up, as he walked closely behind her.

Key rolled her eyes, as she ignored them all. As she attempted to step to the valet, her path was blocked. "Where you going?" he stood directly in front of her.

"Nigga, move," she sneered, attempting to shove past him. He wouldn't budge.

"Stop playing with me, man," he glowered down at her.

"So, Keyasia, I can call you or what?" Mucci stepped to them.

Wale grimaced. "Nigga, if you don't back your bitch ass up. Take that weak shit on. She TSP, nigga," he spat, referring to Take Somethin' Property. Take Somethin' Clique was the infamous name of his squad.

Mucci looked at Keyasia like she'd sprouted two heads and had deeply betrayed him. "She sat with me all that time, and aint tell me shit. I aint with the drama, baby girl."

She bubbled her face with laughter. "Is this clown for real?"

"Yeah, alright, nigga. Move ya bitch ass on, before it be some problems out here," Wale threatened, lifting his shirt, revealing the butt of his pistol.

Keyasia scowled, as Mucci took heed, stepping off. "How the fuck did you get that into the club?"

"Sometimes you just gotta know the right people," he winked.

"Whatever," she huffed, attempting to walk off again. He grabbed her.

"Where you going? Huh?"

"To my car," she gritted. "Can you let me go?"

"Nah, I can't do shit. Let's fuckin' go, before I clown yo ass out here."

"Clown me for what?" she bucked her eyes.

"You fuckin' know. Look at this bullshit you got on," he tugged at her shorts. "We already discussed this shit."

"Ooh, let's make this about me, huh? What about the fact that you was flirting with my associate."

He grimaced. "What associate? That bitch that came to the section aint a friend, associate or nothing else to you. That's dead wood. Delete that bitch's number out of your phone. She selling that stale ass pussy for a rack. I told that hoe that I wasn't with it, and she moved on to my boys. I think Big Block went for it."

"She what?!" Keyasia gasped.

He licked his lips. "You heard me, man."

"That bitch is trippin' hard."

"Yeah, that's how them powder heads get down."

"Powder head? She told you she does coke?"

"Shit, told me?" he lifted a brow. "How 'bout she sat there and did a few lines in our section."

"Wow."

"Yeah, wow. But you'd know this if you wasn't all in that broke nigga's face."

"I wasn't in his face," she denied.

He slid his tongue across his teeth, as his eyes wandered around the lot. "That aint what I saw, but yeah, I'm ready to burn. These niggas is drunk, and shit could go left. So, let's get the fuck."

"Okay," she agreed. "Just let me go get my truck."

He waved his head. "Nah. I said fuck that truck."

She glared at him. "Fuck my truck? Really?"

"Yeah." He nodded. "Run me those keys. Craven will drive your shit back to the spot."

She sucked her teeth. "And how you know that I want Craven driving my shit?"

"Man," he stressed, tilting his head. "Keyasia, quit playing with me. Give me the keys, girl."

For a few seconds, they engaged in a stare down, before she gave in. "Okay," she huffed. "And if he fucks anything up, you're paying for it." She reached into her pockets, and grabbed her valet ticket, before handing it off to him.

"That aint even something you gotta say. Come on, now," he uttered, before turning to his cousin. "Kinfolk, I know we rode together, but something came up. Ride to the crib in her Range. Bring it through in the morning," Wale instructed, handing him the ticket.

Craven stood with a huge grin. "Let me find out you's a sucker for love, nigga. You bailing out on us left and right."

Unconsciously, Key looped her arm around Wale's. "Craven, what's wrong with that? As long as I'm a sucker too we're good, right?"

He nodded. "True. I aint gon hate on it. Alright, I'ma fuck with yall." Craven chunked up the deuces, as he stepped to the parking attendant.

Keyasia glanced to her left, and realized that someone had already pulled Wale's Lambo up to the curb. "Come on, Corinthian. My feet hurt," she whined.

"Good. Them bitches need to hurt," he squawked.

Just as they were turning to leave, someone shouted, "Keyasia!"

She twirled around to see Jas rapidly approaching them. "What?"

"Bitch, where are you going? I know you aint leaving me," Jas breathed, as she posed in front of them. "Did you forget that I rode with you?"

Key shrugged. "No."

"So, where were you going, then? You didn't even tell me you were leaving."

Wale gazed down at Keyasia, wanting to hear her response.

"Well, I aint say nothing, because I was leaving you," Key offered with a straight face, causing him burst with laughter.

"You was leaving me for what?" Jas was in shock.

"Cause you took your nasty ass over there, flirting with my man. And I aint trying to get pulled over by vice for sex trafficking your prostituting ass."

Wale found himself leaning on Key's shoulder, laughing hard. "Man, where did this girl come from?"

Jas was steaming, but was low key afraid of Keyasia. They'd met in high school, back in the burbs, and she'd witnessed Key have quite a few fights. None of the suburban girls could hang with her, and frankly, Jas was intimidated.

"Fuck you, man," Jas grumbled, as she dialed out on her cell.

"Alright," Key agreed easily. "Come on." She tugged Wale along, as they traveled to his car.

Right before they were about to enter the car, he halted her. "Aye, I just gotta say one thing, man."

"What's that?"

"You better not *ever* handle me how you handle these hoes, main," he chuckled uncontrollably.

She giggled. "Man, fuck that hoe. And I don't discriminate. If you don't want that treatment, your ass better stay on my good side."

Chapter 10

"Wait, nigga!" Keyasia screamed at the top of her lungs.

"Nah," Wale slapped her bare ass. "I told you to shut up, and take this dick." He pounded into her from the back.

"Corinthiannnnnn!" she belted, as her head bumped into the headboard. "Stooooooop!" she squeezed her eyes tightly, as he beat the pussy up.

"Hell, nah!" he growled. "I told yo ass not to be wearing them lil' ass shorts, didn't I?"

"Yes, yes!"

"But you aint listen, did you?" he popped her ass again.

"Noooooo!"

"Exactly," he breathed. "You gon learn to listen to me."

"Baby, I'm sorry! I'm sorry!"

"I don't care about no fuckin' sorry," he gritted, as he gripped her hips, as he slammed into her.

"Awwww!" she screeched, as she still somehow managed to throw it back, although he was trying to break her back.

"I don't give a fuck how loud you scream. I aint letting up," he promised, as he ventured as deep as her body would allow.

It was noon, and he'd been fucking her since they'd come through the door at six that morning. Keyasia was receiving her punishment for violating, and she didn't know whether to be pissed, or grateful for the infraction. Wale was going hard, and she'd already busted three times. Her body was now weak, and dripping with sweat.

Deciding that she had to take him down, she rolled her hips, and began twerking as he hit it. "Aww, shit," his mouth fell open, as he stopped moving. Right then, she knew she had him, and went in for the kill. She wobbled her ass, and squeezed her walls around him. Soon, his back stiffened, before he erupted inside of her. "Fuck," he vented, as they both collapsed into the bed.

She smiled brightly, as he kissed her neck. "I thought you wasn't letting up?" she teased.

"G's fuck up too," he snickered.

Just then her cell vibrated on the nightstand. Picking up the phone, she saw that it was her mama, wanting to video chat. "Baby, lift off me. I need to talk to my mama, right quick."

He sighed, as he rolled off her.

She quickly pulled the covers up to her neck, before answering the call. She made sure to hold the phone in an angle that didn't have Wale in the shot. "Hey, mama. What's up?" Key leered.

"Uh, how are you, stranger? I guess you don't live with us, anymore, huh?" Raquel probed.

"Mama," Key sighed. "Why you say that?"

"Cause, little girl, you haven't slept here in ages. Nobody gets to spend a second of time with you."

Wale rested his head on her shoulder. "Yeah, I think she should come visit yall," he offered.

Nicole Jackson

Key was caught off guard, as he revealed his face to her mama. "Boy," was all she could say.

Raquel narrowed her eyes. "Is that…is that Wale?"

Key palmed her forehead. "Yes," she breathed, as if it pained her.

He smiled. "Yeah, I think you may have heard of me as *Corinthian*."

Raquel slid her tongue across her teeth. "I *see*. Why you been letting her keep you a secret?"

"Aye," he shrugged. "I guess I was letting her live, you know?"

"I guess," Raquel smiled. "I can't wait to tell Kevin this."

"Oh God." Key continued to clutch her head.

"Don't try to hide your face now. Yall need to come over here, after you wash your nasty asses. We need to chop it up with you, Wale."

He nodded. "I'm cool with that. When you want us to come through?"

"Today. Me and my sister supposed to be cooking today, anyway."

"Alright. We'll be there," he promised.

"Cool. See yall then," Raquel nodded, before ending the call.

Keyasia dropped her phone on the bed, before rolling over to face him. "I can't believe you."

He laughed, smacking her ass hard. "That's payback for last night. I been playing cool about you hiding a nigga from your people. I mean, I get it. But since you wanna violate, I'ma show you how its really done. Got your ass in the hot seat with ya folks."

She pursed her lips. "Nigga, please. You just don't know. We'll see who'll be in the hot seat. All this time I've been saving your ass, but whatever. Just remember at the end of the day, you asked for this."

******

"Damn, girl, how many damn shrimp did you buy?" Raquel squawked, sitting at her kitchen's nook, as she peeled a jumbo shrimp.

"Seven pounds," her sister Raven responded. "Shit, I should've gotten more. In between your kids and mine, shit, this shit will be gone before we can sit our asses down."

Raven couldn't argue with that. Between the two, there were fourteen children, and they all had ferocious appetites. Then there were their spouses, and friends. There was never too much food whenever they all came together.

"So, when is Key coming?" Raven questioned.

"She's supposed to be here by now. Her ass better not pull a fast one. She's been keeping this boy away for long enough."

Raven grinned. "That nigga must be something else for her to keep him a secret."

Raquel pursed her lips. "She knows that his ass is out there in those streets, and didn't want us getting on her ass about it."

Raven nodded in understanding. "I could see her way of thinking. And I'm really on the fence on how to feel about it. Like, I'd prefer that Jhyrah have a boyfriend that's doing something legal, but I wouldn't go in if she chose otherwise," she referred to her daughter. "Number one, I'd be the biggest hypocrite ever, and I wouldn't want my disapproval to drive a wedge between us. I know how I was at that age, and there was no talking to me."

"True," Raquel agreed. "Keyasia is grown, and definitely has a mind of her own. So, I aint gon run her in the ground about her choices, but I will be letting that nigga know that he better handle my daughter a certain way. And I know Kevin will let that be known off the muscle. Wale has always been cool, but he wasn't fucking with my child, then. That's when all that friendly shit matters none to me. And I really aint worried about hoes with him. I mean, the boy is handsome, but my baby can handle that part. I just know how he *really* is. Hell, he's put in work for Kevin a couple of times…*and* Bee. So, when I say that he's out there, he's *out there.* And in deep."

"That's Jah and Kevin's worst nightmare, right there. Their daughters getting with niggas just like them." Raven shook her head.

"Exactly," Raquel concurred. "And Kevin has always said that Key was gonna be the one to bring home some hardhead, and I could feel it too. And I can tell that whatever is going on between her and Wale is serious, because Lil' Amir has been stopping by, hoping to talk to her, but she's never here. Her ass has been practically living with that boy, and I can just see a damn baby coming. And I'll just fucking die. You hear me?"

"Raven squinted. "I don't know, Quel. Keyasia's a smart girl. And I really can't see her having kids any time soon."

"Yeah," Raquel sighed. "Me and you were smart too. So, what does that mean?"

"Hey," Raven bucked her eyes, as she blankly stared at the shrimp in her hand. "You got me there."

"Yall still aint finished cooking?" Shay, their friend, questioned as she stepped into the kitchen.

"Nah, we was saving some work for your ass," Raquel quipped. "So, put down the Celine bag, and help us."

Shay smirked. "Aye, I aint tripping. I knew you slow bitches needed me."

"Shay, baby, we didn't ride the short yellow bus like your ass. We keep telling you that we were in two different types of special classes. We were in gifted classes. Say it with me, okay? Resource classes are completely different," Quel jested.

Shay giggled, as she sat at the table with them. "Bitch, you really need to get paid for the jokes. But yall got me fucked up."

The three women all sat laughing, until they were rudely interrupted. "Say, Quel, when is the food gonna be done?" Kevin pressed, stepping into the room.

Raquel sucked her teeth. "What, are you planning on coming in here to help or something?"

"Nah."

She sassily snaked her neck. "Then get your ass out of here."

Kevin chuckled, expecting nothing less from his wife. "Alright, man. Hurry up, though. I need you to come break these niggas' asses for me. They're raping my pockets."

Shay shook her head. "I know yall niggas aint playing dice?"

"Hell yeah," Kevin nodded.

"Aww, that's soo cute," Raven cooed. "Kevin is coming to get his woman to fight his battles. Let me guess, my Zaddy is taking all yall coins."

Kevin scratched his head. "Raven, if I aint know no better I'd swear that you and your nigga be burning candles. Nobody's luck is that damn good."

"That's cause I got the Midas touch, nigga. He has a lifetime of good luck, as long as I'm his wife," Raven teased.

Raquel cut her eyes at her sister. "Bitch, please. Bae, tell that nigga to go wash his hands. He probably got her pussy on his fingers, and shit. Midas touch my ass."

"What?!" Shay hollered. "Bitch, you is stuuuupid! Where does this shit come from?"

Raven laughed hard, knowing that her husband Jahrein had indeed just played with her clit on the ride over. She was grateful that her oldest, Little Jah, had driven his siblings over separately in their Escalade, giving them the opportunity to ride there alone.

"What?" Raquel hunched her shoulders. "I'm just saying."

Kevin's shoulders trembled as he laughed at her. He loved her raunchy humor.

"Mama, where's the keys to the car? I forgot my phone," Shay's son, Monster, questioned as he ran into the room.

"Go ask your sister. She had them last," Shay instructed.

"I was trying to, but I can't find her. She was sitting in the living room, but then her and Little Jah went outside together."

"Well, check outside," Raven offered.

Monster frowned, causing his green eyes to darken. "I did. They're not out there. I think they left in your truck, Auntie Raven."

Raven nodded. "They probably went to the store, or something."

"Or they're somewhere humping," Raquel blurted.

"Humping?" Monster repeated.

"Boy, get out of here!" Shay yelled, sparing his impressionable ears. "Wait 'til your sister get back to get your phone."

Monster smiled, after receiving an earful, but also immediately jogged off.

Raven rolled her eyes. "Bitch, stop the madness. Lil' Jah and Josairah don't see each other like that."

"Whatever. If you say so. But I think they like each other. I've seen them interact when they spend nights over here at the same time. I even asked Keyasia if they had anything going on, but you know her ass will lie for them. Hell, they probably got some dirt on her ass, keeping her from breaking the silence," Raquel scoffed, knowing her daughter all too well.

"Well, I don't see it," Shay claimed. "They act like cousins more than anything to me."

"Umm hmm," Quel pursed her lips together.

Kevin licked his lips. "Quel, you messier than a muthafucka, but yeah, hurry that ass up." He strolled out of the room. "I'ma get them to play pool, until you come. Them dice are probably nigga rigged," he grumbled.

"She would have everybody and their mama over today," Keyasia mumbled, as she and Wale stepped through her home.

Wale was rather quiet, as he listened to her ramble. He could detect a bit of nervousness, and it was rubbing off on him. Usually, he didn't concern himself with meeting chicks' parents, but he had too much respect for Kevin to handle things that way.

"Yeah, but this house…main. My nigga Kevin is doing it. I aint think he was living like this. I could see us having something like this one day," Wale whispered, causing a chill to ease up Key's spine. Obviously, he could see them in the future, which said plenty.

"Yeah, I helped them design this house. They built it from the ground up," she informed him.

"That's what's up." He nodded, as he continued to glance around. They'd traveled beyond the living room, which was void of people, but loud voices could be heard in different directions. That told him that people were simply congregating in the other areas within the home.

"Yall finally made it, huh?" Kevin uttered, as he crossed paths with them in the hallway.

Key's heart skipped a beat. "Hey…hey, daddy," she stuttered.

Kevin smirked. "What's up, baby girl? You finally decided to come see us, huh?"

"Yeah," she answered coyly.

"What's up, nigga?" Kevin asked Wale.

"Chilling, main," he offered, as they clasped hands.

"Yeah?" Kevin locked eyes with him. "So, how you end up dealing with my daughter, man?"

Wale smiled. "It's a small world, I guess."

Kevin nodded. "I feel you. But go holler at her mama with her, and then come back to the game room. I wanna chop it up with you."

"Okay," Wale agreed.

"Cool," Kevin voiced, as he ventured further down the corridor.

"I guess," Keyasia sighed, although deep down she was relieved. The first round had gone well.

Hearing laughter coming from the kitchen, she knew that her mother was more than likely there. Therefore she tipped in that direction with Wale trailing closely behind. "Uh, yall are loud in here," she teased, as she entered the room.

All the women lifted their heads.

Raquel smiled. "'Bout time. I was 'bout to report your ass missing."

Wale stood humbly with his hands behind his back. "How are you ladies doing?"

He was a little more comfortable with the females, especially ones as attractive as them. All three women were beautiful to him, and if he'd seen either of them on the streets, before Key…he would've hollered, without a doubt. Raquel looked more like Key's sister, was just as fine, but thicker. The other chick sitting next to her had to be her sister, because they were almost identical. Then the last chick…her ass was so big that he could see it while she was sitting down. Three dimes, for sure.

"I'm fine, cutie," Raven smiled. She leaned over, whispering to her sister, "Niece got trouble on her hands. You said that he was handsome, but *damn*. He can't be nothing but a headache…with his sexy lil' ass. And are those eyes green or hazel?"

"Both," Shay answered, curling her lips. "And he is a fine muthafucka. Niece gone have several *problems* on her hands."

"Yall are so rude," Keyasia spoke up. "Over there whispering like we aint standing over here. And loud too. We can hear yall."

Wale chuckled.

"Girl, be quiet," Raquel waved her off. "And hey, Wale, sweetie. Pull up a chair, and come chat with us."

He nodded, as he did as he was told.

"Oh, Lord," Key grumbled, knowing that those three women had absolutely no filter. There was no telling what they'd say. She stood at the kitchen's island, listening closely.

"So," Raven was the first to jump off the interrogation. "How old are you?"

"I'm twenty-four," he answered, looking directly into her eyes, asserting himself.

"So, you're four years older than Key." Raven nodded. "That aint too bad."

"Is Wale the name your mama gave you?" Shay questioned.

"Nah, it's Corinthian."

"So, I guess she wasn't lying about that." Raquel cut her eyes at her daughter.

Keyasia lifted a brow. "Since when do I lie at all, mama?"

"Shit, you was hiding this nigga, right here. I aint know what to think."

"Yeah, I told her she was tripping," Wale added, coolly, as he licked his lips.

"I can tell you're real smooth with it, too," Raven said easily.

He slid his tongue across his teeth, drawing attention to his soft lips. "I don't know about that."

"Anyway," Raquel butted in. "Wale, be real with me. You really like my daughter?"

He blushed, as he rubbed his chin. "Of course. I wouldn't be here if I didn't. That's my baby."

A chill shot up Key's back, as she played it cool, remaining silent.

Raquel nodded. "I hear that. But I want you to know that I know what you do with Bee. Hell, we all know, and that aint what I want my daughter a part of."

"And she won't be. That's something that I keep away from her. And I'd leave her alone, before I'd have her in the middle of some street shi…I mean, stuff."

"That's all that I ask," Raquel declared. "And I'll save any other talk for another time, but you're smart enough to know that your *work* won't last forever. Are you investing your money? Because as a lawyer, I can definitely point you in the right direction."

"I do a little something," he admitted. "Me and Keyasia was chopping it up, and she convinced me to become a silent partner in a clothing store with my cousin out in the Woodlands."

"Oh, really? Is it opened, yet?"

"Yeah," he nodded. "Keyasia helped out a lot. That's when I realized that she actually had a brain," he chuckled.

"That's cause she's my niece," Raven couldn't resist adding.

"Whatever," Raquel rolled her eyes. "But yeah, if you need any further help, let me know."

"Oh, I will be in touch on that matter. I do need to flip more of my money legitimately." He rubbed his hands together.

Shay examined Keyasia from her head to her toes, checking out her simple Seven jeans and t-shirt get up. "Key, you're all huddled up in a lot of clothes today," she teased, knowing usually Key liked to show skin.

Keyasia glanced down at her clothes, as if she'd just realized what she was wearing.

"I think she looks nice like that," Wale offered, unintentionally telling them everything they needed to know. Her attire was definitely his doing.

Raven lifted a brow. "Are you a little controlling, Wale?"

He hooded his eyes. "I wouldn't say that, but I can be a little jealous. Nothing extreme, but I'm well aware that she's beautiful, and any man would be lucky to have her. But with that being said, Keyasia's grown, and free to dress herself as she pleases…and how I like," he smiled.

"See," Raven pointed. "There goes that suave shit again. That was a cool way to say that she won't be dressing any kind of way with me."

"Well, a little jealousy never hurt anybody. As long as it's not too much," Shay interjected. "It's cute…to a certain extent."

Raquel was a little surprised with how open Wale was, but she appreciated it.

"I see Keyasia is being extra quiet," Raven acknowledged. "I think she done met somebody that can tame her ass."

Keyasia immediately sucked her teeth. "Auntie, you cute and all, but you tryin' it, baby."

Wale snickered.

"Aye, daddy told me to tell somebody named Wale to come here," Scooter interrupted, sticking his head into the room.

Wale scooted his chair back. "Well, I guess that I have to go through my next line of questioning."

Promiscuous Girl: Keyasia and Wale

"You know it," Raquel confirmed, as he stood up, and followed Scooter.

"So, I guess you're my sister's new boyfriend, right?" Scooter quizzed, as they strolled through the house.

Wale adjusted his sagging jeans. "Something like that."

Scooter grinned. "Well, good luck. She's crazy. I don't know how niggas deal with her…and can't seem to leave her alone."

"Can't seem to leave her alone?" Wale repeated, instantly catching that. "Her exes are still around?"

"I wouldn't say that, but they chase her. Even after she does some of the craziest stuff to 'em," Scooter chuckled. "But maybe they know something I don't. Ion care how pretty she is…couldn't be me."

Wale nodded, as they approached an open doorway. He didn't know what to expect from Kevin, as he entered their game room. Kevin wasn't there alone, either. There were several teen boys, and a few other adult men as well. The youngsters were playing the vintage arcade games, while the men were either watching, or playing pool.

"*Well, let me tell you a lil' something about the niggas I roll with. We chin check bitches. We don't go for that hoe shit. Come to the bloody Nickle trying to stunt. Fifty thou say I knock your ass out with one punch…*" Geto Boys' music floated from the built in speakers in the ceiling.

Kevin stood with no shirt, upper body fully tatted, looking no older than Wale. But Wale didn't allow his youthfulness to fool him. He'd actually witnessed Kevin pull a trigger a few times, and knew firsthand that he'd

Nicole Jackson

rightfully earned those two teardrops underneath his left eye.

The unmistakable scent of weed was in the air, as a blunt dangled from Kevin's mouth. He held the pool stick in his hand, as he locked eyes with Wale.

Wale smirked, thinking of how his big homie was out there, living it up in the burbs, but would probably always be a hood nigga at heart. "Aye, what's up?" he spoke to everyone in the room.

"'Sup," everyone replied simultaneously.

"I know those women were talking your ear off, huh?" Kevin guessed, as he took a shot on the pool table.

"You know it."

Kevin nodded, before he glanced up at his boys. "Say, let me pause this game for about five minutes. I wanna rap with him for a moment."

The men all nodded.

Kevin placed his stick on the table, before stepping around to Wale. "Come on, man." He led him out of the room.

Following closely behind him, Wale knew that he wanted to have a man to man. Together they stepped outside onto the back patio, which led to a sizable sparkling pool. Taking a drag off the blunt, Kevin blew smoke through his nostrils.

"What's been good with chu?"

Wale rubbed his hands together, as he trained his eyes on the pool. "Man, you know. The same ole same ole."

Kevin nodded. "I know you and Bee are still doing yall thing."

"We are," Wale readily admitted, sticking his hands in his pockets.

"And you know that I don't want Keyasia getting caught up in none of that, right?" Kevin cut his eyes at him.

Wale immediately nodded. "For sho'. That goes without saying. I wouldn't put her in any compromising position."

Kevin tilted his head. "But sometimes shit is beyond your control."

"True, but that's in anything. It wouldn't matter if I worked a nine to five. Shit happens. But as a man, I'm standing here telling you that I have no ill intentions with your daughter. If I did, I would've backed off the minute I found out that she was your daughter."

"I hear you, man. I hear you. So, I guess you should know that I'll die for mines. I'll kill for her. And I won't stand for no nigga putting their hands on her, or none of that hoe shit."

"Big homie, on God, I hear you. If I gotta beat her, I don't need her. And besides, I doubt Keyasia would let me get down like that, anyway."

Kevin thought about it. "Shit, probably not. She's her mama on one thousand, for sure."

Wale cracked a smile. "Well, her mama must be a handful."

"Nigga," Kevin rubbed his head. "That's the understatement of the century. Talks more shit than the law should allow."

"Well, Key got it honest, then."

"Pretty much," Kevin agreed, as he tucked his lips into his mouth. "But she's straight, though." He studied Wale. "Respect my daughter, man. That's all that I ask. And if you can't do right by her, then leave her alone."

"I got you," Wale claimed.

"Alright," Kevin nodded, extending his hand for a shake. "I'ma hold you to that. A man is nothing without his word."

Wale nodded. "Aye, I can't argue with that."

Kevin cracked a smile. "Bet not, nigga."

Chapter 11

"I'm surprised his ass is on time," Keyasia grumbled to herself, as she dragged her luggage behind her. She was headed towards the exit, and could clearly see Wale's awaiting Benz.

After four days of being in Atlanta, she was back at home. She'd done a video, and two club appearances while there. The money was good, and she'd had a decent time, but everything would've felt better had she spoken to Wale at least once. For four damn days, he'd been M.I.A. and she was quite eager to learn why.

As soon as she sashayed outside, his trunk popped open. He then hopped out of the car, and stepped to the rear end. Keyasia sighed heavily, as she rolled her Gucci luggage to the trunk.

"What's up?" he questioned, as he grabbed the bag, placing it into his car.

Spinning on her heels, she stomped to the passenger's side, and slid in, never uttering a word.

He shook his head, as closed his trunk, before easing back into his car. "I guess you didn't hear me?" he posed, as he pulled away from the curb.

Keyasia studied her stiletto shaped nails. "What did you say?"

"Uh, okay." He nodded. "We playing games today, huh?"

"No," she denied. "There's no games. I just don't really have much to say." She toyed with her phone, scrolling through random things.

"Why is that?" he briefly glanced her way.

She shrugged, never giving him eye contact.

"You…you mad at me, Keyasia?"

She tucked her lips into her mouth, causing those dimples to sink into her cheeks. Unbeknownst to her, he loved whenever she'd do that. She tilted her head, before speaking. "You know…actually, I am."

He smirked. "Why is that? You didn't get the roses I sent you?"

She rolled her eyes. "You know, four dozens of roses would've been cool had I been able to talk to you. I called and texted you several times, and never got a reply." She finally lifted her head, and glared at him. "And then you have the *audacity* to get Craven to call me, and confirm what time my flight was landing."

"Man," he dragged out, rubbing his chin. "That should tell you that I was busy."

She balled up her face in anger. "Busy? Nigga, what kind of fool do you take me for? The same energy you exerted to get your cousin to call me, you could've easily taken thirty seconds, and called me your damn self."

He licked his lips, as he focused on the road. "Yeah, I could have, but I aint wanna talk to you."

Her heart sank down to her stomach. "You didn't want to talk to me? What? What is that supposed to mean?"

"Exactly what I just said. I didn't wanna talk to you," he expressed again.

She gulped. "And why not?"

"Cause I didn't want to pretend that everything is kosher, or argue, so I kept my distance."

She narrowed her eyes. "So, why did you send me those flowers with the card, claiming that you were thinking of me?"

"I was thinking of you," he claimed. "Otherwise, I wouldn't have sent them."

She grabbed her forehead. "Okay, now I'm confused."

He shook his head. "It aint nothing confusing about what I just said. I might have missed you, but I wasn't feeling your actions, so I didn't answer your calls."

"What actions?!" she snapped.

"Ion know why you hollering, and shit. But you know what the fuck I'm talking about. And I don't give a fuck about you bringing up the fact that I do illegal shit. That bullshit you do should be against the law too. You just visually prostituting yourself. Shaking your ass in the clubs in provocative clothes for a few dollars. Taking pictures and being friendly with a bunch a niggas, calling that shit work. And what's crazy is that I know you don't even need the money. I really believe you just love the attention. Shit, sometimes bitches aint supposed to be seen."

"Bitches, huh?" Keyasia's nostrils flared.

"Calm down. That's just a figure of speech."

"I don't give a fuck!" she shouted. "Let me call you a bitch, bitch!"

He snidely snickered. "You feel better now?"

"Man, fuck you. Seriously, you catch attitudes left and right, acting like I need to do everything you say. But I don't put any demands on you. I don't tell you about the fucked up decisions you make, but you trying your hardest to make me feel like a hoe. Like I'm the problem. Nigga, I'm barely twenty years old. Got a whole lot of living to do. And I'ma do what the fuck I want."

"Oh, we know that. That's what you did. Hopped your ass up, and said fuck me. Then you didn't tell me that you was doing a video. I gotta hear the shit from my niggas. And that bitch ass nigga you did the video with made you his WCW. That's all good that people are now assuming that you and him are fucking around, right?"

She frowned. "You know that's just to hype up the video, and get people talking."

He grimaced. "Ion know shit. For all I know, he could've smashed."

With fury, Key reached back, before slapping the spit out of his mouth.

He took the vicious blow with a smile. "Hhhh…okay. You do that shit again, and you gonna have to call your daddy. Somebody's gonna have to see me."

"Nigga, I'll see you. I aint gotta call my daddy," she fumed. "We can tear this muthafucka up!" she loudly clapped her hands.

"You's a rowdy, hardheaded, ignorant broad. But I likes that shit, though. Just keep that same gangsta talk when I hit your ass back," he spoke calmly.

"And like a woman, I'll take that, because I opened that door. But then it'll be over, and you won't have to worry about me getting my daddy. You can just consider me dead to you."

He shrugged. "That's cool with me. Bitches is like buses. Miss one, next fifteen, one coming."

"Well, how about you let them come now?" she folded her arms. "You can do you, as soon as you drop me off. Believe that."

"Baby girl, my mama six feet deep, and I haven't needed her permission since the sixth grade. So, I definitely don't need you to tell me what I can do," he spat, as his cell rang on the dashboard. He grabbed it, and realized that it was Craven. "Yeah?" he answered.

"Say, nigga, where you at?"

"Leaving the airport. Why, what's up?"

"What you mean, what's up? You aint get all those messages?"

"What messages?" Wale questioned in confusion.

"They had to rush Gan to the hospital, and they're saying that she might not make it."

His stomach turned. Gan was his great grandmother, and had been a huge part of his life. "Man," he drawled not knowing what to say. He rarely displayed emotion when something this devastating arose. "What's wrong with her?"

"They say it's heart failure," Craven revealed.

For a few seconds, Wale said nothing. Keyasia cut her eyes at him, as she could clearly hear the entire conversation. Even on Craven's end. "Alright, man. So, yall 'bout to ride down there?"

"Shit, I'm like forty minutes away. I been calling you all morning."

"Fuck," Wale vented. "After my shit just kept ringing, I turned it off. And I damn near overslept, before rushing to the airport. I aint check to see who'd been calling."

"Well, you gonna have to play catch up. Everybody is either already out there, or on their way. We couldn't wait on you any longer."

Wale sighed heavily. "Alright. I'm 'bout to fill up, and hop on the highway."

"Shit, that's exactly what I did. I left straight from the club, nigga."

"I feel you. You aint did nothing wrong. But, yeah, I should be out there in the next four hours. I'm getting this gas, and leaving."

"Alright, bet. See you when you get here," Craven ended the call.

Keyasia really didn't know what to say, as the car grew silent. She definitely didn't want to ask stupid questions, upsetting him. She'd gotten the gist, and knew exactly what was happening, but didn't know where the hell he was headed. After exchanging such harsh words, she was sure that he'd be dropping her off to her truck, which was parked at his townhome. But just as he'd told Craven, he stopped at a gas station, filled up, before traveling down 45. They were probably an hour outside of the city when she decided to say something.

"Uh, where exactly are we headed?"

"Dallas," he answered dryly.

"Dallas, huh? And who lives in Dallas? I thought your family was from Louisiana."

He exhaled. "My great grandma's oldest son moved out there, and eventually gave her a house. He told her that it could be the family's house. Then later my grandmother moved out there to help take care of her mama. So, that's where they live…and that's where I'm going."

"Where *you're* going, huh? So, I guess I'm getting out at the next exit or something."

He sucked his teeth. "Keyasia, I aint in the mood to go back and forth with you."

"And I'm not, either. But you said that's where you're going, as if you don't have my ass in this car too."

"Look, I aint have time to be dropping you off. That shit would've pushed me back a hour, if not more."

"And I'm not disputing that. I know that you need to see about your grandma, so I'm not tripping. You do what you have to do. I just don't want to get to the destination, and feel like I'm stranded."

"Stranded?" he scowled. "The fuck are you talking about? You act like I'm some bitch nigga that'll flip the script and leave you hanging because of a argument. If I rock like that, then I wasn't real from the beginning."

"Whatever," she grumbled.

He glanced at her. "Don't be whatevering me. You better hope one of my cousins don't see how you busted my lip. I aint gon be able to save you."

"I wouldn't give a fuck. Them bitches better have a whole fuckin' army. Cause I'ma slide me a few bitches, and then call for reinforcement."

He screwed his face up. "Keyasia, you aint that fuckin' bad. You can't whup everybody. I got some cousins on my mama's side that'll give you a run. Shit, a lot of my people are from your hood, and will jump your ass in a heartbeat."

She pursed her lips. "Nigga please. I know you kin to Kaydoa, but I know most of his family. That must be ya daddy's side you speaking on now. Fuck them…whoever they are. If Ion know them, then they aint about shit, anyway. Your people are probably some marks."

"And when they whup your ass don't say nothing," he teased, wanting to aggravate her.

She stared straight ahead. "They better come with it. Cause I'ma keep coming, until a bitch lay me out."

Despite his internal turmoil, he grinned. Keyasia was funny. Yeah, she was serious, and meant every syllable uttered, but it was still humorous. Her parents moving out into that huge house in a gated community hadn't changed her one bit. She talked like any other hood girl, who swore she was a knock out artist. He loved that she was multifaceted, and never afraid to speak her mind.

"Nigga, aint shit funny." She waved her hand.

"Alright, man." Just then, his cell rang again. Checking the screen, he saw that it was his grandma. "Hello."

"Corinthian, why haven't you been answering your phone?" his grandma wasted no time.

"I was tired, granny. So, I turned my phone off," he explained.

"Well, your Gan is in ICU, and we need everybody here to help her shake this."

"I know," he revealed solemnly. "Craven told me, and I'm on the way as we speak."

"Good. You're not driving by yourself, are you?"

"No. I have somebody with me."

"Oh, okay. Is Kash with yall?" she asked, assuming that the 'somebody' he referred to was Mona.

"No uh."

"Well, why not? You know how much Gan loves that little boy. And I wanted to see my grandbaby. Ask Mona why she left my baby at home."

He sighed. "Granny, she's not with me, either."

"Oh," his grandma paused. "Well, who's riding with you, then?"

He cleared his throat. "Her name is Keyasia."

"Keyasia? Umm, okay. I guess you and ole Mona are on bad terms, huh? I was hoping you'd stop playing. You've been dealing with her for a long while, and hell, she's the closest thing you've had to a girlfriend. And now you've added somebody new to the equation."

"Oh, Granny, don't start all that," he groaned. "I never told you that I was pursuing a relationship with her. Yall got all attached to Kash, and started making too many assumptions."

"Assumptions my ass. You've been playing daddy, bringing her around, and fucking her. Hell, what was we supposed to think?" she snapped.

"Granny, there you go talking crazy. I'ma see you when I get there, alright?"

"Umm hmm," she grunted. "You just hurry up. Changing women like you change your damn drawls," she grumbled, ending the call.

Keyasia sat, fighting her urges to go off. After hearing about the state of his great grandmother, she wanted to bury the hatchet, at least until her fate was known. But after hearing what she'd heard, she wasn't so sure if she could keep the peace. Consequently, it wasn't long before she caved in.

"Who is Kash?" she questioned with an arched brow.

He gripped the steering wheel a little tighter, as he kept his eyes trained on the road. "He's Mona's son."

"Mona's son, huh? And your family has a relationship with him?"

He gripped the bridge of his nose. "Yeah."

"What about you?" she narrowed her eyes.

"Yeah," he gulped. "I have a relationship with him, as well."

"And exactly what does that mean?"

He exhaled, really not wanting to have that conversation, right then…if ever. "Man, look, it means that while dealing with Mona I grew attached to her son. I provide things for him, spend time when I can, and basically do all the shit that his bitch ass daddy won't do for whatever reason."

She glared at him, as she tilted her head. "And you never thought that this was something that I should know?"

He licked his lips. "Keyasia, let's not pretend that we've discussed everything under the sun. After going to snoop through my shit, and reading Mona's letters, what have you ever directly asked me about, regarding her?"

"Nothing," she retorted.

"Exactly."

"But why didn't you bring it up?!" she shouted.

"For what?" he bucked his eyes.

"Because that's some shit I'd like to know!" she lashed. "That would've helped me to see how complicated shit is between you and her. And then I could've decided if I wanted to deal with all that."

He frowned. "What's complicated about that, Keyasia?"

"A child's involved. I really thought I knew, and understood your relationship with her, but now I feel like I know nothing. And if you've been keeping the fact that you have this relationship with her son, then there's no telling what else you're not saying. She obviously knows your family, and I don't believe you've completely stopped communicating with her."

"I haven't," he admitted with no remorse. "I never told you shit like that. Nor do I have any plans to stop communicating with her. She'll be around, regardless. What I have with her son aint changing. And it damn sure aint up for debate."

"Wow," she stressed. "You've said enough. I definitely didn't know this at first, and I don't think I want to deal with it. So, I guess we'll be going our separate ways, after you see about your grandmother."

He grimaced. "What? We going our separate ways? Over my relationship with a little boy? What kind of self-centered bullshit is that?"

"Don't try to turn this around. You wouldn't like it if I had a child that I never mentioned, would you?"

He sucked his teeth. "That's different."

She scowled. "What? You know what…just shut up talking to me. I said what I had to say. Fuck you from this point on. You and your little readymade family aint gonna worry me. That shit is for the birds. I just fuckin' left a relationship for this bullshit, and you think that I'm about to walk headfirst into the exact situation again? Got me fucked up," she grumbled.

His eyes seemed to darken, as he became infuriated. "I told you that I aint that bitch ass nigga. So, don't bring what happened between you and another nigga into this. I aint gon say that shit again. Fuck that nigga, and I'm not about to pay for his bullshit. That's where you got me fucked up at."

She fumed. "Nigga, you might as well be talking to a wall, right now. I'm not hearing that shit. Like I said, you've made yourself clear, and I'm telling you straight up that I'm not on board. It's over."

He nodded angrily. "Bet that. Fuck it. If it's over, it's over. I aint never lost sleep over a bitch."

"And I wouldn't give two fucks if you did." She folded her arms. Seconds later, her cell was ringing. Lifting her phone, she saw that it was Josairah calling her. After sighing deeply, she answered. "What's up?" she asked, attempting to shake any tension out of her disposition.

"Hey, friend, where are you?" Josairah cheerfully inquired.

"Umm," Key tucked her lips into her mouth. "I'm headed to Dallas."

"Dallas?" she repeated in confusion. "But I thought that you were catching a flight home?"

"I was, but something came up."

"Damn," Josairah breathed into the phone. "I thought your ass was back in Houston."

Keyasia thought about it. "You must've needed me for something."

"Yeah…kind of," Josairah confessed. "I been kinda spending too much time over at Jah's house, and we…you know, wanted to switch it up for a few days."

Key giggled. "Bitch, yall are both getting out of hand. Trying to use me to lay up. You know my mama is on to yall. If she catches yall, she's telling everybody. I didn't know that much fuckin' was possible. But yeah, hopefully, I'll be back in a day or so. Then I'll be at home permanently, and I got you."

Wale cut his eyes at her.

"What do you mean by permanent?" Josairah asked curiously.

"I mean that I'm going to start back sleeping in my own bed. Staying away from fuck niggas, you know?"

"Oh Lord," Josairah sighed. "What did your boo do?"

"What boo?"

Josairah tittered. "Key, is he sitting there with you, right now?"

"Yeah," she breathed. "I'm riding with this lame ass nigga."

Wale slid his tongue across his teeth. "Keep playing with me," he warned. "And tell ole girl that she knew my little cousin was feeling her. That nigga made it seem like they was rocking on some exclusive shit, but you're talking about her fucking some other nigga. Is that how yall little crew get down?" he quizzed. Recently, his cousin Meeko had linked up with Key's friend, coincidentally. Meeko seemed to be immediately smitten by her, and Wale had naively vouched for the girl, thinking that she was one of those good girls. He'd met her once when Meeko had brought her to the hood, and this was when they all realized that the two girlfriends were dealing with the two cousins. But now Wale knew that Key's friend was fucking somebody, and it clearly wasn't Meeko.

"Our crew don't get down like shit," Key spewed. "Josairah was just cool with Meeko. He never even fucked her," she clarified. "And my cousin, whose Josairah's boyfriend, even told Meeko to stop calling her."

"Yeah, tell that nigga he has it wrong. I don't know what the hell his cousin has been telling him," Josairah added, obviously hearing both sides of the conversation.

Wale chuckled to himself. "Shit, I might do have it wrong this time."

"Clearly. But I wasn't talking to you, anyway. So, I don't know why the fuck you decided to insert yourself into my conversation in the first place."

"All I know is that you better take all that bullshit down a notch. I don't know who the fuck you think you're talking to. Cause you gon fuck around and be stranded on the side of the highway," he threatened.

Keyasia sucked her teeth. "Fuck you." She focused on her call. "Josairah, let me call you back, alright?"

"Okay, girl. Let me know if it's a problem, and I gotta make a phone call."

Key pursed her lips. "Trust me, I aint worried. But, yeah, I'll hit you later," she claimed, before ending the call.

"You really trying me, man. If you was any other bitch, on life, yo ass would be missing a few fuckin' teeth. I aint never allowed a broad to talk reckless."

"And I aint never met a nigga that was dumb enough to try me. I wouldn't be able to save that ass from getting buried six feet deep."

"Daddy can't fight all ya battles, and he aint the only nigga with a pistol. I don't fear no nigga walking this earth, and you can take that shit to the bank."

"Look, I really don't give a fuck. So, could you please stop talking to me? Please."

"And fuck you too," he rebutted.

"No thanks." She shook her head. "I pass on that weak ass shit."

"Weak?" he snickered. "So, I guess that's why I got all these scratches on my back, huh? Cause this dick weak, right?"

"Shit, they say fake it 'til you make it."

"Yeah, okay." He nodded. "I'm done with it. I won't say shit else to you."

Chapter 12

Keyasia was struggling to keep up with Wale, as he briskly traveled through Parkland hospital. They'd arrived in Dallas just twenty minutes prior, and he'd come straight there. The two had continued to argue the entire ride, although they both kept telling the other to stop talking. Keyasia rolled her eyes every few seconds, as she studied his bowlegged strut. Even when she was pissed, she couldn't help being wildly attracted to him.

She was feeling a tad underdressed, as she stepped through the hospital in black and white classic Adidas leggings with a matching cropped top. Her long Indian sew-in was swaying across her back, as she twisted. She was hoping that she didn't have to check anybody for getting the wrong impression about her based upon her attire in the setting.

"You finally made it, huh?" someone said, as Wale approached a group of people standing in the ICU waiting area. Amongst the crowd was Craven, his aunt, and a slew of cousins. Several of them continued chatting among themselves, obviously consumed with grief.

Keyasia stepped up, realizing whose voice she'd heard. Seeing her face, he smiled.

"What's up, Key? What you doing with this nigga? Your daddy knows you're hanging with him?"

Keyasia grinned. "Tino, you do realize that I'm grown, right?"

"And what that mean?"

"That I can do whatever I want." She twisted her neck.

Wale waved off Key and his cousin. "How many people are in the room with Gan? Do I have to wait to go in?"

"Granny and Keesy are in there with her," Tino explained. "So, yeah, you gotta wait, man."

"Wait a minute, is that Keyasia?" someone asked, causing everyone else to look up.

Key glanced up and locked eyes with Falen. She was Tino's wife, and someone Keyasia had always considered cool. She knew them and quite a few of their family members back from Fifth Ward.

"Hey, girl," Key spoke, before the two embraced.

"Uh, where's my hug? I know you see me standing here," Toya, Falen's best friend and Keesy's girl, interjected.

"Oh, bitch, you know I got you," Key laughed, as she hugged Toya as well.

Wale stood back, taking everything in. It was clear to see that Keyasia was well loved amongst his people, but he was interested to see how his grandma would respond to her since she seemed to be rooting for Mona.

"Anyway," Wale voiced. "What's Gan's condition, right now?"

"Her breathing levels have gotten better, but everything's still in the air for now," Falen answered.

"Yeah, it's fucked up," Tino breathed, as he stroked his waves with both hands.

"Corinthian, you finally made it, baby?" his aunt quizzed, walking up to him, taking him into her arms.

"Yeah," he sighed, before they released one another.

"I'm glad you made it. Shit, you even made it before Jeremy and Paris with their late asses," his aunt Trina expressed, referring to her son and his wife.

He smiled weakly. "You know how the Big Money Team operates," he used the name he often referenced his cousin and his wife as.

"Yeah, yeah," Trina scoffed. "Their asses still better get here."

"Corinthian, baby, when did you get here?" He spun around, and his eyes landed on his grandma. She wasn't a heap of tears, which was a good sign. "Hey, baby," she spoke softly.

"What's good, kinfolk?" Keesy smiled.

Wale hugged them both, before standing back with his hands in his pockets. "I've been here for a few minutes."

Keesy nodded.

"Well, everybody else has seen her, so you go in now," his grandma offered.

"Okay," he agreed, as he solemnly traveled down the hall.

Keyasia had taken a seat along with Falen and Toya. Seconds later, Trina sat down with her daughter Jerena and her niece Bubble Gum, who'd just arrived herself.

"Lord, I hope Gan pulls through this shit," Falen whispered, as she sat between Key and Toya. She was careful with her words, not wanting the men in particular to hear her. She knew how they wanted to remain strong, but knew that losing their great grandmother would eat them alive.

"Who you telling?" Toya added. "I know Keesy would lose his damn mind."

With Keyasia knowing both women for an extensive amount of time, she felt comfortable speaking on it. "Well, let's just pray for the best."

They both nodded.

"So," Toya cleared her throat. "You done went got yourself a Wiltz, huh?"

Keyasia giggled. "Ion know about that. I thought his last name was Ley."

Falen nodded. "That's his daddy's last name. His mama was a Wiltz, so there you go. You got yourself a Wiltz."

Keyasia shook her head. "Well, Ion see what's the hype all about with the niggas in this family, because they seem to be some big ass headaches."

Toya tittered. "But I bet you aint gonna leave his ass alone, though."

"Shit," Key stressed. "Yesterday I might have agreed with you, but after the ride here…I'm done."

"After the ride here?" Falen arched a brow. "What happened?"

"That nigga failed to mentioned that he's playing step daddy, and then told me that either I accept it or get the fuck, basically."

Toya smirked. "That arrogance will make you wanna kill their asses."

"Literally," Falen concurred. "But I still aint convinced that you're done. Because please believe me, I've said the shit a bazillion times."

"Fuck him," Key grumbled.

Toya pursed her lips. "Uh hmm. Bitch, please. It's something about them niggas. When you go there…them other niggas aint the same. And to quit fucking with him over a child is kind of petty, don't you think?"

"No," Key disagreed. "He never told me, until I overheard him talking about it today. Then I know for a fact that the Mona broad aint ready to let go, so I'd have to deal with drama from her, when he's not even obligated to be there."

"Mona?" Toya sucked her teeth. "Girl, please. That bitch aint shit. I mean, I aint got nothing against her, but she was never gonna get any act right out of that nigga. For one, she's super ignorant and ghetto. And I aint talking about when it suits the occasion. She don't know how to turn that shit off. So, I honestly believe that they'll never be more than they are right now."

"Regardless of them being more, she's still in the picture. And he so-called claimed she's not going anywhere. That alone was a red flag for me, so I'ma move around."

"How long have yall been fucking around?" Toya pried.

"For a few months."

Falen poked out her bottom lip. "I feel you. The respect seems like it's missing in this situation. You didn't know all that from the beginning, and he sounds unapologetic. And I get where he's coming from to a certain extent. He was probably trying to make it clear to you that he's sincere with being there for Kash. That's something that he's decided to do, and nobody is gonna sway him. But it probably came out at the wrong time, with this happening, and he was harsh. Tino have a tendency to do that, and it took me a long time to get adjusted to that shit. But it seems like you and Wale are still fresh, so I can understand you feeling like it's more than you can chew. That baby mama drama can be never ending, and it's probably even more annoying when he's not the biological father. Cause it's like he's choosing to have all the bullshit in his life."

"Exactly."

Toya waved her head, as she scrunched her face. "But you done already had that Wiltz's D. Aint not coming back from that. Keep it real with her, Falen. She aint going nowhere."

Falen smiled. "Toy, this is Raquel's daughter, man. They're crazy as fuck…and Wale is too," she realized. "Oh my goodness. I can only imagine the shit yall will get into."

"Like I said, fuck him," Keyasia reiterated. "I really hope that his grandma ends up being okay, but until we know something, I'ma spare him. But then it's a wrap."

******

Keyasia sat in a lounging chair, as she absently gazed at Wale. They'd left the hospital a few hours earlier, and they were all now back at their grandma's home. The house was two stories, surprisingly large, and decorated in a contemporary fashion. It was obvious that the grandkids had come together to make sure that their elders lived comfortably, because an abundance of money had been invested into the home.

She had been able to fit right in, since she knew several of his family members. It was rather ironic, after Wale had teased her about his family whupping her ass, and they ended up being her people. In fact, Paris, who was Wale's cousin's wife, was very close with Raquel and Raven, therefore she'd often visit their homes, and they had all taken several family vacations together.

Seeing Wale in a family-oriented setting was such a climate change. For the past hour, he'd been wrestling with all his younger cousins in the backyard, and all the smaller children seemed to naturally gravitate towards him. She'd never realized how much he seemed to love kids.

She'd been so lost in her own world that she never noticed when Toya vacated the seat next to her, and Wale's grandma took her place. "What's your name, baby?" she questioned, startling Key.

"Huh?" Key whipped her head around, coming face to face with a woman who definitely didn't seem old enough to have fully grown grandkids. Her rich caramel skin was wrinkle free, as she rocked a nice tapered short hairstyle.

She smiled lightly. "I said, what's your name?"

Key cleared her throat. "I'm Keyasia."

"Keyasia, huh?" she poked out her bottom lip. "Okay. How long have you been involved with my grandson, baby?"

Keyasia chose her words carefully, knowing that she could have a sharp tongue at times. "For about three or four months."

"Is that right?"

"Yes, ma'am." Key nodded.

"How old are you?"

"I'm nineteen."

"Ooh, you kinda young, huh?"

Key smiled awkwardly. "I'm legal."

Grandma snickered. "I know that's right. I guess that's all that matters."

"Yeah, I guess so," Key answered without a hint of laughter.

"So, where are you from in Houston?" she interrogated.

"I'm originally from Fifth Ward."

Grandma arched a brow. "Oh, really? Who's your people?"

"You're from Fifth Ward, right?"

"Yeah." Grandma nodded.

"You probably know my grandma, then. Her name is Dorothy."

"Dorothy that used to live on Nobel and Brewster? The one with the daughters Roz and Vee? And a few knuckle head boys?"

Keyasia gradually smiled. "Yeah. She's my great grandmother."

"Wait, you're Roz's granddaughter, right? Paris was telling me that Roz's daughter had a little girl when she was still a baby herself. You know, she keeps me in the know, because I moved out here when Jay Rock 'nem was still some teenagers," Grandma babbled, lightening up significantly.

"Yeah, Paris is like an aunt to me."

"Baby, it's a small world. Or did you meet Corinthian through Paris or Tino 'nem?"

"No, ma'am. I met him while I was out. I didn't know he was related to any of them, until today."

Grandma shook her head. "I don't know what you young people spend all your time discussing. Been na'done messed around and slept with ya own family. Yall better learn about the other person's family tree."

Keyasia squinted her eyes. "I never really thought about it like that."

"Well, now you know better, baby." She patted Key's hand. "But, yeah, what do you do? You work? You aint out there in them streets like Corinthian, huh?"

"No, ma'am. I go to college."

"College, you say?" she beamed. "That's alright, right there, baby. You have any kids?"

Keyasia snickered. "Boy, I'm really getting a full interview, I see."

"You better know it." Grandma tipped her head.

"Okay. I get it. But yeah, I don't have any kids."

Grandma nodded.

"Now, can I ask you something?"

"Sure, honey."

"What is your name?"

"Baby, they call me Grandma Nina."

"Okay," Keyasia leered.

"Uh huh, but don't pay me no mind, girl. I just had to come over here and see what you was about. It's not often that Corinthian brings girls around. Hell, I done only met one other one, and that was because she just popped up at Paris's party some years back. And that's when I fell in love with her little boy. Then for the longest I assumed that Corinthian was gonna be with the girl, but I guess not. And that aint none of my business. But I likes you."

Keyasia giggled. "Grandma Nina, you're blunt like me."

"Aint nothing wrong with that. And they say that's why my grandkids got it honest." She winked. "And look at Corinthian's ass. He's gonna go cross eyed trying to look over here."

Key's shoulders shook with laughter. "Oh my God."

"I'm serious," Grandma Nina tittered. "He tries to put on a front around me, but I know he be back in Houston, raising hell. Most of my grandsons love them streets, but Corinthian...I know everybody want his ass *off* the streets. While he's terrorizing folks. And ever since he was a little boy his hands would sweat. And you know what they say about people with sweaty hands." She cut her eyes. "Watch ya purse. Shit."

Keyasia was crying laughing, as Wale's grandma went in on him. Before long, it was impossible for him to ignore. "Say, granny, what you over there telling that girl?" he asked from across the yard.

"We talking about your thieving ass," Grandma Nina clarified.

Placing his little cousin, Tina, back on the ground, he stepped over to them. "Granny, I know you over here cracking on a nigga."

"No," Grandma Nina denied. "Me and Keyasia just over here having real talk."

"Real talk?" he lifted a brow, as he studied Key. "Well, did Keyasia tell you that she was done with me?"

Key paused for a moment. She wasn't expecting him to throw her out there like that.

"She's done with ya ass already? What did you do?" Grandma Nina placed a fist on her hip.

"Remember when you called me earlier?" Wale licked his lips, preparing to spill all the tea.

"Uh huh."

"Okay, well, she got mad about Kash," he snitched.

Keyasia gasped, as he threw her under the bus.

Grandma Nina hooded her eyes. "What you mean she was mad about Kash?"

Keyasia pursed her lips, as she glared at Wale. "Really? You're just gonna throw out half-truths, trying to make me look bad?"

"So, you didn't tell me that you was done?" he lifted his chin.

Key laughed despite herself, before focusing on his grandma. "Grandma Nina, you seem like a sensible woman, so can I ask you something?"

"Go ahead."

"Okay. If you're dating a man. You're at his home on the regular. You give him all your free time, and you believe you know him. And then you find out that he has a stepchild that he never bothered to mention. You find out through a conversation he has with his grandmother, while yall are riding in a car. Would you not look at that man differently, and reconsider giving him your time? *Especially*, when your time is a gift, and nonrefundable?"

"Oh, definitely. I would be reconsidering plenty," Grandma Nina agreed.

"Granny, what happened to loyalty?" Wale opened his arms. "*I'm* your grandchild," he emphasized.

She waved him off. "Boy, I don't uphold you in the wrong. That's what I won't do. And if you love and accept Kash the way that you claim you do, he should've never been a secret from the beginning. You never remove someone's choice from the situation. You was supposed to lay all your cards on the table, and then let her decide if she could hang. That's a huge piece of information you left out."

"Right on, Grandma Nina," Keyasia instigated.

"And it seems to me, baby," she faced Key. "You need to get him in line. If you do decide to stick around he needs to have his interactions with Mona and Kash out in the open. Get some understanding. Don't be no fool." She stood up. "Now, I'm done playing mediator. I need a damn drink," she murmured, as she twisted off.

Wale chuckled, as he collapsed into the seat she'd just stepped away from.

"Why are you sitting here, with ya dry snitching ass?" Key chided.

"Cause this my grandma's chairs," he pestered.

She cut her eyes at him. "Aint nobody playing with you. Go'on somewhere."

"You go'on," he shot back.

"Okay." She swiftly stood, and attempted to walk away.

"Quit playing," he snickered, as he pulled her onto his lap.

"Corinthian," she curled her lips. "Let me go. I don't have time for this bullshit," her nostrils flared.

He leaned his head back. "You still got a attitude, huh?"

"Nah, this aint an attitude. This is Ion got time for your bullshit-tude."

"Why you so plexed up?"

"You aint basic. You know why."

"So, you're gonna leave me hanging, when I need you?" he gently rubbed her ass, as he gazed into her eyes. Those green eyes were undeniably captivating, as she felt herself slipping into his spell.

A chill shot up her spine. Him *needing* her sounded musical to her ears. Before she knew it, she was rubbing his waves, submitting to his will. "I'ma ride with you at least until your grandma is okay."

Gradually, he formed a grin like a Chester cat. "I knew yo' ass wasn't going nowhere."

Chapter 13

Wale was resting his head in Keyasia's lap, as they relaxed on his grandma's couch. It was nearly one in the morning, and the living room was in an uproar over the sleeping arrangements their grandma was insisting upon.

His cousin Keesy was the ringleader, refusing to accept her commands. "Ant Nina, I aint no little kid," he argued. "Me and Toy got two kids. Why would I sleep in a room with another grown ass man?"

"It's simple." Grandma Nina bucked her eyes. "Put a ring on it. I don't know what the hell ya waiting for. It's obvious ya ass aint goin' nowhere. But until then…yall unwed asses aint laying up in here!"

Tino chuckled. "Yeah, yall niggas can share beds like the old days, while me and Falen go lay down, and do what grown-ups do," he teased, knowing that the rules didn't apply to him and Falen, because they were legally married.

"Granny, you cold blooded," Jay Rock, another one of Wale's older cousins, added. He and his wife and kids had just arrived two hours prior. His wife, Paris, was exhausted, because they'd just flown into Dallas last minute, and were switching time zones in the process. Therefore, she was out like a light, as she rested her head of curly tendrils on his shoulder, as she lightly snored.

"Cold blooded my ass," Grandma Nina jeered. "It's six bedrooms in here with plenty of beds. Yall make it work. And please don't make me come and check on you grown unmarried folks early in the morning. If ya aint married, then don't sleep in the same bed. End of discussion. And don't give me that shit about yall paid for everything in here. My sisters and brothers aint here, so *I'm* the oldest." She pointed at her chest. "And I'm laying down the law."

Jay Rock eased off the couch with heavy eyes. "This lady on one." He knelt down, shaking Paris awake. "Come on, baby. Let's go lay down."

"Jay," Paris whined with her eyes still closed. "Leave...leave me alone. I'ma just sleep here."

Wale instantly cut his eyes in her direction. He'd already decided that he was sleeping on the sectional, and really was hoping that not too many other people were planning on sleeping in the living room, period.

"Girl, get up," Jay Rock persisted, but she wasn't budging. "Shit," he sucked his teeth, before scooping her off the couch, and into his arms. Like a newborn baby she rested her head on his shoulder, as he traveled through the house.

Keyasia giggled, along with everyone else. "Everybody aint able."

"Pops just trying to get some booty," Jay Rock's son, Jeremy Junior, wisecracked.

"Well, at least they're *married*," Grandma Nina interjected. "But I'm gone to bed, yall. Goodnight." She moseyed out of the room.

Craven stood up, taking a stretch. "Shit, I'm 'bout to lay it down too," he yawned. "You coming Keesy, baby?" he smiled.

"Nigga, fuck you," Keesy griped, as he stood in the middle of the room.

Toya sniggled. "Bae, you might as well go lay down with him. You heard with your auntie said." She eased off the couch, and headed towards the stairs.

"Toy, stop playing with me," he insisted, as he followed her.

Craven wasn't too far behind them.

One by one, people began to venture into different areas within the home, searching for a space to sleep in. Soon, it was just Keyasia, Wale, and Jay Rock's twin sons Jeremy Junior and Jared remaining.

Wale eyed his little cousins, who were just a year or so younger than Keyasia. "Yall niggas aint gon catch one of those bunk beds upstairs?"

"Nah," Jared yawned. "I'm making a pallet right there on the floor."

"Yeah, I'ma go grab some blankets from the hall's closet," Jeremy Junior announced, as he stepped into the hall.

"Come on, man," Wale drawled, feeling like they were intentionally cock blocking. He was already a little uncomfortable with how familiar both twins were with Keyasia. Apparently, they ran in the same circles, and were talking about social settings that he didn't know existed, until the very moment they were uttered.

A few moments later, Jeremy was back, distributing blankets to everyone, before making himself a pallet on the plush carpet. Soon, his twin followed suit, as they were both completely oblivious to their cousin, Wale, mean mugging them the entire time. Then seemingly adding insult to injury, Jeremy decided to make a call, showing no signs of heading to sleep.

"What took you so long to answer the phone?" he questioned rather loudly.

"Nigga, let that girl go to sleep. Got damn," Jared scolded. "You oughta be tired of hearing her voice. Let her breathe. I'm trying to go to sleep."

Keyasia giggled. "You're talking to Jhyrah, Jeremy?"

Remaining engrossed in his conversation, he simply nodded.

"Who is Jhyrah?" Wale probed. "I know I heard you say that name before."

"You saw her before. That's my cousin. You know, Jahrein's daughter."

"You talking about the lil' chick with dimples like you, and the big ghetto booty?" he recalled. "Her real hair is long, and shit? And I think she's a little bowlegged."

"Got damn." Key glowered down at him, as his head still rested in her lap. "You sure was paying attention to her."

He cheesed. "Shit, who wouldn't pay attention? That young buck is super bad. Shit, now I see why lil' cuz gotta check in, before he close his eyes. He gotta keep his eyes on the prize. You aint doing nothing wrong, Lil' Jay Rock."

Jeremy glanced up. "Not too much, nigga. You just focus on Key. Don't be peeping mines."

Keyasia sniggled.

Jared sucked his teeth. "Man, you aint gotta worry about nobody snatching up Jhyrah. Aint nobody finna let her bleed them, like she bleeds you. Giving her all your money. Nigga gotta borrow from her just to eat at school. But I guess after she breaks him off during lunch, he forgets about feeding his face."

Keyasia gasped. "No, Jhyrah don't be giving it up on campus, does she?"

"Shit," Jared stressed. "They might as well make a room underneath the gym's bleachers," he snitched. "That's why that nigga be tricking. That girl is a freak."

Jeremy shook his head. "She can hear you. She said why you telling all her business."

"Tell her it's just payback, because she stays telling my business. I'm still mad about her telling my two bitches about each other."

Wale chuckled, realizing how much his little cousins had grown up. Because he and they lived two different lifestyles, he didn't see them very often, and until then he still viewed them as green suburban kids. Their father had hustled hard to ensure such. But now he knew that they were fucking, and who knows what else.

An hour coasted by, and Jeremy was still on the phone. He seemed to be struggling to keep his eyes open, but refused to hang up. His twin was completely knocked out, and had begun to snore. Keyasia was tired of sitting on the couch, and had just pushed Wale's head out of her lap, causing him to sit up. She then stood up, stretching her limbs.

"Shit, I'm about to go to sleep," she announced to no one in particular, as she grabbed two blankets. After folding up one comforter vertically, she placed it onto the floor.

Wale grimaced, as he observed her. "What chu doing?"

"I'm laying down," she explained sleepily, as she slumped down to the floor.

"But why you laying down there?" he furrowed his brows.

She smiled sheepishly. "You heard your grandma. I can't lay up with you."

He sucked his teeth. "Keyasia, quit playing, man. You can't lay up here, but you gonna lay down there with them?"

She rolled her eyes, as she spread the other blanket on top of her body, before lying on her side. "They're way over there. Nowhere near me. And besides, this carpet feels good."

He frowned, as he slid his tongue across his teeth. "Yeah, okay."

"You need to quit worrying about me," she slurred, as her eyes slowly lowered. "And go to sleep. I know you're...tired."

Within a matter of minutes, Keyasia was completely out of it, and Jeremy had fallen asleep with his phone glued to his ear. Wale was the last man standing. The living room was now dark, and the only light illuminating the room was the smart TV screen. Briefly, his mind drifted to his Gan. He was afraid that he might actually lose her, and he really didn't know how he'd cope with that. After thinking about it, he realized that Keyasia's presence made the burden seem a tad lighter. Not too many women could've brought a smile to his face during such a trying time. There was something about her that always caused him to forget about the perils the world could provide. She offered this weird, chaotic peace that only he understood.

He smiled to himself, as she let out a soft whimper much like the ones she produced whenever he was hitting her spot. Instantly, he'd rocked up. Wanting to forget about his problems, he eased off the couch. Quietly, he tipped over to Keyasia, while unbuckling his belt. Hovering over her, he dropped his jeans to the floor, before stepping out of them. He then lowered himself onto the floor, and slipped underneath the cover with her.

Feeling around, he eventually gripped the waistband of her leggings, and peeled them off her ass. Just as he suspected, she wasn't wearing any panties. Dragging his Polo briefs down to his knees, his hard-on sprung up, as he straddled her, while she lied on her stomach.

"Corinthian, what are you doing?" she asked, still half sleep, as she felt his dick slap her ass.

"Shhh," he placed an index finger to her lips. "Just let me fuck you back to sleep."

"But we're not alone," she whined.

"We know that," he whispered. "So, be quiet." He began to stroke between her thighs, causing her to arch her back. Soon, he was at the mouth of her pussy. With one hard thrust, he pushed inside of her.

"Uhhh," she moaned quietly.

"Huhhhh," he breathed into her ear, while moving inside of her.

Biting her bottom lip, she placed both hands firmly on the floor. Snaking his girth into her, he clasped her hands, intertwining their fingers. "Ummmmm," she purred.

"Why this pussy so wet?" he spoke into her ear, keeping his stroke steady.

"Cause…cause this dick feels…magical."

"I thought you said it was weak?" he dipped a tad deeper.

"I…I was just…ru…running my mouth."

"Is that right?"

"Yeahhhh."

"So, you done with me, huh?" he smashed into her.

"N…no."

"I can't hear you." He quickened his pace, stimulating her clit.

"Noooo," she whimpered.

"Where you going?" he growled, as he lifted into push-up position, swaying through her wetness. Her round ass was slapping against his hard stomach, creating distinctive sounds. But she was feeling so good to him that he didn't care.

Soon, he was straddling her, while her legs were closed, allowing her to feel every inch of him. He was so deep inside of her that she could feel the head of his dick, as it began to twitch.

"Uh, you make me feel so good," she cried. "I'm…I'm about to cum. Corinthian, cum with me," she pleaded.

"Damn, I'm cumming, baby." He plowed into her rhythmically. "I wish we was at home, so I can sleep in this pussy. Wake up, and bust in it all over again."

"Shitttt," she hissed, as her wound began to throb around him, draining all of his semen.

He rested his body on hers, as he felt himself spilling into her. "Why…why this pussy keep calling me? Get me to tripping, and shit," he exhaled, exhaustedly. "And what's crazy is that I know I be tripping. Got me all jealous, and shit. Feeling like a stalker."

She shifted her neck, awkwardly. "But you don't have to be jealous. Ms. Kitty might as well have your name written on it." She gripped his chin, bringing his lips to hers. Sensually, she slipped her tongue into his mouth, as they kissed passionately.

They lied there, kissing for what seemed like forever, while he remained rooted within her. Then as he felt himself slipping in and out of consciousness, he reluctantly pulled out of her. Caringly, he pulled her leggings over her ass, before doing the same with his briefs. He then pulled her into his embrace.

"Corinthian," she spoke barely audible. "What if your grandma sees us like this? Get back on the couch." She rested her head on his chest, making no effort in getting released from his grasp.

He palmed her booty, and squeezed. "Granny will just be bitching. That's one L I'll just have to take."

Chapter 14

"Well, if it aint Ms. Stick and Move."

Keyasia lifted her head in time to see her cousin sauntering into the living room. She grinned, as he flopped down on the couch next to her. "What's up?"

He smiled. "You tell me. You've been the one missing in action."

Keyasia nodded in agreement. She couldn't deny that she hadn't been spending much time around her parents' home, or with her family and friends. It had been weeks since she and Wale had traveled to Dallas, and once they'd arrived back in Houston they'd been practically inseparable. After three days, his Gan's condition had significantly improved, and by the time they'd left she'd been moved to a regular hospital room. With the task of supporting her boo in his time of need, Key had completely placed their entire argument on the backburner. Since then, they had carried on, as if the tiff had never occurred. It was also becoming apparent that Wale didn't want to revisit the situation with him, Mona, and Kash. And Keyasia had definitely taken notice, and it carried weight in her decision to stay at her own home, while he was out of town, handling business.

"Yeah, I'm just trying to get like yall," she teased.

Jahrein Junior scrunched his face. "What you mean?"

Key tilted her head. "Don't play crazy. You and Josairah."

He chuckled, but didn't bother with a response.

"And you must be over here to see her, because I could've sworn Lil' Kevin just left with some thot."

He lifted a brow. "Is Lil' Kev the only person I'm related to in this house?"

"No." she shook her head. "But that's who you primarily came to see, before you started screwing my friend every chance you get."

"So, I never come to chill with you? Or Lil' Ray-Ray?" he asked referring to their uncle, who was in fact younger than them both. He was Raquel and Raven's younger brother that their dad had fathered with Raquel's mother, Roz.

"Nigga, you know damn well that you don't come over here to hang out with that heathen. Every time you and him are in the same room yall argue," Keyasia tittered. "Yall are too much alike. Act just like Ray-Ray's old ass."

"Nah," Little Jahrein denied. "I act like my daddy. That nigga acts like Ray-Ray. You know, he tried to holler at Josairah, even though he knows what it is between us?"

"No shit?"

"Hell, yeah. That nigga got a hold of her number, and was texting her. I was going through her phone and saw the shit."

Key cut her eyes at her cousin. "Jah, you said that shit too casual. Why are you violating my girl like that?"

He grimaced. "How is that violating? She was sitting right there. I didn't do the shit behind her back, and if we kickin' it how we're kickin' it, then it should be nothing to hide."

She narrowed her eyes. "Okay, but does she go through your phone?"

"Yeah," he claimed. "She has. It's a two-way street."

She rolled her eyes. "If you say so. I don't know what the hell you and her got going on. Yall acting like this shit is forever. Like some grown-up shit."

"What you mean by that?" he furrowed his brows. "Do you and ole boy have some grown-up shit going on?"

She nodded with her bottom lip poked out. "Pretty much."

"So, why are you trying to diminish our situation?"

She paused for a second, before gradually smiling. "So, you really are serious about my girl?"

He squinted. "So, you think I'm doing this shit for nothing? As you've said, I've screwed her several times, therefore if that was all I wanted from her, her time would've expired a while ago. I aint gonna lie. The sex is amazing. But she's *amazing*. That's my baby," he beamed.

"Awww," Key cooed. "So, do you think you're in love?"

He licked his lips, as he stroked his waves. "I mean, I mean," he stuttered. "I got strong feelings for her…but love? I mean…"

She giggled. "Look, at you. Getting cold feet already. It's okay. I know how it is. A lot of dudes struggle with talking about their emotions."

He laughed. "Fuck you. You always trying to put people on the spot, man."

"My name's Keyasia and that's what I do," she declared. "But since we're talking, let me ask you something?"

"What's that?" he licked his lips.

"My lil' boo Corinthian revealed that there's a little boy he's taking care of, right?"

"Right." He nodded.

"And the little boy isn't biologically his."

"Okay."

"So, the little boy's mama still wants him, and he said that regardless of how I feel about it, he was going to continue to be there for the little boy. Should I be offended?"

"Offended for what?"

"Because he's basically telling me that it doesn't matter how I feel. And if it came to it, he'd choose them over me. So, either I'ma get with the program or move around."

Jah skeptically lifted his chin. "He actually told you that?"

"No, but that's the message I got from it."

"Key, niggas aint that complicated. If he wanted the other chick, he'd be with her, right? Aint you the one constantly at his crib, and getting all his free time?"

"Yeah."

"Okay, then. From the sound of it, your nigga just sounds like a stand-up dude. A man of his word. If he vowed to do something, he's not switching up just because you stepped into the picture. You should really be more concerned, if he allowed your presence to switch up his behavior with the little boy. Cause then you'd know that he's disloyal."

"True," she agreed. "But what if the little boy's mama becomes problematic? How much drama should I tolerate from somebody that he's choosing to keep around?"

Jah bucked his eyes. "See, I can't call that. I guess it depends on how much he loves the little boy, and if he really cuts for you. If the mama is the roadblock, I think most dudes would walk away, but I doubt she'd push him away. Because like you said, he chooses to come around, and she wouldn't want to change that. Especially, if she still wants him. But knowing you, that girl aint a damn problem. All the women in our family are needy as fuck, and can't deal with women and their dudes interacting. You probably just don't want to deal with the girl, period. And wanna argue the fact that the little boy isn't really his. Ass so jealous that ya skin is turning green."

"Fuck you." She playfully elbowed him.

Just then, a few voices could be heard approaching them, before Kevin Junior, and Amir Junior stepped fully into the living room. Instantly, Keyasia loudly sucked her teeth.

"What you sucking ya teeth for?" Amir wasted no time.

She rolled her eyes. "Lil' Kevin, why didn't you leave your company outside?"

"Key, this nigga is still my boy. It's been like that way before you ever decided to give him the booty. So, I aint acting brand new, just because you curbed his ass." He waltzed over to the couch, and collapsed onto it.

Amir scowled. "Curbed, my nigga?" he asked, causing both Kevin Jr. and Little Jah to chuckle.

Kevin Jr. opened his arms. "Ay, how else you want me to say it? She dropped your ass like a bad habit. Then blocked everybody from you to ya step-mama."

Key giggled at her little brother. He was super messy, and unapologetic about it.

"Alright, nigga. Talk that shit the next time you need some tickets to a concert," Amir threatened.

Little Kev propped his feet on the coffee table. "Shit, from what I heard, my new brother-in-law has connections too. One monkey don't stop the show," he taunted.

Jah snickered. "Kev, you cold blooded for that one."

"Yall niggas got jokes today, I see," Amir grumbled, as he slickly sat beside Keyasia.

She glared at him.

"What?" he lifted a brow.

"Why are you sitting so close, nigga?" she gritted

He smirked. "To bask in your essence."

"This nigga," Kevin Jr. murmured, right before someone rang their doorbell. He glanced over at his sister. "Queen Thot, go answer the door, man."

"Boy, bye. You get it." She waved him off.

He sprung to his feet. "You lazy, dog. You gon be fat when you get older. Watch," he warned, before swaggering off to the door.

Jah scooted to the edge of the couch. Keyasia studied him. "You expecting someone?"

A few seconds later, Josairah twisted into the room.

"Should've known," Key grumbled.

Jah lustfully ogled at his girlfriend, as she rocked a simple, fitted, sleeveless, race-back dress. Although slim, Josairah packed a powerful punch with her little curvaceous body. Her green eyes sparkled, as she laid eyes on her man. But then, she attempted to play it off, as she focused on her girl. "Friiiiieeeend!" she screeched, rushing over to hug Key.

Keyasia allowed the hug to linger for a second, before pushing her back. "Yeah, yeah. You can stop fronting, bitch. We both know you didn't come here to see me."

Josairah hovered over her. "How do you know? You don't think I miss you? You've been spending every waking moment with *Corinthian*."

Keyasia pursed her lips. "That may be so, but you still came here to see *Jahrein*."

"Whatever." Josairah playfully rolled her eyes, before smoothly copping a set next to Jah.

"Uh huh. Look at you. Couldn't even fake the front for a full minute," Keyasia teased.

Before Josairah could conjure up a snappy comeback, Jah gripped her chin, and eased his tongue into her mouth.

"What the fuck?" Keyasia chided. "This here aint no damn hoe house," she quipped.

Kevin Jr. looked at them with disgust. "Uh. I'm telling you now, man. If yall going in my room with that bullshit, I'm charging. You copping me them new Jays tomorrow, Jah."

Jah gave him the okay sign without pulling away from his kiss.

Keyasia shook her head. "Ion even get dick around here. Yall muthafuckas be doing the most. I wish Raquel or Kevin would come home, and catch yall ass. Shit, I'm hating."

"Key, chill out with that." Jah brushed her off, as he finally broke the kiss. He then eased off the couch, before grabbing Josairah's hand, helping her to do the same. "Let me talk to you in private for a second," he spoke softly.

"Okay," she practically gushed.

"Shit, *talk* my ass," Keyasia mocked, while the duo ignored her, as they headed upstairs.

Amir lightly tapped her arm. "Say, let them people do them, man. Quit hating. And stop lying. You know I done smashed you in ya room several times."

She rolled her eyes. "It must've been bad, because I'd damn sure forgotten."

"So, I guess that's why you scratched my back so deeply one time that you left a permanent scar," he shot back.

Before she could reply, her cell vibrated in her pocket. Quietly, she retrieved her cell, and viewed the text message.

Corinthian: *You still at your mommy and daddy's house?*

She hesitated for a second, before texting back. *I guess you're trying to be funny. But yeah I'm at home.*

Corinthian: *I'm really not. Aint that what little girls call their people?*

Keyasia: *Little girl, huh?*

Corinthian: *Yeah. Little girl.*

Keyasia: *Whatever. Why should I stay at the townhouse if you're not there? It doesn't feel the same.*

Corinthian: *That sounds like you miss me or something.*

Keyasia: *Is that a crime?*

Corinthian: *Nah. I aint gon lie. I'm feeling the burn too.*

Keyasia: *And its really messed up that you'll be gone for another three days.*

"Man, who are you texting?" Amir finally spoke up, becoming annoyed with her texting. That had to be a nigga.

Keyasia briefly lifted her eyes to focus on him. "Noneya."

"Let me see." He attempted to grab her cell, but she quickly pulled back in the nick of time.

"What's wrong with you? Don't touch my phone," she snapped, glaring at him. She felt her phone vibrate consecutively, indicating that Wale had replied multiple times. She glanced down at her phone's screen.

Corinthian: *I'll be back before you can blink your eyes*

Corinthian: *Did you get the money I left in your glove compartment?*

Corinthian: *Keyasia???*

Keyasia*: Yes I got it. But I told you that I was good. You didn't have to do that.*

Corinthian*: I did. You know that. But what took you so long to reply?*

Keyasia*: I was distracted*

Corinthian*: With what?*

"Keep disrespecting me," Amir seethed, as he successfully snatched her phone.

"Stop playing!" she blurted in full panic mode.

With her phone, Amir shot to his feet, stepping away from the couch, as he read the texts. "So, you missed that nigga, huh?"

"Amir!" she belted, as she sprung to her feet. "What the fuck?! You're out of line!"

Little Kevin sat back with a grin.

"Well, let me reply to this nigga." Amir typed on her phone.

"Nooo!" she screeched, before diving on him, causing them both to tumble to the floor. "Give me my phoooooone!" she straddled him.

"Damn," he breathed, gripping her ass. "I really miss this shit."

"You do?" she grinded into him.

"Hell, yeah." He licked his lips.

She could feel him hardening. "You need me to help you out?"

"Hell, yeah." He rubbed her booty.

"But I can't." she snatched her phone back, and scrambled to her feet. "The fuck you thought this was?"

Within a flash Amir was standing again, pulling her into his arms. "Stop running, girl. You don't miss me?"

"Amir," she whined, allowing her head to fall back. "We already discussed this. Let me goooo."

"I can't." he shook his head.

"Why?" she stressed.

"Cause I'm still in love," he confessed, holding her tight.

Kevin Junior fell over with laughter. "This that bullshit. Ole pussy whipped ass nigga."

Amir sucked his teeth. "Key, please, come outside, and just let me talk to you. Please."

"Talk about what?" she asked softly, remembering all the love she once felt for him. Then for a fleeting moment she wondered if the love was still there.

"Us."

She sighed heavily. "Amir, I really don't have anything to say."

"Okay." He nodded. "Then you can just listen."

She bit the inside of her mouth, as she rolled her eyes. "Okay." She gave in.

Finally. He felt there was a fighting chance for them. "Come on," he commanded, grabbing her hand, guiding her out of the house. After hitting his locks, they stepped to his BMW, which was parked curbside. Like a true gentlemen, he opened the passenger's door for her, allowing her to ease inside. He then quickly jogged around, and dashed in on the driver's side.

Glancing down at her phone, she realized that he'd just typed gibberish, and hadn't sent any messages. Still, Wale had sent a few more texts, but before she could thoroughly read them, Amir garnered her attention.

"Can you put the phone away for a second?" he implored.

Keyasia slid her tongue across her teeth, as she eyed him. For a minute she thought about telling him to kiss her ass, but she knew that wouldn't get them anywhere. He was determined to get things off his chest, obviously. Therefore, she'd allow him to have the moment, completely. "Okay," she agreed, as she placed the phone in her jeans.

"You seem to be really into this nigga," he acknowledged.

She frowned. "Is that what you brought me out here for? To talk about another dude?"

"No." he shook his head.

"Then what's up?" she studied him. Admittedly, Amir Junior was still handsome as ever. His caramel complexion was still velvety, and he had the prettiest, whitest teeth she'd ever seen on a guy. He was always fresh, and this day was no exception. The Givenchy ensemble he wore appeared tailored to his physique, and his tapered fade was freshly lined up. Then he smelled heavenly. But this was exactly how he carried himself all the time. Even while breaking her heart.

"Okay, Key. I just gotta make this right. I mean, I know I fucked up, but I'm not ready to let go. I tried to let go, but I can't. What I gotta do to make this right?"

She stared straight ahead, as she gazed out of the window. "I really don't know what you want from me, Amir."

"The same thing I've always wanted. Your heart."

Her heart skipped a beat, after hearing him speak those words. "You make it sound so simple."

"It is that simple. If there's feelings left, then there's always hope."

She sighed. "Hope, huh?"

"Yeah. We've been at it for too long. And no other girl can make me feel like you can. Nobody. No other chick can make me smile like you. All I do is think about all the fun we had together. How it was stress free. I can't find that with anybody else. I don't want to."

She laughed despite herself. "You should've been saying all that shit to yourself, before you fucked a bitch naked headed. *You* changed all that. And now nothing will ever be the same."

"But I don't want her. Valerie is just my BM. Nothing more. Nothing less."

"And you still fucked her, after I forgave you."

He drug both palms down his face. "I did. I regret that shit every fuckin' day, man."

She nodded, as she finally glanced his way. "But how did it happen? Tell me the truth. Be real for just once."

He took a deep breath. "Okay. I guess that I was spending too much time around them. You know that you was always closed off when it came to my daughter. So, I would put in my time at Val's house, because I knew that bringing the baby around you would make you uncomfortable. And I toyed with the idea of giving my daughter the complete package. Me and her mama. So, I'd straddle the fence, and play house. But I realized that dealing with somebody just for the sake of a child aint healthy. It just causes resentment."

"It could." Key nodded. "But are you not hearing yourself?"

He squinted. "What you mean?"

"You have a daughter, and you feel that I'm uncomfortable around her. I mean, I'm not disputing that you're right, but that's your daughter. Your child. How could you want to be with someone who doesn't fully accept your child? How could we ever work out, Amir?"

"I…I could keep the two separate, until the wounds heal," he stuttered.

"But what if time doesn't change how I feel? How could we be together? Because I think that's how you've been dealing with this. Hoping. Hoping that I'd come around. Hoping that time would heal everything. When truthfully we were done the moment she became pregnant. But we were stubborn, and held on. We both know what type of person I am. Stubborn as fuck."

"I know," he smiled weakly. "But that doesn't change how I feel about you. Love will make you fight, even when shit seems impossible."

"Yeah," her voice cracked. "Sitting here, I'm realizing a lot. You're right to a certain extent. And maybe five months back I would've been all for it. Ready to give love another try. But you've fucked up, and it led me to another person. Regardless of what you say about him, he hasn't hurt me. He hasn't made me feel inadequate. And it aint fair to give you another chance to fuck up, when he hasn't. It's bad enough that you've done a number on me. You've given me insecurities I once didn't have. And I try my best not to bring that into this new thing, but's it hard." She squeezed her eyes tightly, but tears still managed to escape. "Because you hurt me. And you want me to walk right back to that pain. Like I should just accept your mistake, and embrace it," her voice trembled. "It's not fair." Her shoulders shook, as she cried.

"Come here." He pulled her into his arms. "Stop that. I'm sorry. I'm so, so, so sorry," he apologized.

For a few minutes, Keyasia cried on her ex's shoulders. It was rare that she allowed people to see her truly vulnerable. She used that smart mouth to mask her true self. On the outside looking in, she was this playful worldly girl, who didn't sweat the small shit. She'd act up, and then laugh about it. But she'd then cry her eyes out the moment she was alone. And until that very moment, she'd never really dealt with the pain Amir had inflicted upon her.

"You know," she sniffled, as her head rested upon his shoulder. "I didn't realize how much you having a baby bothered me, until I started dealing with him. I be tripping, putting him in a box, thinking of how you betrayed me."

"I can never apologize enough for that," he whispered. "I never imagined one stupid ass night would change everything for us. Never thought there'd be a time where I'd have to watch you be with somebody else. I swear to God I hate that shit. But if you feel like you need to be with him, right now...I gotta accept that."

She smiled faintly.

"I don't like it, though. And just know that I'ma still love you. Can't change what I feel," he proclaimed, kissing her lips.

"Amir," she gasped, pulling away.

Before he could respond, there was a loud knock on the passenger's window. "Step out of the car, Keyasia."

Her heart plummeted to her stomach, as she recognized the voice. Whipping her head around, she locked eyes with Wale. He stood there with the look of death in his eyes. Without thinking, she pushed the door open.

"Get the fuck out," he commanded, standing in the car's doorway.

Keyasia practically jumped out of the car. "What...what are you doing here?" she stuttered nervously.

"Fuck all that," he fumed. "The fuck you doing in the car with this nigga? Kissing at that."

"No, no, no." she waved her head. "I wasn't kissing him. I mean, he kissed me, but I didn't want him to…" she rambled, trying to explain herself.

"Bitch, you think I'm trying to hear that bullshit!" he growled, practically biting her nose off.

Amir promptly emerged from his car. "Ay, she aint gon be another bitch in my presence."

Wale's nostrils flared, as he pointed. "Bitch ass nigga, I advise you to stay out of my business."

"Nigga, you don't know me." Amir angrily stomped around his car.

"You walked around here like you ready for me. What's up?!" Wale raged, stepping around Keyasia.

"Corinthian, calm down. Let me tell you what happened," she pleaded, on the verge of fresh tears, before rushing to stand in front of him. "I wasn't kissing him. I was just telling him that it's over between us."

He glowered down at her, as she held onto his shirt. "The fuck you take me for? You supposedly left him in the wind a minute ago. The fuck you needed to explain some shit that should already be understood?!"

"The fuck going on out here?" Kevin mumbled to himself, as he cracked their front door. His eyes grew larger when he realized that Wale was out there. "Jah!" he shouted.

Little Jah came racing downstairs. "What's up?" he huffed out, thinking that he and Josairah were about to get busted for having sex in his aunt's home.

"Come here!" Kevin Jr. called out from the front door.

Jah jogged over to his cousin. "What's going on?"

"Look at this shit." Kevin pulled the door open wider.

"Damn," Jah stressed. "Key done got caught in her pimpin'."

"Yeah, and she's struggling to hold that nigga back. Fuck. Let's go out there."

"Yeah, come on," Jah agreed, before they both stepped outside.

"Keyasia, let me go!" Wale shouted, as she held onto him for dear life.

"No!" she refuted.

"Key, move out of his way, man. I want that nigga to run up," Amir spat, refusing to back down.

"What?" Wale grimaced. "Nigga, if I aint halfway fuck with ya daddy, I'd have my pistol in ya mouth! You aint ready for this gangsta shit. I eat niggas like you for breakfast!"

"I'm ready for whatever!" Amir roared. "I aint never needed my daddy to fight my battles."

Wale attempted to charge at him, as Keyasia clung to him, preventing him from getting very far.

"Mir, chill out," Little Jah urged, attempting to guide him back towards the house.

"Man, fuck that nigga. I'll knock his hoe ass out!" Amir spewed.

"Knock me out, then!" Wale challenged, as he broke out of Keyasia's grasp. Rushing Amir, he threw two vicious slugs, both connecting with his jaw.

"Saaaay!" Little Jah blurted, as Amir countered with a slug of his own.

"Man, chill out!" Little Kevin yelled, prying himself between Amir and Wale. "Yall niggas aint in the hood! These white people are probably already on the phone with the laws. And that shit aint a good look. My mama and daddy don't want this type of shit going on in their front yard. Have some fuckin' respect!"

Wale nodded. "Lil' nigga, you right. I'ma respect my big homie's house." He backed off. "But you better pray Ion catch you on the streets, nigga. Your daddy's clout might not be strong enough to protect you," he threatened Amir.

"Fuck you! I'll be ready too. You aint the only one with a gun. Remember that!" Amir sputtered.

"Keep talkin' and you gon have to use it!"

"Corinthian," Keyasia grabbed his arm, as he attempted to step past her. "Let me talk to you."

He snatched away from her. "Aint shit to talk about. I see what it is with you. I'm good."

"You see what?" she panicked. "I didn't do anything. On everything I love."

"How the fuck are you gon tell me like I aint got fuckin' eyes? I seen you kissing the nigga!"

She bucked her eyes. "He kissed *me*! I was letting him know that it was nothing!"

"The fuck was you doing out here, in his fuckin' car? I'm texting, but you aint replying, and you out here with him. There aint shit you can say to make me understand that shit. You talk about how the nigga had a baby on you. But you must like dog ass shit like that. Obviously, I been going about this shit all wrong." He turned to leave.

"But that's why I'm done. I told him that," she expounded, running after him. "Baby, just listen." She grabbed his shirt, just as he reached his car.

"Get the fuck off of me, Keyasia!" he roared. "I'ma fuck around and hurt you! It's taking God himself to keep me from knocking your fuckin' teeth out." There was a deranged look in his eyes. "If you knew where my mind was going right now, you'd get the fuck away from me. I could strangle you with my bare hands, girl." He lifted his head. "Say, Kevin, come get your sister, man." He put his hands in praying position. "Please! I'm trying me best to keep my composure."

Kevin jogged over. "Key, come on." He grabbed his sister.

Wale dropped down into his car.

"Kevin, let me go!" she screamed, as he lifted her off the ground.

"Nah, man. Cause if that nigga hits you, it's gonna go down. Fuck all that," Kevin explicated, making sure that Wale heard him.

Keyasia felt like her world was crashing around her, as she helplessly watched Wale speedily back away from the scene. "The fuck, man. Put me down," she cried. "I was just trying to talk to him."

Once Wale's car had disappeared down the street, he obliged her request, placing her back on her feet.

"Move!" she yelled, shoving her brother away. "You make me sick!" she looked around, spotting Jah and Amir. "All you niggas! I fuckin' hate yall!"

Chapter 15

"I should just let the nigga go. If he wants to leave, then fuck him. There's a million other niggas out here. Who the fuck is he?" Keyasia grumbled to herself. "I don't need somebody like him, anyway."

She sat behind the wheel of her Range Rover, driving around aimlessly. It was nine in the morning, and she couldn't shake thoughts of Wale. She'd left the club around four in the morning, after doing an appearance, but didn't want to go home. Therefore, she'd stopped at IHOP with Taraj, and they'd fed their faces. As usual, Taraj was going on and on about Taz, who was out of town. The entire time Key sat with a grin, pretending she didn't have a care in the world. She couldn't even bring herself to tell her friend that she was going through it.

It had been a week since the fiasco outside of her parents' home, and she hadn't seen Wale since. She'd called, and called him, but he never answered. She'd even stooped as low as calling a few of his boys, and they'd all promised to deliver her messages, although she knew deep down that it was all a shot in the dark. He wasn't fucking with her.

Keyasia grew sick to the stomach, as she realized that he would usually be at home at this time of the day, blowing her back out. She wondered if he was still keeping to his old routine with a replacement.

"Bitch ass nigga," she gritted, before thinking about it. "And my shit is still over there. If he got a bitch over there, fucking with my stuff…He got me fucked up. I'm going to get my shit," she decided, knowing that she would have thought of any excuse to go over there, anyway.

Promiscuous Girl: Keyasia and Wale

Her nerves began to kick in, as she traveled to Wale's home. There was a very real possibility that he could be at home with another chick. Even worse, he could've changed the locks, preventing her from entering his residence. Knowing the type of man he was, she was bracing herself for the latter.

Pulling into his driveway, her heart pounded. Knowing all of his vehicles, she recognized two cars that didn't belong to him. "This muthafucka," she curled her lips, as she gripped her steering wheel. "He didn't waste no fuckin' time."

For a few minutes, she contemplated. More than likely, Wale had some broad in his house, but technically he had every right. He'd made it abundantly clear that he was done with her. She would be in total violation if she clowned him. But Key didn't want to be rational. Yes, she fully understood how he'd mistaken the situation between her and Amir. If the shoe was on the other foot, she would've undoubtedly done the same. But she was innocent, and felt that she was still deserving of him. He needed to understand that. He had to.

"Fuck it," she mumbled, before stepping out of her truck.

A surge of anxiety shot through her body, as she switched up to his door. With shaky hands, she pushed her key into the lock. To her surprise it still worked. Quietly, she tipped into the townhouse. Stepping to the living room, she noticed a pair of stilettos scattered across the area rug. The area rug she'd handpicked.

Her nostrils flared, as she ascended the staircase. At this point she knew that he was laying up with some bitch, but she wasn't walking away. Even if she accomplished

nothing more than causing a dramatic scene, she was going
for it.

By the time she reached the top of the stairs, she
could distinctively hear moaning. It was a female's voice.
Key's hands became clammy, as she ventured down the
hallway. Before she could reach the master bedroom, she
noticed one of the guest's rooms door was halfway open.
She soon discovered that the moaning was coming from
there.

Since she'd never bothered furnishing the room, it
had no bed, and the stark naked high yellow girl was wildly
riding a dick on the carpeted floor. Thinking she'd caught
Wale red-handed, Key barged into the room. That's when
she embarrassingly realized that it was in fact Craven
receiving a ride.

"The fuck?" Craven's head shot up, sensing
someone's presence.

"Oh, excuse me. I thought your cousin was in here,"
she explained, before casually leaving the room.

Not missing a beat, she continued to Wale's
bedroom. She discovered his door closed, and found herself
taking a deep breath. Expecting the worst, she twisted the
doorknob, before entering his room. Her breath was caught
in her throat, until she realized that he laying across the
bed, shirtless…completely alone.

Slowly, she tiptoed to his bedside. She hovered
above him, taking note of the shoes still planted on his feet,
and the two chains around his neck. Usually, whenever
he'd fall asleep like this it meant that he'd had a long night,
and there were a few things on his mind.

His phone was sitting near his head, signifying that
he'd probably been catching every call she made. She knew

that he hadn't bothered to block her by the amount of times his phone would ring, therefore her calls alerted him every time, but he'd never made any attempt to pick up for her.

As if on que, his cell went off, interrupting her thoughts. Groggily, he opened his eyes, as he grabbed his phone. Just as he answered the call, he lifted his eyes, realizing that she was standing there.

He frowned, as he spoke into the phone. "Yeah?"

"So, I see your phone still works." She folded her arms across her chest.

"Say, let me call you back." He never took his eyes off her, as he ended the call. "The fuck are you doing here, Keyasia?"

"Why didn't you answer any of my calls?" she lifted a brow.

"Fuck all that. Answer my fuckin' question. What the fuck are you doing here?" he angrily sat up in bed.

"I came to get my shit!" she shouted.

His scowl deepened. "Your shit? You must be crazy. You aint got nothing in this muthafucka."

"What?" she grimaced. "What happened to all my clothes? My laptop? My make-up?" she stomped over to the walk-in closet. She was preparing to go off, demanding that he tell her where he'd taken her things. But everything was just as she'd left it. All her clothes were still neatly hanging up in the area she'd commandeered in his closet.

"Man, you aint got shit in there," he snapped, as he now stood behind her. "Get the fuck out of my shit."

She twirled around. "What do you mean? Those clothes in there aren't mine, Corinthian?"

"Hell, nah."

"How is that?" she placed her hands on her hips.

"Go call that nigga. Tell him to buy you some shit. I don't recall you buying anything in there, so it's mines. And you better not fuck with nothing."

"Ooh, so you wanna be petty, huh? I don't give a fuck about those clothes. Where the fuck is my laptop? Gimme that, and I'll be on my way."

"That's my laptop."

"Whatever." She rolled her eyes.

"Why are you here?"

She brushed his question off. "Why did you let Craven bring some random over here? He has a whole house, with a bitch in it. He should do his dirt somewhere else. And I thought you didn't like having hoes over here? Shouldn't that apply to your boys and cousins too?"

"That nigga caught me slipping this time," he revealed, before catching himself. "But I don't you a explanation. That aint none of your business."

"Are you ready to talk to me now?" she pressed, as they both stood in the closet's doorway.

"For what?" he glowered down at her. "What are you gonna say that you didn't say in all those texts and voicemails?"

"So, you read all the messages?" she gazed up at him.

"Yeah."

"Then why didn't you respond?"

"Cause I didn't want to."

"Is it that easy for you to leave me alone?"

"I can't deal with disloyalty, Keyasia. Your actions got me questioning a lot of shit."

"But I keep telling you what it is. Why can't you just accept what I'm telling you?"

"Because what you saying don't fuckin' matter!" he barked. "You should've never found yourself in that position for him to make a move. That whole situation don't sit right with me, and I aint got time to baby-sit a bitch. A hoe is gonna be a hoe, and I let hoes be."

"Bitch and hoe? That's how you feel?"

"Aint that what you showed me?" he furrowed his brows.

"I didn't show you shit!" she blurted. "I was just trying to clear the air! But you can run to Mona's house, and claim you seeing her son for hours at a time, right? I'm not supposed to question that, but I can't clear the air with my ex?"

"Right about now none of that shit matters. You can do whatever the fuck you want. It's obvious you been doing that, anyway."

"So, you aint fucking with me no more? That's it?" she searched his eyes for an ounce of compassion.

He shook his head. "Nah, I aint fucking with you, Keyasia. You poison. I can't have a bitch fucking with my head, clouding shit up, when I need to be focused. No matter what you say, I'ma feel like every time you miss a text, or take too long to respond that you in a nigga's face.

That aint no way to carry on, and I rather leave that shit where it's at."

"So, you never felt anything for me, then," she sniffled. "You couldn't have, if that's all it takes for you to throw in the towel."

He shrugged. "You gon say, and feel however. I aint trying to convince you." He spun around, heading back to his bed.

Keyasia's chest heaved up and down, as she fought to keep her composure. She didn't want him to know that he was breaking her down. But to conceal the mounting pressure in her chest was impossible. "I hate you!" she became a ball of fury, as she charged at him, before pummeling his back.

"Man, get the fuck off me," he gritted, as he turned around, grabbing her.

Keyasia completely lost it, as she viciously sunk her nails into his face. "You think you about to go fucking with these hoes?! I'll scratch these green ass eyes out!"

He gripped her hair, as they fell into his bed. She landed on top, and used her knees to climb up his body, until she was able to press a knee into his neck. "The fuck?" he struggled to get out. No other girl had ever come at him like this. She was literally attacking him, and the only way that he'd be able to get her ass off him would be to knock her ass out. He was trying with all his might not to go there.

"You wanna play with me?!" she growled, before biting his finger.

"Hell, nah," he spat, taking control of the situation, flipping her onto her back. Violently, he gripped her throat, and squeezed. "Keyasia, you gon fuck around and make me take your fuckin' life. Keep your fuckin' hands off me," he warned.

Stubbornly, she ignored his warning, while clawing at his face.

"Bitch, you crazy!"

"Fuuuck yooooouuuu!"

After staring down at her, as she went berserk, he realized why she was the first chick to make him really feel like he was normal. Usually, people swore his edges were a tad too sharp for their taste. He'd go into those dark places, and there was no talking him down. And Keyasia was exactly the same way. Her crazy matched his, which made them downright volatile together.

"With ya stupid ass!" he spat, as he released his hold on her.

She hurriedly sat up, while he felt the numerous scratches she'd left in his face.

"I swear, I should shoot your ignorant ass. The fuck you do that shit to my face for?"

She held her head in embarrassment. "I don't know what came over me. I just blacked out."

He bucked his eyes. "And I was about to black out with your ass too."

She gazed at him with the saddest eyes. "I'm sorry."

"Nah, you aint fuckin' sorry. Not with the way you just came at me. I've murdered niggas for less."

"I…I just went crazy at the thought of not having you. I can't accept that." She waved her head, as she gripped his chin.

"Keyasia, get off me, man," he uttered, before she silenced him with a kiss.

It wasn't long before the kiss grew wild, but that did nothing for the severity of the situation in her eyes. She needed to do more. Have him see, and feel her sincerity. She dropped to her knees, while peeling off her clothes. "I need you to understand how sorry I am."

He allowed her to unzip his jeans, as she held his undivided attention. With all the sex they'd had, she'd never been in that position before. Therefore, he sat back, as she unleashed his hard-on. Staring directly into his eyes, she flicked the head of his dick with the tip of her tongue.

"Damn," he moaned just from the sight. He'd been patiently waiting for the day when she'd bless him with some head.

Feeling like she had something to prove, she took him into her mouth. Steadying her breathing, she took him down her throat.

"Fuck." He unconsciously clenched his butt cheeks together. Her expertise had taken him by surprise.

Key went into a zone, as she gobbled him up. She was sloppy with it, allowing him to touch her tonsils.

"Damn." He fell back on his elbows, as he watched her suck the skin off his dick. His toes involuntarily curled, as she bobbed vigorously. He was astonished, as he found himself approaching his peak, although she'd just begun. This was definitely new for him. "Shit. I'm 'bout to bust, but I wanna shoot it on that ass."

After deep throating him for the last time, she anxiously crawled onto the bed. She then lowered her upper body, tooting her ass in the air. Wanting to give him a show, she spread her legs, before simultaneously wobbling her ass checks. Her booty control was a sight to see, and he exploded, as she began toying with her own clit.

"Fuuuuck," he grunted, as he released all over her ass, while she continued to make her cheeks clap. His semen slowly trickled from the crack of her ass to her opening. She sensually wound her hips, beckoning him. He couldn't help himself, as he lowered his head, and began tasting her from the back. Still, she vibrated her ass, driving him crazy.

"Ahhh," she let out, as he stimulated her clit.

It wasn't long before he could feel her pearl twitching, and he quickly sat up, positioning himself. As she came, he forcefully entered her. Immediately, she threw it on him, as he gripped her hips.

"That pussy is gushing," he uttered, as her ass smacked against his abs. She was backing him down, dominating their connection. "Oh, you wanna show out, huh?" he breathed, before coming to his feet in the bed, while remaining deeply rooted inside of her. Straddling her ass, he ventured deeper, causing her to feel it in her stomach.

"Oh, wait!" she screamed, as he began to beat it up.

"Hell, nah. This what you wanted, right?" he slapped her ass. "Huh?"

"Yessssss," she hissed. "But got damn it!"

He was pounding into her, as she gripped the sheets.

"Ahhhhh!" she howled.

His pace remained rapid, until he was jerking inside of her. Sweat dripped down his face, as he collapsed on top of her. She lied on her stomach, as she felt him spilling inside of her. He was heavy, as he rested all of his weight on her back, but she was enjoying every second. He was right there with her, skin to skin, as their hearts raced. Still, she didn't know where this would lead them. Had his mind changed? Was it enough?

Her thoughts were about to drive her insane, before she felt him gently kiss the back of her neck. She melted, as he slowly maneuvered his body off hers, and then pulled her into his arms. She snuggled in, feeling like everything would be alright. Or so she hoped.

Chapter 16

Keyasia had never been so glad to be in bed. Once again she'd done a club appearance out of town. She was in Atlanta, and had been partying non-stop. She'd honestly enjoyed herself, but she needed some rest. In between school, club appearances, and Wale she hardly had time to think.

The past few weeks had been a blur. She'd been on the move, but Wale was still the apple of her eye. They'd been kicking it, ever since the day she'd popped up at his home, but now she felt this weirdness whenever they were apart. Thoughts connected to him were often followed by butterflies, as she tried to ignore what she felt in her gut. His phone seemed to ring longer when she called now. Texts took longer to get responses. And she felt some distance sometimes when they spoke. She was hoping that it was just a phase, and that they'd eventually recover fully. But it was hard to ignore that things weren't completely right with them.

Laying in her hotel's bed, she'd contacted him three times, but his voicemail was picking up. Despite desperately trying to block the thoughts, her mind ventured to what he could possibly be doing. It was now six in the morning in Houston, and he had undoubtedly gone clubbing, as he usually did every weekend. But until recently, he was still reachable around this time.

Wanting to know what he'd been up to, she picked up her cell, and scrolled to his Facebook page. He wasn't big on social media, but would occasionally post a picture at the club. It was crazy how he had roughly seven hundred friends on his friends' list, and would receive nearly six hundred likes on his photos, indicating that most of his friends were women. This time was no different. He'd posted a photo around twelve midnight, and already had three hundred likes. He was dressed in Balmain, looking dapper as ever.

Usually, Key would feel a sense of pride whenever he stepped out fresh, but now she felt jealousy more than anything else. Unquestionably, he'd gone to the club where the vultures were probably pawing at him, and it didn't help that she was hundreds of miles away.

Wanting to see what people were saying underneath his photo, she read the comments. As she suspected, there were several chicks boldly flirting. That was nothing to her, especially since she'd have thousands of comments on her pictures. However, she found reason for pause, as she noticed Mona had left a comment, as well.

She wrote: ***When you see him know that's me!***

Then there was another comment. ***Zaddy is gonna cut up tonight! 5th Amendment we in that thang!***

"He took this bitch to the club?" Keyasia mumbled to herself, as she clicked on Mona's page. "The fuck?"

Her heartrate sped up, as she noticed that Mona's cover photo was a picture of her and Wale at the club. He was wearing the Balmain ensemble, indicating that the picture had just been taken. Then as she scrolled down, she saw all the pictures of Mona and Wale partying together. Admittedly, Mona was looking right. Her hair had been done up in an array of long spiraling curls, and her makeup appeared to be professionally done. She rocked a dangerously short and tight dress with thigh high boots. She was smiling like she had the world in the palm of her hands, as she wrapped herself around Wale in every other photo.

Keyasia's hands began to tremble, as she noticed one post. It was Wale lying in bed, shirtless. Mona had obviously taken it while he was sleeping, and posted it at five that morning. The caption read, ***I'm on some Bey shit today. If he fucks me good I'll take his ass to Red Lobster. He did his part, so it's Red Lobster for lunch #trustmehedeservesit #imsore #workingwithamonster***

Key's entire body went cold, as she felt immense betrayal. She knew that he was probably spending time with someone else, but tried to ignore her suspicions. But now the truth was slapping her in the face. There she was in Atlanta, turning down men left and right, and he was laid up with someone else. And not just any somebody. This was the same chick he vowed to keep around, regardless.

She was seeing red, as she dialed out his number. Finally, it rung, after going straight to voicemail for hours. Still, he didn't answer. Refusing to give up, she called again, and again. After nearly twelve calls, he picked up.

"What's up?" he answered with music and wind in the background, demonstrating that he was in a car.

"What type of bullshit are you on?!" she shouted.

"What you mean?" he asked, dumbfounded.

"Nigga, you fuckin' know!"

"I don't know nothing. The fuck is up?"

"I just saw that bitch Mona's page! She got pictures of yall all hugged up in the club, and one with you in bed. She claimed you just fucked her. What the fuck is that about?"

He sucked his teeth. "Is that what you called me for? I'm thinking you got some kind of emergency out there."

"Are you serious?" she asked in disbelief. "You disrespecting me is urgent like a muthafucka."

"Disrespect? Man, what are you talking about?"

"So, if being hugged up with that bitch in public, or laying in her bed aint disrespect, then what is? Huh?"

"Man," he drawled. "I really aint got time for this. I'm not tied to anybody, and don't owe nobody a explanation. I'm a grown ass man…and single."

She gasped. "Oh, that's how you feel?"

"What you mean? What you thought? We already established what it is."

"So, let me get this right," she breathed into the phone. "You can keep a whole bitch in the picture. Play daddy to her child. And still fuck her, but come at me over my ex, right? Why wasn't you spitting this same single shit when it came to me and other niggas?"

"Keyasia, I was cool on Mona, until…you know what? That shit don't even matter. It is what it is. Like I said, I'm single."

"But that bitch is laying claim to you on her page, though," she fumed.

"I can't control what she put on the internet. That's her page."

Keyasia grimaced. "Are you for real? I can't believe what the fuck is coming out of your mouth…but you know what? You got it. I'ma step aside, and allow you to do you in peace. You be good." She ended the call.

For a few minutes she blankly stared at her phone, as she came to grips with what had just taken place. After all the potential she saw in them, this was how they ended.

Nicole Jackson

He'd played her completely to the left, and she never saw it coming. Not to this extreme. He was so callus, as if he never cared. Yeah, he was probably feeling some type of way about the Amir situation, but judging by the way he ran back to Mona, Amir had done her a favor. The first infraction she commits, and he's laying with the next girl. Key told herself that he would've eventually pulled that stunt, regardless. Maybe he shared something special with Mona. Who knows?

Key's stomach became queasy, as she thought of the future. A future without Corinthian in it. The whole sound of that felt cold, and hurtful. And this was different from what Amir made her feel. Undoubtedly, he'd disappointed her, but she'd kept it moving. But now with Wale…she felt lost. She didn't want to walk away. She still wanted him, but was wise enough to understand that if she stayed at that point, she'd be offering herself up as his personal doormat. Being weak wasn't something Keyasia could conform to, no matter who the man was. So, there was no other choice. She had to let go, even if being without him made her feel physically sick.

******

Heartbreak had never been hidden better. For a month now, Keyasia had been partying from coast to coast, even missing a few classes, unbeknownst to her parents. She was drinking a little heavier, and smoking exotic to calm her nerves. She was down for anything that would keep her preoccupied, and away from her phone. She couldn't allow herself to slip-up and call Wale.

It was now as if they'd never happened. Since their phone conversation, she hadn't contacted him, and he hadn't called her, either. By all indicators, he was still living life, clubbing, and stunting. Every other night he was in somebody's club, posted up with a new girl. Curiously,

Key had checked out a few chicks' pages, after they'd tagged him on Facebook. Each broad was in some fashion claiming him, and even arguing with other women over him. Then Mona would post pictures of him sleeping in her bed every other night, completely ignoring what he did on the other nights he wasn't with her.

Keyasia was grateful that she was not a part of the circus. Obviously, Mona was perfectly willing to publicly make a fool of herself, just to let the world know that Wale still chose to screw her. She threw self-respect right out of the window, in the name of making sure the next woman knew that she didn't have him fully to herself. Nobody did. And the only winner in that situation was Wale. He was openly fucking whomever he pleased, and they all anxiously awaited their turns, while despising any other woman getting a feel of the dick too. None were smart or bold enough to hold him accountable, clearly creating a monster.

Key told herself that she'd made the right decision. Wale wasn't the type you planned a life with. He was the one to call when you wanted a good time, and your back broken in. Unfortunately, she'd made the mistake in thinking that she was special to him, but she'd taken those rose tinted goggles off. It was now clear that he was the typical, game-running, immature, afraid of commitment little boy. Guys like him came a dime a dozen.

"I see your ass is back to the naked life," Raven quipped.

Keyasia smiled at her aunt, as they stepped into Starbucks. Indeed, she was back to her usual attire, having no one around to protest her fashion preferences. This day she wore tiny green and yellow Ralph Lauren logo running shorts, along with a matching sports bra. They'd just taken a jog at a neighborhood track, before deciding to grab a treat. Her body was in excellent condition, and she'd recently shed a few pounds, after parting ways with Wale. She'd been gaining "relationship pounds", but that was a thing of the past. Her strong legs and thighs were toned, while her ass still had a nice bounce to it. Her deep caramel skin appeared baby soft, as she had subtle tattoos around her hips, and one on her side, traveling from her waist to her breasts. She was universally enticing, as her beauty transfixed every man in the vicinity, regardless of race. Trouble in the love department had done nothing to stop her glow.

"Auntie, those little shorts you got on are a little suspect, too. What would Uncle Jah say about this whole booty shorts sports bra combo you having going?" Key teased, as they stepped to the end of a line.

"Shit, he'd probably cuss me out, but what's new?" Raven giggled. "It keeps us fresh. He gotta know what he got." She winked.

"Umm hmm," Key pursed her lips.

"So, what's going on with you, and ole boy?" Raven questioned.

"Who?" Key squinted.

"You know. Wale."

"Oh, I don't know. I told you that I was done with him."

"Yeah," Raven tucked her lips into her mouth. "But people say a lot of things. That don't make it true."

"Well, it's true in this case. Aint nothing happenin'."

Raven lifted her chin. "Is it because of Mona?"

Keyasia scowled. "How you know her?"

Raven gave her a guilty smirk. "From Facebook."

"So, you and my mama been lurking, huh?"

Raven's eyes danced in her head. "Why you say that? Who said anything about your mama?"

"Cause I know yall. Yall get together, and be messy. And if you know that he's dealing with Mona, then you know that he's talking to several other girls too. But you wanna ask me if I'm still dealing with him. I'm offended. I know yall know that I'm not that crazy. If he's moving like that, then surely I'm not sticking around."

Raven nodded. "I know that's right. But what changed everything? I mean, cause it seemed like he was serious about you. Was it the Amir kissing you thing?"

Keyasia gasped. Up until that moment, she thought that her brother, and cousins had kept the incident to themselves. Neither of her parents had brought it to her attention, which caused her to think that she was out of the woods. "Who told you about that?"

Raven stroked her long ponytail. "Umm…it was Zyrie," she revealed, referring to Amir Junior's step-mother, and a good friend of Raven's.

"Is that right?" Key folded her arms. "And what did she say?"

"She was just telling me how Little Amir was pissed at your boyfriend, and said that they had a fight. And don't worry, I didn't tell your mama. I know Raquel would've been pissed that they was doing all that in front of her house. And when I asked Little Jah he said that they were able to get control of the situation. I was just glad that it didn't escalate into something more serious." Raven whispered, "I heard that Wale is a little loose with the trigger finger, and I know that could get downright ugly. I know Big Amir can get stupid himself."

"Yeah," Key sighed. "I just hope that they both continue to keep their distances from each other…and me."

"Girl, please." Raven waved her off. "I don't know about you and Amir. That probably is over. But you and ole Wale? I think you'll be back, and he will too."

Key cut her eyes. "I don't know where you get that from."

Raven shrugged. "I know what I know. Your mama said it too. I don't even recognize you when he's around. That nigga done tapped into something else. And whatever it is, Amir couldn't or wouldn't reach it."

"Whatever." Key rolled her eyes, before she felt a tap on the shoulder. She twisted around.

"Small world, huh?" Bash smiled.

"Yeah, it is. This is a long way from Atlanta, huh?" Key smirked. She'd met him a few months back, and knew that he lived in Atlanta. He was a young producer that had a few recent hits under his belt. They'd met at a party, and had conversed a time or two. He'd also expressed interest in working with her, claiming that he could get anyone on a track and make them sound noteworthy.

Bash stood before her, looking delectable. He wore a simple, yet stylish Lacoste unit. He had a medium brown complexion, and a nice sturdy build. The fact that he was incredibly handsome was the icing on an already impeccable piece of cake.

"It is," he answered. "But you know the H has always been my home away from home."

"Oh, I really didn't know that."

"Well, you learned something new, huh?"

She lifted both brows. "I suppose I did."

"Yeah, and I've been meaning to catch up with you."

"Why is that? You have some work for me?"

"No." he shook his head. "Honestly, it's personal."

She gave him a perplexed look. "Personal?"

"Yeah," he rubbed his chin. "I told Lil' 5th to relay the message, but I guess he didn't get a chance."

"Relay what?"

He cleared his throat. "That I wanted to take you out."

"Really?" she gave him a skeptical look. Industry guys weren't usually her cup of tea. That world seemed so fake and superficial to her, therefore she only indulged on a money and entertainment level.

"Yeah. And he was telling me how you really didn't like dudes in the music game...outside of Amir. I know that you were with him for few years, before he started getting radio play."

"What are you getting, Key?" Raven interrupted, as it was their turn at the front counter.

"Give me an iced skinny vanilla latte," Key instructed, before focusing on Bash again. "You sure have been doing your homework, huh?"

"When you wanna ace the test, you'll study for it first, right?"

"Right," she agreed.

"Okay, then. I was curious, so I did a little research. I noticed how you never seemed to entertain anybody, and I honestly liked that. The game hasn't changed you, and that's a rarity. And now I'm letting you know that I'm not on any bullshit. I don't know much about you, but I'm crazily attracted to you, and I really want to get to know you. Like take you on a real date. None of that industry bullshit. Just two people chilling, and feeling each other out."

"Ay, I like that answer," Raven barged in, offering her two cents.

Key cut her eyes at her aunt. "Really?"

Bash smiled, as he rubbed his hands together. "Hey, I need all the help I can get. But for real, shawty. Give me a chance."

Keyasia inhaled, as she contemplated. Bash was cute…and she did need to keep herself distracted. He could be exactly what the doctor ordered. "Umm…okay. You got one little date to show me what's up."

******

"Uh, how long are we gonna sit here?"

Wale unhurriedly took a toke off his blunt, as he glanced her way. "Until I put my shit in drive, and pull off."

She sucked her teeth, as she shook her head.

Wale shrugged her off, as he thought about how he was deleting her number the moment he dropped her off at home. It had been a brief week of kicking it with her, and he was over the experience.

Nicole Jackson

The chick sitting in his passenger's seat was a part-time reality TV star, named Kree, and she wanted to be famous more than anything on this earth. All she talked about was celebrities, and their lifestyles, wanting to be more than she was. The most she'd done on television was appear as a friend of a regular cast member on a few popular Black reality shows, but she swore she was Hollywood.

Kree was a yellow chick that was cute, but had a few enhancements in the body department. At first glance, she seemed like someone worthy of being snatched up, but her conversation killed that notion. After dealing with Key, Wale had a false perception of what dealing with "Instagram models" meant. She was grounded in reality, and the world hadn't changed her, but after meeting Kree he knew that there weren't many Keys walking around.

"Is that the new Maserati?" she damn near broke her neck, as the car pulled into the lot.

Wale blew smoke from his nostrils. "Looks that way to me."

"Yeah it is." She snapped her head around. "My friend Ashley and her boyfriend just copped his and hers last month."

"That's what's up." He nodded.

"Yeah, they're the ones with the penthouse in Millionaires' Row in Miami."

He sighed, before licking his lips. "That's cool, lil' mama. But what you got? Ion wanna hear about the next people."

"Well, well," she stuttered, causing him to smirk.

"You know what? Don't even worry about it."

Just then his cell vibrated in his lap. Picking up the phone, he realized that it was Mona. Disappointedly, he dropped the cell back onto his lap. It was never the right person texting these days. And he didn't know what it was going to take for Mona to realize that he wasn't fucking with her on that level. Yes, he'd talked all that shit to Keyasia, claiming that Mona could post whatever she wanted. But the moment he'd hung up with her, he'd called checking the shit out of Mona. He had no idea that she'd taken pictures of him sleeping, and then posted it. Her sneakiness had pissed him off, and fucked up things between him and Keyasia. Still, his pride wouldn't let him pick up the phone, and plead his case, especially after she'd recently played him. What kind of message would that be sending her, then?

"Now, are you ready to go?" Kree questioned, grabbing his manhood.

Eyeing her hand, he took one last puff from his blunt. "Yeah, I think I am," he answered, grabbing her hand, before flinging it back to her side of the car. "But I'ma need you to keep your hands over there."

Chapter 17

"I got your ass right where I want you," Keyasia gritted, as she aimed her gun. It was dark, but she knew it was him.

"But bae, I was just playing. Come on, don't shoot me," Bash pleaded.

"Too late." She pulled the trigger, tagging him.

"Aw, damn, you aint gon let a nigga make it with nothing, shawty," Bash groaned.

Key giggled uncontrollably. "Nigga, I told you that I was a beast in laser tag."

"Yeah, him and Jah are some sore losers," Josairah joined in, laughing.

Little Jah sucked his teeth. "Girl, I let you win."

"Yeah, yeah," Josairah waved him off.

"But uh, the game aint over, until somebody's won it all. So, sorry Jah-Jah!" Keyasia blurted, as she turned her gun on Josairah. Before she could react, she pulled the trigger.

"Ahhhh!" Josairah screamed.

Jah chuckled. "That's what your dramatic ass gets."

"Shut up," Josairah pouted, as she shoved him.

"Don't be mad. Stay on guard next time," Key taunted, wagging her tongue.

"You really think you're hot shit, huh?" Bash questioned, as they all strolled towards the exit.

"I don't think anything," Key boasted, as they stepped into the lighter part of the facility.

It was almost hard to believe that she'd gone on several dates with Bash, and he'd been a fresh breath of air. He was actually taking the time to date her, keeping things light-weight. Things had been nice, and she'd been genuinely smiling. Bash was everything she needed for the moment.

"I need another drink," Bash announced, while they were removing the laser tag gear.

"Me too," Keyasia agreed.

"Shit, we all can," Josairah added with a grin. She was down to get tipsy, although they were all under the legal drinking age, with the exception of Bash.

"Shid, you young muthafuckas aint about to get me thrown out of here," Bash teased.

They all shared a laugh, knowing that they'd all been drinking throughout the night without any issues of identification.

"Well, we're getting one more, before we burn," Little Jah announced, as he wrapped his arms around Josairah's waist.

Keyasia pursed her lips. "What's the alibi tonight?"

"Me and you are clubbing, and Jah is too. I'll be home by six in the morning," Josairah explained.

"So, that means we'll be finishing our night alone," Bash winked.

Key sighed, wishing that her cousin and her girl could stay longer. She'd been purposely having double dates to keep Bash at bay. He'd been a perfect gentlemen, but there was a lot of sexual tension between the two, and she'd been using others to distract them both. She knew that she was attracted to him, but wasn't sure if she was ready to get intimate. Although, she kept her feelings private, she was very much in touch with them, and knew that she wasn't over Wale. And until she was, she didn't want to complicate her life.

Still, three hours later, she found herself back at his condo, on his couch, allowing him to nibble on her neck. Her temperature began to rise, as he palmed a breast. His lips were so moist and soft, causing her eyes to roll into the back of her head.

"Damn," she bit her bottom lip.

"I want you so fuckin' bad," he breathed into her ear.

"Okay, okay, wait a minute," she halted him, pulling away.

"What's the problem?" he asked in confusion.

"Look, I really like you. But I got some stuff going on internally and I'm just not ready. And no matter how much you kiss and probe, my position won't change."

He gripped her chin, and gently caressed her face with his thumb. "Is it Amir?"

She slowly lowered her eyes, as she shook her head. "No."

"Okay," he licked his lips. "I can respect what you're saying, but what if I just want to make you feel good?"

She lifted a brow. "How is that, if I'm not ready to give it up?"

He gazed at her lustfully. "I just want to taste you."

"Taste me?" a chill shot up her spine.

"Yeah, that's it. Nothing more. Nothing less."

"But what's in that for you?" she looked skeptically.

"Getting personal with the most intimate part of you. That shit turns me on, honestly."

"Bash, I don't know…" she got out, before he put a finger to her lips.

"Shhh," he hushed her. "Just let me do me, shawty. Please." He smoothly lifted her shirt and bra.

She watched closely, as he lowered his head, before drawing a nipple into his mouth. "Umm," she bit her bottom lip. It felt like he was making love to her breasts, as he flicked his tongue, giving her a sample of what was to come.

"Let's take this off," he whispered, before completely removing both her bra and shirt. Her entire upper body was fully exposed, as her nipples hardened in the air conditioned room. He slowly peeled off her jeans, revealing her perfectly shaven kitty. He marveled at her young seemingly untouched nakedness, as she seductively posed for him, without an ounce of shame.

Keyasia enjoyed enticing him, as he eyed her like she was on his dinner plate. Wanting him to get a full view of what she had, she stood up. He was then able to take in every dip and curve. "And you think that you'll be able to restrain yourself, when I say that you can't slide inside of this?"

He sighed heavily. "It'll be hard, no pun intended, but I can manage," he claimed, as he stepped to her, easing his hand between her thick thighs. Using an index finger, he slid between her plump lips, and located her center. "What about you?" he quizzed, as he stroked her clit.

"Uh," she slid her tongue across her teeth, while erotically twirling her hips.

"You sound ready," he offered, as he played in her wetness.

She smiled wickedly, opting not to reply.

"Come here," he commanded, grabbing her hand, while keeping the other between her thighs. He sat on his couch, before guiding her to straddle his shoulders.

She braced herself, balancing on the wall behind the couch, as his tongue found its way to her pearl. "Aw, damn," her mouth dropped.

Rhythmically, she grinded into his face, turning him on.

With both hands, he clenched her ass cheeks, as he fed himself large doses of her honey pot.

"Damn, do that shit." She began to rock her hips.

He worked his tongue vigorously, until he could feel her thighs shake.

"Yessss," she hissed, as she scratched his wall. She was riding the hell out of his face.

He slurped loudly, allowing her to hear exactly how wet she'd become.

"Uhhh," she began to buck her hips.

Soon, he could feel her clit throbbing, as her thrusts became wild.

"Ummm," she moaned, as she creamed all in his nostrils.

He continued working his tongue even well after she'd reached her peak.

"Okay, okay," she trembled. "That's enough." She attempted to climb off his shoulders.

"Nah, where you going?" he smirked.

"I'm tapping out," she breathed. "Shit. What more can you do, nigga?"

He chuckled. "That ass can't hang. What you thought this was?"

"Alright," she exhaled, finally freeing herself from him. "You got me. You did that." She flopped down on the couch next to him.

He gripped her thigh. "So, does that mean that you're gonna let me feel you for a second?"

She eyed his hand on her thigh. "It was good." She grabbed his hand. "But not that damn good," she snickered. "Better luck next time, nigga."

******

"We be talkin' stick talk. And we be talkin' bricks too. We be talkin' lick talk, and I'ma fuck ya bitch too. I aint got no manners for no slut. I'ma put my thumb in her butt…"

Club Pure was rocking, as the crowd poured in. Wale was in his section, popping bottles as usual. He and his boys had just hit another lick, and it was time to celebrate. For his people he smiled, but was truly struggling to enjoy himself.

There in the middle of the club he was flossing his usual two chains around his neck, Givenchy threads, and a fat bank roll, but something was missing. It was becoming harder by the day to ignore that he missed her. There were women everywhere, but none were Keyasia Williams. They simply didn't compare.

Staring at his phone, he was beginning to really feel like a sucker. For the past few days, he'd check her Instagram every hour, on the hour. He'd study every picture, hoping that he didn't spot some nigga in the background. Judging from the smiles on her face, she was good without him, and he wasn't taking it well, as he gulped down Cîroc, straight from the bottle.

Wale felt heat on the back of his neck, as he spotted her. He had to blink his eyes to ensure that they weren't playing tricks on him. She'd come through with some nigga flanked on her arm. Then she had the audacity to look ravishing with a bun at the crown of her head, while the back of her hair was long and bushy, and hung freely. The little tie-dyed blue denim booty shorts she wore left little to the imagination, along with the netted cropped blouse that revealed a white thin halter top underneath. Everything from her accessories to her Giuseppe's scandals were blinged out. Key's curves were like loud sirens, and it simply wasn't fair to the other women in the club. She'd shut the scene down.

Then the dude with her went for the Robin's gaudy blingy look, matching Key's swagger to the letter. He was holding her extra close, leaving no doubt that they were in the building together. Adding insult to injury, it was as if one of the club's hosts were in on a bad joke, as she seated

Key and her companion in the section adjoined with Wale's.

With his antennas already up, Craven elbowed his cousin. "Look at ya girl."

Wale nodded, keeping his eyes trained on Key. "I see her."

"Well, what you gon do?"

He smirked, "Buy 'em a bottle."

Keyasia sat with an uncomfortable smile on her face. She'd done everything within her power to avoid that man, and now there he was; less than ten feet away. Knowing Wale, she didn't know what to expect. He wasn't someone you could always read, and it was obvious that Bash was completely oblivious to the storm that could possibly be brewing.

"They're about to bring us a bottle," Bash spoke into her ear, as she tried to avoid eye contact with Wale. He was sitting across from them, boldly staring at her.

"Okay." She nodded, just before the waitress approached them with two bottles.

Bash grimaced, as he watched her sit both bottles before them on a little coffee table. "Thanks, sweetheart." He stood up. "But I only ordered one bottle of Cîroc," he informed her.

"Oh, I know. He paid for the other one," the waitress pointed in Wale's direction.

"Oh," he hesitated. "Okay." He sat back down, and focused on Keyasia. "You know that nigga or something?"

"Who?" she faked confusion.

"That nigga over there in the next section. The one that's looking over here at us, right now."

She glanced in the direction he pointed. "Uh, yeah. I know him."

"Well, he just bought us a bottle."

"He did, huh?" she asked dryly.

"Yeah, but how do you know him?"

She scratched the back of her neck. "I was seeing him at one point."

"Oh, yeah?" he furrowed his brows. "How long ago was that?"

"I don't know." She crinkled her nose. "About a month or so."

"A month or so…" he thought about it. "Is he the issue you call yourself working out?"

She cut her eyes at him. "Why you gotta say it like that?"

"How else do you want me to say it?" he snapped. "Are we in the section next to a nigga you was just with?"

"I wasn't *just* with anybody," she clarified, but it was useless. She knew exactly what he meant.

He angrily shook his head, before grabbing a bottle. He fixed himself a drink, and quickly guzzled it down. Following suit, she did the same. They ignored the tension between them, as they had drink after drink.

Soon, Wale's section was spilling over into theirs, as everyone partied. Bash was still feeling salty, as he stood up, bobbing his head to the music. The liquor had gotten into Key, as she swayed to the music, waving her drink in the air.

She couldn't help but laugh when she heard, *"Red light. You know I can't make this thing that official. Believe we had a great night. But I aint the type to tell you that I miss you. Shit, you don't like that I make this easy. Leaving. After sexing on the floor. Baby, I know you need me, like I need you. But I'm not the one you want to love..."* Nicki and August Alsina's song should've been Wale's damn anthem. The lyrics were so fitting to the nigga he was…to most girls. *"So, just pop a couple of bands with a nigga like me. Loving at the same with a nigga like me. You used to them, but aint no love in me..."*

When Nicki's verse came, she couldn't help but rap along, as she brazenly glared right at him. "I guess you know, I'm here to save you. Me and them girls, we aint the same, boo…You can't treat me like you treat them. Yes, I am the crème de la crème. Yes I am from one to ten to ten ten. You fronting in them streets. You saying we just friends. You can't front like this aint way realer. I know that you hard. I know that you a killer. I know you started off a dope dealer, but let your guards down. Your niggas know that you feel her…"

Being the arrogant asshole Wale was, he didn't shy away, but instead blew her a kiss.

She rolled her eyes, while attempting to stifle a grin. Somethings would never change.

When the deejay played her song, it was a wrap. She sprung to her feet. "Ayyyye! Cut it! Cut it! Cut it! Them bricks is way too high, you need to cut it!"

From clubbing together previously, Key also knew that Craven loved the song, and wasn't surprised to see him performing. He was too cool, as he bobbed his shoulders to the beat, as he motioned his fingers in a cutting motion. He then went old school with it, doing a little shoulder lean, before folding his arms across his chest, with his Louie shades shielding his eyes, as he rapped the lyrics.

"Water whipping. Looking like I'm fishing. Base boiling in the kitchen…" he pretended to stir up, as he bumped shoulders with Key. "How it go, lil cuz?"

She joined right in. "Dirty money on me. Got a scale up on me. I don't fuck with phony. 'Bout to sell a pony. All these niggas on me. All these bitches on me. They say my prices good, muthafucka show me!"

Craven chuckled, as he threw an arm over her shoulder.

Their entire clique was showing out, stunting, tossing money in the air.

Somewhere along the line, Bubble Gum had stepped onto the scene, and the second she recognized Key, she ran over. "Keeeeey!" she squealed, as they embraced.

"Hey, girl. I missed you," Keyasia admitted, before they released one another.

"Me too. I was just asking about you."

Bash took another chug from his cup, as he eyeballed Key. All of a sudden, it was a family reunion, as she became chummy with everyone in her ex's section.

"She say I'ma dog, but it takes one to know one. Alright. And I can go for hours, and believe me, had to show one. Alright. See, I prefer the floor. Not the bed. Feindin' for me. I can get it wet…" Kevin Gates was now in rotation.

Keyasia was feeling it, as she hopped on a couch, feet first. Bending over, she wobbled her ass. She'd reached her limit a while ago, and had surpassed drunk. There was absolutely no shame, as she dipped low, making her ass twitch.

Bash took another sip of liquor, as he watched Wale post up behind her. Key was oblivious to his presence, as she moved illicitly. Wale was wasted himself, as he struggled to stand up straight. Holding a bottle full of vodka, he pressed himself against her perched ass. Feeling someone on her, Key whipped her head around. She was surprised to find him there, and was too tipsy to put up a front.

Seductively, she rolled her hips, as she placed a dip in her back. Her moves were fluid, as he found himself staring down at her waist, as she moved like a snake. Displaying her skills, she began to tick her ass to the beat.

After a while, he felt that she was going too far, as he gripped her hips firmly. "Chill," he commanded.

Placing her feet back on the floor, she stood up, keeping her back to him. "Why you trying to stop me?" she giggled. "I'm just getting started."

"You doing a little too much in these little ass shorts," he spoke in her ear.

"You sure?" she rocked her hips.

"Hell, yeah." He wrapped his arms around her waist.

"Whatever." She shrugged him off, as she gripped the bottle he was holding. "Gimme some."

He allowed her to turn his bottle up.

"Slow ya roll," he slapped her ass, before flopping down onto a couch.

"Here," she handed him the bottle back, before he pulled her onto his lap. At that very moment it was like the deejay had become her personal theme song player, as he threw another song into the mix.

"I'm feelin' myself. I'm feelin' my…I'm with some hood girls, looking back at it, and a good girl in my tax bracket. Got a black card, and let Sak's have it. These Chanel bags is a bad habit…" Beyonce and Nicki blasted from the speakers.

Keyasia spun around, straddling Wale. Letting loose, she popped her back, dancing hard on him. He vehemently shook his head, before gripping her ass with both hands. "Stop that."

Bash was now under the influence himself, as he watched Keyasia grind all over some nigga she claimed to be done with about an hour ago. His ego had taken a direct hit, but it wasn't that serious. Ladies were lined up around the corner to get at him, so he'd take the nick on the chin, and keep it moving.

Craven found the scene hilarious, knowing that Keyasia had totally disregarded her little friend. Deja vu like a mutha. She and Wale drunkenly fondled each other, until the lights brightened, and the deejay urged everyone to take their asses home.

By this time, Bash had disappeared into the crowd, as Keyasia glanced around. For a second, she felt a twinge of guilt, realizing that he'd done nothing to deserve her behavior. She made a mental note to apologize to him the moment she had a chance.

"You looking for your boyfriend?" Wale inquired with a hard face. The playful demeanor had suddenly vanished.

"What boyfriend?" Keyasia slurred.

"That nigga you came in here with. Don't play stupid with me."

A chill eased up her spine. "I'm not playing anything. And he's a friend."

"Did you fuck this friend?" he frowned.

"Really, Corinthian? You ask me that as if you haven't been doing you?"

He waved her off. "Stop deflecting. Did you fuck him, Keyasia?"

She sighed, rolling her eyes to the ceiling. "No, I didn't fuck him."

He studied her face, looking for any signs of deceit. "You better not be lying." He poked her temple with his index finger.

"Corinthian," she breathed, as he was so close to her face that their noses were touching. "Everybody is leaving. Why are we still standing here?"

"I don't give a fuck about all that," he growled. "You heard what I said. Let me find out you lied to me, Keyasia. You gon have to call your daddy for me then. Cause I promise I'ma fuck you up."

"And if I fucked him, I'll let you have that one. Now, let's go. Damn."

He eyed her for a second, before seemingly coming to his senses. "Come on." He grabbed her hand.

Together they exited the club on wobbly legs. "Cor…Corinthian, I don't think we gon make it. You didn't drive, did you?" she asked sluggishly.

"Nah," he shook his head. "We got a party bus." He nodded, gesturing at the bus that was already parked curbside.

"Oh," she arched her brows in surprise. "What's the occasion?"

"Do it have to be a occasion?"

She poked out her bottom lip. "I guess not."

"Damn, Keyasia. All that ass is out," Meeko commented, rather loudly.

"Man, you better back yo bitch ass up with all that. The fuck you think this is?" Wale fumed, feeling like his cousin had crossed the line. There had never been any interaction between him and Keyasia that gave the impression that the comment was appropriate.

"Kinfolk, I was just fucking with her." Meeko put his hands up in surrender.

"Yeah, alright, nigga. My radar is going off. Niggas get that liquor in them, and the truth comes out. You paying too much attention to my bitch."

Craven stood back, shaking his head.

"Craven, you know I was bullshitting. Tell your cousin that he's tripping," Meeko urged. They'd often refer to Wale as the other's cousin, being that they were related to him on opposite sides of the family.

"Nigga, keep me out of that one. You said what you meant, shit," Craven chided. He knew exactly how quick-tempered Wale could be, and he wasn't going to receive the brunt of his fury. Besides, Meeko did seem to have a certain fixation with Keyasia, and her entire little crew, swearing they were some bad bitches. Always bragging about her, and her friend, although the friend didn't seem very interested in him.

"Exactly," Wale piped. "But you better keep your fuckin' distance, lil' nigga. Let me catch you getting out of pocket again, Meeko."

Keyasia stood silent, as Wale checked the fuck out of his cousin. She wasn't mad at him, after Meeko had childishly called her out. Hell, if her ass was out that was her business, although deep down she knew that the shorts were a bit much, even for her.

"Come on, man," Wale placed a palm at the small of her back, ushering her onto the bus. They then flopped down onto the seats. "You know you out of line for those shorts, though?"

"What?" she frowned.

"You heard me. I could tell that nigga was weak by how he let you step out the crib. Aint no way in hell you would've pulled that shit off with me. I aint even want you dancing in that shit. You tripped the fuck out, coming through in this bullshit."

She pursed her lips. "You niggas kill me. Any other bitch could have this same shit on, and yall would all be scratching and pawing at her. But you condemning me like I committed a fuckin' homicide."

"Why sell yourself short like that? We aint talking about any other bitch. I'm talking about Keyasia, and I carry a different level of respect for her. You're too pretty to have it all out there. Leave that to the bitches who have to try harder."

"Who? Bitches like your hoe, Mona?" she questioned sarcastically.

"Yeah, like her," he agreed, not falling into her trap.

"Whatever." She rolled her eyes.

"Girl, fuck all that talking. Yall got plenty of time for that," Bubble Gum interrupted. "Come turn up with me, before this bus pulls up to the hotel."

"Hotel?" Keyasia glanced at Wale. "Yall got a hotel for the night?"

"Yeah." He shrugged.

She gripped the collar of his shirt. "And who the fuck was you taking there? You didn't know I'd be at the club."

He chuckled. "Chill out, man. I was gonna go back there by myself."

"Yeah, fuckin' right!" she seethed. "You was gonna bring one of those bitches back from the club, huh? Tell me so I can slap the fuck out of you," she dared him.

"Keyasia, let my shirt go."

"I aint doing shit, nigga!"

"Alright." He nodded. "Alright." He gripped her hand. For a second, she thought that he was going to bend it or something, until he intertwined his fingers with hers.

Her heart skipped a beat.

"Stop playing with me," he whispered, before easing his tongue into her mouth.

It wasn't long before she'd straddled him, as they kissed wildly. Wale's boys were all grinning, as they realized that he had a soft spot for Keyasia. No other chick had been able to get him to be so open or passionate. She was different to him, and it was becoming crystal clear to his comrades. He'd bitten the bullet.

Within minutes the bus pulled up to the Four Seasons. "Okay, let's go," Wale breathed, pulling away for their intense kiss.

Keyasia nodded, before standing up, and allowing him to do the same. Together, they exited the bus with his crew right behind them. As usual, Craven had a girl with him who wasn't the girl he lived with, but everyone else had their main chicks with them.

Being that they'd all checked in earlier that evening, they headed directly to the elevators. Key attempted to hide her disdain, when she realized that she and Wale were headed to the top for to the penthouse presidential suite. She couldn't help but think about who he could've possibly brought there had she not come along.

When the elevators slid open, she couldn't keep it in. "I see you, sparing no expenses. That bitch would've loved this."

"Watch out, main. You know I only give *you* the best, Keyasia."

"Nigga please," she scoffed, while he used his key card to gain access to their living quarters. She stepped into the room with an attitude, until she noticed the gold Reese's Pieces spelling out 'Sweet like Keyasia'. "What the fuck? When did you have time to get them to do this?"

He smiled, loving her reaction. "Don't worry about all that."

"You think you smooth, huh?" she wrapped her arms around his neck.

"Nah," he denied. "Ion know what you talking about." He lifted her thighs, making her wrap them around his waist.

Feeling secure in his grasp, she removed her arms from around his neck, before clutching both of his chains. Playfully, she removed the jewelry, and then placed them both around her neck.

"What you doing with my shit, huh?" he asked, kissing her lips.

Her body was going into overdrive, anticipating becoming acquainted with him again. With little effort, he tossed her onto the king-sized bed. She giggled, as he reached into a bucket of ice, and grabbed a bottle of Cristal. He wasted no time popping the cork, before taking the bottle to the head. Seductively, she crawled to the edge of the bed, and stood on her knees.

"Gimme some."

Stepping to her, he placed the bottle to her lips, as she took it to the head. For several minutes, they continued to indulge in the Cristal, chasing the high that had slowly faded during the ride over.

Soon, they were both heavily intoxicated, as music pumped from a state-of-the-art sound system. The two had drunkenly stepped out to the hot tub area, with their clothes still on. Key was still sipping from the bottle, as she held onto the ledge of the Jacuzzi, twerking.

"Fuck up some commas. Fuck up some commas, yeah. Forty thousand to a hundred thousand. A hundred thousand, another hundred thousand. Three hundred

thousand to five hundred thousand. A million, let's have a money shower…"

She threw her ass in a circle, as Wale recklessly tossed bills all over her ass, while filming the entire scene. She was sloshing water all over the place, as she performed for him. He smiled as she wobbled her ass cheeks better than the dancers at V-Live. And her booty was really hanging out of those shorts.

Knowing that he was filming her, she was extra with it, as she removed her shirt and halter, becoming topless. Still, she managed to keep both chains on, as they now rested between her perky breasts.

"You like watching, huh?" she asked, gazing into his eyes. "Well, you better not blink." She slowly peeled off her shorts.

As if on cue, the music switched to something more fitting to their current situation. *"Don't play with her. Don't be dishonest. Still not understanding his logic. I'm back and I'm better. I want you bad as ever…"*

Now completely naked, she sat on the ledge of the hot tub, and spread her legs. She then licked her index finger, before bringing it between her legs. With his full attention, she slid the finger between her slit, stroking her clit. Hypnotically, she rolled her hips, causing his jaw to drop.

They locked eyes as she sat the bottle down, and then proceeded to rub a nipple. She twirled her hips one too many times for him, and he couldn't take anymore.

"Fuck this," he grumbled, as he put his phone down. Splashing water around, he eased next to her, and replaced her hand on her clit with his tongue.

"Uh, shit," she gasped.

His head looped around between her thighs, as her breasts heaved up and down. She'd nearly forgotten how he could set her body ablaze. Absolutely no one did it better.

By the time he pulled away, she was quivering. Her heart was racing, as her clit thumped at a rapid pace. Watching him remove his wet clothes had her vagina going into convulsions. Thoughts of taking him into her mouth ran through her mind, but before she could make a move, he was back between her thighs, sliding inside of her.

"Uhhh," she grunted, hating that due to lack of sex, she'd closed up. He was pushing through tightness, killing her.

Wale was silently rejoicing, feeling like she'd stayed true, and had kept his pussy on lock. Still, he needed her to feel him, as he gripped her shoulders, and ventured as deep as her body would allow.

"Ahhh!" she screeched out, clawing at his back.

"It'll be alright. Just relax," he urged, as she wrapped her legs tightly around his waist.

The pain slowly subsided, and then pleasure ensued. They kissed sloppily, as he maneuvered through her wetness. Her toes curled, as he hit her spot. It was inevitable. She was about cum, as he continued to deliver the death stroke. He snaked in and out of her, until her levee overflowed. She felt delirious, as she climaxed, while he continuously stimulated all the right spots.

She wrapped her legs tighter around him, refusing to let go. Nothing in life should ever feel this good. How the hell was she going to ever live without it? The way he moved inside of her…shit, they were never breaking up. Fuck what he thought.

Chapter 18

Keyasia's eyes fluttered open, as she heard a phone buzzing on the nightstand next to the bed. She attempted to reach for it, wanting to see if it was her phone, but she couldn't move. Wale was lightly snoring, and had a death grip on her. She simply laughed, as he practically held her in a headlock.

"Corinthian," she spoke directly into his ear.

"Huh?" his eyes popped open.

"One of our phones are ringing, and I can't reach the nightstand."

He frowned. "Fuck them phones."

"That's easy for you to say. What if it's somebody looking for me?"

"So?" he shrugged. "They'll just be looking."

She smirked. "Really? Even my mama and daddy?"

"They'll see you when they see you."

"You funny. I bet you won't say that to my daddy's face," she tittered.

"Bet." He furrowed his brows. Right then, a cell vibrated on the nightstand again. He sucked his teeth, as he picked up a phone. It was Keyasia's, but he still answered. "Yeah?"

"Ay…uh, is Keyasia around?"

"This," he checked the screen of the phone. "Bash, right?"

"Yeah."

"Oh, alright. She busy, my nigga. Is there something I could help you with?"

"I'm saying…you, you her secretary or some shit?"

"I'm the nigga answering her phone. What's up?"

"Man," Bash stressed. "You must be the nigga from last night, I guess."

"You guessed it right. But I was giving you the benefit of the doubt. I just knew the sucker ass nigga from last night would have too much pride to call her after that. I mean, did you call to see how much dick I put up in her, or what?"

There was silence.

"Hello?" he glanced at the screen again, and seen that ole boy had hung up.

"Corinthian, there you go with that bullshit," she sighed, but he could tell by her tone that she could care less about what he'd just told that dude. He wasn't her focal point, and that was cool with Wale.

Seconds later, his cell was ringing, and he lazily picked up. "Yeah?"

"I was just checking to see if your ass was up. You know it's about to be checkout time, right?" Craven spoke into the phone.

Wale yawned. "Shit, yall can go. I booked another night, before I fell out earlier."

"No shit?" Craven chuckled. "You and Key up there making up for lost time, huh?"

"Get out my business, nigga."

"Whatever. I think she got your nose wide open, on some real shit. You was kissing all on her in public and shit. Since when we started doing that shit?"

"Anyway," Wale cut him off. "I'ma fuck wit ya."

Craven continued to laugh. "Nigga don't wanna hear that shit. Holler at you later, sucker."

"Fuck you," Wale spat, ending the call.

Keyasia was giggling, after hearing the entire exchange, while still lying in his arms.

"Oh, that shit is funny to you?" he eyed her, until his cell rang once again.

They both stared at the phone, as Mona's name flashed across the screen.

"Answer it," Key urged.

"Man," he hesitated.

Realizing that he was stalling, she accepted the call, immediately activating the speaker option.

He sighed, "Yeah?"

"So, you finally pick up, huh? Damn, I could've been over here dying for all you knew," Mona complained.

"But obviously you still breathing, so what's up?" he snapped.

"So, according to the internet, you was cutting up in the club with that bitch last night."

"Man," he drawled. "Mona, go'on with that bullshit."

Promiscuous Girl: Keyasia and Wale

"Go'on with what bullshit? Was you or was you not in the club with her?"

"What kind of fucking question is that? Obviously, you saw it on some of my people's pages, which means you saw the pictures. The fuck are you looking for me to confirm? You saw the pictures."

"That bitch must be around somewhere," she assumed, making Keyasia want to go off, but she knew better. They needed to talk more, so that she could see what the hell was going on between them. "You back fucking with that Instagram hoe?"

He chuckled. "Watch out, man. Her name is Keyasia. We both know that. But yeah, I'm fucking with her. So, what?"

"You stupid ass nigga!" she imploded. "I knew it. I fuckin' knew it. I could tell that you was weak behind that bitch, but I kept trying to tell myself that I was tripping. You running behind a bitch that love to be in any nigga's face that can hold a mic."

"Mona, chill out, man. I'm really trying to spare your feelings. For real," he warned.

"Spare my feelings?!" she raged. "There aint a muthafuckin' thang you can say to hurt me, nigga. You the fuckin' duck, running behind a hoe. Stupid, lame ass."

"Alright, I'm a stupid, lame ass nigga. I got you. But what that make you? Cause I know that I can fuck with her, until I get good and tired. And then if I wanted to, I could still come back to your ass. And you'd take me willingly. Stupid, lame, and all."

"Nigga, fuck you!" she spewed. "I hate your bitch ass! You aint gotta worry about me or my fuckin' son. Since you wanna fuck with that hoe. We don't need you!"

"Mona, who the fuck you take me for?" he asked calmly. "Do you honestly believe that I'll chase you down to help you take care of another nigga's child? It aint that serious, lil' mama. You aint hurting me. The only people who'll lose is you and Kash. I promise."

His words had quickly sobered her. He'd never threatened to walk away from her baby. This was serious…He was serious about her. She was about to have an anxiety attack. "Look, you know that I would never stand in the way of you and Kash's relationship."

"Alright, look, from now on, don't call me about shit, unless it pertains to Kash. Anything else is irrelevant between us. You got me?"

There was a pregnant pause.

"You got me?" he repeated.

"Yeah," she gulped. "I got you."

"Good. Not get the fuck off my line," he spat, ending the call.

Keyasia lied there, saying nothing. Really, she didn't know what to say. Was she okay with his responses to Mona? For the most part, yes, but she'd much rather them have no contact at all. Still, they just weren't in the space for her to make such demands, yet. Wale was known to flip the script on her as well, so who was she to make demands?

****

"Come on, Keyasia. Move them feet."

Keyasia rolled her eyes, as she pouted. "I can't believe you have me out in public like this."

Wale frowned. "Like what? You look good to me."

"This muthafucka got jokes," she grumbled to herself, as they stepped outside of the hotel's lobby. Thankfully, the valet had already pulled his Benz up front. She would've surely died right there on the spot if she would've been forced to stand in front of a five-star hotel dressed in her current attire.

"I'm for real. You look good to me. I like how that shirt is all baggy on you, and those shorts are damn near to your ankles," he teased, as she stood there in his clothes.

"Corinthian, I am not in the mood to play with you," she gritted, before sliding into his car, while he tipped the parking attendant.

He then eased into the driver's seat. "Who said that I was playing? I like this look. You all sporty, and covered up. Why don't you like it?" he asked, as he pulled away from the hotel.

She sucked her teeth. "Are you crippled, blind, or just flat out crazy? These clothes are swallowing me whole." She waved her hand over her clothes for emphasis. "I could've just had my clothes dry cleaned by the concierge, but noooo. You wanna play games with my shit."

"What you mean?" he narrowed his eyes, playing ignorant to the fact.

"Nigga, you know," she snapped, whipping her head around. "My damn clothes came up missing, and it was just me and you in the damn room."

He cracked a smile. "I told you that I accidentally threw that shit away."

"And you say that like it's no big deal. Do you know how much all that stuff costed?"

He pretended to ponder on it. "Hmm...it couldn't have been too much for a few pieces of strings. I mean, the shit barely classified as clothes."

"Whatever," she huffed, as he cruised the streets. It was a little past midnight, and was the first time they'd left the hotel in three days. They'd been held up in that penthouse, doing unspeakable things to one another, and had finally decided to make a little food run.

"Shit, I wish it was a little earlier. We could've swung by Steak 48. We both dressed for the occasion."

She cut her eyes at him, knowing he was being funny. Steak 48 was an upscale restaurant where there was a dress code, and most times a reservation was necessary. "Nigga please. You know damn well they wouldn't even let me in the building with this bullshit on. And I would never go any damn where like that, even if I could. Stop playing me."

"Whatever," he rubbed his hard abs. "But I do want a steak or something. Let's fall off in IHOP."

She frowned. "You got to be out of your rabid ass mind. I am not going anywhere in public dressed like this. Period. So, drive this muthafucka through somebody's drive-thru and call it a night. The fuck you think this is?"

He snickered, enjoying every second with her. He'd never been able to laugh with a broad he fucked, until her. She was somebody he could tolerate, even when sex wasn't on the menu, and that had never been the case before.

Keyasia was cool to kick it with on all levels, providing a certain euphoria he was unfamiliar with.

"Matter of fact, don't you love them damn Jack-in-the-Box tacos? There's one up ahead. Stop there."

He shook his head. "Any other time you complain about how that shit is so unhealthy, but now you wanna stop there, huh? Anywhere so that you won't have to get out of the car."

She smirked, before sneezing. "Exactly." Absently, she opened his glove compartment, searching for a napkin to wipe her nose. Luckily, there was a few napkins, sitting right over a nine-millimeter pistol. Grabbing a napkin, she closed the compartment, while shaking her head. "I should've known you'd be riding dirty, like you aint a damn convicted felon. Do you ever take a day off?"

He checked his rearview mirror. "Aye, I rather be judged by twelve than to be carried by six. I can get out of jail. Aint no coming back from death."

"If you say so," she sighed, rolling her eyes. She knew there was no talking sense into him when it came to matters of the streets. "But yeah, stop at Jack in the Crack."

"Alright," he agreed, before checking his rearview mirror for the third time. "The fuck is really good," he grumbled, as he saw the same black Taurus behind him. He'd switched lanes a few times, and was traveling at a low speed on a pretty low traffic street, yet this car remained behind him. There was no urgency in bypassing him, or a need to occupy any of the other three empty lanes on the street.

Wale threw on his blinker, and the car did the same. He slowed, as if he was turning into Jack-in-the-Box, but

Nicole Jackson

drove past the driveway entrance at the last minute. The car behind him did so, as well.

"Why did you pass it up?" Keyasia questioned in confusion.

"Keyasia," he spoke carefully. "Pass me the heater."

"What?" she whipped her head around. "I'm not putting my damn prints on that."

"Keyasia," he said in a serious tone. "Hand me my gun."

Catching his tone, she did as she was told, handling the gun with a napkin. "Are you gonna tell me what the fuck is going on?"

Wale gripped the gun with his finger on the trigger, as he glanced at the rearview mirror for the millionth time. They were still there. Following them. "Keyasia, I need you to listen to me carefully. Get down on the floor for me."

"Do what?"

"Keyasia, please. Do what I asked you. Get the fuck down on the floor!" he demanded forcefully.

Without another word, she eased out of her seat, and onto the floor of the car. Right then, Wale mashed on the gas, before taking a sharp turn on a side street. The Taurus burnt rubber, attempting to keep up.

"Fuck!" Wale vented, knowing at that exact moment that his suspicions were correct. Thinking quickly, he hit another block, and jotted down the street, leaving the Taurus behind. He hit another corner, and then another. Checking his rearview mirror, he realized that he'd lost the car following them.

He sighed with a little relief, hoping that they could get back to the hotel without further incident. Slowly, his car approached a four-way stop. Just as he came to a stop, he saw the Taurus zooming down the cross street. At the speed the car traveled, he knew what was next.

"Fuuuuuck!" he let out, as the car drove past him, dumping.

BLOW! BLOW! BLOW! BLOW!

"Ahhhhhhhhh!" Keyasia screamed at the top of her lungs, as glass shattered around her.

With pure rage, Wale fired back, striking a dark shadow within the car. The Taurus then skirted off the block, and Wale did as well in the opposite direction.

"Them muthafuckas!" he vented, pummeling the steering wheel of his car.

Keyasia was literally trembling, as she remained on the floor, too terrified to move.

"On everything I love, I'ma find them bitches, and kill their whole fuckin' family," he spewed.

Keyasia whimpered, as he mashed the gas, exceeding 100 mph on the dash. Wale's mind was racing, attempting to piece together what could've possibly happened. Frankly, there were too many adversaries to really rule anyone out, and that alone was diving him crazy.

About fifteen minutes later, he pulled up to a rather old home, and parked in the driveway. Slowly, Keyasia rose up, checking out their surroundings. Moving at a fast pace, Wale had already exited his now bullet riddled car.

"Keyasia, come on!" he shouted, as he stalked over to a late model Lexus, popping the trunk.

Cautiously, she eased out of the Benz, while constantly looking around. Her eyes bucked when she noticed what he'd retrieved from the trunk of that Lexus. "What…what is that?"

Placing a clip into the weapon, he answered, "A chopper."

She gulped, seemingly realizing for the first time that she was in love with a real live gangster. What the hell had she gotten herself into?

"Man, quit just standing there. Get in the fucking car!" he barked.

Like a child who'd just been chastised, she opened the Lexus's door, and slid in, without uttering a word. Within a flash, he was in the driver's seat, starting the engine. Key nervously eyed the huge gun that sat in his lap, as if it was about to jump up and bite her.

Grabbing a burner phone out of the ashtray, he pulled out of the driveway. While gripping the steering wheel with one hand, he used the other to make a call.

"Who dis?" Craven spoke into the phone, after picking up.

"Man," Wale drawled. "Be real with me. Which one of you dumb ass niggas put the hotel's location on their page?"

"Huh?" Craven asked in confusion. "What you mean?"

"I mean, which one of yall was dumb enough to tell the world what hotel we was staying in?!" he raged. "Because some niggas in a fuckin' Taurus just dumped on me and my bitch."

"No shit?! You bullshitting. Yall wasn't hit, huh?" Craven questioned with concern.

"Nah, we wasn't, cause I was busting back. Their bitch asses got somewhere, then."

"As you should. As you should…but damn, main. I aint gon lie. A few of us posted pictures from the hotel, after we'd left. I swear to God I wouldn't have done that shit, had I known you was gonna stay for more days. And what's crazy is, somebody was asking about you on Facebook, and Big Block's bitch called herself trying to be messy on the thread, saying that you was still there at the hotel. I knew she said the shit because Mona had commented, and she probably wanted her to see it. Not knowing the kind of information she'd just given the haters."

"See, what the fuck I be talking about?" Wale fumed. "I keep telling you niggas. We in the fuckin' streets. We aint got no fuckin' business on the internet, giving play by play on our moves. I been telling yall for the longest that the most yall should do is post a pic, after you done shook the spot…at the club at the most. But yall can't see that shit. Too fuckin' busy trying to stunt on a bunch of broke muthafuckas. And done fucked around, and put a nigga's whereabouts out there for anybody to see."

"And that's our bad. We all fucked up, dog. I sincerely apologize for that. On God. And you know we gon ride on whoever them bitch ass niggas is….you think they was trying to rob you?"

"I doubt it. They came straight blasting, after following us for a minute. That shit seemed like a hit, or some shit."

"What the fuck, man. You didn't see nobody's face or at least recognize the car?"

"Shit, if I even had a hunch, I'd be at whoever mama's front door, as we speak."

"Hell, yeah. I feel you."

Keyasia sat there listening to Wale talk casually about taking innocent people's lives, and she was praying that it was just the shock of the entire incident speaking for him.

He was racing through the streets, traveling outside of the city limits. Keyasia knew that he wasn't headed to his townhouse, because it was in the opposite direction, on the other side of Houston. Soon, they were in the small town of Conroe, Texas.

Naturally, she figured he was going to lay low, and find some sort of motel to crash at for the remainder of the night. Therefore, she was surprised when he pulled up to yet another home. This one was a quaint, neat, little home that looked to belong to some old retired couple.

After using the clicker that was attached the sun visor in the car, Wale pulled into the garage of the home. "Come on," was all he offered, as he hopped out of the vehicle, with the chopper in tow.

Reluctantly, Keyasia exited the car, and followed him, as he used a key to enter the home. Stepping into the living room, she found that it was fully furnished with simple contemporary black leather and stainless-steel couches.

"Whose house is this?" she asked, remaining near the door she'd just walked through.

"Mine," he answered casually, before leaving her standing there to obviously secure the perimeter. He then returned to the living room, and grimaced. "Why you still standing there by the door?"

"Cause. You just bring me to this house. A house that you've never mentioned. And it has furniture. Why would you have furniture here, but not where you regularly rest your head at?"

"I have furniture there too, Keyasia."

She sighed. "You know what I mean. You didn't have furniture at first. But you got this little house all equipped and shit."

He flopped down onto the couch, and placed the chopper right next to him. "I lived here first, Keyasia."

"Way out here in the boondocks? Why?" she gradually moved towards the couch.

"Because," he breathed, dragging his palms down his face.

"Because what?" she carefully sat on the couch with him.

He stared at her. "Why you acting like I'ma bite you or something?"

She shrugged. "I'm still shook."

He nodded in understanding.

"Answer my question, though," she pressed.

"Alright, you wanna know, huh? Well, fuck it." He shrugged. "When I first got out, I was living with Mona. But I didn't want to be there, cause she had just put another nigga out, and he really didn't want to accept that it was over. The nigga was on some crazy shit. Climbing through the window, while we was in bed and shit, so I shot his ass," he revealed.

Keyasia was definitely thrown off by his confession.

"But the nigga didn't die or nothing. And he was from the streets, so he didn't tell the laws nothing. But we was beefing tough, after that. Had like three shoot-outs. And I was telling myself that I had to be the craziest nigga alive. I mean, I wasn't even beefing over Mona. Honestly, she was just something to do, until *I* could do, ya feel me? And after seeing how she'd lied to me, while I was in jail, claiming that she was in love, and only wanted me. But was really with her BD the whole time, I knew that she couldn't be trusted, regardless of her choosing me over him when I got out. That meant that I had to move around. So, I went right back to what I know. I was hitting licks, but that shit don't always come how you want it, when you want it. And that means that I had to find alternatives. Any nigga getting it, was a target. I was kicking in doors, catching niggas slipping at red lights. It didn't matter. It's survival of the fittest in the streets, and a nigga like me was gonna eat…by any means necessary. I was wildin'. I aint gon lie. And with the way I was moving, I wanted to rest my head far away from the streets I raised hell in. Keep a low profile. So, I found this house out here," he explained. "At first I was still trying to get my money up, so I just rented it. But then I won for a nice piece of change, and fucked around and bought this bitch. Eventually, I wanted something better, and had switched up my hustle, so I went back into the city, and snatched some new shit up. I considered selling this house, until I really thought about it. The whole time I lived here, I never had company. My niggas never had a reason to travel out here, and I always visited the hoes at their house. This is the perfect duck off spot. And with the shit I do, there was no telling when I'd need something like this. Which came in hand tonight. Nobody knows where we are.

Not even my people." He thought about it. "Shit, for all I know, it could've been one of those niggas who set me up."

Keyasia shook her head in disbelief. "I can't believe what I'm hearing, right now. Like really, Corinthian? You really lived recklessly."

He paused, as he studied her face. "I can't believe *you*, right now. I guess, you've been caught up in what you saw, which was a nigga you're fucking."

"What?" she scowled, feeling offended.

"You know what I'm saying, man. All you know is that I fuck with you, and you seen me in the club, or hanging on the block. That's all chill shit. The shit I choose to expose you to. Everything else is left out in the streets. I don't own a gun that I never busted, Keyasia. You know why I smile whenever people bring up these wild ass stories about how I tripped out, and shot a nigga in broad daylight? You never heard me deny it, right?" he furrowed his brows. "It's because all that shit is true. For a long while, after my mama was killed, I didn't give a fuck. I'd pop a nigga for looking at me the wrong way. I'd rob niggas, and then hang on their block, waiting on them to make a move. On some ignorant shit, honestly. But luckily, I got some family and big homies that really give a fuck about me, and finally talked some sense into me. They told me to leave that dry bullshit to the birds, and chase a check. I listened, but I am who I am. I trips out from time to time. And if a nigga call his self in the game…Ion have no mercy on 'em. It's shoot or be shot. That's the only way to survive out here. Then I aint crazy, either. I'm at a point that I scratched, and stepped on a few heads to get to. Niggas want what I got. I decided to stop taking from niggas who out in the struggle just like me, and just take from these businesses that got insurance, anyway. But now I'm a target for lil' niggas who was hungry just like I was. And I can't be mad at that. It's a part of the game, but that's why I stay ready at all times. And here you is, thinking I keep a pistol close for show, or some shit. Like none of it was real. Like I got a legal ass job, and niggas aint waiting to catch me slipping. That's something you convinced yourself of. Now you looking at me like I'm crazy, and done blindsided you with some shit. I been this nigga from the beginning, but that wasn't what you focused on. And that aint my fault."

Keyasia sat, digesting it all. Reality was quickly sinking in, and she'd definitely ignored anything that wasn't to her liking, when it came to him, and now there they were. He was a crazy nigga with a host of enemies, but that wasn't what frightened her. She was scared shitless about the fact that even with all this new information, and that night's shooting, she was going to still fuck with him. Regardless.

She was in too deep with him. And there was no coming back for her. If it wasn't his homicidal ass…she didn't want it. Even if it defied all common sense.

Chapter 19

"Three in the morning. You know I'm horny. So, won't you come over my place, and put a smile on my face. Leaving the club, shawty, hurry up. So, we can get this party started, and take off our clothes now…" Chris Brown's melodic, hyper-sexual voice floated through the air.

Keyasia was lying across the bed on her back, gazing up at the ceiling fan. The breeze from the fan provided a little chill, as she had goosebumps all over her completely naked body. She wasn't thinking about much, but was beginning to feel a tad nauseous, and the feeling was occurring too often for her comfort.

Before she could head to the bathroom to see if any food was going to come up, she could feel him crawling onto the foot of the bed. Without saying a word, he grabbed her legs, and maneuvered his head between her thighs. Gripping her hips, he leaned in, licking her clit.

"Umm," she moaned, as her eyes rolled into the back of her head.

Nastily, he devoured her, as she rolled her hips.

Although, he'd done this a million times over, it never grew old. Wale was indeed a pussy monster, driving her crazy with multiple orgasms. For an entire week, they'd been holed up at his little hideaway, supposedly laying low, and with nothing else to do, he'd been fucking her into an oblivion.

"Oh, shit," her mouth dropped, as he flicked his tongue rapidly. "Uhhhhhh," she grabbed his head, as she opened her legs, practically into a Chinese split. "Baby, wait!" she gasped, as he took her, before she was ready.

Nicole Jackson

Her damn stomach rumbled, as he brought her to a thunderous climax. "Ooooohhh." Her legs trembled.

At that very moment, she could feel her stomach do flips. Knowing what was next, she jumped out of Wale's grasp, and scrambled to the bathroom in the nick of time. Dropping to her knees, she hurled everything she'd eaten into the toilet.

Wale squinted, as he slowly approached the bathroom's doorway. This was Keyasia's fourth time randomly throwing up, and he was now re-examining what he first perceived as coincidences.

"You…you alright?"

"Yeah," she answered, before spitting into the toilet. "I think it's those tacos. They don't agree with my stomach."

"Yeah?" he folded his arms. "So, why do you keep eating them? I mean, you was swearing that you hated Jack-in-the-Box tacos, but now I can't buy none without you eating them first."

She shrugged. "I don't know. They taste different now, so I like 'em."

"You sure that's all it is?" he lifted a brow.

"Yeah." She stood up. "What else could it be?" she glanced at him.

He stood there, staring at her, letting her know that he felt her question was dumb.

She cleared her throat. "Well, that's all it could be."

He continued to glare at her, as she decided to rinse out her mouth. She could feel his eyes burning a hole through her, as she pretended that he was no longer standing there. Eventually, she sat on the toilet.

"I gotta boo-boo," she announced, hoping that would send him running.

He wasn't moved, though.

Thankfully, one of their phones began to vibrate in the room. Reluctantly, he headed to grab the call. "It's Sye calling you," he broadcasted.

"Oh, bring it here. I been meaning to call her."

Answering the video call, he stepped back into the bathroom, handing her the phone.

"Hey, girl," Key smiled into the phone, as Wale stood there, studying her.

Sye smirked. "I see you still locked down."

Keyasia scratched the back of her neck, knowing Sye was probably unaware that Wale was still within earshot. "Girl, yeah. I'm sitting here, about to take a dump," she replied.

Wale scrunched his nose, when she actually farted. "Man," he drawled. "You dug in deep to produce that bullshit. But you got it," he scoffed, finally vacating the area.

"Whew, finally," she breathed, as she quickly lifted off the toilet, and closed the door behind him.

Sye giggled. "Girl, was he still in there with you?"

"Bitch, yeah. Like damn, nigga. Let me use the fucking bathroom in peace."

"Girl, if that aint the conversation I have with Baby like all the damn time."

"Oh, you know I know. Once that nigga came around, we had to look for your ass with a flashlight. Nigga had you gone off the D."

"Whatever," Sye rolled her eyes. "I can recall you being stuck like glue to Amir, yourself."

Keyasia pursed her lips. "Please. It was never the deep, and that's ya girl's man. Ion want nothing to do with her BD."

Sye sighed. "Girl, bye. Val is my girl, but I stand by my word. I didn't and still don't approve of her fucking with Amir. For one, that was just stupid on her behalf. Like, it's a million niggas at school, but she goes after him. We all knew that boy was in love with you, and I don't know what made her think that she could change that. Shit, she's going through hell, right now. He comes through, gets some ass, and then won't answer her calls for days. Half the time, Zyrie deals with her, regarding their daughter. Then she wants me to sit and listen to her crying and complaining. I keep telling her that she brought it on herself. She said that she feels that he punishes her on purpose, because you left him. And he actually has the nerve to say it to her face. Girl, she hates the sound of your name."

"Well, I don't have any sympathy for the bitch. She's lucky that I never put my foot up her ass."

"True. But I'm glad that you took it like a G, and went snatched another nigga up. Got his ass somewhere sick," Sye wagged her tongue.

"I know," Keyasia barely got out, as she hopped off the toilet, and threw up once again. "Fuck," she spat, puking her brains out.

"Ewe, are you throwing up?" Sye questioned, as Key placed the phone on the countertop, preventing her from seeing anything.

"I was," Keyasia answered, before going to the sink, and rinsing her mouth out. She then picked her phone up.

Sye crinkled her nose. "Girl, are you okay over there?"

"Yeah," Key breathed.

"You sure? You didn't let him knock you up already, did you?"

"Did you get that doctor's excuse from your aunt?" Keyasia asked, ignoring her question. Sye had an aunt that worked in the medical field that had the hook-up on doctor notes, and was supposed to be getting some for her, because she'd missed several days of school. Without that, she'd flunk out of this semester, for sure.

"Yeah, I got it. Whenever you come to school, I'll have it for you. But you better get your shit together, or just drop those classes, because you really can't afford to miss any more days."

Keyasia took a deep breath. "I know, but my mama and daddy would kill me, if I did that. School is the only thing keeping them off my ass."

"Well, leave that nigga at home for a few hours, and go do what you gotta do," Sye suggested.

"I am…I mean, I will. But he's been tripping, lately. Remember, I told you some crazy shit happened, and he's extra paranoid, right now. The only time he leaves here is when we have to make a food run, and he gets mad any time I mention leaving. I've told my mama so many lies, because I'd usually come home to see her, even if I'd go back to sleep at his house. But he hasn't been trying to hear all that. Shit, I might have to actually fight his ass to leave here, especially on my own."

"Damn, what the hell went down, to have him tripping like that?"

Key shook her head, indicating that she couldn't tell her over the phone. With them both dealing with men from the streets, Sye immediately caught on. Her man, Baby, had definitely schooled her on talking reckless over the phone.

"Well, is your car there?" Sye probed.

"Yeah, he took me to get it a few days ago."

"Okay, then, wait 'til he's sleeping or something."

"Yeah, that's what I'll probably do," Keyasia agreed, but sounded unsure. Sye could clearly see that her friend was a little frazzled.

"Key, are you sure you're good? Your energy seems a little low. Are you sure you're not pregnant over there?"

Keyasia smiled weakly. "I aint that damn crazy. Girl, please. I wouldn't let his wild ass catch me slipping like that."

"Right, right. Well, I'm about to go feed this child of mine. I'll talk to you later."

"Alright, girl," Key attempted to sound cheerful, before ending the call. Immediately, her smile faded, as she dropped her face into the palms of her hands. "Oh my God," she whimpered.

The thing she'd been ignoring for nearly two months, was finally catching up with her. Her period was late. Two months late. And she'd known this from the very beginning, but while she and Wale were on the outs, she didn't want to face that type of reality alone. So, she'd ignored the obvious, and was now looking at things completely different, after getting shot at. It wasn't just about the state of her and Wale's relationship. Hell, bringing a baby into the equation seemed almost laughable with the lifestyle he lived. He seemed to be the furthest from ready, as any expecting father could be, and she couldn't fathom bringing a baby into that madness.

Suddenly, finding out if she was with child or not, seemed to be a pressing matter, and she had to get to the bottom of it. Attempting to shake off her anxiety, she prepared herself to deal with Wale. Pulling the door open, she stepped back into the bedroom.

He sat at the edge of the bed, talking on his phone. She could tell that it was about business from his tone. By the time he'd ended the call, he was frowning, and appeared rather tense.

"What's wrong, baby?" she questioned, as she walked over, and sat on his lap. Unconsciously, she began to stroke his waves, as he wrapped his arms around her.

"Them niggas act like they can't do shit on their own," he vented.

"So, you're gonna have to step in?"

"More than likely, but I aint really feeling that when I still don't know who shot at us. I don't trust nobody, but I gotta get this money."

"But do you really? I mean, you don't seem to be hurting for money. Maybe you should just chill."

"Keyasia, you really think that it's that easy? I got a lot of shit. A lot of bills. I live a certain lifestyle, and leaving the game right now…wouldn't be wise, financially."

"I hear you," she caressed him. "And I'm here for you, either way it goes."

"Oh, yeah?" he kissed her lips. "You riding?"

She gently smiled. "Of course."

******

Keyasia was surprised to finally hear the sound of Wale snoring. He'd tired himself out from running the dick up in her for hours. She herself was exhausted, but had business to handle.

Slowly easing out of his arms, she prayed that she didn't wake him. She breathed a little easier, when she realized that he'd remained asleep. Quietly, she moved around the room, hurrying to dress. It was sad that she was leaving with sex still all over her, but that was the only way she'd be able to leave peacefully. Besides, she figured she'd run and grab a test, then take it in a public restroom. And once it came back negative, she could come slide back into bed with him, without him ever realizing she'd left.

She briefly glanced back at him, as he tossed and turned in his sleep, without her next to him. The only time he didn't seem to be restless was when she was right there, in his arms. Undoubtedly, his spirit was troubled, and she didn't want to add to it. Therefore, she kept her fingers crossed, as she went to face her problems head on.

Roughly an hour later, she was in Jack-in-the-Box's restroom, crying her eyes out. She'd been hoping against hope, but it was real. She was pregnant with her Corinthian's child. Just a month ago, she would've been shaken by the news, but would have also undeniably accepted that she would now be a mother. The past week had changed her entire mind frame. Regardless of how he made her feel, how great he'd fuck her; he was not ready to be a father.

After tossing the test, she cleaned herself up, and attempted to shake her emotions. She then left the restroom, and ordered herself four tacos. She was all over the place, crying and eating, as she walked back to her Range.

At that moment, she didn't know what to do, or who to talk to, but knew that she couldn't be around Wale. There was no way in hell that she could conceal her somber mood, without him questioning the cause. Therefore, she headed to her parents' home.

By the time she pulled into the driveway, it was pouring down, raining. As if on cue, her cell rang. It was him.

"Hello," she answered.

"Where the fuck you at?" he fumed.

"I'm over here at my house," she explained.

"Your house, huh? Why you aint say shit? With all this shit going on, leaving without telling me aint cool, man."

"I know," she sighed. "You was just sleeping so good, and my mama called all hysterical. She was on some crazy talk, saying she'd been dreaming about me. So, I came over here to ease her mind."

"Yeah," he breathed, listening to her. He wanted to go off, and tell her to bring her ass back, but he understood that any sane parent would begin to worry, if their child had gone MIA for as long as she had. Unlike him, she had concerned parents, and still felt obligated to respect them, and ease their worries. "I hear you. Go ahead, and deal with them."

"I am, and then I'll be back. Do you need anything?" she asked, hoping to have him believe that everything was cool on her end.

"Nah. Just hurry ya ass up, and come back."

"Okay, I will," she promised. "It's raining cats and dogs out here. I'm about to run into the house. I'll call you back once I make it inside."

"Alright," he said dryly.

"Okay, bye." She ended the call. Putting her phone into her pocket, she pushed her car door open, before easing out, and then sprinting to their front door.

Using her key, she let herself into the house. The moment she stepped into the living room, Raquel lifted her head, feeling her presence. Silently, she studied her daughter, taking in her features. For a fleeting moment, she'd thought of Wale keeping her away, because he was beating her ass. But judging from the glow on her daughter's skin, that definitely wasn't the case. Keyasia was intact, and seemed to have picked up a pound or two, as she stood there in her natural state. Her weave and lashes were absent, and she looked no older than fifteen.

"Well, who do we have here? I know that aint my daughter. She's too busy to spend time with her family, spending every waking moment with a little knuckle head," Raquel chided.

"And hey to you too, mama," Keyasia smirked, before sauntering over to sit on the couch.

Raquel poked out her bottom lip. "I guess that nigga aint over there losing his mind. You look to be in good condition. But I can't believe you letting your real hair breathe." She pointed out.

Keyasia had thick, wild, curly hair that could be quite unruly. Most people considered it beautiful, as it flowed beyond the middle of her back, but it could be difficult to tame. It was now positioned at the crown of her head in a huge, puffy bun, making her look exactly like the little girl Raquel remembered from years ago.

"Yeah, I need to go to the beauty shop. I've just been so busy with school, and everything," Keyasia lied.

Raquel narrowed her eyes. "So, you've been going to school like this?"

"Yeah."

"Is that right?"

"Uh huh."

"Okay, we'll go with that, for now. Hopefully, you're telling the truth. Cause if I find out you're lying, we'll have some real problems."

Her stomach became queasy. "Alright, mama."

Their conversation continued, as they caught up. Soon, their entire family was in the living room, laughing. Keyasia had been gone for so long that everyone was glad to see her. The house was definitely a lot quieter without her.

A few hours passed by, and she was no closer to being ready to go back to the hideaway with Wale. So, she took a long bath, and thought to herself. She cringed, as she came to the conclusion that she needed to look into abortion facilities, before it was too late. Thinking about how he was so observant and paranoid, she figured the sooner she dealt with the situation, the better.

She also knew that it would be difficult to follow through with her plans, while in Wale's presence, therefore she'd have to stay at home for a few days. So, when he video called her, while she was in her bedroom, she delivered the news.

"It's still raining out here, and it's flooding by the freeways, so I'll have to sleep out here tonight."

He grimaced, as he nodded. "Okay. It is flooding all around the city, so you do need to stay where you're at."

"I know," she sighed. "So, I guess you'll probably smoke a few, and fallout for the rest of the night, huh?"

"Nah." He shook his head. "Rain makes for easy work. I'm about to meet up with Craven 'nem in a minute."

"Really, Corinthian? You gonna go out there in this weather? Is it really that serious?"

"My residuals are always that serious, Keyasia."

"That's crazy," she grumbled, realizing that she'd never really paid much attention to how often he'd place his freedom on the line for the almighty dollar.

"Why you acting like this is new to you? How many nights have I left to go to work, with you right at the crib with me?"

"Too many to count, but still. Sometimes stuff gets old."

"And what does that mean?"

"Like, why don't you consider doing something else? Something with less risks. I mean, do you ever really think about the future? You can't do this forever."

"Man," he drawled. "Keyasia, I can't do that, right now. It's more than maybe you understand, but I gotta do what I gotta do. There's people who depend on me."

"What you mean? I'm sure all of your boys can take care of their selves."

"Not them. I'm talking about people like...Kash."

She gulped. There it was. He already had previous obligations, and was a slave to them. That would only intensify with a new baby to provide for. Then that whole Mona/Kash thing didn't seem to be going anywhere. Why would she want to permanently tie herself to that situation? "Well, I guess you have to do what you have to do for your little *family*."

"Why you gotta say it like that? You a part of my family, too, right?"

Her heart skipped a beat. "Oh, I didn't know. I mean, you've made it clear, time after time that Mona and Kash comes before everybody else."

"Nah, you's a lie, right there. Mona just comes along with Kash. So, I tolerate her. My only concern is him

Nicole Jackson

and you. And I never told you that he comes before you. So, I don't know where you're going with that bullshit."

"I was just going by what I was told. And I hear you, but you don't have to take care of me, Corinthian. I can take care of myself, and my mama and daddy would never allow me to go without."

"And that's cool, but that don't change my stance."

"I just wish you'd realize that I don't care about how much money you have. I'd love you, anyway."

He furrowed his brows. "You'd love me, anyway? Did you just tell me that you love me, Keyasia?"

She blushed, as she tucked her lips into her mouth, causing her dimples to anchor into her cheeks. The sight hardened him, instantly. "Yeah, I guess I did. I thought you knew."

"You just assumed some shit, huh?"

"Yep."

"Well, I guess I love your crazy ass, too."

She giggled, as her clit thumped. "Crazy?"

"Hell, yeah. You thought I didn't notice that you's a little throwed off?"

"And you aint?"

He chuckled. "That's how I know you crazy too. You fuck with me, so what that makes you?"

"Whatever," she playfully rolled her eyes.

"Fuck," he glanced around the room. "Where the fuck is my bitch?"

"Your what?" she frowned.

He looked up at the phone. "I'm looking for my Nina."

Once again, he'd brought her down from those clouds. Keeping a gun close at all times, wasn't a normal way to live. "Alright, Corinthian. I'm about to lay down. I'm sleepy," she yawned.

"Alright, man."

"Okay. But make sure you call me whenever you're finished…working. I don't care what time it is."

"I will. Get some sleep."

"Kay. But Corinthian…"

"What's up?"

"I mean it when I say that I love you. So, be careful. I'd lose my mind if something happened to you. So, don't fuck around and break my heart. Come back in one piece."

He grinned. "Alright, Keyasia. I'ma try my best to do that…and I love you too."

"Okay, bye-bye," she ended the call. For a few minutes after, she sat on her bed, staring at the walls. She took a deep breath. "It wouldn't be my life, if I didn't make shit extra hard for myself."

Chapter 20

Keyasia sat in her Range Rover, staring at her phone, as Wale called. It had been nearly two weeks since she'd seen him face to face. For the first few days, it had been hell conjuring up different excuses as to why she couldn't come back to the spot with him. Luckily, by the fourth day he was headed out of town to work. He'd been on the road for a little over a week, but was now back in town.

She sighed heavily, as he hung up and called right back. "Fuck," she vented, before answering the call. "Hey."

"Damn, what you got going on? You tied up or something?" he immediately questioned.

"No, I just got out of class."

"Yeah? Well, where you going now?"

She shrugged. "Probably home."

"Home? Damn, I aint seen yo ass in weeks, and you going home? It's like that?"

"No, it's not like that," she denied. "I do miss you, but I didn't know if you were ready for me to come over."

He squinted. "Why wouldn't I be?"

She smiled meekly. "I don't know. I guess I'm tripping. You're still at your duck off spot?"

"Nah. I got the cameras and other shit installed at the townhouse. So, I'm back in the city."

"Oh, okay. Well, after I swing by my house, I'll be over there."

He sucked his teeth. "Really, Keyasia? Can't that wait? Like I *really* need to see you *now*."

Her heart pounded in her chest. "Okay. I'm on the way."

"Alright. Don't be too long," he stressed.

"I won't," she promised, ending the call. "Fuck." Her chest heaved up and down. The time was up, and she now had to face him.

It had been two weeks since she'd stepped into the abortion clinic and terminated her pregnancy. Two weeks since she'd began telling him lie after lie. And she wasn't positive he'd miss the look of guilt written all over her face.

Since the day she'd left the hideaway, she'd been an emotional wreck, crying non-stop. After getting rid of their baby, she'd been in shambles, feeling like the worst person walking the earth. The sight of little babies was enough to break her, and she'd been desperately trying to get a handle on herself. Two days prior, she'd just stopped bleeding, and didn't want any remnants of her decision to be noticeable to Wale. Therefore, she was a ball of nerves, thinking he'd see right through her.

About forty-five minutes later, she arrived at his home. Using her key, she gained entry into the townhouse. Before she could fully step through the living room, he attacked her.

"Corinthian," she struggled to get out, as he kissed her feverishly.

"Corinthian, what?" he breathed, lifting her off her feet.

"I can't even come all the way through the door," she giggled. God, she'd missed him, and didn't realize how much until that very moment, within his arms.

"Hell, nah. You was taking too long," he growled.

Judging by his tone, she knew what was on his mind. He was ready to fuck her senselessly, but she wasn't sure if she was ready. For one, she didn't know if she'd feel differently to him, and she didn't want him thinking that she'd stepped out on him. Secondly, she was fully aware that she could end up pregnant again, and she'd been hoping to hold him off, until her doctor gave her birth control in a few days.

With her back pinned against the wall, there was little she could do to fend him off. His kisses had become wild, as he tugged at her sweat pants. She panicked, not wanting him to get to the kitty.

"Baby, wait," she panted. "Put me down."

Wanting to see what she was up to, he placed her back on her feet. Gradually, she lowered to her knees, unbuckling his jeans. Once she was gripping his massive hard-on, preparing to take him into her mouth, he halted her, tucking his dick back into his boxers.

"Wait, wait. Bae, the head is good. In fact, it's muthafuckin' superb, but that aint what I need, right now."

She gazed up at him. "So, what is it that you *need*?"

"To feel you."

She gulped. "But Corinthian…"

"Shhh," he hushed her. "Just stand up for me." He helped bring her to her feet. Grabbing the tip of her chin, he swirled his tongue on the side of her neck. "You don't want me to slide inside of you, Keyasia?" he whispered. "Huh? You don't like my touch no more?"

Her eyes rolled into the back of her head. "I love your touch."

"You let somebody else feel my pussy?"

"No." she waved her head. "Never."

"Then show me what it is, then," he urged.

"I think I can do that," she breathed, before grabbing his hand, guiding it inside of her pants, and then her panties.

Like second nature, his finger tickled her pearl. Lowering his head, their lips met, as he eased his tongue into her mouth. He quickly grew excited, as he felt how wet she'd become. Before she could attempt to stall him, he had both her pants and panties at her ankles. Still, he continued to stroke her clit. Using his feet, he pushed her panties completely off.

Breaking their kiss, he looked into her eyes. "Pull this dick out."

Gazing into his green eyes, she was spellbound. Without thinking of anything else, she reached into his boxers, and uncovered his hard-on. Slowly, she stroked him.

His mouth fell open, before he was able to gather his composure. He swallowed hard. "Put it in that pussy."

Surprising him, she threw a leg onto his shoulder. With his dick in her hand, she steered him inside of her. Gripping her hips, he shoved himself deeper into her. Working her magic, she popped her back, meeting his strokes. She was so wet that she could feel her own juices trickling down her thigh.

"Grrrr," Wale fought to keep his composure. She was putting that pussy on him. Feeling like she was making him weak, he roughly shoved her against the wall. Twirling his dick inside of her, he pounded into her.

"Ahhhh!" she let out a high-pitched scream.

"The fuck you thought was gon happen?" he gritted. "You thought I was just gon let you fuck the shit out of me? Huh?"

"Yeahhhhh," she whimpered, as he gave it to her good.

"This can't be no one-sided shit. Hell, nah."

"Okay, okay, okaaaaaayyy."

He smiled. "Yeah, I likes that shit. Even when I put pressure on it, you fuck me back. Fucking a nigga like you missed him. You missed me, Keyasia?"

"Yessssss," she purred.

"Yes, what? Huh?"

"I...I...I missed you. I love you. I need yooooouuuu."

"Damn," he grunted, as his dick twitched, while she pulsated around him. "Blasting at the same damn time, huh?" he chuckled.

"Yeah," she answered faintly, feeling like a complete fool. In a matter of seconds, he was able to get her to do everything she promised herself she wouldn't. It was like temporary insanity. In between his alluring green eyes, that long fat dick, and the way he caused her heart to skip a beat…she'd never stood a chance. But deep down, she knew there would be consequences for her actions.

******

"I'm hearing voices in my head, I think I'm schizophrenic. I swear they're saying let's get it from a another planet. Thirty sixty thousand times will do a somersault. Do it right, and you can lead your whole summer raw…" Young Jeezy's voice blared throughout the room.

"Ayeeeee!" Black Reign boasted, as she wagged her tongue.

"Uh oh, just when they thought it was over! My girl can still get down on them hoes!" Keyasia shouted, egging Black Reign on, as she wobbled her ass, while standing on her kitchen's counter top. Key was right along with her, straight cutting up.

It felt like old times, as Keyasia and Black Reign were able to link up. Although, they'd always been cool, they'd never really hung as they grew older. But since Wale was Black Reign's cousin-in-law, the two were seeing each other all the time, and an old childhood friendship was now rekindled.

They'd been drinking, and getting lifted on a little herb for a better part of the day. So now they were high, and clowning around. They were like two loud, obnoxious, teenaged girls who were acting up, while their parents were away.

Wale and Kaydoa had been catching up, along with Meeko in the living room of Kaydoa's home. For quite a while, they'd been hearing music, and giggles from the kitchen. Finally, after getting hungry, they'd decided to see what the hell was going on.

Kaydoa shook his head, as he found his wife dancing on the kitchen's counter. He wasn't surprised, because it was in her playful nature, whether she'd had a few drinks or not. Wale had to chuckle at Keyasia, as she danced hard, doing a split on the counter, while rapping along with the song's lyrics.

"Guess what my mama told me? She hate my partners. But guess why she hate 'em, though. Cause all of 'em robbing…"

"They got their own music video going on," Meeko commented, checking out both women.

Wale observed Meeko, as he seemed to lock in on Keyasia, as she twerked. He even licked his lips, and wore a little smirk. There was no telling where Meeko's mind was going. "Aye, aye," Wale spoke up, stepping fully into the kitchen. "That's enough, man. Come on, get down," he instructed, literally removing Keyasia off the counter, throwing her over his shoulder. "Pull this down." He actually tugged her shorts further down her thigh.

"Corinthian, really? These damn shorts are damn near to my knees. What the hell can anybody see?" she questioned, while upside down.

"Shut up." He popped her booty.

"Stop!" she grabbed her butt cheek. "That shit hurts!"

"So," he popped her again. "What you in here showing out for? Dancing all nasty. Sometimes I think you strip on the side."

"Nigga, you got me fucked up! That's something I'd never have to do, when I can just dig in your pockets."

"Is that right?" he chuckled, knowing she was just talking shit. "Well, dig this." He spun around in a circle, while she was still upside down.

"Corinthian, stoop!" she yelled. "I'm about to throw up-ahhhhhhh," she hurled all over the floor.

"Shit," he expressed, as he hurriedly placed her on her feet.

"Damn, you made me throw up," Keyasia groaned, holding her stomach.

Black Reign sat down on the kitchen counter. "Well, you threw up earlier, and Wale wasn't even in the same room. And what about the other day?" she pointed out.

Keyasia glared at her.

"What?" Black Reign put her hands up. "I'm just saying. Maybe it's more to your little stomach sickness."

Kaydoa cut his eyes at Wale. "You put a baby in her, nigga?"

Wale eyed Keyasia. "I don't know. Did I, Keyasia?"

Key smacked her teeth. "Corinthian, don't let them fuck with your head. You know damn well I'm not...pregnant."

"Ion know nothing. Why you throwing up and shit?"

"I don't know," she snapped. She hated how they were putting her on the spot. She didn't even want to begin to assess the situation right then and there. Hell, she was almost sure she knew what it was, but she wasn't ready to face that kind of reality, yet.

Once again, she was in another predicament. Against the doctor's advisement, she'd gone right back into her routine of having unprotected sex with Wale. She was supposed to get on the birth control shot, but realized the day before her appointment that she had a test in one of her classes that she couldn't afford to miss. Therefore, she had to change her appointment date, all the while Wale was fucking her raw, cumming in her countless times. After missing her period, she was too afraid to go to the doctor, feeling like she'd hear something she wasn't ready for. Her dumb ass was more than likely pregnant again.

"Say, if I was you I'd have her pee on a stick, man," Kaydoa suggested. "Don't let her be like Jasmine," he referred to Black Reign by her government name. "She was pregnant with Kaylah, getting high and shit, swearing she aint realize that was my baby kicking, instead of gas."

"Uh uh, Kaydoa, don't do me," Black Reign interjected. "I really didn't know I was pregnant. Did I do that shit with Junior, though?"

"Hell, nah. Cause I would've put my foot up your ass. You knew better. Had you take the test, before that period was even due. I knew I had put him in there."

Wale smirked, thinking about the fact that he'd never attempted to pull out when fucking Keyasia. He was actually surprised that they hadn't had any slip-ups, yet.

"I gotta go to the bathroom," Keyasia blurted out, before clutching her mouth, racing out of the room.

"Yeah, kinfolk, you need to have her pee on a stick," Kaydoa reiterated.

Wale nodded. "Black Reign, where yall paper towels at? I need to get this fuckin' puke up."

"It's right there," she pointed.

"Nigga," Kaydoa paused, as Wale grabbed the paper towels, and proceeded to clean up Key's throw up. "You aint tell me that you was in love and shit."

"Huh?" Wale glanced up.

"Main, you heard me. You down there on the floor, scrubbing up this girl's puke. That's love, nigga. You doing that shit in thousand-dollar jeans, like it's nothing."

Wale shrugged him off.

"Aww, Wale loves his Key," Black Reign cooed. "Aint nothing wrong with that."

"Shit, you a damn lie," Kaydoa refuted. "If that nigga loves her…and she can deal with him. On a regular. Then they're both crazy. And two crazy muthafuckas don't have no business together."

Wale smiled. "Yeah, okay, nigga. Don't worry about me, and my broad. And if two crazy muthafuckas don't belong together, then tell me what the hell you doing with Black Reign's looney ass?"

Chapter 21

Keyasia felt like she was on the top of the world. It was the winter time, but the sun shined brightly. Chloe glasses shielded her eyes, as her girl, Taraj, rode shotgun in her new Ferrari. Well, it was actually Wale's, but he'd put it in her name. He claimed that he'd copped the vehicle for himself, yet he'd allowed her to choose the car, and he'd never driven it.

"Say, I love this car, man. Did your daddy get it for you?" Taraj pried, knowing Key already had a relatively new Range Rover that costed at least a hundred thousand.

"Nah, my daddy would swear I'm too young for such an expensive car," Keyasia answered.

"Well, who helped you get it? I know you didn't use all your money to make it happen," Taraj assumed, knowing Keyasia had plenty of help from both parents.

"Well, this is Corinthian's car, and I just like…use it."

Taraj giggled. "Corinthian? But I saw the insurance card. This shit is in your name, and you've been driving it. Aint no nigga just gone let somebody use his new, high ass car as soon as he gets it. Sounds like he bought it for you to me."

"Whatever," Keyasia sighed. "Mine, his, same difference."

"I guess. You and this dude be doing the most, and I still haven't met him."

"That's cause the minute we're done working, you're running home to Taz's ass. I mean, I aint mad at that, but you don't be on the scene."

"Ewe, you make me sound so lame."

Keyasia giggled. "Well, I'm not trying to. I can dig what you and Taz have. That nigga loves your dirty panties. So, I can see why you want to be around him. Yall make each other happy."

Just then they pulled up to Taraj's condo. She smiled, when she noticed her man's Benz parked outside. He and their son were supposed to have a little bonding time, while she shopped with Key.

"Taz and the baby must be back already," Taraj guessed, as they exited the car.

"Aww, I miss my wittle Tazerin, with his cute ass," Keyasia cooed, as they stepped to Taraj's front door. After unlocking the door, they stepped inside.

"There goes your mama," Taz smiled, as he held his son in his arms. "Say 'bout time, Junior."

Taraj sucked her teeth. "Nigga, I'm back early, and yall are still supposed to be gone."

Taz studied her, as she sauntered over to him. "We missed you."

"Aww," she cooed, before kissing their baby, and then her man.

Keyasia watched the whole scene, feeling emotional. Briefly, her mind ventured to the baby she once carried, and couldn't help but imagine what he or she would have looked like. Then the fact that she was once again pregnant came to the forefront of her mind. She'd found out about a month prior, and hadn't told Wale, yet. She was still sort of on the fence about what she wanted to do, but seeing Taraj with her family gave her hope. She knew that although in a different field, Taz was in the streets, but he was a good father to his son.

Lifting her phone, she texted Wale. He'd left town nearly a week ago to hit a lick. She'd been missing him like crazy, and couldn't wait for his return in two days.

What are you doing? She texted him

Trying to get back to you. He replied.

It's taking too long.

I know.

Feels like I can't breathe…

Damn. It's that deep?

Yes.

Well I gotta hurry up huh?

Definitely. And I got something important to tell you too.

Important? What's that?

Not in a text. Face to face.

Alright. You got my mind racing. Trying to figure out what's up with you.

Well it's nothing bad…I don't think. But we'll see.

Okay. I guess we'll see

"What's up, Keyasia? You can't speak?" Taz questioned.

"Oh, hey, Taz, what's up?" she asked, as she sat down on their couch.

"Nothing, much, man. What's been up with my boy, Amir Junior?"

She rolled her eyes. "Now see, your ass is trying to be funny. You know damn well that I don't fuck with him like that."

"Damn, you cold on 'em, huh? Yall was in love not too long ago."

"Shit, it's been a minute. That nigga had his little baby with ole girl, and that was really all she wrote for us."

"Girl, I have to wonder about a lot of these niggas, and the bitches they choose to lay down with," Taraj chided, rolling her eyes. "Be finding the lamest bitches on this earth," she threw a slug at Taz.

Recently, they'd discovered that he had a little girl with a chick he'd dealt with before ever meeting Taraj, and she wasn't very receptive to the BM. Taraj had a past herself, but hers had been forced upon her, while, Lani, the BM had been a willing participant in her hoe-ness. Therefore, Taraj was leery of her coming along drama free, and was waiting on her ass to get out of pocket.

"Aw, there you go with that shit," Taz drawled. "You know that was just something to poke on. You know you the only one to ever get more. If she aint you, I swear Ion want her."

Taraj gushed, as Keyasia cheesed, loving how Taz was so open for Taraj, and didn't care who saw it. Wale had his moments, in his own way, but never really verbal, especially in front of people. She couldn't wait for them to get to that point, like Taz and Taraj.

"Boy, you better stop talking like that, before I have to take your ass back to the room, right quick," Taraj warned, with lust filled eyes.

"Shit, what you waiting for?" Taz growled.

Taraj spun around. "Friend, can you keep an eye on Tazerin, right quick?"

Keyasia laughed. "You muthafuckas is something serious, but, yeah, I got the baby. Yall better be lucky yall made a gorgeous child, because yall know I don't like kids like that."

"Appreciate ya," Taz thanked her, quickly handing over his son to her.

"Umm hmm," Key pursed her lips, as they scurried upstairs. She bounced their bubbly baby in her lap. He was the perfect mixture of both his parents, with silky hair, and tight eyes. "Hey, Tazerin," she sang. "You are too adorable. Can I let you in on a secret? I'm gonna have a little you pretty soon. Yes, I am."

She had a one-side conversation with the baby, until her cell rang. Checking the screen, she saw that it was her aunt Raven. "Hello," she answered.

"Hey, I just emailed you about a job. They're offering a nice piece of change," Raven reported.

"Oh, okay. That's cool. I hope it's not an immediate job, because Corinthian is coming home in two days, and I need my schedule clear."

"Coming home? What you mean by that?" Raven quizzed.

"I mean he's out of town, and he'll be back in two days," Keyasia reiterated.

"Huh? Key, are you sure about that?"

"Sure about what?"

"About him being out of town."

"Why you asked that?"

"Because," Raven hesitated. "I…I'm mutual friends with quite a few of that girl Mona family members, and she tagged some of them in a post. Her son is having a huge birthday party today. Wale supposedly paid for damn near a hundred guests at Schlitterbahn in Galveston. I really don't how much he actually did, but she's praising him for shelling out all the cash for her baby's day, and how they're taking over the damn water park. And he's there with them. Every person there have on Ninja Turtles t-shirts with the little boy's name on it, including Wale. The girl Mona is posing in pictures with his family, down to his grandma. Shit, I just talked to Paris, and she said that her, Falen, Toya, Tino, Keesy, and everybody are there."

Keyasia's heart plummeted down to her stomach, as her neck grew hot. "What?" she let out faintly. "Let…let me call you back. I gotta see what…what's going on," she stumbled over her words.

"Alright, go ahead," Raven encouraged, wanting to make sure that her niece wasn't getting played for a fool.

"Okay." Key hung up, and immediately scrolled to Mona's page on Facebook. Sure enough, the first thing she saw was Wale clearly there on photos, celebrating Kash's birthday. Like Raven described, he wore a Ninja Turtles t-shirt that said 'Father of the birthday boy'. "This dirty muthafucka," she gritted.

Her hands were trembling, as she scrolled through photo after photo of Wale, and his entire family. Keyasia was floored that he'd do something like this behind her back. His actions had diminished their relationship to basically nothing. She felt like the outsider. Like some side chick that he dealt with occasionally, but he was now with his real family.

She stared at all the pictures, becoming angry at the people she personally knew that were in attendance at the party. Even Wale's grandma had made her feel comfortable, but now she felt it was all fake. Grandma Nina was going to deal with whomever Wale brought around, and she didn't discriminate.

Tears clouded her eyes, as she watched a video of Wale hugging Kash. He and Kash both wore matching Lacoste swimming trunks, as he handed the little boy a fat bank roll. "My lil' nigga gon ball on 'em like his daddy, huh?" Wale boasted, as everyone else laughed.

While filming Wale and her son, Mona playfully slapped Wale's ass. "Daddy needs a treat for pulling this one off."

He simply smiled. "Stop playing, man."

Tears streamed down Keyasia's face, as she placed her phone down. "I hate this nigga. I aint keeping this fuckin' baby. He got all the fuckin' family he needs, right here."

******

Wale was exhausted, as he pulled up to his townhouse. As soon as he'd come into town, he had to rush to Kash's party. He'd given Mona the money to throw the shindig, and she'd invited his entire family. Initially, he thought that he wouldn't make it, but at the last minute the crew collectively decided to do a job a few days earlier, giving him room to come home sooner than expected.

He'd been moving at a fast pace, and just wanted to get some sleep. He was glad that the Range and the Ferrari were both parked out front, indicating that Keyasia was already there. He always slept better with her in his arms, so he knew that he'd get a good night's rest.

Traveling to his front door, he knew that she wasn't expecting him, and couldn't wait to see the look on her face. He also considered the fact that she could possibly already know that he was back in town. Mona was a social media junky, so he knew that she was very vocal about the party. Then he considered that people like Paris were very close with Key, and had probably told her about it. He was hoping that it wasn't the case, but it was what it was.

He hadn't mentioned the party, because he knew that subject was touchy for him and Keyasia. Then when he ended up going to Kansas for a job he couldn't refuse, he figured there was nothing really to tell. He wouldn't physically be there for the party, anyway. Yes, he knew that his family would be there to rep him, but that was something that he'd never kept from Keyasia. His family, especially his grandma, truly saw Kash as one of their own, and were there for all special moments, like family should be. In fact, there were constant interactions with Kash and his family, even when Wale wasn't directly involved. His cousins with children Kash's age would often scoop him up from Mona to spend the weekend at their homes. Wale sometimes just avoided speaking on it with Keyasia to avoid any uncomfortableness. But he'd always maintained that he was going to be there for Kash, and Key never asked about the what, when, and where.

Stepping into his residence, he was caught off guard by the amount of bags piled up near the front door. After closely inspecting the items, he realized that everything belonged to Keyasia. "The fuck?" he mumbled to himself.

As if on cue, she jogged downstairs with three pairs of shoes in tow. She stopped at the bottom of the stairs when she realized that he was standing there. "Hey."

He frowned. "Where you going?"

"Uh," she hesitated. "I was going to take a few things to my mama's house. I…I wasn't expecting you today, so I was going to stay at home, for now."

He narrowed his eyes. "Keyasia, you never bring clothes to or from there. You got shit at ya people house to wear. And this is definitely more than clothes for a few days. It looks like everything you have here."

"Oh, does it seem like that?" she asked, attempting to fuck with his head.

"Yeah." He nodded, glaring at her. "So, are you gonna tell me what's up with that?"

She swallowed. "I'm going home. That's what's up."

"Going home? With all your shit, huh?"

"Yeah."

He aggressively stalked over to her. "What kind of fuckin' games are you playing? Huh?"

"Games? There's no games. That's not what I do, but you seem to be a pro at it. Running around, throwing elaborate parties, playing house, and then come to me like you really fucking with me. Nigga please. I'm going back to my muthafuckin' house where I belong. So, you can miss me with the bullshit," she fumed.

"Man," he stressed. "You blowing shit way out of proportion. I came home early, and was gonna surprise you. Yeah, Kash had a party today, and I thought I was gonna miss it. But I made it at the last minute. Did me and you talk about it? No. But when do we ever discuss him, Keyasia? You heard me when I said that I was going to be there for him, and then you went right on, acting like he don't exist. You never seem interested in what's going on with him. I can tell you about a program at his school, and you change the subject. I mention that I gotta take him to the barber shop, and you roll your eyes. So, I don't talk about him, and that don't equate to sneaking behind your back. Obviously, you don't wanna hear about him, anyway. But now you tripping, because I was at his party?"

Her nostrils flared. "Oh, make it sound like I'm crazy. Like you wasn't being deceitful. Let me go throw a whole party for somebody, and then casually stroll in here later, telling you that you never bothered to ask about it. I bet you'd be giving me the side eye. It's clear you have a whole life that I'm not a part of. That shit comes across sneaky, and dishonest."

"Okay, if that is how you feel, I can't dispute that. That's how it comes across to you. That don't make it a reality. Kash is my little nigga. I got a lot love for him, and I can't apologize for that. But I can acknowledge that I should have told you. That's my bad, but let me ask you this."

"What?" she folded her arms across her chest.

"If I would've told you about the party, would that have made you feel better? Or would you still be standing here mad?"

She thought about it. Honestly, she was uncomfortable with his relationship with Mona's child, regardless. Therefore, if he would've told her that he was back home, but headed straight to Kash's party, she would've more than likely been in her feelings. "Look, I don't know what I would've done. But I know that I wouldn't be able to claim you're a liar. And you think that Mona's behavior towards you was cool? She was slapping your ass and shit, and you basically laughed it off."

"What? I don't know what you talking about. So much shit was going on that I wasn't paying her no attention. Where you getting this bullshit from?"

"From her Facebook page. She was filming you, when she touched your ass."

He shook his head. "This petty bullshit will drive a nigga crazy. Mona was just being Mona, Keyasia. I probably brushed her off, and didn't think twice about it. I haven't fucked with that girl in God knows when, and she probably just wanted to put on for the internet."

"So, I guess I can go to Amir's daughter's party, and let him rub on my booty, huh?"

"Okay." He nodded. "I see where you going with this. Maybe I need to have another talk with her. I give you that, but is this enough for you to walk out on a nigga?"

"You tell me what I should do, then, Corinthian. Should I stay around and keep allowing you to make me feel like this?"

"Feel like what?" he invaded her space, getting directly in her face.

"Feeling like I'm fucking with the enemy. Like I don't know what you do whenever you go out into the world. Like you don't take me serious enough to consider how you move, and if it'll affect me."

"But that aint the case. You think I do this shit with every broad? You think I have them in my house, let them see me go in the safe, and trust them with my shit when I aint around? You think I go around telling girls to grab the newest Ferrari, I pay for it, let her have legal claim to it, and never drive it myself? Nothing about my actions show you that I'm just bullshitting with you, Keyasia. Or that I don't take you serious. And what makes you think that I'd invest all that into you, just to let you walk out the door? You think it's that easy? And if it's that easy for you, then you aint true, anyway. But you had already convinced me at first, so yo ass is stuck, either way it goes."

"But I aint gon be your fool, either. Corinthian, I watched my mama, auntie, and cousins go through it with their men. I saw them crying and fighting for their love, and I would always say, 'Not me. I'd never be that weak for a man.' Loving a man doesn't mean losing my self-respect. I aint signing on to be one of those chicks that lets a man drag her through the mud in the name of love. I can't be that girl. I won't let you turn me into that girl."

He gripped her face with both hands. "And I'm not trying to take you there. There aint a master plan to break you. I just wanna know that you really fucking with me. Even when I do shit that pisses you off. I mean, you can be mad. Fuck me up. Act up. Clown. I don't give a fuck. Just don't leave me."

She closed her eyes, as she grew emotional. She wanted to walk out that door, and leave him standing there, looking crazy. But her feet wouldn't move. Thoughts of being without him seemed almost paralyzing. She couldn't take herself through that type of anguish. Not right then. She wasn't strong enough.

"Okay," she breathed. "I won't leave you."

He gently stroked her cheek with his thumb. "Ever?"

Her belly rumbled. "Ever."

Nicole Jackson

******

The birds were outside chirping, as Keyasia lied on her back in bed, while she nibbled on a saltine cracker. Morning sickness was kicking her ass to the point where she had to keep crackers at her bedside. It was like Wale knew something, and just wouldn't say it, as he floated in and out of consciousness, while rubbing her stomach.

Key was a little envious, as he seemed to have no problem sleeping. She was restless, as her mind was hard at work. Later that day, she was scheduled to have an abortion, and was still on the fence about what to do. There were so many variables to consider, and she was utterly confused.

"Keyasia, what did you have to tell me?" Wale questioned with his eyes still closed.

"Huh? What are you talking about?"

"Yesterday. In that text. You said you needed to tell me face to face."

"Oh…I don't even remember, honestly," she lied.

He opened his eyes. "You eating crackers again?"

"Yeah, my stomach won't settle."

"I wonder why." He stroked her belly with his palm.

"I don't know."

"Umm…maybe," he began, until one of their cells vibrated on the nightstand beside him. Reaching over he grabbed the ringing phone, discovering that it was Mona calling him. Usually, he'd send her calls to voicemail, and return her call whenever Key wasn't around. But he wanted to do things differently, and become transparent with his actions. "Yeah?" he answered.

"Hey, did you get my text?"

Keyasia's ears perked up, as she heard Mona's voice crystal clear.

"Nah. Why? What's up?" Wale questioned.

"You gave Kash everything he asked for on his birthday, except the one thing he won't shut up about."

"And what's that?"

"You know he begged for me, you, and him to go out to have dinner together."

Keyasia was glad that she was facing the wall, because Wale couldn't see the snarl on her face. *Dinner together? Like, really bitch?*

"Oh, yeah," Wale exhaled. "Honestly, that shit did slip my mind."

"Well, he haven't forgot about it. That's all he talks about. Every damn morning he goes on and on, asking when you was taking us."

"Oh, yeah?"

"Yep, and this morning I think I figured out why," she claimed.

"Why you say that?"

"Because as I was driving him to school, he asked me if you were gonna always be around. He said that he understands that you aint his binocular father."

"Biological father, you mean?" he corrected her.

Nicole Jackson

Promiscuous Girl: Keyasia and Wale

"Yeah, whatever. But anyway, he said he understands that, but wanted to know if you'd always be around. He recognizes that you got a little girlfriend, and everything. He talked about how he barely sees you these days, and that he was so glad you was able to make it to his party. And he fucked me up when he asked if you and that girl ever had a baby, would you forget about him. You know I can't bullshit him, so I told him that I hope you wouldn't. But in life we never know."

"Man," he drawled. "Mona, what the fuck are you talking about? When have I ever not been a man of my word? Me being with somebody aint got nothing to do with Kash. And if I had a baby, then that would just mean that I got two kids now. I fuck with Kash, because I fuck with him. Not because I don't have my own kids or some shit. He *is* my kid. That shit aint negotiable."

"Okay, I hear you. If you say you're here to stay, then that's what it is. But what are you gonna do to ease your son's mind? Are we going to dinner?" Mona quizzed.

Keyasia cringed, after hearing Mona refer to her child, as Wale's son.

"Look, I aint gonna say that we're going today or tomorrow. I got some runs to make, but I got him this weekend. We'll link up, and take him to eat."

"Okay, cool. Then we can sit him down, and help him to understand that we'll always be family, regardless."

"For sho'," Wale agreed.

"Okay, we'll see you this weekend. Oh, and Grandma Nina said for you to call her. I just got off the phone with her."

"Alright."

"Bye." Mona hung up.

Keyasia closed her eyes, pretending that she'd dozed off. She was fuming, and didn't want to face Wale, right then. He'd done nothing more than talk to Mona, about her son, but that conversation had her reeling. It was a cruel reminder of what could be to come. She could very well have his child, have to deal with his profession, all the dangers that come with the hustle, and be forced to tolerate him being Mona's Super-Save-A-Hoe. Nothing about those particular circumstances were appealing to her. In fact, with all those hurdles they had to leap over, there no was guarantee that their love would survive. And then she'd find herself raising a child all by her lonesome.

The more she thought about it, the more she came to the realization that she and Wale weren't ready for a child together. There seemed to be no end in sight with his criminal activity. Mona was a nuisance that seemed to be a permanent fixture in his life. A nuisance he chose to keep around, as well. Key had personally witnessed most of the women in her life deal with baby mama drama, and it was a never-ending battle. She didn't want that in her life. It was too much.

Seemingly, as she wrapped her mind around the fact that she was about to terminate another pregnancy, all her food threatened to come up. "Shit," she hissed, as she hopped out of the bed, and raced to the bathroom. She heaved everything she had into the toilet.

Wale squinted, as he eased out of bed. Slowly, he approached the bathroom's doorway, and watched her. For over a month, he'd been suspecting that she was pregnant. Then after chopping it up with Craven, as he complained about how his girl was bitching because she was on her period, he realized that he couldn't recall the last time Keyasia had had a cycle. It had been several months, and she had obvious pregnancy symptoms. At this point, he was just waiting for her to confirm it. He already knew what it was, and figured that her ass would have to come clean, sooner than later.

"You alright?" he asked her.

She nodded, as she wiped her mouth with tissue.

"You sure? Because it seems like you've been throwing up every morning. You sure there aint something more to it?"

"I'm positive," she lied, while avoiding eye contact. She climbed to her feet, and tipped to the sink. "I just got a weak stomach," she claimed, before lowering to rinse out her mouth.

He was about to kick his interrogation up a notch, until he heard a cell ring. Spinning around, he stomped over to the nightstand, and saw that it was Craven calling him. "What's up, nigga?" he inquired, just as Keyasia's phone vibrated. Picking up her phone, he saw that it was her alarm going off in the form of a Gmail alert, indicating that she had a Planned Parenthood appointment today.

After glancing back, he placed her phone down, making sure that he never fully opened the alert. Eventually, it ended on it's on, and Keyasia was now in the shower, presumably never hearing it go off.

Wale sat down at the edge of his bed, half listening to his cousin ramble on and on. He was really waiting on Keyasia to come out of that bathroom. Fifteen minutes later, she stepped back into the room with a towel wrapped around her. Without saying anything, she prepared to get herself ready.

"Aye, hold up, Craven," he halted his people. "Keyasia, where are you going?" he asked her, as she pulled a Moschino t-shirt dress over her head.

"Huh?" she paused.

"I said, where are you going?"

"Umm…" she stalled. "I'm about to meet with my auntie. She wanna show me these contracts for this little deal she's been working on for me."

"Oh, yeah?"

"Yeah."

"And then what you're doing?"

"I don't know. I know that I gotta stop to get me some pads." She grabbed her belly. "My stomach is cramping. I think that I'm about to start my period."

If she'd bothered to look his way, she would've seen that his jaw was twitching, as he listened to her feed him bullshit. "Your period, huh? Where was that muthafucka all these other months?"

"What?" her eyes bucked, as he caught her off guard with his question.

"You heard me."

"Oh, sometimes my period is irregular. It's been like that since I was a little girl."

Wale fought against himself to cuss her out. As bad as he wanted to confront her, he wanted to know what she was planning to do even more. If he just came out with the accusations, she could feed him bogus stories, and he'd have no way to dispute it. No. He had to see how far she'd go with her lies.

Grateful that he'd let up with the questions, Keyasia dressed in peace, and then stepped over to him, kissing his lips. "I'll be back."

His green eyes darkened, as he nodded. All the while, Craven was still on the phone, and caught his attention, after he'd watched her switch out of the room. "You heard me, kinfolk?"

"Say, what?" Wale focused on the call.

"I said that I'm about to pull up. You aint leaving right now, are you?"

"Nah, nah. You know I don't move around this time of the morning."

"Good. Well, come open your door."

"Alright," Wale agreed, as he stood up. Grabbing the first thing he saw, he threw on some basketball shorts, and a wife beater. He then traveled downstairs.

By the time he reached his front door, Craven was already standing on the stoop. Stepping to the side, Wale examined the car his cousin pulled up in. "Nigga, what you doing in that old ass Benz?"

"Jazel is in my fuckin' 750," he referred to his girlfriend. "The Escalade is at the body shop, and the Porsche is at Jazel's mama's house. Yana's old ass been having my shit for a week now," he talked about his girlfriend's mama. "When I leave here, I'ma drive by there, park this Benz, and take my shit. She got me fucked up, on the cool."

Wale chuckled at his cousin. He had the weirdest relationship with Jazel and her mama. He interacted with her mama, as if she was a broad he grew up with. He'd call the lady all hours of the night for virtually nothing, hang with her, and smoked weed with her. Then Jazel was a wild little thick chick, he'd snatched up. People often made the assumption that Craven had some timid girl at home, who allowed him to walk all over her. That could be no further from the truth. The real reason he had some much free time to fuck bitches was because his girlfriend loved to run the streets. She club hopped more than him, and would spend his money faster than he could make it. Truly, Craven and his girl were one in the same, but refused to let each other go.

"Well, your ass needs to buy her another car. That's why she won't stay out of yours," Wale pointed out.

"Shit, she wrecked the last car I bought her. She begged and begged for that Audi. I got that bitch for her, and what she do? Ram that muthafucka into my Escalade."

Wale roared with laughter. "Quit testing the waters with her, man. You know that girl is crazy than a muthafucka. Every time I see her, she ask me, 'Wale, why you won't let me come to your house? I aint gon try to set it on fire like I did when you was living with that bitch Mona. But you know that hoe was trying to hook Craven up with her friends.' I mean, she say that shit every single time. Always reminding me of how crazy you gotta be to still be with her. I knew she was off her rocker when she shot at you, grazing you with that bullet."

"Nigga, fuck you," Craven chided. "I fucked her up too. Don't forget that part."

"You fucked her up?" Wale furrowed his brows. "Before or after she chased you through the hood? Or what about that time she kicked Mona's cousin's door down? She had all them bitches in there shook, and had you stuttering. I aint never seen you scared like that. Niggas in the streets can't shake you like that. So, I already know who to call, when I need somebody to get on your ass. Jazel whups yo ass once a week."

"Yall niggas love to claim my bitch is crazy. But I bet you won't say that shit to her face."

Wale grinned. "Hell, nah. I aint gon say shit to her face, unless I got my pistol close by. I'll have to shoot it out with her ignorant ass. I'm still tripping off her beating yall's old neighbor's ass. Didn't you say that lady was old enough to be her mama?"

Craven cheesed. "Yeah, but she was finer than a muthafucka. I let that hoe suck my dick, and 'til this day I don't know how Jazel found out. But all I know is that she dragged that lady up and down the sidewalk."

"That broad is violent. The fuck was Yana smoking when she was pregnant with her?"

Craven licked his lips. "Shit, aint no telling."

"Yeah, that car is bringing down the property value, since you pulled it in the driveway…" Wale jested, until it dawned on him. That was definitely a car Keyasia wouldn't recognize. "But say, let's swop, right quick. You grab one of my cars, and I'ma make a run in that ancient ass Benz."

"The fuck you trying to do?" Craven questioned, knowing that typically Wale wouldn't be caught dead in a '08 model vehicle.

"Don't worry about all that," he waved him off. "Just let me see the keys."

Craven gave him a weird look, as they exchanged keys, but Wale had no time to address that. He was already on the phone, calling Keyasia.

"Hello," she answered.

"Aye, how far have you made it?"

"I stopped to get some gas, so not too far. Why?"

"I really need you to double back, and grab my clothes from the cleaners. I know they'll be closed by the time you make it back, and I gotta make a run."

She sighed heavily. "Really, Corinthian? I was damn near to the freeway."

"But you just said that you wasn't that far."

"Ooh, Lord, you get on my nerves. Okay, Corinthian, I'm turning around to get your clothes now. Are you happy?"

"For sho'. But let me call you back." He hung up.

Craven watched curiously, as his cousin fiddled with his phone, going into some app. "Nigga, do you got some kind of GPS on that girl?"

Wale's eyes remained trained on his cell. "Mind ya business."

Craven shook his head, as Wale scooted his feet into a random pair of tennis shoes, before jogging out to Jazel's car. "Lock the door behind you," he called out, before dropping down into the car.

Wale backed out of his driveway like a bat out of hell. He had just a few minutes to catch up with Keyasia at the dry cleaners. Hopefully, he'd catch her, as she was leaving, and tail her to her destination. Having a back-up plan, if he was to miss her, he'd then use the app on her cell to GPS her whereabouts. This was possible, because unbeknownst to her, he'd placed a hidden app on her phone weeks prior, therefore he always knew where to find her. He'd done this during his heightened paranoia, thinking it could potentially save her life. And now he was going to use it to catch her in a lie.

Pulling the car up to the curb near the local dry cleaners, he caught a glimpse of the Ferrari, exiting the lot. Keeping a safe distance, he followed her. He shook his head, as he realized that she was heavy footed. She was zipping through the traffic on the streets, breaking the speed limits.

As he tailed her, he felt this surge of nervous energy flow through his body. He still held onto hope that she could possibly be meeting her aunt somewhere, until she pulled into the parking lot of a Planned Parenthood. Not wanting to risk her catching a glimpse of him, he waited on the road, until she'd slid out of the car, and jogged into the building. He then jotted into the lot, parking the car.

"The fuck is she doing?" he asked himself the obvious. He was having a hard time believing Keyasia was living this foul, lying to his face. "I know this bitch aint doing what I think she is."

He sat gripping the steering wheel for several minutes, attempting to gather his thoughts. It felt like his mind was in a haze, and nothing happening at the moment was real. "Nah, it gotta be something else," he tried to convince himself, as exited the Benz.

His body seemed to have a mind of its own, as he marched into the building Keyasia had entered. Glancing around, he saw a few women, and one familiar face. Robin.

Robin was a chick he'd met through Craven's girlfriend, Jazel. The two were old friends, and she'd always flirt with Wale whenever she was in his presence. Robin was a cute medium brown skinned chick with a nice ass on her. Still, he had never given her the time of day, because Jazel had admitted that the girl used to have a nasty coke habit. That made her a liability he couldn't afford. Still, she resembled an upstanding citizen, as she strolled around the help desk.

Wale furrowed his brows, as he saw how well-groomed and polished Robin's loud, ghetto ass appeared. "What's up, Wale?" she asked, as she approached him.

"What's up? I didn't know you work here."

"Yeah, I've been here for almost two years. What are you doing here?"

He studied her for a second. She could probably help him figure some shit out. "Dropping my people off," he lied. "Why, where you going?"

"To lunch," she batted her lashes.

"Well, let me walk you to your car."

"Cool," she smiled, as they moseyed out of the building. "So, which chick did you bring here, and is she your gal?"

"Nah, I aint got no gal," he replied, choosing to answer the question she really cared to hear about.

She grinned. "Okay. So, which chick did you drop off? Three different ones just walked through the door."

"Why you wanna know?" he lifted his chin.

"Because I'm curious."

"Okay." He nodded. "Which one you think it is?"

"Hmm." She placed a finger on her chin. "One girl had a nappy weave, and had no ass, so I don't think it was her. But then there was this mixed girl with long hair, and a brown skinned girl with some hair down to her ass. Now, I do believe that hers was fake, but the shit looked natural. Both girls were pretty attractive, but I know you don't seem like the super reckless type, when it comes to hoes, so I'ma go with the mixed one."

He squinted, but snickered, hoping to throw her off. "What you mean by reckless? What you got against brown skin chicks?"

"Nothing. The last time I checked, I was brown skinned, so obviously there's no issue with that. But that brown skinned girl was dressed to the nines in expensive labels. Bitch looks like she shits out a golden coin, but is using the fucking abortion clinic as birth control. Twice in less than sixty days? I mean, come on."

Wale's jaw tightened, as he felt sick to his stomach. Keyasia must have lost her rabid ass mind. He couldn't believe that she'd do something like this. He could barely see straight, as he left Robin right where she was standing. God, must've truly been on Keyasia's side that day, because he'd left his home in such a haste, that he'd forgotten to grab his gun. Otherwise, there would've been a bullet waiting on her, the moment she stepped out of that building. She'd done the unthinkable. The unforgiveable.

Chapter 22

Idly, Wale sat in his Audi, in his driveway, with the lights out, taking huge gulps of Cîroc directly from the bottle. It was a bit past midnight, and he'd been drinking for hours. He was hoping that the liquor would numb him, but it had only intensified his rage.

He thought about all the women he'd disregarded, never allowing them in. He knew that he'd been guarded, and was unapologetic about it, but he'd never taken Keyasia through those type of changes. He'd been as real as he knew how, but it wasn't reciprocated. She'd handled him like he was any other man, and did what she wanted. He'd never met a woman more selfish.

It had been hours since he'd left the clinic, raced home, and hopped in another car. Keyasia had called him a handful of times, but he didn't answer. He was honestly at a loss for words. She'd killed two of his babies. For a second, his mind tried to play devil's advocate, suggesting that perhaps those babies weren't his, but he knew better. It had become habitual to watch those closest to him, and he'd watched Keyasia like a hawk. Even when she was out of town, he had eyes and ears everywhere. Not to mention, he had full access to her call log, unbeknownst to her. She'd been walking a straight line. She'd been on her best behavior, even on her social media pages, because he'd sneakily gotten her passwords to all that too. He really thought he had a loyal one. Somebody to hold on to. But she'd shifted his entire mindset.

When he'd told her that he loved her, he'd meant it. Sure, he'd said it to a few other chicks before, but that was to get whatever he wanted at the moment. Keyasia was different. He'd think about her, and it would bring a smile to his face. Whenever he'd hit a lick, he'd think about the

Nicole Jackson

next thing he could buy her, because he wanted to be the one to put a smile on her face. When he was with his boys, he'd mentally countdown to the second he was back with her. She was it for him. But now, as he sat outside his own home, he felt nothing but contempt for her.

His eyes hooded, as his body became weary. He was exhausted, and wanted nothing more than to crawl into his bed, and go to sleep. Staring at the Ferrari, parked in front of him, he knew that she was inside of his home, and that was why he couldn't bring himself to get out of the car. He wasn't sure that if he was to go inside that he wouldn't take one look at her, and blow her brains out. He honestly didn't know how much restraint he had, and didn't want to black out, and strangle her to death.

Deciding that it was best for the both of them, he backed out of his driveway, leaving. He had to go, before he'd do something they'd both regret.

******

Keyasia's eyes fluttered open, as she slowly realized that the sun was now out. Rolling over in bed, she discovered that she was alone. "The fuck," she grumbled, as she sat up, and read the alarm clock. It was ten a.m. and Wale still wasn't there. That was highly unusual for him, as her heart pounded in her chest. Clutching her phone that was lying next to her, she checked for any missed calls from him. There were none.

Consumed with worry, she dialed up his number, and listened to his phone ring. Eventually, his voicemail picked up. She then hung up, calling him again and again. Finally, he answered.

"Yeah?"

"Yeah?" she repeated, becoming infuriated. "Where are you? Did you end up going to work last night?"

"Nah," he replied with music in the background.

"Then what are you doing?"

"I'm chilling, man. Hanging and shit."

"Hanging? So, you been up all night, just hanging?"

"Nah. I stopped somewhere and got a little sleep," he revealed.

"You stopped somewhere?!" she beseeched. "Why wasn't that somewhere your fuckin' house?!"

He sucked his teeth, as she screamed at the top of her lungs. "Say, the last time I checked, I was a grown ass man. I don't answer to you, or anybody else. So, lower your fuckin' voice."

"I aint lowering shit! What type of bullshit are you on? You think I'ma put up with this?"

"Do it sound like I give a fuck about what you'll put up with?"

Keyasia was floored, as he spoke to her disrespectfully. "Corinthian, do you hear yourself? Tell me what the problem really is," she urged.

"The problem is you calling my phone a hundred fuckin' times, coming at me like I'm your fuckin' child. You got me fucked up, and like I said, I'm chilling. I'll be through there whenever I get around to it."

"Corinthian, do you not hear how disrespectful you sound?" she questioned.

He said nothing.

"Hello?"

Still nothing.

Removing the phone from her ear, she realized that he'd hung up. She was pissed, as she called him back, but he refused to answer. After twenty minutes of unsuccessfully trying to reach him, she decided that she was going to pack up her shit, and go home.

After grabbing just a few items, she realized that she was still rather tired. Lying back down, she promised herself that she'd leave, as soon as she was done taking a nap.

When she finally awakened it was now once again dark outside. She was shocked that she'd slept for so long. Looking at the alarm clock, she realized that it was nine o'clock at night. Glancing around the room, there were still no signs of Wale. Picking up her phone, she saw that a few people had called, but none were him. Dialing him up, she listened to his phone ring.

"Yeah?" he answered.

"So, you're still on that bullshit? It's about to be another day, Corinthian."

"On what bullshit?"

She huffed. "Why are you playing games? When are you coming home? I'm tired. I don't want to argue."

Hearing her say that infuriated him. The bitch wouldn't be tired, if she wasn't letting them physically suck babies out of her ass. "Man," he drawled. "What are you talking about? I told you earlier that I was chilling. That shit aint changed…" he trailed off, as he focused on people in the background. "Nah, nigga. We falling off in that bitch around twelve. We got the biggest section in that muthafucka. Craven got Jazel to run down to the mall for us. We all wearing Ferragamo tonight."

Keyasia was incensed, as she listened to him make plans for the club in the middle of the week, while she was talking to him, no less. And if Jazel had picked up their clothes for them, then she was definitely going out with them, yet he hadn't extended the invitation to her.

"Fuck this," she mumbled, hanging up. "He really got me fucked up."

Feeling stupid for calling him to smooth things over, she hurriedly grabbed a few things, along with her laptop, before storming out of the house. To show him that she didn't need him, she hopped into her Range, leaving the Ferrari behind. She wasn't about to kiss his ass, and if he wanted to flip the script that was cool. Two could definitely play that game.

******

Keyasia had been blindsided by Wale's sudden change. He'd switched up so fast that she was surprised she didn't have whiplash. She'd ran home to her parents' with the assumption that he'd call, demanding she bring her ass back to the crib. Two weeks later, that call had never come. Instead, he was turning up with his boys, shaking and moving, never bothering to pick up the phone to see if she was still breathing.

Key was shocked by the fact that she now appeared to be single again. With his sudden change of heart she could only assume it to be another girl, because there was no other plausible explanation. For five seconds, she told herself that he'd done her a favor, but by the sixth second she realized that he and whatever bitch he was dealing with had her fucked up. He couldn't just come along, open her up, and then walk away. It wasn't that damn simple, and she wasn't going down without a fight.

So, on her quest to confront Mr. Corinthian, she was riding through his hood, hoping to spot him. After dealing with him, she knew the Acres Homes area like the back of her hand, and all his hang-out spots.

After an hour, she was becoming frustrated. She'd already stopped by his townhouse, and knew that he wasn't there. He also wasn't hanging out on the cut, and neither were any of his boys. That meant that they were probably all together somewhere, and she was determined to figure out where. Thinking of who could help her out, Jazel entered her mind.

Jazel was crazy, as hell, and Key loved it. However, Wale had been adamant about the two not becoming too cozy, swearing that her being friends with Jazel would just bring drama and confusion. Naively, Key had heeded his warnings, but now she wondered if Wale didn't have his own selfish reasons for keeping them apart. Maybe Jazel knew things that she didn't, and he wanted to keep it that way. Who knows? But she was about to see what ole girl could do for her today.

Scrolling through her phone, she located her name, and dialed her up. After a few rings, she picked up.

"I was checking my screen to see if this shit had malfunctioned. Like, I know this aint Keyasia calling me. What's up, though?"

Key giggled. "Is that how you answer your phone all the time?"

"Something like that. But what you calling me for? You looking for that nigga Wale? Cause he's right over here in my living room with the rest them annoying ass niggas. No need to thank me. Just bring me some chicken strips from Whataburger, and we can call it even."

"Bet," Keyasia agreed. "I'll be there in like thirty or forty minutes…with your food, mam."

"Alright, bye," Jazel hung up.

Key tossed her cell onto the dashboard, and mashed the gas. Like most of his boys, Craven lived out in the burbs, and she couldn't get there fast enough. Twenty-five minutes later, she pulled up to Craven and Jazel's home with Jazel's Whataburger in tow. Spotting Wale's Audi, she knew that he was still there, and she was just hoping that he didn't have some broad with him. Not that another girl would stop her, but she preferred less hassles.

Shooting Jazel a text, she asked her to come open the door for her. She couldn't risk one of the guys seeing her, and not letting her in. She'd witnessed Wale and his boys run interference for one another a few times, and she didn't want to be forced to cuss one of their asses out.

Before she was fully on the porch, Jazel opened the door, allowing a cloud of weed smoke to seep outside. "You right on time with this food," she smiled, before puffing on a blunt.

"You got the munchies, huh?" Keyasia laughed, handing her the bag of food.

"Yes mam," Jazel concurred, standing there in some very provocative booty shorts. She was the epitome of a black stallion with her smooth chocolate skin, and voluptuous tight body. She was a solid size fourteen with ass for days, and had no problem showing it off. Then she was a beauty, equipped with tight eyes, and was a cross between a young Taral Hicks and a tender Kenya Moore. She often opted to wear long bundles of weave, but this day she hadn't bothered doing much to her head, as her natural hair was bundled up in sloppy bun. The thing was, it worked for her, as she had super long curly hair, and the messiness only exposed how nice her hair naturally was.

Keyasia stepped into the house, and immediately all eyes were on her. There was a mixture of people there in the living room. She noticed quite a few of Wale's boys, a nice sum of their girlfriends, and some additional chicks she'd never seen before. Since Jazel had willingly allowed her to come over, she assumed that none of the girls were there for Wale by way of her. Still, something told her that he'd come through with a bitch, as some light skinned girl sat awfully close to him.

Craven cut his eyes at Jazel. "What you did, man?" he whispered.

She bit into a chicken tender. "Got her to bring me some Whataburger. You didn't feel like driving, remember?"

"You always being messy, man."

"Whatever. I bet next time yo ass will just go get my food. Trying to front for these niggas," Jazel scoffed.

"What's up, yall?" Keyasia spoke to everyone.

Wale glared at her. "What you doing here, Keyasia?" he asked her, fighting the urge to cuss her out. He couldn't believe that she'd come through in that tiny neon green and back Nike ensemble. The shorts fully exposed her thighs...where she'd newly tatted his name. He couldn't believe his eyes. She actually had his government name engraved across her left thigh.

"I came to see you," she declared, causing the girl sitting next to him to frown. "But do you have a problem with that?" she gestured at the girl with a head nod.

"Who me?" the chick pointed at her chest, while a few other women smirked.

"Yeah, you. Cause you had this ugly ass look on your face like it's a problem."

"Wait, wait, wait," the girl waved her hand. "Who is she talking to?" she glanced around the room.

"She's talking to your ass," Jazel instigated with a mouthful of food.

Big Block chuckled. "See, that's why I love coming over here. My girl don't be giving zero fucks. Jazel knows she's messy, and is proud of it."

"Well, let me clarify something for you," the girl spoke up, looking squarely at Keyasia. "I came here with this nigga, right here. We call ourselves talking, so hell yeah, I'ma look at some random broad crazy, who comes through, begging to talk to him."

"Begging? Oh, there's no begging going on here. And I really don't give a fuck what you call yourself doing with him. I said that I need to talk to him, and you aint gon do a muthafuckin' thing about it. Before I *clarify* how weak your beautician is with that bullshit ass sew-in, when I snatch a patch out of your fucking head. You don't know me, bitch," Keyasia growled.

"Oh, shit!" Big Block hopped off the couch, getting hyped, while everyone else laughed. "That sound like fighting words to me!"

Keyasia boldly sauntered over to Wale, hovering above him. "That bitch aint ready." She shrugged, focusing on his face. "But can I talk to you for a minute, Corinthian?"

"Corinthian? Who is Corinthian?" the girl blurted, causing half the room to burst with laughter.

Keyasia shook her head. "Obviously, somebody who aint really fucking with you. So, don't worry your nappy lil' head about it, baby."

Jazel giggled so hard that her shoulders trembled. "I knew it was a reason I liked her ass."

Wale's little companion shot to her feet. "Bitch, you don't know me like that!" she barked with a tremendous amount of base in her voice. In that short amount of time, Keyasia had caused her to lose her cool. Initially, she thought that maybe she could outwit her, but her mouth was too reckless to endure. Her insults were coming left and right, and she was bold with it, standing merely inches away from her.

"And bitch I don't wanna know you," Keyasia spat. "You sure your name aint Jesse? You look just like this boy I went to school with, and you sound like him too. Aint no biological woman walking around with this amount of testosterone." She glanced down at Wale. "Corinthian, you switched to the other side on me?"

That comment brought him to his feet. "Man, Keyasia, stop playing with me."

"You stop playing with me!" she screamed, catching everyone by surprise. She'd been relatively calm, until that exact moment. "Bring your bitch ass outside, and let me talk to you!" she demanded.

"Who the fuck do you think you talking to?" he gritted.

"Yeah," the girl attempted to put her hand in Keyasia's face. "Who the fuck are you talking to?"

Without thinking, Wale flung her hand away, before shoving her back. "Chill out," he warned her.

"Yeah, before I pop you, hoe," Key added.

"Say, Keyasia, go'on with all this bullshit. How the fuck are you gonna show up to these people's house with drama? You know I aint with this dry ass shit," Wale squawked.

"So, you aint gon step outside so that we can talk about this?" she questioned, completely ignoring his lecture.

"Hell, nah. Take your ass home, somewhere. I'll call you in a lil' minute," he instructed.

Keyasia appeared to be preparing to rebut, but she paused. "You know what? You're right. Call me." With that, she spun on her heels, and headed towards the door.

Meeko snickered once she stepped out of the house. "Damn, all you had to tell her was that you'd call her? I thought it would be a little harder than that."

Big Block shook his head. "You niggas is sleep. I seen that wild eyed look she had. That girl aint going nowhere. Shit, yall better hope she aint going to the car to get a chopper."

"Exactly," Jazel spoke up. "Cause if I was her, I'd air you muthafuckas out."

Big Block scrunched his nose. "We aint talking about you. We know you crazy. That's why Craven can't take your ass nowhere. You get kicked out of every place you go. His damn grandma banned you from her house."

"Boy, bye. Me and Nina worked all that out. She knows that I didn't cut Craven that deep at her house. He was just exaggerating, trying to get her to feel sorry for him," Jazel alleged, causing everyone to roar with laughter once again. The sad part was that she was as serious as a heart attack.

BOOM!

"The fuck was that?" Craven stomped over to the front door, and snatched it open. There he could clearly see Keyasia kicking a huge dent in the side of Wale's Audi. "Kinfolk, you might wanna come handle this. She out there vandalizing ya car."

"Man," Wale stressed, as trudged over to the door. He shook his head, as Keyasia put all her weight into it, as she drop kicked his car, repeatedly. "I'm gon fuck this hoe up," he mumbled, stepping outside. "Have you lost your fuckin' mind?" he questioned, as he approached her.

"I told you to come here!" she belted. "But I guess you too busy trying to impress that bitch in there!" she charged at him, swinging on him. She caught him in the mouth twice.

Wale was hot, as she popped his ass, but ever alert, he noticed a patrol car headed their way. Thinking quickly, when she took another swing, he wrapped her in his arms, giving the police the impression that they were just a couple playing around. "Chill out," he whispered into her ear. "The laws are coming."

Keyasia's body trembled with anger, and he could feel it. "I can fuckin' kill you," she seethed, speaking directly into his ear. "I should bite your bitch ass, right now."

For some reason, her anger amused him. It was ironic how she was the one going off, although she'd betrayed him. "And you really believe that I'ma stand here, and let you do that shit?"

"And you really believe I give a fuck?" she dug her nails into his skin.

"Alright, alright," he forcefully removed her hands off him. "You going too far with this, Keyasia. You gon make me fuck you up."

She locked eyes with him, as her lips curled. "Fuck me up. I don't give a fuck, Corinthian. Matter of fact, tell that hoe in that house to come outside, and see me. Tell her you mine, and that shit aint gon change. Never. Fuck you think this is?"

He was pissed at himself, as a chill shot up his spine. She wasn't going down without a fight, and he'd be lying if he claimed that her determination didn't turn him on.

"Look, man," he licked his lips. "Let's go to the car, so you can tell me what you gotta tell me." He grabbed her hand, leading her back to her Range. Opening the door for her, he nudged her. "Get in."

Reluctantly, she climbed into the truck, as he stepped around, and got in on the passenger's side. She sat, glaring at him.

"Okay, you got me out here. Say what you gotta say."

She sighed heavily. "Why are you playing games, Corinthian? You go from telling me you love me, to acting like you can't be near me. I mean, I don't get it. Why the sudden change?"

His jaw clenched, as he thought about their unborn kids. She had the audacity to feel victimized, convincing herself that he was doing her wrong. She had nerve, and his emotions were still too raw to go there with her. If he'd told her the deal, then he'd have to really address what he felt, and he wasn't ready. And she definitely wasn't ready, because he'd probably pop her in the mouth if she said the wrong thing.

"Look, Keyasia, I backed up, because I needed to get myself together. I don't wanna go into details, but I'm battling with some demons. The shit was too heavy for you not to feel the burn. So, I did us both a favor. Trust me."

She screwed her face up. "Dealing with some demons? The fuck is that supposed to mean? Do you see the word stupid written across my forehead? Don't insult my fuckin' intelligence. You just got that little boy syndrome. You scared of the closeness. Shit was getting too deep for you, so you sabotaged us. Call it what it is."

"Man," he stressed. "You don't know what the fuck you talking about. I promise."

"Oh, but I do," she insisted. "You running off scooping up these corny ass bitches," she jabbed, as she noticed his little companion and two other girls switch to a Lexus, and hop in. "Driving cars older than them, and shit," she chided, watching them pull off.

"Watch out," he attempted to conceal a smirk.

"Don't be laughing, cause it aint funny. You lucky I didn't come through and assault you."

"Whatever, Keyasia. Keep on looking for trouble, and I'ma give it to you."

"You're the one looking for trouble, entertaining these hoes," she persisted. "You tripping."

"I'm tripping, huh?"

"Yes."

"How am I tripping?"

"Dealing with these tricks. Saying fuck me. Like they can replace me. Or fuck you better. Can they do that, Corinthian?"

He stroked his goatee, refusing to answer that question.

"Answer me," she commanded. "Can they fuck you better? Huh?"

He cut his eyes at her. "I don't know. You tell me."

"See," she got out, before taking him by surprise, as she leapt over to his side of the truck, straddling him. "You really got me fucked up," she clutched his throat.

He laughed at her, as she attempted to rough him up. Reaching on the side, he pushed a button, reclining his seat. Gripping her hips, he gazed into her eyes. "When did you get that tattoo?"

She gulped, releasing his neck. "A few days ago."

"You doing shit like you love a nigga."

"I do," she offered with no hesitation.

He cautiously eyed her. "Ion know if I believe you. Show me."

He didn't have to tell her twice, as she smothered him with a deep, passionate kiss. With both hands, he clutched her ass, rubbing her booty. As she grinded into him, she could feel him grow an erection.

Feeling like she needed to prove something, she lifted up, and peeled off her own shorts. She then wiggled them down her thighs, before lifting one of her legs completely out of them. Before Wale could blink his eyes, she was undoing his jeans, pulling his one-eyed monster out. Lowering her head, she took him into her mouth.

"Ooh, shit," his mouth fell open, as she deep throated him.

Sloppily she sucked him up, allowing her saliva to trickle down to his balls. When he began to grip her hair, she knew she had him, but that wasn't how she wanted to end it. Allowing him to plop out of her mouth, she straddled him again. With her hands on his shoulders, she tooted her ass onto the tip of his dick, before sliding down. Swirling her hips a few times, she then proceeded to fuck the shit out him.

"Whoa," he huffed, as she rapidly bounced on him.

"That bitch can fuck you like this?" she breathed. "Huh?" she held his face with both hands, kissing his lips.

"Hell, nah," he admitted.

"Nigga, you alright in there?" Craven knocked on the window.

The sun had just gone down, and Keyasia had dark tint on her ride, so he wasn't sure what the hell was going on.

"Yeah, man," he answered, while Keyasia sat completely down, rocking her hips, taking every inch of the dick.

Keyasia giggled, as Craven headed back to the house. She sat up, continuing to fuck him. "They act like I lured you out here to kill you or something."

He smiled. "Maybe you did." He gripped her hips.

"You funny, huh?" she licked a finger, before bringing it between her legs. Seductively, she rolled her hips, as she stroked her own clit. "Uhh, this dick is filling this pussy up. I just wanna cum all over it." Her head fell back. "Fuck meeee," she purred.

Lifting his ass off the seat, he pounded into her, causing her to gush onto the bottom of his shirt. She was super wet, as his dick made her pussy fart.

"Uh! Uh!" she let out, as he hit it hard, making the truck rock. "I'm 'bout to bust, baby!" she screamed.

"Huuuuuh!" he gritted his teeth, as he erupted inside of her.

"Ooouuuu," she trembled, as she climaxed.

His back crashed into the seat, as he attempted to catch his breath.

"Whew," she sighed, after crawling back to her side of the vehicle.

Tucking his dick back into his jeans, Wale grabbed the door handle. "I'ma call you."

Key's heart dropped down to her stomach. She was hoping that he'd tell her to follow him home, where they could follow up with round two. "Okay," she swallowed hard.

Opening the door, he eased out of the truck. After zipping his jeans, he strolled back to the house. Stepping inside, everyone focused on him.

"The fuck yall looking at?" he asked.

"Shit, you," Big Block spoke up. "I was hoping you wasn't about to sit down on these people couch with that girl's cum all over your shirt, and shit."

Wale glanced down at his shirt, and sure enough Key's secretion had soaked his shirt. He lifted his head, as everybody laughed at him. He didn't give a damn. "Fuck yall. I was going home any fuckin' way." He turned to leave out the door.

Chapter 23

It was hard to believe that three months had coasted by, and Keyasia found herself stuck in a weird situationship with Wale. Ever since that evening she'd had sex with him in her truck, he'd been straddling the fence with her. Keeping his word, he'd called her the following day, but there were no talks of when, and where he'd see her again. Eventually, they linked up again, nearly two weeks later.

At this point Keyasia knew what it was. He wasn't trying to be tied down. She now rarely spent nights over at the townhouse, and whenever he'd go out of town for work, she'd stay at her own home. He never asked her to stay, anymore, and when he'd return he wouldn't bother calling her. Sometimes she'd randomly run into him at the club, after thinking that he was still out of town. He'd made it perfectly clear that she was no longer the first person he wanted to see when he made it back home.

Their relationship transformation had her suffering internally, but she tried her best to mask her hurt. Every blue moon she'd get full of that liquor, and ask him why he'd changed up on her. He'd never give her a plausible explanation. The most he could give her was a nice fuck, and gifts. The gifts, and money was still tossed her way, but them…they'd lost their intensity. And it had her slowly dying inside.

She never thought that she'd find herself in these set of circumstances, and too weak to walk away. Wale was doing him, and didn't care about how it made her feel. The chick she'd had a run in with at Craven's was still in the picture. It was now a known fact that most times when he wasn't with Key, he was with ole Carmen. The two knew about each other, both knew that they were fucking him, and both refused to leave the situation.

Nicole Jackson

Keyasia had been tolerating Carmen's presence for a nice little second, but was fed up. As time passed, Wale seemed to have less and less time for her. He was spreading himself too thin, and Key seemed to be getting the shortest end of the stick, as she felt that her position was reducing to some form of a side chick. She couldn't take it, anymore, and today he was going to know exactly what was on her mind.

Looking out for her, Jazel had sneakily shot her text, letting her know that Wale, the crew, and all their girls were at Pappadeaux's eating. Needless to say, Key was fuming, as he now preferred kicking with some other bitch, while hanging with his boys. But it was cool, because she was intending to fuck up everybody's night.

"There's his fucking Lambo, right there," Key pointed, as Sye pulled into the lot of the restaurant.

Sye nodded, as she whipped into the spot next to the Lamborghini. "I just hope that nothing gets out of hand, because I got my heater on me."

"What?" Key whipped her head around. "Your heater? Sye, you packing?"

"Yeah," Sye answered easily. "I keep my thang on me. My Baby won't let me leave home without it."

Keyasia shook her head. "I swear ever since you got with his ass you think you's a gangsta."

"Girl please," Sye waved her off. "I been official with my pistol grip. My daddy showed me how to shoot when I was like twelve."

"I guess."

"For real. Ask Jazel. She met my daddy before," Sye offered. Coincidentally, Jazel was her man's, Baby, cousin, and they were pretty close.

"Oh, I believe you. I heard about how you was shooting at Baby's old hoe."

Sye smiled. "I'm still waiting to see that bitch Randi again. I might just whup her ass all over again."

"This bitch here," Key tittered, attempting to conceal the fact that she was nervous. It wasn't that she was afraid of Wale or Carmen, but something in her heart told her that this confrontation would be different. It definitely seemed like it was the end of the road for them, and she knew that she couldn't remain in the situation as it stood. "Let me go in here," she sighed, before easing out of Sye's Benz.

Wanting to upstage the competition, Keyasia looked camera ready. Her hair hung to her ass, and had been curled to perfection. Her fire red distressed Cavalli jeans appeared painted on, her white blouse exposed her entire back, and her Chanel sandals brought serious volume to her thick legs.

She waltzed into the restaurant like she owned the place. Remembering what Jazel described, she headed to the left. Venturing to the back of the place, she spotted them, and their table.

"Aw, shit," Meeko chuckled, spotting Keyasia approaching them.

Jazel slyly smirked, grateful that her girl never disappointed her. Key was always willing to put on a show, much like Jazel would do herself. She was loving every second of the foolery.

Nicole Jackson

"What?" Big Block turned around. "Aw, fuck. And I aint even ordered my food yet. Her ignorant ass is gonna get us thrown out of here."

"Who?" Wale looked up, spotting her. "The fuck?" he sucked his teeth.

Carmen rolled her eyes, as she leaned over, speaking into his ear. "What the hell is she doing here?"

"Say, let me holler at you, big homie," Keyasia demanded, stepping to their table.

"How you doing, Keyasia?" Meeko practically sang, as he lustfully ogled at her.

Wale frowned. "The fuck you doing, nigga? Aint shit change. It aint that type of fuckin' party."

"And what does that mean?" Carmen wanted to know, as she folded her arms over her small breasts.

Wale waved her off. "Anyway. What you want, Keyasia?"

"Oh, I don't think you want to have this discussion out in the open."

"Okay." He nodded. "Well, as you can see, we about to eat. So, I'ma fuck with you on the rebound."

Her stomach became queasy. "On the rebound? No, nigga. You gon talk to me now!"

Everyone in the vicinity turned to look their way.

"Wale, main, step outside and talk to her. Cause yall gon fuck around, and have these people call the laws. You know we don't need that type of heat over bullshit," Craven reasoned.

"Exactly, before I act a fool in this muthafucka. Flip this table over on your hoe ass," Keyasia threatened with fire in her eyes.

Angrily scooting his chair back, Wale stood up.

"No uh," Carmen shook her head. "You aint going out there with her by yourself. Not today. I'm so fuckin' tired of her bullshit. Bitch can't understand when a nigga don't want her ass."

"Well, come outside," Keyasia waved her over. "Please do, so I can slap those nappy edges straight. Try me tonight. You done caught the devil at home today, and I'll eat your ass alive."

"Alright, man," Wale stomped around the table. "Come on. Let's go outside."

Carmen stood up, and he caught it. "I'm going too."

"Nah." He shook his head. "You stay in here. That parking lot be swarming with laws. So, just chill out, and order some food. I'll be right back."

Obediently, she sat back down, causing Keyasia to giggle. "Yeah, sit down, bitch. Just like a well-trained mutt," she taunted.

"Keyasia, come on," he ordered, leading her out of the restaurant.

The moment they were out in the lot, she went in. "So, you taking that bitch on dates and shit?!"

He glanced around, before focusing on her. "Lower your voice, man."

"No!" she clapped her hands dramatically. "Don't tell me to lower my voice! I'm tired of you fuckin' disrespecting me!" she roared.

"Man," he drawled, stepping deeper into the lot, traveling to his car. "Why you out here doing all this clowning, Keyasia?" he questioned, once he was standing in front of his whip.

She rotated her shoulders, as if she was preparing to bat for a baseball team. "The question is why are you making me clown. How the fuck am I supposed to react when I hear that you taking this bitch out to eat? What type of bitch you take me for?"

He shook his head. "Ion take you for nothing. I'm a grown, single man, out eating with my people. I don't you no explanation. How many times do I have to tell you that shit?"

She stepped in front of him. "And who did you discuss this *single* business with?"

He rubbed his goatee, as he looked at her with those piercing green eyes. "Don't I move like a nigga who's unattached? Or are you just ignoring that part?"

"Fuck you!" she lashed, shoving him so hard that he fell back onto the hood of his car. Unflinchingly, she continued with her attack, as she clawed his face. "I'm tired of you playing with me, bitch!" she swung, hitting him with multiple slugs.

She was coming so hard that Wale forgot that she was a female for a second, as he grabbed her, body slamming her onto the hood of his uber-expensive car.

"Hey, hey!" Sye hopped out of her car, practically jumping on Wale's back. "Get off her!"

Just then, both Craven and Big Block stepped onto the scene. They'd come out to make sure that things weren't getting out of hand, and found their boy wrestling with two relentless broads. They were tagging his ass, as he wrapped his hands around Keyasia's neck.

"Nigga, chill out, before the laws come," Craven pleaded, as he attempted to grab his cousin.

"Get the fuck off me!" Wale snatched his shoulder away, refusing to release Keyasia from his grasp.

Using her heel, Sye clucked Wale in the head. "Let her go, muthafucka!"

"Aye, aye!" Big Block shouted, snatching Sye away from his boy.

"You better keep your hands off me, you big muthafucka!"

Craven stepped in front of Big Block. "Dog, chill out. That's Jazel's cousin. My fuckin' people. And her nigga can get stupid right with us."

Wale and Keyasia were oblivious to their little sideline tiff, as they tussled, before she sank her teeth into his arm. Gritting his teeth, he gripped her weave, and viciously slung her into Sye's Benz.

"You got me fucked up, bitch ass nigga!" Keyasia spewed, as she scrambled to get in Sye's car, and pop the trunk. She then ran to the rear of the car, retrieving a jack. "I'ma show you," she seethed, before reaching back, and then smashing the jack into his driver's window of Wale's car.

"This hoe gone make me hurt her. This the fuckin' third time she done busted my window out," Wale calmly grumbled, maintaining a safe distance from Keyasia. If she ran up again, there would be no saving her.

"Okay, Key, baby. That's enough," Sye stepped in, ushering her back to the car. "Let's go, before the police come."

"Okay," she nodded, before peeking at Wale. "Fuck you, you bitch ass nigga! You aint never gotta worry about me no more. I fuckin' hate you!"

He nodded with a menacing glare. "And I hate you too, bitch."

"Damn, what the fuck done got into yall?" Craven asked. Even he was thrown off by his cousin's bizarre switch up with Keyasia. One minute he acted like he couldn't breathe without her, then the next he'd get pissed any time someone mentioned her name.

"Fuck her," Wale waved him off. "With her stupid ass."

The men stood watching, as Keyasia and Sye hopped into the Benz, and skirted out of the lot.

Wale and Craven stood in silence, while Big Block shook his head. "See, that's why I stick to mediocre broads. Them fine, pretty bitches are ignorant as fuck. Aint no way. Yall niggas can have that."

******

Wearing Versace biker shorts and sports bra, with matching sunglasses, Keyasia was stylishly heartbroken. She, Raven, and Taraj were in L.A. on business, and she'd been pretending that she didn't have a care in the world. She smiled, cracked jokes, wanting people to believe that she was unbothered. But as they sat in a bar, having drinks she was becoming pissed. It was like the deejay was her antagonist, playing songs that echoed her dead ass situationship with Wale.

"We aint going steady. We just be fuckin' 'round. Yeah, the sex great, but damn, bae. We fuckin' round. Girl, you got me hot. Poppin' up at my spot. You out yo got damn mind. What the fuck is you thinkin' 'bout…" Rocko's voice blared from the speakers.

"Somebody need to fire that damn deejay, playing that whack ass song," she squawked.

Raven danced in her seat. "Shit, fuck what you talkin' about. That shit is jamming," she claimed. "Yeah, that pussy good. I aint gon lie. But if you was looking for a dude, girl, I aint your guy," she rapped along with the song.

"Ayyyye!" Taraj wagged her tongue, as she too danced in her seat. "Girl, you know better. You not my main squeeze. It aint like we go together," she rapped.

"Whatever," Key rolled her eyes. "Yall are lame just like the nigga on this song."

"Is there ever a time where you aint talking shit?" a deep voice questioned.

Keyasia looked up, noticing Bash, standing behind her. "Oh, hey," she spoke. Guilt immediately washed over her, as she thought about the last time she'd seen him. She'd totally disrespected him for Wale. "How have you been, Bash?"

He smiled, looking handsome as ever. His Gucci ensemble was on point, and he smelled delightful. "I been straight, shawty. What's been up with you? Still working out your little issue?"

She cracked a smile. "Aw, there you go."

"Yeah, there I go," he chuckled. "Can I sit down?"

Taraj and Raven looked at each other, giggling.

"Yeah," Keyasia answered. "Have a seat. I been wanting to talk you, anyway."

Chapter 24

"Got damn it," Wale sang to himself, as he noticed a girl with a fat ass walking down the sidewalk. Everywhere he looked, there were dimes walking around. Hell, if he'd known that colleges had all the bad bitches he would've signed up years ago.

He was pushing his Audi through TSU's campus, searching for her. He knew it was time for her to get out of class, and he was trying to remember the building she usually came out of. It had been damn near a month since he'd last seen Keyasia, and he wasn't going on another day.

When she'd came through Pappadeaux's raising hell, he swore that he was done with her. He was tired of sparing her, and he hated how she'd kick up dust, like she wasn't the cause of his switch up. He didn't even want to punish her, anymore. He just wanted to be done, but that was easier said than done. After the first week, he couldn't sleep, and all his food tasted nasty.

Wale felt like a lame, as he went through the motions over a selfish girl, who only *thought* she loved him. In his mind, there was no way that she could truly love him, and do what she'd done. Then the fact that she did it twice, with no hesitation, had him feeling like he never really knew her. Sadly, that didn't change what he felt for her, though. That type of love doesn't disappear overnight, and he was stuck. He wanted somebody that clearly wasn't good for him.

His common sense had been telling him to stay away from Keyasia, but that week had been a rough one. That day was the anniversary of his mother's death, and only Key could lift his spirits at a time like this. Therefore he ignored the practical thoughts in his head, and went with his heart. And his heart had led him there, at her school, outside of her English class.

Not wanting to miss her, he sat on the hood of his car, facing the English building. Different chicks were breaking their necks, as they strolled past Wale, trying to get a second look. Dressed in all white Valentino, with non-prescribed Cartier glasses, and Giuseppe's on his feet, he was dazzling.

He couldn't help smiling, as he spotted her sauntering up the sidewalk. He swore they had to be some kind of kindred spirits. She was wearing the hell out of a simple white fitted dress accompanied with gold high top Giuseppe sneakers. She was completely oblivious to her surroundings, as her face was buried in her phone. Several guys walked past her, nearly running into the bushes, checking out her fat ass.

Soon, she was just a few feet away, and she still hadn't noticed him. "Get your nose out that phone, before you fuck around and trip over your own damn feet," he startled her.

"The fuck?" she stopped, and looked up. "What are you doing here?"

He stroked his goatee. "I stopped by to see my gal. I wanted to scoop her up, and chill with her for a few."

She arched a brow. "And she has class in that building?" she pointed.

"I don't know, Keyasia. You tell me."

"Huh?" she gave him a look of confusion, until it dawned on her. "Oh, my God. It's the anniversary of your mama's death, isn't it?"

He was a little surprised that she remembered, as he nodded.

She sucked her teeth. "I guess. Carmen wasn't available."

"Carmen?" he screwed his face up. "What she got to do with this? She don't even know my mama's fuckin' dead. Less along, *when* she died. The shit aint that deep."

"Whatever." She rolled her eyes. "Look, I gotta go," she claimed, as she attempted to step off.

He smoothly grabbed her hand. "Wait. Let me talk to you." He pulled her closer.

"Talk to me about what?"

"About you coming over, and kicking it."

She narrowed her eyes. "Come kick it with you? But you hate me, remember?"

He shook his head. "I was just following your lead. Telling you what you told me."

"But what reason did you have to be mad? You was there with another bitch, shitting on me. So, why was your aggression matching mine?"

He licked his lips. "Believe it or not, I have my reasons. I see now that you only see shit from one angle. You aint no angel, Keyasia. I got a few issues with you, but maybe I should address the shit differently. Still, aint nobody sitting around, wanting to dry fuck you over."

"And what are those issues?" she bucked her eyes. "You say that, but won't offer a real explanation."

He studied her face. "I don't think you really want me to go there, because it might be no coming back.

Talking about it could bring out some real ugly shit. You cool with that?"

She swallowed hard. Did he know? How? "Okay, look, we don't have to talk about any of that heavy bullshit today. What are you trying to do in your mama's memory? Wanna go get her some balloons and flowers?" she asked, wanting to change the subject. Something was telling her that she didn't want to open Pandora's Box with that other conversation.

He smiled, "Yeah, that sounds like a plan."

******

"Corinthian, if you don't stop playing!" Key squealed.

Wale ignored her, as he stood behind her, attempting to pull her shorts further down her legs. "Nah, be still. I'ma pull these fuckin' shorts out of ya ass."

She giggled uncontrollably. "My shorts are not that damn short. Stop!"

"Yes they are, man. I know I should've made you try 'em on. They looked longer, before you pulled them over all this ass."

"They're the perfect length. Stop playing," she persisted.

Big Block stepped out of his front door, to find them playing around like two big ass kids. "Man, are yall gonna come in, or just fuck around out here all day?"

Keyasia sucked her teeth. "Big boy, you always grumpy. I know you gon let us live."

"Whatever, Ms. Psychotic." He threw a hand up.

Wale chuckled. It was now an ongoing joke that he and Keyasia were both mental. For nearly a month now, they'd been good, almost as if they'd never fallen off. They were inseparable, acting like they'd die if they had to go more than a few hours without each other.

This day was no exception. Big Block's ten-year-old son was having a Jump Man themed party, and since Wale was the God father they'd come through, together. Tam, Big Block's BM, had insisted that everyone wear Jordan apparel, sticking with the theme of the party. So, Wale and Key were both rocking white, red, and black Jordan's, matching Bull's snap backs, Jordan tees, Robin's shorts, with long white, red, and black Jordan socks.

"Yeah, I got your psychotic," Keyasia sneered.

"Baby, don't fuck him up," Wale smiled, tossing an arm around her shoulder.

"Whatever," Big Block replied, as they stepped into his home. "And you better have him a good gift in that bag." He playfully shoved the back of her head.

"Fuck you." She gave him the finger.

Big Block rubbed his hands together, as he checked out Key's backside. He couldn't deny that Keyasia was like something right out of his dreams, and if his boy wasn't crazy about her…That shit didn't even matter, as Wale seemed to have some silent alarm on him, alerting him to whenever another man was watching his bitch. Because he'd glanced back at Big Block, giving him the death stare.

"Nigga, what you looking at?" Wale questioned, stepping to the right, obstructing the view of Keyasia.

"Man," Big Block stressed. "Aint nobody thinking about that girl. Nigga, you tripping."

"Yeah, okay." Wale nodded, as they traveled through his house. Eventually, they made it to the backyard, where the party was in full effect.

"Hit the Quan! Ayyye!" Big Block's son, Maurice Junior, yelled. He was the spitting image of his father, and the life of the party.

Some kids were dancing to the music, while others were either playing on the basketball court, or jumping in the huge bouncers. There was a professional deejay there, playing the latest dance rap. Tam had gone all out, even getting some men to perform on the court in a Harlem Globetrotters-esc fashion.

"Lil' Maurice, you getting down, huh?" Wale laughed. He was always entertained by Big Block's son. He was ten going on twenty, and was pretty blunt, much like his father.

"Unc, this how I'ma do your lil' girlfriend right there," Maurice announced, as he did the Quan, acting like he was hitting it from the back.

Keyasia's jaw dropped. "Is his lil' ass talking about me?"

Wale snickered. "Yep."

"Hey, Keyasia," Tam sang, as she approached them. She was a high yellow, tatted up, thick, Plain Jane, girl from the hood. She'd been with Big Block since middle school, and they had four kids together. She and Keyasia had met a while back, and they had taken a liking to one another. She was the exact opposite of Big Block, and one of the friendliest chicks Key had ever met.

"What's up?" Key spoke. "You outdid yourself with this party, girl."

"Why thank you." Tam patted her weave.

"Well, Tam, I guess your ass didn't see me standing here, huh?" Wale teased.

Tam waved him off. "Boy, bye. You aint nobody. But yeah, Key, there's drinks, and a full bar over there. Feel free to get whatever you want."

"Okay." Keyasia nodded. "I got you."

"Good, yall enjoy," Tam encouraged, before switching off.

Deciding to cop a seat, they sat at a table with Tam's cousins. Although there was plenty of room, Key sat on his lap, as he held onto her waist. Quietly, they whispered, playfully cracking jokes on the other party-goers. Unconsciously, Wale caressed her ass, as he seemed to cling to every word she uttered.

"I see that yall beat us here," Craven interrupted, as he approached them.

Both Key and Wale glanced up. Craven was standing there with Jazel, and Kash. Wale smiled, after laying eyes on his little man. "Appreciate you for stopping by to grab him, kinfolk," he offered. "Lift up." He tapped Keyasia's butt, causing her to stand. "Look at your shoes, man." He leaned forward, tying Kash's new Jordan's.

"It took us forever, because we brought him the clothes you sent, and he had to change into it, and shit," Jazel interjected.

Wale nodded, stroking Kash's fresh tapered fade. "And I see you ran him by the barbershop like I asked."

"Yeah, that nigga Nard cleared the chair for him," Craven reported.

Nicole Jackson

Keyasia stood silently, not really knowing what to say. She'd never met Kash in person, and felt uncomfortable. Admittedly, he was a handsome little boy, and Wale had him fresh. Surprisingly, he had the exact same attire as she and Wale. Since she'd gone shopping with him when he bought their clothes, she figured that he'd only gotten them something. But as she thought about it, after they'd collectively decided what to get, he'd urge her to continue shopping, while he stayed behind to pay for things.

"That's what's up." Wale stroked his goatee, before gazing down at Kash. "You good, lil' man?"

Kash nodded.

"Okay, cool. Well, this is Keyasia," he introduced.

Kash looked up, and studied her curiously. He'd heard his mama mention the woman's name a million times, and she always referred to her as ugly. Therefore, he was surprised to see Keyasia, and learn that his mama was wrong.

"Is she your girlfriend?" Kash quizzed.

Wale glanced up, locking eyes with Keyasia. "Uh…you can say that."

Kash smiled, deviously. "Well, she's pretty."

Keyasia beamed. "Thank you. You're handsome, yourself, cutie."

"Thank you," Kash replied, before spinning around. "Ooh, can I get in one of those bouncers?" he jumped up and down, excitedly.

"Yeah, go ahead. Take off your shoes first," Wale commanded, as Kash was already racing towards the bouncers.

"I'ma take plenty of pictures, cause his mama said that she wanted footage," Jazel announced, referring to Mona. "So, come on, Keyasia and Wale. Let me take yall picture."

Everybody laughed.

Wale shook his head. "Craven, why you aint leave her ass at home?"

"The same reason you brought Ms. Psychotic," Craven shot back. "Yeah, nigga, you can't joke about me having a crazy broad no more. Shit, welcome to the club. Now her and Jazel can both hide in the bushes together."

Wale smirked, "Fuck you."

"Uh-oh," Keyasia shouted, as she started dancing. The deejay had just started something, spinning every kid's favorite song. "Watch me whip. Now, watch me Nae-Nae!" she did every dance move accurately.

Like a stampede, the children all ran over, joining in. They were all doing the Nae-Nae, and Keyasia was leading the pack, as she got too into it. She was oblivious to the fact that Kash was now right beside her, going in as well. Jazel couldn't resist, as she recorded every second. Wale was cheesing, as Kash danced with Keyasia, feeling like he could actually have the best of both worlds, peacefully.

Everyone had stopped to watch the kids dance, including the men. Other women had joined in, but he caught several dudes eye-balling Key. He brushed their lustful glares off, deciding that he'd address it later.

Stepping directly in front of him, Keyasia captured his full attention. Incorporating a playful slap to his face, she kept dancing, never missing a beat. She was unwittily seducing him, as their eyes locked. Not being able to resist it, he groped her ass, as he slobbered her down.

"Ewe," Jazel cringed, still filming it all. "This is a kid's party," she giggled, knowing that a few chicks were going to be pissed when she uploaded the video, and tagged both Key and Wale. Especially Carmen. Jazel had recently accepted a friend request from her, and all she did was post memes about women holding onto men who didn't want them. Jazel knew that she was taking digs at Key, therefore she wanted her to have egg all over her face. Hell, she'd already nicely warned the girl, telling her how Wale wasn't going to leave Keyasia alone, and vice versa. But some people had to learn the hard way. And Jazel would be just the one to deliver the hard truth.

"Alright, alright," Maurice loudly interrupted, grabbing Keyasia's hand. "Unc, let her go. She's doing the dances, and I need to copy off her. You can have her later."

Wale was in stitches, as Maurice's young ass literally pulled Key away. She giggled, as she commenced to dancing again. With her having younger siblings, she was a natural with all the kids. They gravitated to her, and Wale took notice of this. He couldn't help but think about their unborn babies. At that moment, he felt this overwhelming urge to just ask her why, but in his heart, he knew that going there wouldn't end well.

A few hours breezed by, and the party was whining down. Key was now seated, as Wale played with Maurice and Kash. She noticed how attentive he was. It amazed her how he was never too hard to put that hood persona to the side. It was as if he knew that those kids looked up to him, and he took the role model thing seriously. He would kid with Kash, but was also stern when needed…like a father. Keyasia became choked up, as she realized that killing their babies was probably the worst mistake of her life.

Yeah, some unknown people had shot at him, but as far as she knew there hadn't been any further incidents. Sometimes she questioned if the whole ordeal hadn't just been random, with some idiots attempting to rob them. Maybe Wale shooting back had changed their minds, before they were able to successfully execute their plans. Who knows? But what she did know was that had that day not occurred, she would've carried his baby without question. Now, she just prayed that her secrets remained buried, and that she and Wale would completely move on.

"Alright, yall niggas better come to the club, man," the deejay, Zale, declared, after packing up all his equipment.

Mostly everyone had left, except Wale's main crew of friends, and they were just sitting around, joking.

Big Block waved him off. "Zale, how many times are you gonna say that shit? I mean, do you just want me to pay you, and make sure you squared away?"

Zale frowned. "Nigga please. That aint what we agreed on. I came here at the last minute, because you needed a favor. And now I need one. All yall niggas come through, buy some bottles, and tell all your boys," he requested, knowing that them showing up to the club he worked at would be much more profitable, than getting paid for a deejay gig. TSC being in the building would attract the women, and the women drew the men in. That all translated into money for Zale.

"Alright, Zale, main. Next Tuesday we'll fall off in that bitch. We got you," Wale offered.

Zale graciously nodded. "Appreciate you, Wale. Cause I could tell Big Block's ass was about to renege."

Big Block shrugged. "Shit, Tuesdays is usually my chill nights, and Tam be tripping."

Craven chuckled, exposing his bottom grill. "But I thought you said she don't run shit?"

"What you say, Craven?" Big Block spoke loudly. "You aint going over what bitch's house, again?"

Craven's smile quickly faded. "Okay, fuck nigga."

"Uh huh," Jazel nodded, as she chewed on a stick of gum. "Big Boy telling on that ass, huh? Let me find out," she warned. "You was cutting up not too long ago, and I was too. But we agreed that shit is over, right?" she gave him a pointed look.

"Right." He agreed hurriedly.

Wale narrowed his eyes. "Wait, Jazel. What you mean by you was cutting up, too?"

Jazel rolled her eyes. "Mind your business, Wale. And I'll think about minding mine." She slyly winked.

"Yeah." Craven lifted his chin. "The fuck did you mean by that? You better be talking about how much you was going to the club. Cause Ion wanna have to beat yo ass."

"Boy, bye." She waved him off, popping her bubble gum. "You better stop letting Wale pump you up. You know exactly what I meant. We already talked about it."

"Well, quit trying to make it seem like you was out there fucking around."

"Whatever." She folded her arms.

Keyasia found the whole scene hilarious. Craven was the biggest whore around, and had the nerve to get jealous. And from what she could tell about Jazel, the chick definitely had some skeletons in her closet. Recently, when they were hanging, Key saw just how popular Jazel was. She knew men everywhere, and her phone was a hot line. So many dudes were calling her, and she was clearly entertaining them, but who could blame her? Craven was fucking everything moving. They seemed to be two peas in one messy ass pod.

"Anyway," Wale exhaled. "We gotta go out of town, and won't be back until Tuesday. So, that's right on time for you, Zale."

Keyasia looked at him sadly. "You didn't mention going out of town. When are yall leaving?"

He stroked his goatee. "Tomorrow. I thought I told you," he lied. He'd purposely never mentioned it to her. Her cell had been on silent a tad too much for his liking, and he wanted to catch her ass slipping. Leaving in and out of town without her being able to put a clock on him would definitely aid him in catching her off guard.

"No, I definitely would have remembered that."

"Oh," he shrugged. "Well, yeah. We're going out of town. We'll be gone for a little over a week."

"Well, damn." She threw her hands on her hips. "Thanks for the heads up. Now, what the hell am I gonna do since you'll be gone?"

"How about get a damn life," Big Block pretended to sneeze.

Keyasia and Wale were so keyed in on each other that neither of them had heard the voices around them.

They were consumed with skepticism. She thought of him going off to be with another girl, while he thought about what lie she'd tell next. They both swore they were staring at a liar.

Wale stood with a hard face. "Just be good…"

She smiled. "Well, you know I'ma do that anyway…"

He cut her off. "And don't do no sneaky shit behind my back."

Her heart skipped a beat, as her smile slowly faded. "My sentiments exactly."

Chapter 25

"You sure it's cool, cause I don't wanna impose?" Taraj asked Raquel.

"Girl, bye," Raquel waved her off, as she flopped down onto her couch. "He'll be good here."

"See, I told you," Keyasia yelled from the kitchen.

Taraj rolled her eyes, as she sat down on their couch. She couldn't believe that she'd allowed Key to talk her into going out on a Tuesday. This was usually her chill nights, but Key had insisted that she hit up this spot with her. Club Faces was cool, but it was a little different from the clubs they'd been frequenting as of late. It wasn't a hole in a wall, but wasn't quite large enough to have sections.

"Tazerin, you hanging with me tonight?" Raquel hugged the baby.

"Yep." Tazerin nodded. He'd always liked Raquel.

"Where yall going?" Raquel asked, glancing up.

"Faces," Taraj yawned.

"Faces?" Raquel scrunched up her face. "Girl," she drawled. "I smell some bullshit." Taraj smiled. "Why you say that?"

"Since when Key like going to small clubs like that?"

Taraj pursed her lips. "That's what I was saying."

"Hmm, I think I know. It must be about that nigga Wale."

"Wale?" Taraj lifted a brow. "Who is that?"

Raquel shook her head, as she rolled her eyes. "Some little wild nigga that Keyasia loses her mind over."

Taraj searched her mental rolodex, trying to recall Key mentioning this Wale character. Nope. The name didn't ring any bells. "Why haven't I heard of him?"

"Aint no telling." Raquel shook her head. "She probably don't talk about his ass, because she's embarrassed. It's really crazy. I mean, my baby can pretty much have any guy she wants, you know? She's smart, pretty, and charismatic. The life of the party, just like I was at her age. But she's smarter, because she actually learned from the mistakes she saw me make. She handles her business in school, so there's no complaints there, but her taste in men…God. Now I know exactly how my mama felt when I used to run the streets, chasing after Kevin's ass," Raquel vented. "Of all the niggas running around here, she wants to deal with this boy. He's into all types of shit. Ole pistol packing, rowdy, ruthless muthafucka. And Key loses her mind over him, chile."

"Uh," Keyasia huffed, stepping into the room. "Mama, don't start with that."

For the past few months, her parents, particularly Raquel, had become more vocal about the disdain for Wale. Initially, she'd been neutral, until the back and forth between them began. Wale's involvement in the crime world was already a bit much, but to compound that with him flip flopping with different girls, disrespecting her daughter, she wasn't feeling him. Frankly, she felt that Key could do better. Still, Keyasia was grown, so she spoke her piece, but never actually butted into her business.

"Whatever," Raquel waved her off. "I'm talking to Taraj."

"Umm hmm," Key pursed her lips together. "You ready, Raj?"

"Yeah," Taraj scooted off the couch. "Bye, booski," she knelt down, kissing her baby.

"Bye ma-ma," Tazerin, waved.

"I'll be back later," Taraj promised.

"Okay, bye-bye," he waved so cutely.

Keyasia tried her best to focus on anything else. Every time she'd see an adorable baby, she'd think of what she'd done. Guilt was definitely riding her back.

Wanting to shake off negative thoughts, she attempted to focus on the night ahead of them. "Let's turn up," she boasted, as they both climbed into her Range.

Taraj nodded, but didn't say anything. There was just too much on her mind.

Keyasia knew that her friend was going through some things, and she felt that it was her duty to cheer her up. As solid as Taraj and Taz's love was, they were at odds, and he'd left their home. Although Taraj hadn't verbally admitted it, it was obvious that she was sick without him. Key also felt a little guilty, because several of their issues stemmed from their video and appearance gigs. She knew that their little hustle could awaken insecurities within the strongest man, so she wasn't surprised that Taz had some issues with what Taraj was doing. However, she never thought that a simple music video would lead to them breaking up.

A few weeks back, they'd gone to Miami and starred in a video. Taz had given Taraj a surprise visit on set, and was infuriated to learn that Taraj would have to kiss the rapper in a scene. Apparently, it proved too much for him, because he left Miami without uttering a word to her. Then when Taraj eventually arrived back in Houston, Taz was M.I.A., only to later be found at his hideaway. Taraj lost it when she discovered his baby's mother in his shower, and beat the girl senselessly. Of course, she assumed that her man had cheated, but everyone else swore that she had misread the situation, including Keyasia.

With the way Taz carried her girl, Keyasia didn't even need to know the facts, to know that he wouldn't shit on Taraj like that. She'd seen the love in his eyes. She'd witnessed him respect Taraj, even when she wasn't physically present. She saw how he'd go out of his way to make sure that no one around Taraj had any ill will. Those weren't attributes of some dude that would leave his family to lay up with a promiscuous ex. It just didn't add up.

"I am," Taraj nodded.

"Nah," Key shook her head. "I'm serious. Ion like how you been moping around. You really tripping with yourself."

"How is that?" Taraj faced her.

"You acting like it's the end of the world, because you and Taz aint seeing eye to eye. Really, you worrying about a whole bunch of nothing. Truthfully, there's girls who would kill to have what yall got," Keyasia expressed, really speaking for herself. Although, Wale could make her feel like she was on top of the world, he was inconsistent. Almost as if he took joy in building her up, only to tear her down. Therefore, she didn't know what to make of things, and he was so unpredictable that she couldn't see beyond the next few days with him. She'd give anything in the world to be able to proclaim indefinitely that they have the real thing. With Taz, Taraj didn't have to wonder. She knew. Everybody did.

Taraj grimaced. "Why do you seem so confident in what this nigga feels for me?"

Keyasia leered. "I've seen it before."

"With who?"

"With my mama and daddy. I see how my daddy loves my mama. He has that unconditional, ride or die, I'll lay down my life for you kind of love for her. And when you're around him you'll see it in everything he does and says. I know my old man aint the most righteous, but the way he loves Quel…man. But to answer your question, that's how I know. Everybody won't ever get to have that kind of love. You should consider yourself lucky," she stated solemnly.

"If you say so," Taraj swallowed, secretly hoping Keyasia knew what she was talking about.

Although, the club was on the smaller scale there was still valet parking, which Key took full advantage of. As soon as the duo eased out the truck, men grabbed their hands left and right. Not trying to do too much, they both wore t-shirt dresses, with booty shorts underneath. Their hair was dramatic with huge curls framing their faces.

The Louboutin booties they sported brought flair to the simple, trendy outfits. The club was jam packed, but Keyasia could care less. She just couldn't wait to lay eyes on him. Wale had been gone all week, and he'd called her a few times. Still, it wasn't like he once would. Key was praying that they could soon get their old thing back.

She was tired of feeling uneasy. She hadn't been able to relax with him, because of how he'd switch up at the drop of a hat. There was no use in pretending. She loved him, and felt super susceptible to getting hurt by him. It was so deep that she refused to check any of his little groupies' pages, afraid of what she might see. She was desperate, welcoming any distractions. Therefore, she'd given plenty of her free time to Bash.

He'd been in town for the past few weeks, and had taken out Key on a few dates. She was pleasantly surprised that he didn't hold any grudges against her, after how she'd behaved in the club with Wale that night. He admitted that he was teed off, but also acknowledged that things between him and Key hadn't gotten deep enough to take real offense. He claimed that he dug her enough to move past that incident. Of course, Key was flattered, but recognized that she was simply entertaining him to pass away time…and possibly alleviate the stings from Wale's indiscretions. He was simply the right guy at the wrong time.

Taraj was feeling a tad irritated, and she wore it all over her face. It had been a long while since she'd been to a spot where there was no designated area for her to sit. Standing up in one spot was killing her feet, but she was enduring it for her girl.

Keyasia was bobbing to the music, when she noticed them. They were hard to miss, as they shitted on every other dude in the club. With a smile, she greeted the entire Take Somethin' Clique. They were stunting as usual, wearing different variations of Louie shades. Butterflies brewed in the pit of her stomach, when she laid eyes on him.

Playing games, Wale attempted to strut past her, but she grabbed his hand, refusing to allow him to blatantly ignore her. Deep down, she felt like a lame. Yeah, Zale, had mentioned the club in her presence, but it was never established that she'd come along. Wale hadn't invited her, but she needed to see him.

Their interactions immediately alerted Taraj, because the Keyasia she knew never had to vie for a guy's attention. Never. The dude was flanked by several men. He stood a little over six feet, and was wearing Louie shades like the rest of his crew. He had a peanut butter complexion, thick waved up hair, diamonds on all his teeth, a nasty thick diamond flooded bracelet adorned his wrist, and two gaudy chains rested around his neck. He was extremely bowlegged, had on Robin's jeans, and Giuseppe's on his feet. His body was littered with tats, including one on his temple. Definitely eye candy.

"Hey, man," Wale chuckled, hugging Key tightly. "You good?" he teased, knowing exactly what he was doing, when he tried to stroll past her.

"Yeah," she nodded, as she considered cussing his ass out.

"Cool." He nodded, as he glanced around the club. "We got a few bottles. I'ma get a waitress to bring yall one."

Keyasia rolled her eyes, obviously not liking his response.

He furrowed his brows. "What's wrong?"

"Don't worry about it," she pouted, suddenly feeling emotional. This cat and mouse game was getting old. Why the hell would she and Taraj need their own bottle, when she'd clearly come to be with him?

With a grin on his face, he leaned forward, whispering into her ear. "I see you love popping up on a nigga. What if I would've had my other bitch with me?" he chuckled.

Instead of her usual snappy comeback, she sucked her teeth, as her feelings were truly hurt.

Gazing down at her, he noticed the defeated expression on her face. "Why you looking like somebody pissed in ya cereal? I can't joke with you now? Huh?"

Like a little girl, she silently shook her head.

Taraj stood watching, curiously. The dude that Keyasia hadn't bothered to formally introduce was obviously comfortable, as he spoke with his hand on her waist. Then a few people squeezed behind them, pushing everyone closer together, and Key unconsciously rested her head on his chest. Taraj lifted a brow, really wanting to know what this nigga had done to her friend.

For a short while, Wale was bombarded by different people, and he chopped it up with them all, while managing to hold on to Key's waist. Then once again, he was perched at her ear, holding a private conversation.

"You wanna tell me what you been up to, while I was gone?" he posed.

"Nothing," Key practically whined.

"You sure?"

She scrunched up her face. "Why are you asking me that?"

"Everything in life got a rhyme and reason to it, Keyasia. I don't do nothing for the hell of it. I aint fickle. Your actions just make me react. But you wanna play stupid, right now."

The back of her neck grew hot, as she wondered what he was getting at.

"Uh huh. Look at you. You aint got nothing to say now. Do you?"

"What am I supposed to say? I didn't do anything," she claimed in a childlike voice.

"So, you wanna keep lying to me?" he furrowed his brows.

"You asked me what I did, and I'm telling you nothing. What else do you want me to say? I mean, I told you about anything work related, so I'm confused, right now."

His head fell back, as he gazed up at the ceiling. "Ion know why I bother with this shit."

"Bother with what?" she pressed for answers.

He sucked his teeth. "Fuck this shit." He attempted to walk away.

She grabbed his shirt, feeling like she couldn't breathe. "Where you going?"

For a few seconds, he stared at her, as she clenched his shirt. As much as she lied, he was surprised her nose hadn't grown. He was hoping to spot an unattractive feature. A flaw. There were none. She was gorgeous, and being that close to her made his dick hard. It never failed. Everything in him wanted to walk away, and never look back at her ass. But something kept calling him, and like always…he had to answer.

Leaning in, kissing her lips, he asked, "Why you won't let me go?"

"Cause," she spoke lowly. "I didn't come here for you to leave me. Stay here with me," she uttered, almost pleadingly.

Taraj was speechless, as Keyasia transformed into a person she didn't recognize, right before her very eyes. That popular, outgoing, party girl was now a little kitten, as she clung to ole boy. It was cute, but also very telling. He had her. Taraj definitely knew the feeling.

"Spend all day thinking. All night wondering. Why love has to change? You kiss me, but it's not real. Tell me what happened. Are we living a lie, baby? Or is that magic gone? Do you feel the same way you used to, girl? Ooh, tell me. Is it wrong for us to love like this? How deep is your love..." Keith Sweat's voice belted throughout the club.

Wale became pissed, as Zale's bitch ass played that song. Keith Sweat's whining ass was begging some ungrateful bitch to love him. That shit was for suckers. Love was for suckers. Women weren't built like they used to be. Like his mama was. Now they were liars, schemers, and manipulators, including Keyasia. *Especially* Keyasia.

"You run your fingers through my hair. You tell me you love me. You act like everything between us is alright, girl. But you know, you know that it's not true. You love me? Or do you wanna leave me, baby. Tell me, girl. I can take it. Something is not right, no, no, no. Tell me how deep is your love..."

Wale couldn't take it, anymore. Unlike Keith Sweat, he didn't have to ask. He already knew the bitch didn't really love him. So, after tonight he was done with holding everything back. It was time to let her ass have it.

"Say, I'm about to go the car, and roll up. Meet me out there in a few minutes," he instructed, speaking into Key's ear.

She hesitated, before nodding. She could tell that something was off. He wasn't his usual charismatic self, as he left all his boys behind, exiting the club alone. She waited exactly five minutes, before deciding to catch up with him. She considered telling Taraj that she'd be back, but her girl already seemed uncomfortable, and was only there for her. Therefore, she decided to have Taraj tag along, and prayed that her conversation with Wale didn't take a left.

"Come outside with me," Keyasia urged, seemingly breaking into Taraj's thoughts.

Nicole Jackson

"Okay," Taraj glanced around, realizing that Key's little friend had disappeared. Together they squeezed between people, making a beeline to the exit.

Once outside, Key looked left to right, until she spotted his Lambo. "This way," she gestured with her head, before they sauntered over to the exotic car. "Get in the back, Taraj," she instructed, as she pulled the door open, sliding into the passenger's seat.

Taraj eased into the backseat, realizing that Key's little friend was in the driver's seat, puffing on a blunt.

"Ms. Keyasia," he spoke smoothly, almost in a sing-song manner. "What's up with it?"

"Nothing," Key sighed, feeling like he was about to be on some bullshit. He was just in the club questioning her, but was now on some friendly shit. She knew it wasn't genuine. "But Corinthian this is my friend Taraj. Taraj this is Corinthian."

He shook his head. "There you go with that shit. It's Wale. But yeah," he glanced back at Taraj, and took off his shades, exposing the most beautiful hazel green eyes she'd ever seen in her life. "How you doing, Taraj? I done heard a lot about you."

"I'm good," Taraj spoke, carefully. Now it all made sense. Key's Corinthian was also Wale...the dude Raquel didn't seem to like. "But why they call you Wale if you don't mind me asking. You don't look nothing like that rapper."

He smiled. "That was my name before I'd ever heard of that nigga. It was really Wild-Lay. My last name is Lay, and they kept saying that I was wild. You feel me?"

She nodded. "I got ya."

"Real," Wale turned around in his seat.

"So, Keyasia, this is the dude Corinthian that you're always arguing on the phone with? Didn't he buy you that Birkin bag the other day?" Taraj asked, low-key calling Key out.

"Really, bitch?" Key whipped her head around, squinting her eyes at Taraj.

"What?" Taraj asked in confusion.

"Nah, don't try to hush her now," Wale spoke up, becoming heated. "But nah, Taraj. I didn't buy her a Birkin bag. Wrong nigga."

"Boy, it aint like that. I told her that it was from you, until I realized that you didn't send it," Keyasia attempted to clarify.

"Yeah, okay. I'm just the nigga that bought the Gucci, Louie, and Prada bag. The Versace shades, purses, and shoes was me too," Wale griped. "But you know, Key. She got 'em lined up around the corner, so it's easy to get us confused."

"Corinthian, really?" she cut her eyes at him. He was definitely on one, because that was not how she rolled. Recently, she was hand delivered a Birkin bag on the set of a video, with a note stating that the sender had a crush on her. Naturally, she'd assumed it came from Wale, but when Bash called her, he explained that it was from him. She'd forgotten to tell Taraj about the mix up, though. Still, it was nothing like he was inferring.

Wale gave her an evil glare. "You know I'm just fucking with you, hot girl. I understand that a girl got fans out here, and shit. Trust me, I understand." He winked.

"Okay," Key sighed. "What about you? I've been hearing about you flying to Atlanta, dealing with that hoe from Love and Hip Hop," she pointed out, although the gossip was old as hell. She'd heard about this a while back, and they'd had several make-ups to break-ups since then, but she'd never mentioned it. Until now. Letting him know that he did absolutely too much to ever point a finger at her. Kree was clearly just the tip of the iceberg.

"And," Wale causally shrugged, as he sat there, rolling up another blunt.

Keyasia's stomach did flips. There it was again. That wishy washy shit. They were good before he left, but now he wanted to show his ass; in front of her friend, no less. "What you mean, *and*?" she scowled.

"You heard me, man," he spoke evenly, leaning against the door. He wasn't the least bit fazed by Key, wanting to piss her off. Embarrass her even.

"So, you aint gonna even deny fucking with the bitch?" she fumed.

He shrugged. "She's a friend. Just like you a friend. I got a few of 'em. Fuck. I mean, what you want me to say?"

Keyasia glared at him. "Are you fucking her?"

"Man," he licked the blunt paper, sealing in his weed. "I aint about to go there with you, Keyasia."

She angrily shook her head. "I don't know why I keep fucking with you."

"I don't know, either." He nonchalantly shrugged.

"Yeah, okay," she pursed her lips together, as her cell vibrated in her hand. Her emotions were all over the place, and she wanted to make him feel how she was feeling at the moment.

Dropping her eyes down to the screen, she realized that she had a new text. It was Bash, asking is she could come over. Focusing on her phone, she replied to the text. Soon, she was going back and forth with the texts, while Wale sat, smoking his blunt. Then without warning, he snatched the phone clean out of her hand.

"Who you texting, man?" he growled, attempting to play it cool. His reaction would've been completely different had Taraj not been in the backseat. She was Keyasia's saving grace, for sure, as he thought about smashing her head through the glass window. Violent thoughts were running rapidly through his mind.

"Give me my phone, Wale!" Key shouted. "Damn!"

"Oh," he nodded, cutting his eyes at her, wanting to slap her. "I'm Wale now, huh?"

Refusing to give her phone back, he read her texts.

Her heart raced, knowing that wasn't about to end well. Bash could be quite explicit, as he'd revisit times where she'd ride his face. "For real? You really gonna violate my privacy?" her chest heaved up and down.

"Yep," he nodded, as he continued to read, while grinding his teeth. "Okay. I see. You spent a night at that nigga's house, huh? He bought you a Celine bag...and that Birkin bag. He misses you, and want you to sit on his face again. Okay," he nodded.

Key felt sick to her stomach. Taraj held her forehead. Keyasia's ass was caught red-handed.

"Oh my God," Key dropped her head in her palms.

"Don't oh my God now," Wale seethed, as he jabbed her head with his index finger, causing her head to bounce around.

"Keep your fuckin' hand off me!" she snapped, feeling like she was about to lose her mind. How in the hell did this turn around on her?

"What you gon do about it?" he gritted his teeth. "Huh? Call your daddy. I got something hot for his ass. I'ma anybody killer, baby," he asserted, placing a chromed glock on his lap. "Matter of fact, call that bitch ass nigga you was just texting. Tell him to come see me."

She swallowed hard. "Look, I aint got time for this. Give me my phone, and I'ma get the fuck out of your car," Keyasia offered. She wasn't about to argue with him. Corinthian unquestionably had a few screws missing, and she didn't want to do anything to incite him. She'd never been caught up like this, and she honestly didn't know what he'd do to her.

"I aint giving you shit," he shook his head. "I paid for this muthafucka. Go get somebody to take it from me," he dared her.

"Get somebody for what?" Key frowned. "Just give me my phone."

"Let me show you what I feel about this phone." He lifted the phone, and using two hands he folded the cell in half, destroying it.

Keyasia gasped, "So, you just sat there, and broke my phone?"

"Hell yeah. Go get that nigga you was just texting in my face. Tell him to come holler at me."

"You're so fuckin' stupid!" she yelled, as her voice cracked. She was on the verge of tears.

"Here," he reached into his pocket, pulling out a knot. Without batting an eye, he tossed the entire thing into Keyasia's lap. "Go get another phone, *thot*."

"I don't need your fuckin' money!" she hurled the cash back at him.

Calmly, he placed the money back in her lap. "Don't throw nothing else at me. Keep this shit. I aint gon repeat myself, girl," he spoke with a curled lip. She could see the fire in his eyes, and knew that she needed to let him have the moment.

"Whatever," she rolled her eyes, attempting to open the door.

He hit the locks. "Where you going?"

"Corinthian, let me out of here," she gritted.

"So, now you in your feelings? But it was all good when you was lying to my face. I asked you if you was fucking that nigga, and you lied. You know the penalty for lying to me, Key?" he gripped a strand of her hair. "Huh?"

"I really don't give a fuck," she twisted her neck, talking tough, when she really wanted to make a run for it.

"Alright, man," he nodded. "Keep talking," he warned.

"Let me out of this muthafuckin' car," Keyasia fumed.

"And you wonder why I do the shit I do," Wale carried on. "A nigga aint finna be out here looking like a fool. You in and out of these clubs, and think that I'm about to take you serious? Get the fuck outta here. You aint to be trusted. Niggas constantly in your face, and you swear up and down that you aint fucking. You lie to me time after time. Then I'm laying down with you naked headed. I'm the muthafuckin fool for that one. And don't think I aint know about that little trip to the clinic. You got your people thinking you got your shit together, but you out here killing babies. *Two* of 'em. Yeah, look stupid," he nodded, taking Keyasia's breath away. "Thought I didn't know, huh? I keep telling you. Money can buy any information. And you aint that slick. But the killing part is you keep letting a nigga nut in you. You aint even woman enough to say you don't want a baby, and demand that I wrap it up. You just have me drop a seed, and then kill it. Trifling ass lil' girl. But I'm just as bad, though, cause I can't stop fuckin' with you. I aint gon lie. The pussy too good. But I'ma keep giving these other hoes the dick too. Fuck it. We'll be two hoes together."

She snidely laughed, but was truly hurt, and embarrassed. Something was telling her that he knew, but to hear him say it…fucked her up. The cat was out of the bag, right in front of Taraj, when she hadn't told a soul beforehand. "So, that makes you feel good to put me on blast? What…are you exposing me? Cause I really don't give a fuck," she seethed, not wanting to sound weak in front of her friend. "And I aint a hoe. That's you, boo. Yeah, I let that nigga eat my pussy. But he *never* fucked, and I know you saw him begging for it. I guess it was my silly ass way of keeping it real with your dog ass."

"Keeping it real?" he frowned, refusing to believe that she could be that ignorant. "So, killing a nigga's babies is keeping it real?"

Nicole Jackson

Every time she heard him say that, it chipped away a piece of her soul. She'd actually killed their babies. That was the ugly truth. But she couldn't let him break her. Not here. Not now. She had to keep up the front. "Boy, you really can't leave well enough alone, huh?" she huffed. "But since you must know, I got them abortions when your stupid ass got into a gunfight with me in the car."

"What?" he narrowed his eyes. "That don't even make sense. I got into the gunfight once, but you had two abortions over the same incident?"

She gave him an evil smirk. "I aborted one baby, and went to ya house while you was laying low, and let you put one right back in me; a week later. I'm like you. I can't stop fuckin with you. The dick is too good."

Taraj gasped, as she caught all that tea.

Wale clenched his teeth, as she'd finally confessed her secrets, and showed no remorse. "Keyasia, I'ma let you out my car, before I have to really see your daddy for knocking all his daughter's teeth out her mouth."

"Fuck you," she pushed the door open.

"Take that money with you. Go shopping, thotty. It's on daddy," Wale spat, as she got completely out of the car.

Taraj shook her head, as she was now out of the car, as well.

"Don't say shit to me," she gave him the finger.

"Yeah, okay," he spat, as he caught a glimpse of her fat ass. Right then, he could feel himself growing weaker. It was insane. She didn't even deserve the dick, but how could deny himself the pleasure of feeling that snatch? "Fuck it," he grumbled to himself. "Go drop ya bestie off. Then go to the crib. I'll be there in a few."

"Tuh," she sucked her teeth, as she twisted off, but was sadly elated that he still wanted to end his night with her. Especially after taking all these new revelations into consideration.

"Keyasia!" he shouted her name.

Glancing over her shoulder, she asked, "What?"

"Play with me if you want to," he warned.

Shaking her head, she rolled her eyes, before stepping to the valet. It was taking everything in her to not break down right there.

"Girl, that shit was crazy," Taraj commented. "I see what Quel was talking about. You and him be doing the most."

Keyasia frustratingly held her head, holding back tears. "See, I told you. You aint believe me." she cut her eyes at Taraj. "You're lucky."

Chapter 26

Keyasia had never been less unsure of herself, as she sat up in Wale's bed, awaiting his arrival. After everything they'd said back in the parking lot of Club Faces, any sane person would have steered clear of him. But she couldn't see herself walking away. Her hope was that since the truth was out, they'd finally deal with it, and move forward together. However, knowing exactly who she was dealing with, she knew things wouldn't be that simple.

Her heart was pounding, as she listened to him stomp through the townhouse. Stepping into the room, he was clutching a bottle of Cristal. Standing right in front of the bed, he chugged the champagne down.

Without thinking, she climbed out of bed, and stood before him in just her lace panties and bra. "Corinthian, now that I've had time to think about it, I was wrong…" she got out, but he placed a finger to her lips, silencing her.

"Shhh," he hushed her, before kneeling down to place the bottle on the floor. "I don't want to talk, right now." He hastily stripped down to nothing, slinging his clothes across the floor. "Later for that shit." Standing up straight again, he gripped her face with both hands, sloppily kissing her lips.

Aggressively, he pushed her onto the bed, straddling her. Roughly, he removed her bra, and then snatched off her panties. She attempted to lovingly stroke his face, but he shoved her hand away. Gripping her wrists, he pinned her hands to the bed. With his knees, he pushed her legs apart.

"Corinthian, seriously, listen. I'm sorry…" she got out, before he shoved his tongue into her mouth.

Palming a tit, he slid inside of her.

"Umm," she moaned, as he pushed through her gushiness.

Grabbing her legs, he propped them onto his shoulders, before firmly gripping her shoulders, locking his arms around them. With her balled up in that position, she was defenseless, and he drove into her.

"Ahhhuuuhhh," she screamed, as he pounded into her.

He was balls deep, as they could both clearly hear him swishing through her wetness. Loudly, his balls slapped against her ass, while he beat the pussy up.

"Wait, Corinthian! Wait!" she yelled out hoarsely.

"Shut up." He gripped her throat.

Knowing exactly what he was doing, she allowed him to release some steam. She'd take that punishment, if that was what needed to happen. Still, he eased up, when he looked down at her face. He could tell that he was going too deep, and a little too hard.

"You…you see what you got me doing?" he breathed, removing his hand from around her neck, as he continuously moved inside of her. "Why you making me handle you like this?"

"I don't know." She stroked his face, and this time he didn't stop her. "I'm just stupid sometimes. Can you forgive me?"

He gulped, as she tightened her muscles around him.

"You heard me, Corinthian? I said I'm sorry," her voice cracked.

There it was again. She was making him feel shit he didn't want to feel. It would only lead them into places they didn't need to venture. Places too deep, and complicated for him. Places that would have him wanting to cause bodily harm…even if was to her.

Nicole Jackson

Wanting to block her out, he zoned out, hammering into her. Her shrills intensified, as he hit her spot. She bucked her hips, seemingly refusing to be ignored.

"Uhhh," she panted, as her pussy began to fart. "Oh, God, Corinthiannnnnn."

Standing on his knees, he put his back into it, causing her skin to loudly clap into his. They both sweated profusely, as they switched positions. Somehow Keyasia ended up clutching the top of the headboard, hopping up and down on him, as Wale sat with his legs tucked underneath him.

Showing out, she was crotched over him, literally dancing on the dick. Involuntarily, his mouth fell open. She was going in, determined to make him understand that no one would ever fuck him better. She was snaking the hell out of her midsection, before hitting him with her signature move. Making her booty jump, she stopped working her hips, as she tightened her muscles around him.

"Fuuuck," he grunted, as he erupted inside of her.

Knowing that she had him, she bounced up and down, while he skeeted loads into her.

"Shit," he breathed, falling backwards, onto his back.

Seductively, Keyasia turned to face him with her legs gaped open. Lifting his head, he could see his thick semen seeping out of her. "Damn, that dick was good," she whispered, easing a finger into her slit. After swirling her finger around, she brought the finger to her mouth. "Umm," she moaned. "And that cum tastes so sweet."

He allowed his head to fall back, as he gripped his dick that was saturated with her juices. Without thinking, he began stroking himself.

"No, I got it," Keyasia insisted, removing his hand, before taking him into her mouth. Channeling Super Head, she stroked him with both hands, while she locked her jaw around him. She slurped loudly, as she slobbered him down.

"Fuck," he vented, gripping her head. It wasn't long before he was gritting his teeth, as he fucked her mouth. She took it in stride, deep throating him. "Damn," he gasped, as he felt himself exploding, once again. Like a champion, she was gulping his babies down, as some of it dripped down to his balls.

Taking him by surprise, she lowered her head, licking every drop of cum off his balls. She then proceeded to lick her hand, making sure that she tasted everything he'd shot out, while still managing to stroke him. She'd gotten flat out nasty with it, giving him chill bumps. He hated how she knew exactly what to do to him.

"Alright," he drawled, feeling like she'd sucked the life out of him. "I get the point. You got it." He removed his dick out of her grasp. "Come on." He pulled her on top of him. "Let's go to sleep," he slurred.

Laying her head on his chest, she breathed easier. Then when he wrapped his arms tightly around her, it was a wrap. She melted in his embraces, thinking that everything would be alright.

******

Keyasia slowly opened her eyes, awakening with a smile on her face. After the crazy night before with Wale, she was happy with how they'd ended the night. Glancing to her left, she was expecting to see him lying right beside her, yet all she saw was a pair of boxers in his place.

Sniffing the air, she could smell the scent of fresh soap, indicating that he'd just gotten out of the shower. Sitting up in bed, she took a long stretch. As she yawned, she could smell the stench of her own breath, and could also feel the stickiness between her thighs.

Deciding that she'd wash her ass before anything else, she climbed out of bed. With absolutely nothing on, she tipped to the bathroom. Choosing the quicker route, she chose to shower, and then brushed her teeth. After she was thoroughly freshened up, she grabbed one of Wale's tees, pulled it over her body, before jogging downstairs.

By the time she'd reached the bottom step, she could clearly hear that he was on the phone in the living room.

"Wale, for real. When are you getting dressed? You need to come over here," some chick whined.

Judging by how loud the sound was, Key assumed that he was video chatting with someone. She knew that he couldn't see her from where he was seated, so she decided to stop, and listen for a second.

"Man," he drawled, still sounding exhausted. "I told you I'ma be there in a lil' while."

"No, you won't. Did you forget that I can see you? You just sitting there in your damn drawls," she pouted.

At this point, Keyasia was positive that his disrespectful ass was talking to Carmen.

"I know. I'ma come through just like this," he lazily chuckled.

"Hey, I aint tripping. That makes for easy access. I can just hop right on it."

Keyasia balled up her fists, wanting to fuck them both up.

"Look, you wanna see," Wale brazenly offered, panning the phone over his dick, whipping it out. "You got my shit hard right now." He demonstrated, wagging it in the camera.

"Did this muthafucka just do what I think he did?" Keyasia fumed, practically flying around the corner, making herself visible. "The fuck are you doing?!" she raged.

Sucking his teeth, he sighed loudly, as he pulled his boxers over his hard-on. "Say, I'ma call you back."

Carmen grimaced. "I know damn well you aint got that bitch over there! Every time I ask to come, it's always some kind of excuse…"

Shaking his head, he ended the call, while Carmen was still blabbing.

Keyasia stalked over to him. "What type of shit is that?! You in here playing with your dick, with a bitch, while I'm right upstairs in your bed?! How disrespectful can you be?!" she reached back, before slapping the shit out of him.

He shot to his feet, grabbing her hands. "Chill the fuck out!"

"Don't tell me to chill!" she snatched her hands out of his grasp. With fury, she swung on him, catching him in the mouth.

Viciously, he shoved her back, causing her to stagger. "Keep your fuckin' hands to yourself, before I beat the shit out of you!"

Her chest heaved up and down. She was furious, but something in his eyes told her that he meant it. That day was going to be the day that he'd lay hands on her. Looking into his eyes, she felt hatred staring back at her. This was not how it was supposed to be. Those weren't the actions of a man who loved her. Thinking of how he'd been making her feel, she began to tremble. Her shoulders shook, as she broke down. Against her will, a tear slipped from her eye, before she collapsed into sobs.

"Why do you keep doing this to meeee," she bawled, dropping to the floor. "I…I…I told you that I was sorry. But I can't take this no more. You can't just keep stepping all over my heart."

He stood frozen, as she cried from the depths of her soul, not caring as snot dripped from her nose. It was fucking him up, and that infuriated him. Once again she was the victim, and he was to blame. No. He couldn't let it go down like that. She needed to know the real.

Holding his head, he shook it. "Look, I can't do this no more, Keyasia."

"Do what?" she sniffled.

"Do this. Me and you. Us." He pointed back and forth between them. "I can't stand to listen to you boohoo, like a nigga is really doing you dirty. You really got a lot of fuckin' nerve."

Her mouth fell open. "I…I got a lot of nerve?" she pointed at her chest. "How?"

"The fuck you mean, how?" he snarled, callously. "Why the fuck you think I asked you about what you was doing while I was gone? Huh?" he scrolled through his phone, before exhibiting the screen to her. In his phone was a picture of her and Bash at Cheddar's together. Bash's arms were intimately wrapped around her. For the life of her, she didn't know how he'd gotten the picture, as someone had obviously sneakily taken it. "It was because I already knew."

Her lips quivered. "But I promise to God that I just ate with him, and then I went back home. Nothing happened."

He frowned. "You really believe I'm hearing that shit? Especially after you lied about fucking with him?"

"I swear, I swear I didn't lie. We have never had intercourse."

His scowl deepened. "Bitch, do you hear yourself? Is letting him eat your pussy supposed to make the shit better?"

"No." she waved her head vehemently. "I'm just telling you that it was never that serious, and I have never fucked another man since the day I met you."

"I doubt that shit, but it really don't even fuckin' matter. You just keep showing me time after time that I can't trust you. Then you wanna make this shit about these other hoes. Them bitches is irrelevant. But I'd be damn if I let a hoe fuck over me, so I was doing shit just to get at you. And now that shit is played out too."

She slowly stood up. "Get at me for what, Corinthian? I mean, why would you wanna hurt me? What did I ever do to deserve this?"

"The fuck you mean, Keyasia!" he shouted. "You fuckin' went behind my back, and got two fuckin' abortions! Killed not one, but two babies. And now you expect me to let that shit go?"

"How was I supposed to know that you even wanted kids?" she attempted to reason.

He screwed his face up. "What type of fucking question is that? Do you take me for some kind of illiterate muthafucka? How the fuck can I be fucking you night and day, with no condom, never pulling out, and not be alright with you having my baby? You told me you wasn't on birth control, but you didn't know if I wanted kids? Nah, you aint that fuckin' stupid, and if you was that confused all you had to do was fuckin' ask."

She stood perfectly still, swallowing hard. "And if I would've told you, then what? What would your answer have been?"

He lifted his chin up. "I would've told you that you got me fucked up. We made them, and we gon take care of 'em."

She nodded, as fresh tears brimmed her eyes. "And I'm sorry. I shouldn't have made those choices without you. Lord knows, I'd give anything in the world to do that shit over. But I was scared, Corinthian. I was pregnant, and you was trying to figure out who tried to kill you. I mean, you still haven't figured that out, and I couldn't see us bringing babies into that. I really thought the time wasn't right, and the shooting had me shook. But after that I realized that it didn't matter what was going on, I was in love. And I was gonna take the good with the bad, and if we made more babies, then so be it."

He gave her a look a disgust. "You was in love? You lied to my face, but you was in love? You don't even know the fuckin' meaning of love. How the fuck you love me, but wasn't even really fuckin with me?"

"Baby, I was always fucking with you," she insisted. "What are you saying?"

"You was fucking with me so tough that you decided that I wasn't good enough to be the father of your kids, right? All the money, and gangsta shit was alright, but when shit got real to you, you run off and kill my child. But you was fucking with me? And you love me? Shit, if that's what you call love, then Ion want no parts of that shit."

"B…But I thought I was doing the right thing," she cried. "And I'm so, so, so sorrrrrryyyy. Wha…what you want me to do? Baby, I'll do anything."

"That's the problem. You can't do shit!" he lashed. "I kept telling myself that if I didn't go there with you that we could get past this shit. A nigga was that stupid behind your trifling ass that I didn't wanna confront you, scared that I might actually hurt you. I aint never spared nobody like that. And fucking with these hoes to make you feel it, was never good enough. That shit still don't amount to what you did. To what you took," he vented. "And what's crazy is that I never came at you fucked up. From jump, it was team us. On my life, I aint fuck another bitch, until you did what you did. I really thought you was the one, and didn't give a fuck about what nobody thought about it. And what you turn around and do? Kill my fuckin' kids! But now you wanna cry cause you don't like the way I'm handling you. I can't even have a real situation with the next bitch, because I let you bring all them problems. And that shit is backwards, because you had your fuckin' chance. You wasn't true, and I can't deal with no disloyal ass bitch. That's why this shit will never work."

"But…but we can fix this. I can, I can make this right," she panicked, grabbing his hands.

He yanked his hands back. "You can't fix shit, Keyasia. Sometimes I look at you, and I swear I hate yo ass. Fuck playing games. Fuck making you suffer. I just want you out of my fuckin' life. It's over," he spoke with finality. "I don't care. You can take all your shit. Even that fuckin' Ferrari. I don't want none of that shit. Just you get that shit, and get the fuck out."

"No, no, no," she shook her head. "I don't wanna go. Please just hear me out. We can make this work."

"Apparently, you aint hearing me. I don't want you. I can't stand to look at your fuckin' face, half the time. So, grab ya fuckin' shit, and get the fuck outta my house."

"Corinthian, nooo," she sniveled. "I…I don't wanna leave you. I won't," she declared.

"What the fuck you mean, you won't?! Huh? I said get the fuck out!" he shoved her back.

"Stooop it! I'm not leaving!"

"You aint leaving? You aint fucking leaving?! You must take me for a fuckin' pussy!" he roared, before flipping over his glass coffee table. The glass shattered as it crashed into the hardwood floor, causing Key to jump back.

"Corinthian, calm down," she pleaded.

"Don't tell me to calm down! Bitch, get the fuck outta my house!"

"No," she shuddered.

"Keyasia, keep fuckin' pushing me! You gon make me hurt you. Get the fuck out!" he raged, pacing back and forth. Feeling frustrated, he charged at her, slamming her against a wall. "You think I'm fuckin' playin?!" he spewed, before reaching back, and then slamming his fist into the wall next to her head, creating a hole. "Huh?!"

"Baby, just calm down," she whimpered.

Furiously, he grabbed her neck. "What did I just fuckin' say? Get the fuck out of here, before I kill you in here. Leave this muthafucka, and fuckin' never come back. Or I'ma do something real bad to you."

The tears wouldn't stop falling from her eyes, as she nodded. He was breathing like a dragon, as he released his hold.

"Now go!" he clenched his teeth.

Holding her mouth, she ran upstairs. Hurriedly, she scrambled around the room, grabbing the clothes she'd worn there. Once she had her purse, and keys, she jogged downstairs, then straight out of the front door.

In just a t-shirt, she dashed to her Range, and hopped in. Her heart was racing, as she sat, clutching the steering wheel. She sniveled uncontrollably, until she was all out hyperventilating. Her body grew hot, as she had a meltdown.

"Oh, my God," she sobbed. "This, this, this can't be life. Ahhhh. Noooo." She buried her face in the steering wheel, feeling like life as she knew it, was over.

Chapter 27

Carmen lied on her back, hating the awkward silence. She finally had him there with her, in her bed, but his mind seemed to be miles away. It was disheartening that her best efforts seemed to be futile. They were stuck in the same place, although she'd been dealing with him for months now.

She kept hoping that they'd grow closer, because she saw so much potential in them. Still, her hope was waning, as she struggled to even get an arousal out of him. Their last sexual encounter was great, until she blurted out that she loved him. Instantly, his dick went limp, and he became incredibly distant. It was hard to ignore that something was holding him back. Or someone.

Turning to face him, she noticed that he was laying there, blankly staring into space. She couldn't help but wonder what he was thinking. "Wale, why are you so quiet?"

He shrugged, gazing up at the ceiling. "No reason."

"You sure about that?"

He nodded. "Yeah."

"So," she hesitated. "You're not over there thinking about *her*?"

He was caught off guard by that question, as he shifted his head to look at her face. "Where did that come from?"

She sighed. "It's not hard to figure out. When we first met, you told me that you were single, but then she pops up. You never really put her in her place. She seems to know you in a deeper way than I do. But you tell me it's nothing. Stupidly, I listened to you, even though the shit didn't feel right. I get my feelings all caught up, and then one day you just stop calling. I contact you, and can't get a reply. You disappear for a whole month. I'm not stupid, and I'm friends on Facebook with your people. I saw all the videos and pictures. You was with her. Hugging and kissing. And then out of nowhere you call me, while she's at your house. Obviously, it's way more than you told me. And I'm really beginning to believe that you're playing games just to fuck with her."

He shook his head. "I think you just reading too deep into shit."

"Is that really the case?" she searched his eyes, seeking clarification. "Or are you not telling me the truth? Trying to downplay what it is with her. You think people haven't told me what it is?"

He frowned. "I don't know why you'd listen to Jazel. I told you that girl is cra…"

"No, it wasn't her," she cut him off. "I mean, she always had smart stuff to say, swearing that you're never gonna leave Keyasia alone, but that's to be expected. I know she doesn't like me for whatever reason. So, I would never take anything she says into consideration. No, I'm talking about your people."

"My people?" his scowl deepened. "The only people you met were my boys. And if you listen to what another nigga gotta say…man, nine times out of ten they were trying to fuck you."

She shook her head. "On everything, it wasn't even like that. You know I club in the same spots that yall like to hit up. So, I would run into a lot of your boys, and every time I'd run them down, asking about you. And one night I caught Craven in the club. Him and Jazel were there together, both drunk as fuck. Anyway, I asked about you, and he drunkenly said that you were at home with your bitch. Then Big Block was stumbling all over the place, and he co-signed what Craven said, claiming that I'm playing stupid. According to him, I knew damn well that you was with ya crazy wifey, and would get at me when you could. I mean, they said that shit like it was something I was fully aware of. And that's when it hit me. That's why they never really get involved when she comes around, and busts out your windows, or cause a scene. They know that's how yall get down, and that you're obviously not going to stop dealing with her. I was the only one too blind to see that."

"Man," he drawled. "You tripping."

She smiled despite herself. "And that's all you can say to that, huh?"

He said nothing.

"I mean, be honest with me. Tell me what it really is. I have eyes, Wale. I know she's attractive. Hell, I would be lying if I didn't admit that the ignorant bitch was pretty. But you brought me along, while you had her. There's something you're not saying. I mean, are you just one of those dudes who's afraid of commitment?"

"Nah," he denied. "I hollered at you, because I was digging you. But yeah, I was with her first, and we were kicking it tough. Real tough. But then she did some fucked up shit, and I called myself leaving her alone. So, I saw what was up with you, but she wouldn't let go. Honestly, that's when I just started bullshitting you and her, and that shit wasn't cool. You hadn't done none of the shit she had, and I eventually decided to stop going through the motions with her, and called it quits completely. So, that's my bad for dragging you along for all that," he apologized.

She was stunned that he'd actually stopped the games, and told her the truth. But it didn't feel like a celebratory moment. She needed to know more. "I appreciate the apology, Wale. But can I ask you what she did?"

He sighed heavily. "She went behind my back and had two abortions."

"Oh, wow," she gasped. As crazy as it may have sounded, his revelation made her jealous. She was seeing firsthand that what he and Keyasia had was totally on a different level. Keyasia was getting rid of babies, while Carmen couldn't pay Wale to fuck her unprotected. Key had a sure-fire way to solidify a permanent position in his life, and chose to terminate it. Carmen, on the other hand, would have ran with the opportunity. Why didn't he see her in the same light? Or suitable to carry his child?

"Yeah, she fucked my head up with that," he admitted.

"That's crazy. I would never do something like that to you. In fact, I'd be honored that you'd even choose to have a child with me," she confessed.

He nodded, as he carefully regarded her. Carmen was very pleasing to the eye. Her olive skin was soft and smooth. She had a medium frame with just enough of everything, and she carried herself with plenty of class. She wasn't some gold digger seeking a come up. She had a real career as a nurse, which provided her a quite comfortable lifestyle. She had a home she was buying, and had no children. Overall, she was a catch, and Wale could've seen something more for them…if he'd never met Keyasia.

Key had definitely fucked up the game for everybody.

******

"He's still not answering?" Keyasia questioned.

Solemnly, Taraj shook her head. "Hell, no."

"Well, I'm sure he'll call you back," Key surmised, as they both sat on Taraj's couch.

More than ever, the two found themselves clinging to each other, especially since Josairah had gone to California to attend school. Taraj's relationship with Taz was rocky at best, and she'd just divulged to Keyasia that Taz had been spending more time with his daughter and baby's mother, because the daughter had been molested by the mama's boyfriend recently. Consequently, Taz had initiated a war with the boyfriend, King, as the two gunned for one another in the streets.

With all the madness going on, Taz was adamant about Taraj keeping a low profile, and after bumping heads with him several times, she'd taken heed. So now, most days, Taraj and her son were literally stuck in the house, and Keyasia would come over, keeping them company.

Taraj was on an emotional rollercoaster, since Taz had made a surprise visit home the night before, fucked her to sleep, only for her to awaken, and find that he was gone again. She was reaching her breaking point, as she called around searching for him.

Keyasia had been diligently on her bestie duties, providing a shoulder for Taraj to lean on, while she was silently dying on the inside. She'd expressed the fact that Wale had dumped her, but had neglected to mention how deeply it affected her. She'd use smiles, and jokes to mask her true feelings, but she could feel herself rapidly unraveling.

"Girl, fuck that nigga," Taraj pursed her lips. "If anything I'ma find his bitch ass, and break a fuckin' leg."

Keyasia tittered. "I hear you with your violent ass."

"Shit, sometimes you gotta make them feel you by any means necessary," Taraj scoffed. "We need to just get in the car, and find his bitch ass. Then fuck him up. And after we're done with him, we'll run up on Wale's ass. He can get it too. These niggas got us fucked up, friend."

Keyasia shook her head, as her stomach became queasy from merely hearing his name. "Yeah, that would be some wild shit, but I'm good," she said weakly. "And you know that you're supposed to stay home, until that beef shit is handled."

Taraj paused for a second. Usually, whenever she was on some bullshit, Key would be right along with her, down to ride on a nigga. "You good?" she arched a brow. "You mean to tell me that you don't wanna pop up on that nigga, and punch him in the head for playing with you?"

"I mean, what good would it do? It's over," Key replied blandly.

Taraj frowned. "How is it that you just accept that, but keep telling me that me and Taz will work shit out? Why is there no fight in you for your own relationship? Cause after that whole club scene, I know you love his ass. And you're just gonna let him walk away like that?"

Key bit her bottom lip. "I guess I can tell you to hold on, because you and Taz will never be done. He would never allow it. But Corinthian…that nigga aint fucking with me. He's made that clear."

"I hear you, but I still say let's do a drive-by on his ass. Make him hear you out, you know? Or are you really cool with yall being done?"

"I wouldn't say that I was cool with it, but I can't change it."

"You never know, until you try," Taraj insisted.

Keyasia grew angry. "Taraj, the nigga aint fucking with me. Just let it go," she snapped.

Taraj was thrown off by Key's attitude. "Well, damn, bitch. Don't bite my head off. I was just saying."

Keyasia shook her head. "You know what, I'm tripping. I shouldn't be taking my frustrations out on you. I'm just going through it, and I would love to believe that there's a fighting chance for us. Even after the way he threw me out of his house," she gulped. "And honestly, in the back of my head I thought that nigga really loved me, so he'd never fully walk away. Because on or off, I could walk right in his house whenever I wanted to…with my key. Then I'd go in his closet, and my shit would still be there, hanging up. So, for the first few weeks, I kept telling myself to chill. Let him calm down. But then one morning I got to missing him so bad that I couldn't take it. I said fuck it, and went over to his house, unannounced. That's when I found out that he'd changed the locks, and when I tried to call him his phone was disconnected. Right then I knew that all the clowning, arguing, and tears wouldn't change a thing. He's finished. It's really over."

"Damn," Taraj murmured, feeling bad for her girl.

Keyasia sat for a while, with a glazed over look. She wanted to remain strong, and put on a brave face, but she couldn't keep it in. The thought of being without him was slowly killing her, as she thought about the constant agony she felt. Feeling it in her chest, her lips quivered, as tears clouded her vision.

Taraj was speechless, as the tears slipped from Key's eyes. For as long as she known the girl, she'd never so much as batted an eye over anything. Sure, she'd act out, talk crazy, but then it was over. This time was different, though. She had to be broken.

"Aww, girl, don't cry." Taraj scooted over, wrapping her arms around her friend. "It'll be okay."

"No, it wooooont," Key bawled her eyes out, as she clung to Taraj. "I can feel it. I will never be the same. And I don't wanna do this without him. I just want the pain to go away. It hurts, so, so, bad," she confessed. "I fuckin' hate myself, because I did this. I should've told him about the pregnancies. I should have been honest, but I was scared," her voice trembled. "I thought about his lifestyle. How my mama and daddy would react. How it would change my life. And I panicked. I was so fuckin' stupid, and now he don't want meeeee."

"It's alright, it's alright," Taraj's voice cracked. "We don't need them niggas. We have each other, and I'm here for you. If he can't recognize what he has in you, then fuck him. Don't let him break you down. You're too strong for this." she wiped her eyes. "Shoot, got me over here crying."

Keyasia smiled through the tears. "You stupid," she sniveled. "I wasn't trying to make you cry."

"It's okay. I just know how that pain feels. I had a lot of days where I wanted to give up on everything…but it's definitely a lot easier since I have a friend like you," Taraj admitted.

Key squeezed her tighter. "Aww, I'm glad that I could be a comforter for you. And you make me feel better too," she giggled.

"Good," Taraj breathed. "We can get through our issues together, and say fuck Taz and Corinthian. Hell, we can maybe even find us some new boos, and go on double dates together."

"Yeah," Key sighed. "We'll do that…eventually. But I don't know when. Because right now I can't see it. I don't want nobody but Corinthian." She had to be honest with herself. "His bitch ass got my heart, even if he don't want it."

Chapter 28

"See bitches think they slick, but then they act like niggas. Go fuck off, then come back, and act all sentimental. Bitch. Pack your bags, get out my house. You know the buiz. And you bet not have no nigga around my fuckin' kids. Bitch..." Yo Gotti's *Second Chance* pumped from Wale's stereo system.

He gripped the steering wheel of his Audi, as he drove through the streets of Fifth Ward, with his big homie, Bee, riding shotgun. It had been a while since they'd hit a lick together, and Bee was constantly on the go, therefore they were taking this time to catch up.

They'd known each other for years, and always tried to maintain a friendship that transcended beyond their hustle together. Wale really saw Bee more as an older brother, and felt that he owed him for putting him on, years back. They'd met at some chicks' apartment, both smashing girls that lived together. At the time, Wale was hustling on the streets, slanging coke. The issue was that everybody wanted to move dope, therefore the grind wasn't always lucrative. So, after getting acquainted with Bee, and seeing him ball out, he wanted in. He knew exactly what Bee was into, thanks to the broad he was smashing, and her big mouth. Therefore, he approached Bee about getting put on, and surprisingly Bee was cool with it.

For years they did their thing together, and along the way they discovered that Wale was the cousin of Jay Rock. Jay Rock and Bee had been feuding over Paris for years. Apparently, they'd all grown up together, and Bee was Paris's first love, but she'd moved on with Jay Rock, while he was incarcerated. Eventually, Bee was released from prison, and it was rumored that Paris was backsliding with him, after some confusion with Jay Rock and his baby mama. Wale had heard so many versions of the situation that he didn't know what to believe, but thankfully Bee's issues with his cousin never spilled over into their relationship. Truthfully, both Bee and Jay Rock were two levelheaded dudes, who knew several of the same people, and would've probably been cool, if they didn't both love the same woman.

Sometimes Wale had to laugh, and ask what Paris had between her thighs, because although Bee hadn't been with her in years, he still clearly loved her. And that was the main reason he and Jay Rock couldn't be in the same room together.

Staying true to his nature, it wasn't long before he had to ask about her. "You seen Paris lately?"

Wale shook his head, as he smirked. "Nigga, there you go with that shit. You do realize that broad is married to my cousin, right?"

Bee sucked his teeth. "Man, go'on with that bullshit. Fuck Jay Rock's cock blocking ass. I aint trying to fuck with her, no way. I just asked if you seen her."

Wale licked his lips. "Aye, that's on yall, anyway. But yeah, I saw her last weekend. They was at Tino's house. She was cackling with the rest of them, so I got the fuck."

"Who is they? And what were they cackling about?" Bee questioned, curiously.

Wale stroked his goatee. "Paris, Falen, and Toya was all in my business, asking me about what happened between me and Keyasia. Paris's messy ass was the ringleader, cussing me out. Talking about I'm a hoe, and her niece was gonna get another nigga on my ass."

Bee grimaced. "Damn, you aint fuckin' with her no more? Shit, I'm like Paris. The fuck did you do?"

Wale frowned. "Now see, you sounding like them. Why everybody wanna look at me? How you know she wasn't the problem?"

"Cause, nigga, I know you. You was probably fucking all these hoes, and the shit got old. I know lil' cuz aint putting up with that."

"Man, fuck a hoe. It didn't have shit to do with that. Her ass was the one who couldn't be trusted."

Bee furrowed his brows. "No shit? What, she was out there fucking with one of those rapping niggas, or some shit?"

"Honestly, I don't know what the fuck she was doing. I caught her in a few lies, but that shit was nothing compared to hoe ass stunts she pulled."

"What kind of stunts?"

Wale shook his head. "As much as I don't fuck with her, I aint gon put her business out there like that."

"Aw, come on, main. This me you talking to. Anything you say will remain between me and you. Besides she's grown, so it damn sure aint my job to tell her business."

"Alright." Wale nodded. "She ran off and killed my babies. Had two abortions, and never told me shit. I found out in the wildest way. It was pretty much downhill from there."

Bee scratched his head. "Damn, I wasn't expecting you to say that. I knew her lil' ass was fucking, but damn."

"Yeah." Wale focused on the road.

Nicole Jackson

"And I know that nigga Kevin would've probably lost his mind if he knew some shit like that."

"Probably so." Wale shrugged. "But like you said, she's grown. He would've had to eventually accept it."

"True," Bee agreed. "That's all a part of life." He thought about it. "So, that's enough for you to be done with her?"

"I mean, yeah. She showed me that I can't trust her, and her getting abortions was just flat out stupid. If she didn't want to get pregnant, then her ass should've been on birth control. Aint no way she never considered what could happen with the way we was popping it."

"I hear you. That's why it's not making sense. There gotta be something you aint mentioning."

"What you mean?"

"I'm saying, it sounds like she was cool with having your lil' one. Cause like you said, she aint a dummy, and had to know what fucking raw would mean. So, why would she let you get that far, then turn around, and get rid of the babies? Twice at that."

Wale exhaled, as he contemplated. "Well, alright, we was leaving the hotel one night, and some niggas followed us. I caught a glimpse of them in the rearview mirror, and got her to pass me the heater. Then I bent a corner on their asses. Somehow they caught up with us, and let off some rounds, so I busted back. 'Til this day Ion know who them niggas was, and Keyasia claimed that situation made her scared to have the babies."

Bee couldn't believe his ears, and he knew that his cousin Kevin would have had a heart attack, if he'd known that his daughter was caught up in a shootout. The man had worked hard to provide his kids a better life, only for his daughter to end up with some dude, dragging her back to the very place he'd fought to climb out of.

"Say, man," Bee began. "You say that shit a little too calm for me. We talking about bullets flying, and you wonder why she started questioning if yall could raise a child together. Shit, in the past I've had a few situations with bitches in the car, and as soon as the shit blew over, them hoes was gone. Aint no sane broad gonna be cool with that, unless she's in the streets with you, and even then she might fold. Fuck, honestly, I'm surprised she stayed around after that."

Wale swallowed. "I hear you, but what if it was you? What if your bitch went off, and killed your baby? Would you still be with her?"

"I mean, I would probably be pissed once I found out, and even trip out for a while. But then I'd come down to reality, see how she could feel like the time wasn't right, and do what I gotta do for her to understand that she'll never be put in that predicament again. Even then, we both know that's something I'd never be able to guarantee. Frankly, nigga, from the sound of it, you wasn't ready for a baby, and she made that tough decision for the both of yall. Yeah, I know she should have told you, but it is what it is."

Wale narrowed his eyes. "And this is coming from somebody who's still in the streets. So, you saying that you don't want kids, until you're out the game, right?"

"That aint what you heard." Bee shook his head. "But what we both know is that Ion got no kids. So, whatever I do is on me. I can be reckless than a muthafucka, cause I aint responsible for nobody but myself. Still, I'm old enough to realize that if I had a family, then my moves would have to change. There's no way that I could have a whole different set of circumstances, and expect my life to remain the same. So, maybe Key felt like you wasn't up to changing, and having a baby with you could be asking for trouble," he offered. "Having a baby of your own aint like that situation you got with Mona. You go get Kash on your own terms, when you feel like it, in a kid friendly setting. Imagine having a little person with you all the time, in all your cars, at your house, even when you got beef in the streets. That baby would be vulnerable, and could easily pay for your sins."

Wale listened intently, really digesting it all. He'd been so consumed with anger that he'd never stopped to consider what Keyasia must've felt, after getting shot at. In fact, they hadn't discussed it further beyond the night the shooting occurred. Perhaps, he'd been a tad irrational, with his way of thinking, still that didn't change the deep betrayal he felt from her aborting his children.

"Alright, I see your point, big homie. But let me ask you this."

"What's up?" Bee cut his eyes at him.

"Would you be so forgiving if it was Paris? I mean, as hard as yall went back in the day, what if she would've killed yall's unborn child?"

Bee smirked. "Man, the older I get the more I realize that love is a powerful thing. After all the shit that went down between me and Paris, I could hate her, right now. Shit, she chose another nigga, and now I gotta sit back and watch her give this man everything I ever wanted from her. And I aint shame to say that I love the shit out of her, but there was a time when I had her, and would get caught up in the petty shit she'd do. Cause believe me, her ass aint perfect. Still, what we had sometimes only comes once in a lifetime, and now that I know that I'll never be able to have her in that way again, I swear that none of that bullshit matters. Yeah, I've fucked up in the past, and she did too. She did some shit that made me want to kill her at times, but I'd take all that today. On God, I'd forgive her, and we'd move on. So, this is coming from a nigga who had the bitch he needed, and let her slip out of his hands, over some dry ass beef. But I don't know. Maybe what you had with my little cousin aint that deep, and you'd be alright with her moving on with her life, and getting with the next nigga."

Wale had no words for that. Anger had propelled him to completely cut Key off, and he'd never really stopped to think about the future. He was living in the moment, focusing solely on what he felt right then. But as time went on, he felt lost and confused. He still thought about her constantly, and didn't realize how big of role she played in his life, until he tried to live without her. He was still wrapping his mind around the notion that they were really over, so he definitely hadn't gotten to the point of seeing her with someone else. Truthfully, he wasn't sure if he could bear witness to her entertaining another guy without exploding.

"Man," he drawled, frustratingly rubbing his forehead. "Ion know what the fuck to think or do. All I know is that Keyasia was driving me crazy. Shit, she still is."

Bee chuckled. "But you said that you could handle her. I told yo ass she was live wire."

"Whatever, nigga," Wale chided, pulling up to the curb in front of Coke apartments. "Get yo ass out of my car."

Bee pushed the door open. "Alright, boi. I'ma fuck with you. I'm finna hop in my car, and run by one of these hoes' house, and grab something to eat."

Nicole Jackson

Promiscuous Girl: Keyasia and Wale

Wale shook his head, as Bee hopped out of his car. "You better slow your old ass down, before one of these *hoes* put you out of your misery."

"Aye, we all gotta go some way," Bee jested.

"Yeah, okay. Fuck with me," Wale uttered, as he pulled off.

He was in deep thought, as he navigated through the streets. He exhaled loudly, hating that he was right back where he'd started, still stuck on her. For a second, he considered taking everything back, and giving it another try. But he also recognized that he couldn't be with her, if he couldn't move past what she'd done. Therefore, the question was, could he forgive her?

Breaking his thoughts, his cell vibrated in his lap, right next to his nine millimeter. Picking the phone up, he saw that it was Craven calling.

"Yeah, what's up, nigga?" he answered.

"Say, where you at?" Craven questioned with urgency.

"Leaving Fifth Ward. Why, what's up?"

"Have you been on the internet today?"

Wale grimaced. "Nigga, I know you aint call to tell me about what happened to some bullshit ass rapper on social media. The fuck I care about what's on the internet?"

Craven huffed in frustration. "What? Man, you tripping. I'm asking, because I saw some shit about Keyasia, but Ion wanna run with rumors. You know them Black gossiping blogs be printing lies, and shit."

"So, what it's saying? What, that she's fucking with one of them rappers?" he guessed, knowing that rumor had been thrown out there several times before.

"Nah, man," Craven sighed. "They're saying…they're saying…man, Ion even wanna say it. Cause I aint gon speak the shit into existence, if it aint true."

Wale's stomach did flips. "Say what, nigga? Spit it out!"

"Okay, look. I'ma shoot you a link, and you can read the shit for yourself."

"Nigga, you tripping. Why can't you just tell me yourself?"

"Cause, dog…I aint finna bring no he say she say like this to you. Check out the link, read it for yourself, and then find out what's really going on."

Wale sucked his teeth. "Alright, nigga. Send the fucking link." He hung up. He couldn't understand why Craven was being so overly dramatic, making shit more difficult than it had to be.

When his phone beeped, indicating that Craven had sent the link, he pulled over on a back street, parking at a curb. He frowned when the link read: *Two Instagram models allegedly gunned down in a Pappadeaux's parking lot in Houston.*

Sweat began to form on his forehead, as he clicked on the link. It felt like the wind had been knocked out of him, when he saw a photo of Keyasia and her friend Taraj, smiling together. With trembling hands, he read the article.

"Details are still coming in, but close sources are reporting that Instagram models Taraj Victorian and

Promiscuous Girl: Keyasia and Wale

Keyasia Williams became victims of gun violence last night, outside of a popular restaurant in Houston, Texas. Currently, the conditions of the women are unknown, but it was alleged that one of the women had to be airlifted to Memorial Hermann Hospital. We'll keep everyone posted, as we follow this story."

"Wh…what the fuck?"

Wale's breathing became erratic, as he frantically dialed Keyasia's number. Hearing her voicemail immediately pick up caused his heart to drop down to his feet. Hanging up, he called her again, and again to no avail.

"Fuck!" he vented, as he speedily pulled away from the curb, burning rubber in the process. His chest became tight, as he jotted down the street. Not knowing her fate was killing him, and he was determined to find out, all the while praying that it wasn't true. It couldn't be. God wouldn't be that cruel to allow this to happen again, because he seriously didn't know if he'd be able to bounce back this time. This couldn't be life.

******

Wale's stomach was in knots, as he marched into Memorial Hermann hospital. He'd been unsuccessful at reaching Keyasia, sending him into full panic. Thinking that there could be a possibility that he'd never see her face again was terrifying. Devastating. Heartbreaking. And downright deadly for the people who'd violated.

Just as he was approaching the emergency help desk, he spotted a familiar face.

"Wale, what are you doing here?" Paris questioned, as she stepped over to him.

Seeing her there, with obvious tears in her eyes, and knowing that she had a personal relationship with Keyasia was alarming. Momentarily, his voice was caught in his throat. He couldn't breathe.

Struggling to keep his composure, he palmed his mouth, before sliding his hand down his face. "I…I was trying to see if…umm Key…Keyasia was…" He fought to get out, and then he saw her.

Raquel and Keyasia stepped out of the double doors, leading into the waiting area. Quel held her daughter closely, as she was an emotional wreck, sobbing uncontrollably. "It's okay, baby," Raquel sniveled. "She's not done fighting."

"Huuuuuuh," Keyasia wailed, as she knelt over.

Raquel shed silent tears, as she rubbed her daughter's back, providing whatever small comfort she could. Paris rushed over, attempting to console Keyasia, as well.

Wale stood, breathing easier, seeing that Key still seemed to be physically in one piece. However, seeing her in such anguish had him feeling some type of way. Without putting much thought into it, he stepped over to her.

Raquel was surprised to see him there, since Keyasia had explained that they were no longer an item. "Hey," she spoke, as she eyed him.

"Hey," he replied, right before Keyasia stood up straight, coming face to face with him. She continued to cry, as he pulled her into his arms. "Stop that crying," he whispered into her ear. Slowly, she wrapped her arms around him, as he rocked their bodies side to side.

Raquel leaned over, whispering into Paris's ear. "What is he doing here? You called him?"

Paris shook her head. "Seems like somebody must have told him about the rumor that Keyasia was with Taraj, because he was looking for her. He seemed shook, like he'd thought that something had happened to her."

"Umm." Raquel poked out her bottom lip, as she studied the way Key was clinging to him. She knew right then what it was, and was now trying to process the fact that her daughter had soul-tied with a street nigga.

"Come on, yall, let's step out of here," Paris urged, tapping Keyasia's shoulder. All eyes were on them, as their melodramatic scene played out in front of strangers.

Key nodded, as Wale released her. They then all collectively exited the facility. Paris and Raquel both purposely walked ahead of them, giving them space to talk.

Still sniveling, Key stepped to the left, near the entrance, posting up against the wall. Wale followed suit, while Raquel and Paris sat at a nearby bench. Attempting to wipe her flowing tears, she gazed up at him.

"What are you doing here?"

He stroked his goatee. "I read that you was...you know. And I came here to see what was up."

"Yeah?" she sniffed. "My mama told me that people were spreading those lies."

He nodded. "So, what happened?"

She rubbed the side of her face, as her eyes closed. "My friend Taraj, her son, and a friend named Trell was shot. They shot her just two hours, after I left her house. I was just with her," her voice cracked. "Taraj was shot three times, lost a lot of blood, and they're struggling to stabilize her. And now they're saying that she might not make it," she wept.

"Damn," he grumbled. "That's fucked up." He hugged her once again. "Is her son alright?"

She nodded. "Yeah, he's alright, but Trell didn't survive," she revealed. "I just don't know what I'll do if my friend dies," she blubbered into his chest.

"Keyasia," someone called her name, causing her to look up.

"What's up?" she sniffed, finding Taz standing there.

Wale stood saying nothing, as he recognized the look of devastation written all over the dude's face. He didn't personally know Taz, but they'd seen each other around. They were both known to be thorough in the streets, and had heard several stories about each other.

"Did Taraj tell you why her and Trell was going to Pappadeaux's?" Taz questioned.

"No." Key shook her head. "When I was there she never mentioned going anywhere with him. But I know Trell had been talking to her here and there. She was venting to him, and he kept telling her that you was just handling business. Then when I left she was mad at you, talking about how she was going out to find you. I'm guessing Trell talked her out of doing something crazy, and they decided to hang at Pappadeaux's together."

Grabbing the top of his head with both hands, Taz exhaled. "Fuck, man. Something kept telling me to go home. I should've followed my first mind. I should've followed my first mind," his voice became shaky. "Fuck." He stomped out into the lot, burying his face into his palms.

Wale shook his head, as they watched Taz pace back and forth. "This shit is crazy."

"I swear to God, I'ma murk me a nigga tonight," Jarell gritted, as he stepped out of the hospital. Following closely behind him was Josh, and Danny Boy. Together they all lumbered over to Taz, seemingly attempting to calm him down.

Wale recognized all three men, and knew that they hustled together. Danny Boy was an infamous enforcer, who pumped fear into a lot of so-called certified street niggas' hearts. Therefore, Wale knew that the men weren't weak, and blood was sure to spill in the streets in retaliation of their people's attack.

"Poor Taz. I know he's going through it. Him and Taraj don't really have much family outside of each other. And them fuckin' people shot her, and their baby. I can only imagine what's he's feeling, right now," Keyasia sympathized.

Wale felt like he was in the twilight zone, as Bee's point earlier came full circle just an hour later. It didn't matter what a man's pedigree was, his loved ones could still pay for his sins. Taz had undoubtedly done plenty of dirt, but probably never thought that his family would pay for his dirty deeds. It was sobering for Wale to witness a young cat, much like himself, face the possibility of having to bury the mother of his child. It was the very thing that someone like him often avoided thinking about. And the exact situation Keyasia feared happening to them.

"Yeah," Wale scratched his head. "Some reality checks like a muthafucka."

Somberly, Keyasia nodded. "I gotta sit down." She grabbed her forehead, as she headed back into the hospital. He was right behind her. Absently, she chose the nearest available seat, before he sat next to her.

For long spells, they said nothing, as she leaned on him, thinking of her friend. Hours tipped by with Taraj's condition being unchanged. Keyasia was exhausted, as she fought to keep her eyes open.

Raquel gathered her belongings, preparing to leave. She and Keyasia had come together, and she hated to rush her, but she had a very important meeting bright and early the next morning. As she was about to let Key know that they needed to leave, she realized that Key was significantly calmer. Although she had her reservations about Wale, she was positively grateful that he'd been there to assist her child in her time of need.

Treading closer to them, she asked, "Wale, can I speak to you for a minute?"

Immediately, he nodded, before standing up. Together he and Raquel stepped out of Keyasia's earshot, as she looked at her mother suspiciously.

"Look," Raquel started. "I'm about to leave, because I have some business to handle. Keyasia rode with me, and I'm not sure if she's ready to…"

"You don't even have to speak on it. I got her," he cut her off. "You can go ahead, and leave. I'll wait with her, until she's ready to go. And then I'll take her where ever she needs to be."

Raquel nodded, as she tucked her lips into her mouth. "Thank you. I really appreciate that."

He shook his head. "You aint gotta thank me. I'm here because I want to be…and need to be."

"I hear you." Raquel poked out her bottom lip, before she tipped over to Keyasia. "Baby, I'm about to go," she announced, bending over to kiss Key's cheek. "You know I have that meeting in the morning. Love you. Call me when you leave here."

"Okay," Key responded faintly.

"Alright." Raquel straightened her back. "I'm gone."

Wale reclaimed his seat, as Raquel sauntered off. He glanced around, noticing that several of the people who'd shown up for moral support for Taraj were either in their own little worlds, or knocked out sleep. Checking his watch, he realized that it was now one in the morning.

Keyasia cut her eyes at him. "What did my mama say to you?"

He nonchalantly shrugged. "Nothing, really."

"Whatever," she yawned.

"You seem sleepy. You don't wanna go catch a few hours of sleep?"

She sighed. "I am a little tired, but I don't wanna leave, and then something happens. It's bad enough that Taz 'nem left. They're probably out there collecting souls, and shit," she grumbled.

"But your people, uh what's her name? That chick that was at your mama's house that time…"

"Shay," Keyasia answered.

He licked his lips. "Yeah, Shay and her people are here, holding it down. I'm sure she don't mind calling you if something changes."

Seemingly having supersonic ears, Shay lifted her head, as she sat across from them. "Yeah, Key, go ahead and go home for a little while. You look tired. I promise to call you if anything happens."

"I don't know." Key scratched her neck.

"Girl, if you don't get your *drowsy* ass out of here," Tasha, Shay's sister, spoke up. "We'll call your ass, shit."

"Whatever." Key playfully gave her the finger. "I guess I'll go, then." She stood up.

"Alright," Shay smirked. "Yall drive safely."

"Uh huh." Key waved them off, as Wale eased out of the chair. "Don't forget to call me," she reminded them, before they strolled off.

Quietly, they walked back to his car, and slid in. Keyasia exhaled loudly, shaking her head. "I still can't believe this is happening," she mumbled to herself. Clutching her forehead, she held back fresh tears.

Gradually, Wale grabbed her free hand, interlocking their fingers. "It's gonna be alright, man. And even if shit doesn't go as planned, you'll be alright. I promise you."

She breathed. "I hope you're right."

Without letting her hand go, he proceeded to exit the lot. Never bothering to ask her if she okay with it, he traveled to his home. She really didn't know what his intentions with bringing her there were, and refused to put much thought into it.

Sluggishly, Key stepped into his townhouse, realizing that everything was exactly how she'd left it. Not being able to focus on anything else, her mind was preoccupied with Taraj, as she stoically went to take a shower. Then once she was done, she wrapped a towel around her body, before re-entering his bedroom. There she found him, sitting at the head of the bed, smoking a blunt, wearing only boxers.

Taking it upon herself, she went into his drawers to grab herself a t-shirt. Dropping the towel to the floor, she gave him a full view of all her nakedness. He adjusted his dick in his boxers, as he fought arousal. He swallowed hard, as she pulled his shirt over her head. His erection instantly vanished when she turned to face him, and he noticed her tearstained face.

She sniffled, as she climbed into the bed with him. There was a nice amount of distance between them, as she rested her head on a pillow. Deciding to put the blunt out, he placed it in the ashtray, resting upon his nightstand. He then leaned over, grabbing both of her hands, guiding her on top of him.

"Lay down, man," he whispered, gently pushing her head onto his chest. She shuttered, as he wrapped his arms snuggly around her.

She felt immense security within the confines of his arms, but her heart was heavy. Softly, she whimpered, dropping tears. The beating of his heart slowly calmed her, as her eyes lowered. Eventually, she fell asleep right there, with her head on his chest, within his arms, as he refused to let her go.

Chapter 29

The ringing of Keyasia's cell awakened her. With her head still resting on a pillow, she blindly fumbled around, until she clutched her phone. Popping her eyes open, she saw that it was Shay calling. Immediately, she sat up, before answering.

"Hello." She braced herself for the worst.

"Hey, you must be in the bed," Shay assumed, detecting the sleep in her voice.

"No. I'm up. What's up?"

"Well, our girl is stabilized, and is in here talking shit," she reported.

"Thank the Lord," Keyasia rejoiced, as the room seemingly grew brighter.

"Exactly," Shay concurred.

"Okay, tell her that I'll be up there in a minute. I'm on the way."

"Alright," Shay agreed. "See you when you get here."

Keyasia ended the call with her spirits lifted.

"She's better?" Wale questioned, standing in the doorway, startling her.

"Damn, you scared me." She held chest, as she glanced back at him.

He smirked, as he ambled over to the bed. "My bad."

"Okay, well, um, I guess after I get dressed you can take me to my truck."

He furrowed his brows. "You sure? Cause, I mean, I can just take you directly to the hospital. Unless, you really need your truck right now, or something."

"No...I...I'm not trying to inconvenience you. I really don't know how long I'll be there..." she sighed. "Look, I'ma cut the bullshit. I know that you showed up to the hospital yesterday, because you thought that something had happened to me. I get it, and I really appreciate the concern. But I also know that you decided to end things between us. And frankly, I'm not trying to play on sympathy, hoping to keep you around. Because when the dust settles it'll be back to the basics, and I don't want to bullshit myself. Why avoid the inevitable?"

"Okay." He nodded, moving directly in front of her. "Since we're being honest, I'ma keep it real with you. I was mad as hell at you, and would do spiteful shit to see you hurt. You wounded my pride when I saw that you didn't want kids with me. I was fucked up in the head, and we probably needed to part ways, right then. I needed to see shit for what it is. On both ends. And yesterday when I was questioning myself on if I'd handled shit with you the right way, I got a call from Craven. He let me know that they were saying that you was shot, then suddenly none of that other shit mattered. I just needed to know that you were okay, and prayed to God that it wasn't too late to tell you how much I love you. And seeing your home girl's boyfriend going through what he's going through, I could really see exactly what you meant when you told me you was scared. So, as fucked up as I felt when I found out about those abortions, I understand. Now, I'm just ready to move past all this, and do what makes me happy. And Keyasia, you make me happy. I want us to be together. All the way. No living in the past. None of that in between shit. No side hoes. No wingmen, waiting for a nigga to fuck up. Just us."

Keyasia sat for a second, momentarily speechless.

He glowered down at her. "You aint got nothing to say?"

Gradually, she smiled. "Yes." Springing to her feet, she jumped on him, wrapping her arms around his neck, and her legs around his waist. "I love you," she confessed, raining kisses all over his face.

Gripping her ass with both hands, he kissed her back. "I love you too."

"Forever?"

He grinned. "You know a nigga aint going nowhere."

******

"So, how are you feeling?" Keyasia questioned.

Squirming around, Taraj sat up in the hospital bed. "I'm alright. Just ready to get the hell out of here."

It had been nearly a month since she'd been shot, and her body had been through several changes, but she was now days from being released from the hospital.

Key smiled, as she sat at her bedside. "I know Taz, and Tazerin will be happy when you do." She pointed out, knowing that Taz, and their son had basically moved into the room with her. After getting grazed by a bullet, her baby was still healthy as ever, and would tear that hospital room up.

"Shit, me and them both. It's hell trying to fuck in this little ass bed," Taraj claimed, causing Key to roar with laughter.

"Bitch, them bullets aint cooled that hot ass down, I see. Don't fuck around and get pregnant, while your ass is supposed to be on bedrest."

"Hey." Taraj shrugged. "When I need it, I need it. What can you do?"

"How about try keeping those legs closed?" Keyasia teased.

"Shit, I do," Taraj claimed. "And then Taz steps into the room, and them muthafuckas just spring open. I don't know what's that about."

"Just nasty." Key shook her head. "But for real, I'm glad to see yall back at it, stronger than ever."

"Yeah," Taraj beamed. "But my baby is still stressing."

"For what?" Keyasia frowned.

"Well, I been meaning to tell you, but Taz's ass is always sitting around, being nosey," she alleged. Indeed, Taz was usually right there with her, giving her absolutely no privacy with any of her visitors. It just so happened that this particular evening, Taraj had convinced him to go get a haircut, and to take their son with him.

"Okay." Key nodded, urging her to continue.

"He found out that King wasn't the person who sent those dudes to shoot me," Taraj revealed. "Turns out that those dudes were his baby mama's cousins, they used her car for their getaway, and the police have a warrant out for her arrest. People started putting two and two together, when everybody realized who Trell had shot, before they killed him. Lani's cousin died on the pavement that night too, directly linking her ass."

"What the fuck?" Keyasia gasped. "What type of evil shit is that bitch on? I know damn well that if those niggas were her cousins, using her car, then she had to be in on it. They need to find her ass."

"I know," Taraj agreed. "That hoe went off the grid, and ran off with Taz's little girl. I think the laws are half assed looking for her, and I'm willing to bet that her trifling ass is still in Houston somewhere, hiding out. They say that her scam artist ass already had five different warrants, before this. So, that hoe is a pro at ducking the police. People are also saying that she and cousin named Bleed have been known to hit licks together. I'm guessing that he was probably one of the two other dudes who tried to rob me."

"Wow," Key stressed. "That's some crazy shit. That bitch took hating to a whole new level. And I know Taz is ready to put them muthafuckas to sleep."

"Hell, yeah. But it's a hard pill to swallow, when the bitch is his baby mama. I mean, either he's gonna catch up with her, and deal with her, or the laws will. Either way, she'll still be his baby's mama. Not to mention their little girl. He keeps saying that he wants to go get his daughter, and have her live with us."

Key lifted a brow. "And how do you feel about that?"

Taraj sighed. "I really don't know. Hell, the little girl don't even seem to like me. So, I could see there being a lot of uncomfortableness. But I guess we'd have to get adjusted to one another."

Key nodded, realizing that when a woman loved a man, sometimes she had to deal with the bullshit that comes along with him.

"Anyway, later for all that," Taraj waved off. "So, what's been up? What's the tea?"

Keyasia grinned. "Nothing major."

"Well, what about Josairah? I haven't talked to her, since she came to visit me, before going back to L.A.,"

Key folded her arms. "Did she tell you that her and Little Jahrein broke up?"

"No, she didn't mention that. What happened? Because them muthafuckas was hot and heavy."

"Little Jah was on that bullshit. Apparently, he was fucking Jhyrah's friend Nancy, while she was away at school."

"You know what, I felt like it was something fishy going on between him and that girl." Taraj pointed a finger.

"Exactly. I saw some shit that didn't look right, but if I would've told Josairah, Little Jah would've sworn that I was trying to sabotage their relationship. So, I decided to mind my business. I figured that whatever he was doing would eventually come to the light, anyway."

"True. But how is she handling it? I mean, is she cool with them being done?"

Keyasia thought about it. "I don't know. Honestly, I think she's hurt, and he won't stop calling her. I didn't believe that he was really serious about her, until she dropped his ass. Now that nigga be moping around like a sad puppy."

Taraj giggled. "Well, that's good for his ass."

"Yep." Keyasia took a stretch. "I love you, friend, but I gotta go," she yawned. "I'm sleepy." Slowly, she stood up, preparing to leave.

Taraj sucked her teeth, as Key moved towards the door. "Bitch, who do you think you're fooling? I know that you're about to run downstairs, hop into that Rover, and chase that nigga down. So, go find your ugly ass *Corinthian*," she teased.

Keyasia gave her the finger. "Fuck you, but you have it wrong, anyway. I'm not about to go downstairs to go looking for Corinthian, bitch. Because he's already out there waiting on me." She winked, before exiting the door.

******

Wale pulled into Mona's apartment complex, and parked. Lowering the volume on his stereo, he called her.

"Hello."

"Aye, I'm outside."

She sucked her teeth. "For what? I already told you what it was. My son aint gone be around no other bitch."

He cleared his throat. "Look, man, come the fuck outside."

She huffed. "Yeah, okay. I'm coming."

Ending the call, he glanced to his right. "You good?"

Keyasia pursed her lips together. "Yeah, I'm alright. She just better stay in line."

He nodded, as he watched Mona step out of her apartment, and switch up to his car. He then pushed his door open, before easing out. Shutting the door, he was ready to deal with her.

Mona frowned with her arms folded, as she noticed that he hadn't come alone. "Why did you bring her to my house?"

Wale grimaced. "What's up with the attitude?"

"What you mean?" she fumed. "You got one of your bitches outside of my house. You think that I want these hoes knowing where I live? The moment some shit pops off, or they get mad that you're over here, they'll be popping up and shit. I don't need that kind of drama at my crib."

"Whoa, whoa," he halted her. "What's all this talk about bitches, and they? Cause she aint neither one of those." He pointed at Keyasia. "And you aint got to worry about her popping up over here, because I don't have no reason to be here. From now on, I'ma come get Kash. That's it."

Mona's jaw tightened. "And what that got to do with you bringing her here?"

He stroked his goatee. "I brought her here, because I wanted her to see for herself that we aint on no bullshit. I'm here for Kash, and you need to know that he will be around her."

"What if I'm not cool with that, though?"

"Then that's gonna put a strain on me and Kash's relationship. And when he asks you why he don't see me, you'll have to tell him that it's your fault. Cause regardless of what you feel, Keyasia aint going nowhere."

Mona's heart sank, but she tried to play it off. She'd been putting up with his bullshit, hoping that one day he'd carry her the way he was carrying Keyasia, right then. "You niggas aint shit," she spewed. "I was the bitch that held you down when you was in jail. I wrote them letters, and put money on your books. Shit, I even put my own baby daddy out to make sure that you had somewhere to rest your head. But what you do? You get on, and get with the next bitch who aint been there for none of the struggles."

Wale glanced back at Keyasia to see if she'd heard any of Mona's rant. Thankfully, she seemed to be preoccupied with something across the parking lot, as she gazed out of the window. Focusing back on Mona, he snarled, "Stop bullshitting yourself, man. Yeah, at one point I halfway fucked with you. And when I went to jail I thought that you was really down for me. You wrote all those letters, swearing you love me. You was waiting. All that shit. But you forgot to mention that you had gotten back with ya BD, and he was living with you. Then when I got out, you waited until the day I was released to put him out. You didn't think twice about putting me in a compromising position, never bothering to tell me that the nigga had been staying there. So, it was your fault that he was in feelings. I mean, who wouldn't be, after he was just living there one day, and you moved somebody else in the next? Right there you showed your true colors. So, I don't know how you thought that we was gonna be together, and I was gonna trust you. I'd be the muthafuckin' fool, then."

"Whatever." She rolled her eyes. "My dumb ass should've stayed with his ass. Instead of dealing with yo selfish ass. But it's all good, cause he's in my apartment, right now, begging for another chance," she wickedly smile, hoping to awaken some form of jealousy.

Wale shrugged. "Good. Maybe now you and him can get yall shit together, and you can stop stealing out the stores for a few crumbs. And he can help take care of his son."

She quickly shook her head. "But I told him that just because he's been coming around lately, don't mean that I'm stopping what you and Kash have. You've been the only consistent man my son knows, and he aint got nothing to do with that."

"I don't have a problem with that as long as you don't try to start no confusion in my life. Respect the fact that I got somebody, and keep this strictly about Kash."

Reluctantly, she nodded her head. "Okay."

"Cool. Now send Kash out here. He asked to come with me for the weekend."

"Whatever." Mona rolled her eyes, before stomping off.

As she ventured back into her apartment, he dropped down into his Audi. Glancing at Keyasia, he attempted to gauge her attitude, but he couldn't read her.

She arched a brow. "Why are you looking at me like that?"

"Just trying to figure out what you're thinking," he admitted.

"I'm thinking that Mona better be lucky that you was able to check her ass without my help."

He smiled.

"And I'm feeling like it aint no coincidence that her baby's daddy is over here, and that same black Taurus from that night we left the hotel is parked outside."

"What?" he frowned.

"Right there." Key pointed. "Aint that the same car?"

Wale carefully studied the car. "Hell fuckin' yeah."

She bucked her eyes. "Small world, huh?"

"I'm ready!" Kash excitedly announced, as he opened the back door. With his backpack in tow, he eased into the backseat.

Wale locked eyes with Key. "This shit crazy." He thought about the irony of the situation. Mona's BD had shot at him over his BM, and jealousy of Wale's relationship with his son. Him doing so had ultimately propelled Key to abort their babies. So, there he was picking up the son of a man who'd caused him to lose his own potential son. The universe could be quite cruel.

Peering into the backseat, Wale asked, "What's up, man? You been enjoying having your daddy back around?"

Kash's cheerful demeanor immediately shifted. "No. I don't like him living with us. All him and mama do is fight. He's mean, and he keeps telling me that I'ma stop going places with you, because he was getting rid of you."

Keyasia shook her head.

Wale smirked. "Don't worry about that, man. I think he meant that the other way around. Somebody told me that he's leaving tonight."

******

Wale studied his phone, while sitting shirtless, between Keyasia's thighs. They were on Big Block's picnic table, in his backyard, and Key had her ass on top of the table, despite Big Block telling her that nobody wanted to eat next to her booty. She blatantly ignored his nagging, as she used a brush to stroke Wale's waves.

As Wale's cell rang, both he and Key gazed down at the screen. It was Mona calling. "Yeah?" he answered, as he lifted his head, spotting Kash on the court, playing ball with Maurice.

"Hey," she sniffled. "Um, I was calling to ask you if you could keep Kash for a few more days. I know that you was gonna drop him off today, but I found...I found his daddy dead outside in his car last night," her voice quivered. "And I gotta deal with the police, find out how he's gonna get buried...too much," she rambled.

"Damn, that nigga is dead? No, bullshit?" Wale questioned, while Key continued to brush his hair.

"Yeah," Mona sniffed. "Somebody shot him in the head."

"Damn, that's fucked up."

"I...I know."

"Man, me and that nigga may have had our issues, but I'm sorry to hear that. And you go ahead, handle your business. I got Kash. In fact, I'll take him back and forth to school if I have to."

"O...okay. And don't tell Kash right now, please. I gotta figure out a way to tell him myself."

"You aint even gotta say it. I wouldn't do that."

"Alright, well, I'll call you later."

"Okay," he agreed. "Take care of yourself, man."

"I'll try." She hung up.

Still brushing his hair, Keyasia asked, "What happened?"

Wale casually shrugged. "She said that somebody killed her baby daddy."

"Oh." Key poked out her bottom lip. "That's crazy."

"Yeah, it's a cold world."

"I know," she breathed. "Can we go Pappasito's when we leave here? I'm hungry."

He glanced back at her, thinking of how she was more like him than she realized. They were both on the same page, giving zero fucks. Fuck Mona's baby daddy. Yeah. What the hell were they eating for dinner tonight?

Chapter 30

"Bitch, I'm telling you. We need to plan a trip. This cold weather is for the birds."

Keyasia cut her eyes at Black Reign as they sat at her kitchen's island. "Girl, aint nobody trying to catch a flight right now. I'm cool on traveling for a while."

Jazel grinned. "Keyasia, how did you let that nigga get you so sprung that you'd back away from all that free money you was getting? From what I can tell, those club appearances and videos was paying pretty good. But now you don't wanna catch a flight. Let me find out that Wale's ass got you literally grounded."

"Whatever." Key waved her off. "Corinthian doesn't have anything to do with it. I'm just focusing on school. It's a new semester, and I was fucking up last semester. I'll focus on my grades…"

"And that nigga," Black Reign added. "Don't leave that part out."

Keyasia rolled her eyes. "Bitch, I know you gon let me. Damn."

"Ewe," Jazel cringed. "She gone rep that crazy ass nigga to the fullest. They both aint wrapped too tight. The other day she facetimed me while she was on the toilet, shitting. And he was right in the bathroom with her, sitting on the counter, smoking a blunt. Like I know it was funky as hell in there, but there his ass was. Then when they started kissing, I couldn't take it no more. I hung up on her ass."

Black Reign tittered. "Sometimes it be like that. You go through different phases. There's times when them niggas work your nerves, and you just wanna go hang with your friends or whatever. And then it's those times, where yall are just vibing, doing nothing, but loving every second of it. I believe that you can only do that when you're friends with your man. Aint nothing wrong with it. Hell, when he can tolerate the smell of your shit, then you know his ass aint going nowhere. He gotta love your musty ass panties."

They all giggled, before being interrupted. "What yall in here laughing about?" Meeko questioned, as he waltzed into the kitchen.

"Nothing," Black Reign answered dryly.

Jazel sucked her teeth.

Key smiled. "Just chatting."

"Yeah?" Meeko eyed Key, rubbing his hands together, as he licked his lips. "You talked to your girl, lately?"

Key arched a brow. "Who? Josairah?"

"Yeah."

"Oh, yeah, I talked to her earlier today."

He frowned. "Well, why she aint answering my calls? She way out there in L.A., carrying a nigga's baby, but be acting like she can't pick up the phone."

"I don't know," Key claimed.

"Well, is she fucking with some other nigga?" he pried.

Keyasia's eyes danced in her head. "How would I know that?"

"Wait a minute. Who's pregnant with whose baby?" Black Reign interjected in confusion.

Meeko beamed with pride, sticking his chest out. "Josairah's pregnant for me. You didn't know?"

"Hell no." Black Reign shook her head.

Jazel cringed. "Ewe."

Meeko glared at Jazel. "What you making that face for? You wasn't saying that when I was running your cousin this dick. She aint know shit about shopping at Neiman Marcus', until I started fucking with her. And you definitely wasn't saying *ewe*, when I hooked your ass up with Craven."

"Nigga, please. Go'on Meeko. Don't nobody wanna hear that shit."

"Exactly," Black Reign agreed. "And what the hell does Neiman Marcus' have to do with anything?"

"I'm saying," Meeko began.

"Say, nigga, what you doing in here? All the men are in the game room," Wale interrupted, standing in the doorway. "Aint nothing in here for you."

Meeko snorted, as he headed out of the kitchen. "Nigga, always thinking somebody trying to fuck with his broad," he grumbled.

"Whatever, home boy. Just carry yo ass up out of here," Wale sneered.

Keyasia sat shaking her head. He didn't even attempt to hide the fact that he watched all his boys around her.

"Keyasia, let me see your phone, right quick. Mine is dead."

Jazel narrowed her eyes, as Keyasia willingly handed Wale her phone. She tapped her nails on the granite counter top, as he strolled off with it. "I guess, you letting that nigga go through your phone. Do he smell your pussy when you come through the door too?"

Keyasia smiled. "If he wants to smell my pussy all he has to do is breathe. Cause my juices are still on his top lip."

Black Reign fell over with laughter. "That's my bitch, main. I swear. I wasn't expecting that one."

Key shrugged. "I'm just saying. Corinthian can use my phone anytime he wants, and I guarantee you that I can use his too."

"Ya feel me?" Black Reign high-fived her.

Jazel smirked. "I aint gon lie. You's a bad bitch. I never thought I'd see the day when Wale fucks with a broad the way he fucks with you. You broke the mold, bitch."

Keyasia popped her invisible collar, boastfully. "You know me," she curled her lips. "I'ma keep 'em in line," she clowned.

Black Reign laughed. "Whatever, hoe. Tell her that she wouldn't understand. We be putting that good Fifth Ward pussy in these niggas' lives. Aint no coming back from that."

"Bitch please," Jazel pursed her lips. "This south side pussy is where it's at. Yall north siders aint hitting on nothing."

Key tittered. "Bitch, you don't even believe that one. But on another note, why do yall seem so annoyed by Meeko? Yall don't fuck with him like that?"

Jazel smacked her teeth. "Girl, that nigga is annoying as fuck. He always bragging about something. I'm like save that for them hoes in the streets, cause who you stunting on? Craven damn sure aint hurting for nothing, but we aint gotta talk about it. And if he fall off tomorrow, I'ma be right there, helping him get back on. Shit, I've done it before. So, I hate to hear niggas like Meeko run his mouth. Then he low key tries to play me, bringing up the fact that he used to fuck with my cousin, and how I met Craven through him. Like I wasn't a live bitch when he met me. A bitch been getting it out the mud. Then my brothers gon help me when I aint got it. Big bro on like a muthafucka. I'm talking seven eight figures, and Meeko wanna toss around where he shops at. I mean, who gives a fuck?"

Black Reign fluttered her lashes. "Aw, there she goes with that big bro shit. Bitch, nobody asked you about Keyon's ass."

Jazel giggled, before sneakily looking around, ensuring that the coast was clear. "Black Reign, it's just too painful to hear about your old boo, huh?"

Black Reign dramatically tossed her long thick hair over her shoulder. "Bitch please."

Key was enjoying this, because she always found it interesting how so many people she knew lives would intersect. Although Black Reign and Jazel were both dating men related to Wale, they hadn't met through their spouses. They'd met years back, through a mutual friend, Dookey Baby. The two had long ago cut ties with Dookey Baby, but remained close friends. At one point, during an off period with Kaydoa, Black Reign had met Jazel's brother, Keyon. For a short while, Black Reign and Keyon had an intense fling, until Kaydoa ran up, cutting their thing off. Approximately, a year later, Jazel was introduced to Craven, and the rest was history.

"But anyway," Black Reign continued. "What the hell is Meeko talking about? I know damn well Josh's daughter aint having his baby. With his lame ass."

Keyasia shook her head. "Girl, Josairah supposedly told that nigga that the baby was his, but I don't know. That bitch is in California at school, and avoids him most of the time. And I know for a fact that they only fucked once. Hell, she was just going with my cousin, Jahrein."

Black Reign crinkled her nose. "Little Jahrein is young, but got more than Meeko's bullshit ass. Why would your girl downgrade like that? Shit, if anything I would've been having a baby for his lil' fine ass. Big Jah and his sons know they're some handsome muthafuckas." She fanned herself. "Whoo."

Jazel snickered. "You better not let Kaydoa hear you saying that."

Keyasia whispered, "I said that's what she supposedly told him. She never told me that was his baby. Shit, when I bring him up, she changes the subject. And she won't tell anybody her due date. Honestly, I think the bitch is playing games. That probably is Little Jahrein's baby, and if it is, all hell is gonna break loose."

"I know Raven would lose her mind," Black Reign added.

"Yep," Key agreed.

"So, since that's your girl, what would you do if the baby came out, looking like your cousin, but she keeps insisting that it's for Meeko?" Jazel wanted to know.

Key shrugged. "If that baby comes out looking like my cousin, her ass won't be able to hide it. My cousin's mama and her mama hang out together. Trust me, they'd spot that shit a mile away. But if I saw her letting another nigga take care of a baby I believe to be my cousin's, I'd tell her to tell the truth, or I would have to blast her ass. But I doubt it would come to that. Still, I'ma make sure to tell her to stop bullshitting with Meeko, cause he seems too invested. Shit, keeping it real, I don't think Josairah gives two fucks about him."

Black Reign nodded. "Yeah, if that aint Meeko's baby she needs to stop the bullshit. Because if she know like we know, she's better off not dealing with his ass. I heard he likes to fight his bitches."

"Oh, really?" Key arched a brow, "I didn't know that."

"Yeah, and he's the grimiest out of all his boys too," Jazel offered.

Key frowned. "Why you say that?"

"Meeko is the only member of TSC that still be robbing. Since the clique is getting a little money, they hang with money, and Meeko be smiling in those niggas' faces, and will be the one to set them up. Him and Craven stay bumping heads over that. Meeko be the cause of a majority of their beefs in the streets, and he always tells Wale to cut him off. He's too greedy."

Keyasia sat soaking everything in, telling herself that she'd have to keep a watchful eye on Meeko, for her girl's sake. Still, she wouldn't run back, filling Josairah's head up with gossip, because nobody's word was gospel. But if she personally saw a need for concern, she'd definitely put her friend up on game.

******

"What you think about this, Keyasia? Everything looks legit?"

Keyasia stood over Wale, as he sat at the desk, sifting through papers. They were at the clothing store Wale co-owned with his cousin, Harold. Harold was pretty much a square, who'd gone to college, and was determined to make something of himself. Stepping out on a limb, he'd thrown everything he had into the store, but still somehow came up short. After mulling it over, he approached several of his cousins who he knew had disposable illegal income. Out of everyone he consulted, Wale was the only one who showed any interest in his proposal. With Keyasia's urging, they'd gone into business together.

Wale was far from a dummy, but Keyasia's knowledge of contracts, and numbers far exceeded his scope of knowledge. After all, her mother was a lawyer, therefore he trusted her judgement, and she had yet to steer him wrong in matters of investments.

Harold stood near the desk, quietly. He wanted to remain transparent, so he offered no objections as they combed over the profit margins he'd calculated on a spreadsheet. He was used to Wale bringing Keyasia there to ensure that he was receiving his proper cut from the proceeds, but was holding his breath, because she'd always find a reason why Wale was entitled to more money.

"Umm," Key tucked her lips into her mouth. "Harold, what's this expense, right here?" she pointed out.

Harold tipped closer to the desk, and peered down. "Oh, that's considered an expense for the store. It can be written off."

Keyasia frowned. "I mean, I hear you, as far as tax breaks are concerned. You could definitely write that off, but we're talking about the agreement between you and Corinthian. Technically, that money you spent was personal, and you took the store's profits to fund it."

Harold gulped. "Yeah, well…"

"So, you owe him five thousand dollars," she cut him off. "No, wait." She flipped through the sheets. "That's just for one month. You've done this thee months in a row. So, that'll be fifteen grand."

Wale smirked, as Harold wore a scowl. He knew that his cousin felt that he was smarter than him, and would probably cut a few corners, in regards to their payouts. Truthfully, if he didn't have Key, Harold would have succeeded in beating him for a few bucks. Would he have withheld all of Wale's money? No. But he definitely would've given just enough to let Wale see that the business was actually profitable. Luckily, Harold's wild ass cousin had scooped up a girl with some actual sense, rendering his educational advantage useless.

Harold narrowed his eyes at Keyasia. Initially upon meeting her, he'd assumed that she was merely another pretty face, coming along for the ride, as Wale's illegal hustle provided a pretty glamourous lifestyle. Of course, his presumptions had been debunked a minute ago, and he had half the mind to ask her if she had any sisters just like her. However, his curiosity remained mere thoughts, because history had taught him that Wale would explode on him, if he even thought that he was looking at Keyasia in a disrespectful manner. Still, Harold couldn't help fantasizing about finding his own version of a Keyasia; a chick who was the complete package.

Key stood there, looking radiating. Wearing a simple black mini skirt and cropped top get-up, her curves were jaw dropping. Her hair was framing her face, and was adorned with soft curls, cascading down to the top of her round backside. Her brown thighs were super thick, but also well defined, and toned. Although, her look was soft and inviting, her presence was always huge in the room, even when she wasn't speaking. Yep, Harold definitely needed his own version of a Keyasia.

While Key held her cell in her hand, it rang. Checking out the screen, she saw that Josairah was calling her. "Bae, I'ma step outside, and talk to Josairah," she announced. "I'll be back."

"Okay," Wale answered, as she left the office.

Harold grabbed a chair, and sat down. "I'ma go to the bank, and grab the rest of your money today."

Wale nodded.

He folded his arms across his chest. "But I see that you and ya lil' mama are back on good terms. I remember a few months back you said that you were done with her."

"Aye, you know how that is. Break up to make up, but we done with all that bullshit."

Harold smiled. "You said fuck that, huh? Decided you was gonna keep her smart ass around. Her ass don't miss a thing," he grumbled.

"She's on her job like she's supposed to be," Wale bragged.

Harold gave him a weird look.

"What, nigga? Why are you looking at me like that?"

"Ever since yall made up all those months back, you seem different. She aint got you going soft, does she?"

Wale heartily chuckled. "This nigga asked me if she got me going soft. Says the nigga who's scared to walk out into the parking lot by his self at night. I can't make this shit up. I swear."

"Aw, there you go." Harold waved him off. "I'm just saying, man. I'm fully aware that me and you are two different people. I can't even compare apples to oranges. But I noticed that you are different. You used to be on some wild shit. Twenty four seven. And now you're calmer. I haven't heard about you having beef on the streets. Meeko claimed that you don't really go to the clubs with them, anymore. I mean, damn, I never thought I'd see the day."

"Yall niggas be gossiping like some bitches. Overthinking and shit. I go out, but I'm my own man. Ion have to fall off in the club every time the rest of them niggas choose to. And besides, being with my bitch all day versus some hard heads is beneficial. Now, you think about that, while you run to the bank to grab the money you owe me." He winked.

"Corinthian, come here," Keyasia commanded, as she barged back into the room.

"What's up?" Wale stood up, and followed her out the door.

She spun around, facing him. "Josairah's about to pull up. She's going to leave her car in the lot, and we're gonna go to my cousin's kickback."

"What cousin?" Wale grimaced.

"You know, Little Jaylen."

"Oh, the spot ya *people* like to hang at, huh?"

She sighed heavily. "Corinthian, please don't start."

"I aint starting," he denied, as his mind wandered. "But, yeah, go'on go. I'll see you back at the crib."

She hesitated. That had been too easy. "So, you're cool, right?"

"Yeah, I'm straight. Come on. Let me walk you outside."

"Okay…" she squinted her eyes, wondering what he was thinking. "Let's go."

She led the way, as they ambled through the store. For a second, Wale lost his train of thought, as he watched her hips sway left to right. Sometimes he swore that Key's ass was a gift specifically made for him, sent directly from God.

Once outside they noticed that Josairah had already arrived. Key twisted to her Range, as Josairah parked next to it.

"What's up, Belly?" Key smiled, as she watched Josairah wiggle from underneath her steering wheel.

Wale leaned against the Range, as he observed Josairah. Meeko had been going on and on about him and her getting together. He was claiming that she was having his baby, but something was clearly off about the situation. Up until recently, Josairah had been avoiding Meeko like he had the Black Plague. Needless to say, that was highly unusual behavior for a woman supposedly carrying a man's child. Then Meeko didn't even know the baby's due date,

Promiscuous Girl: Keyasia and Wale

which further aroused suspicion. Long story short, Wale was having a hard time believing that the baby was actually for Meeko, but he'd kept his opinions to himself.

"How you doing," he spoke, as Josairah stepped to the passenger side of the Range Rover. He couldn't deny that pregnant looked good on her. She appeared to be at least eight of nine months, had glowing skin, healthy hair, and was all baby.

"Fine," Josairah replied coyly.

"So, what are you and my cousin having? A boy or a girl?" he quizzed.

"Umm, *I'm* having a boy," she stressed making sure to exclude Meeko out of the equation.

"Damn. You cold, man. Don't be showing my kinfolk no love."

Josairah hunched her shoulders, before climbing into the truck. "That's what he has a mama for."

He was tickled with her feistiness, always appreciating a smart mouth. From what he could tell about Josairah, she seemed intelligent, and a tad high maintenance. Meeko was sometimes simple minded, having a one track mind, fascinated by the look of things. He never talked about what women made him feel, or what they brought to the table. It was always about their looks, or what they wore. All superficial things. However, Josairah didn't strike him as a chick who'd want that kind of guy as her man. And she unquestionably didn't seem too enthused whenever Meeko was mentioned. It was painful to see, but she just wasn't in to him.

"I'll call you later," Keyasia promised, before sliding into her truck.

Nicole Jackson

Promenading around her opened door, preventing her from closing it, he glowered down at her. "You about to go kick it, huh, hot girl?"

Immediately, she knew that he was on some bullshit. That was the only time he referred to her as a hot girl. "Corinthian, don't make it sound like that. I'm only going to hang with some friends and family. Most of them go to TSU, and I'm sure it's gonna be laid back. I'll probably be back at the townhouse, before ten tonight."

"Yeah, okay," he lowered his head, kissing her lips.

Gripping his head, she slipped her tongue into his mouth. Passionately, she explored his mouth, until he produced a moan. She then released him, coming up for air. Lewdly, she gripped his erection through his True Religion jeans.

"Why you playing with me, Keyasia?" he grinned, as his hazel greens sparkled, while he allowed her to grope him.

"No, why you playing with me? Acting like I aint got all I need, right here in my hand," she rebutted, giving him bedroom eyes.

"Uh, did yall forget that I'm here?" Josairah spoke up.

Key kept her eyes trained on Wale. "My bad, girl, but let me handle my womanly duties, right quick."

Wale hungrily licked his lips. "Come here, Keyasia. Let me talk to you in the store for a second."

Her clit thumped. "No, Corinthian. I have to go. I'm not about to let you fuck me in the bathroom again. That damn hand soap burns my coochie, and I aint about to walk around smelling like a pail of cum."

Nicole Jackson

"What the fuck?" Josairah mumbled, feeling like she was watching the intro to a hardcore porno.

He chuckled. "Well, let me get a few pumps. I won't bust."

She giggled. "Hell no." she released his stiffness. "I'll see you later."

He sucked his teeth. "You on that bullshit. Teasing a nigga."

"Uh huh. Yeah, I know."

He stepped out of the doorway, closing the door for her. "You be good, man. And tell my nigga Lil' Jaylen that I said what's up."

Key pursed her lips, feeling as though he was being sarcastic. As far as she knew, Wale didn't know Jaylen like that. "Whatever." She started her engine.

He stepped back, before she backed out of the spot. He watched the Range exit out of the lot, before dialing a number on his phone. "She must think I'm crazy," he mumbled to himself. "I'ma always stay two steps ahead."

Chapter 31

"Keyasia, you talking all that shit, but I bet you won't take another shot."

Key rolled her eyes at Jaylen Junior. Every time she'd hang at his home, he'd try to get her drunk. He'd been living in the home his father owned for a few years, and all his college buddies, and cousins loved chilling there. Key hadn't been there in quite a while, and was now making up for lost time.

"Jaylen, you must not know me. I aint never scared, nigga," Key slurred, before downing two shots of tequila back to back.

Little Jah chuckled. "Jaylen, nigga, you love to see people shit faced."

"Hell, yeah," Amir Junior agreed, as he gripped a pool stick. "But he's the main one who can't hold his liquor."

Keyasia giggled, before using her pool stick to take a shot on the pool table in the middle of Jaylen's dining room. From the beginning she'd known that there was a possibility that her ex would be there. Jaylen Junior and Amir Junior had been friends for years, and when Key was still with Amir, they'd often come there, use one of the extra rooms, and fuck the night away. Therefore, she'd hesitated in accepting Jaylen's invitation, but ultimately decided that she wouldn't allow Amir to deter her from hanging with people she loved.

Surprisingly, Amir had been on his best behavior, causing her to let her guard down. Of course, he'd voiced the fact that he'd missed her, but had been respectful of boundaries. They'd all been able to laugh freely, without tension in the air. It undoubtedly gave Keyasia hope that one day she and Amir would get to a place of being friends again. Regardless, of their relationship not working out, they'd known each other for years, even before they were in a relationship. So although, Key was no longer in love with him, she still had love for him. And if Amir was willing to accept, and respect the fact that she'd moved on, they could definitely be cool.

"Key, you can't play pool, drunk or sober," Little Kevin teased. He'd just gotten there, although it was approaching midnight. He'd come through with his girlfriend, Talia, hoping to eventually creep off to one of those backrooms and have his way with her.

"I bet that I can beat yo ass," Keyasia challenged her brother.

"You wish. I aint poking you, so I aint got no reason to let you win. So, put your money where your mouth at."

Key scratched the side of her neck. "Well, I left my money at home."

Kevin snickered, knowing she was lying. "Yeah, right. You know that I was gonna beat that ass." He glanced around. "But where is Josairah? I thought you said that she was riding over here with you?"

"She's in the room sleep," Jahrein Junior spoke up.

Kevin narrowed his eyes. "You sho' be keeping up with her. You gon keep ya BM close, huh?"

Everyone laughed.

"Yeah, I been meaning to ask you about that, Jah. Is that your baby or nah? Cause I'm beginning not to believe this story about her fucking with that other nigga," Amir added.

Keyasia eyeballed her cousin, awaiting his response.

Jah smirked, as he stroked his waves. "You really gon put me on the spot, huh?"

"Shit, I'm just asking," Amir shrugged.

Jah licked his lips. "According to my math…yeah, it's my baby. But yall keep this on the low. Cause I already know my mama gon kill me. At least I can chill in peace, until she gives birth. After that…" he shook his head. "Yall just pray that Raven don't strangle my ass to death."

Keyasia giggled. "For the first time, one of yall are being honest. All that damn sneaking and lying yall like to do. Don't make no sense."

"That's Josairah with all that shit. She does it so much that it's rubbing off on me."

"Well, what about ole boy?" Amir questioned. "The nigga that's supposed to be her baby daddy."

Jah shrugged. "What about him? His bitch ass aint taking care of no baby of mine. I just been letting Josairah get her shine on. I know her spiteful ass is still mad about Nancy, so she gives him some play. But fuck his pussy ass. The last time I saw him I threw my drink on him, and he was getting worked up about it. And I swear I was gonna slide his ass. Matter of fact, I'm itching to see him, cause I'll still pop his ass."

Keyasia smirked, as her cousin talked about Meeko. She'd heard about the incident with Jah and Meeko at Chacho's. Little Jah had allowed jealousy to get the best of him, and had tried to fight Meeko, because he was there with Josairah. Meeko had claimed that Jah was sticking his chest out, because he had an entourage with him. However, Keyasia knew better. She and Jah shared the same bloodline, and weren't afraid of too many things. Jah unquestionably would have behaved the same exact way if he'd been there alone. Meeko was simply looking for any excuse as to why he'd allowed a significantly younger cat to publicly embarrass him. He'd even gone as far as attempting to involve Wale, telling him how he was going to seriously hurt Key's cousin. Wale then promptly put Meeko in his place, making it clear that he wouldn't choose sides, and the only action he'd endorse was Meeko calling out Jah to fight. Anything beyond that would put everyone in a compromising position, and Wale wasn't for it.

"Freak hoes, freak, hoes. Bounce that ass make your knees touch your elbows. Free coke. Free dope. Lay it down. Niggas kicking in your front door…" Future blasted from Jaylen's stereo system, catching Key's attention.

"Ayeeeee!" she boasted, wagging her tongue. "That's my shit!" she yelled, as she twerked.

Amir smiled, as he watched her. He'd missed her vibrant personality tremendously. After that altercation with Wale she'd shut him completely out. No matter where they'd see each other, she had nothing to say, and would usually leave to avoid being in his presence for long. So, he'd nearly forgotten the type of energy she'd bring to any occasion. It was intoxicating, causing him to crave what they once had.

"Man," Amir drawled. "You know your ass can't dance," he jested.

Laughing, Key playfully shoved him. "Fuck you. You used to love it, remember? The first time I gave your ass a roll-up you asked me to be your girlfriend. I popped my booty on you, and changed the game."

"Akkeykeey," he mocked her laughing. "That shit aint that funny."

"But it is," she insisted. "Amir, why you bullshitting yourself?" she sat on the pool table, swinging her legs back and forth.

For a second he absently gazed at her, wanting to ask for another chance so badly, but he didn't want her attitude to switch up.

"What's up, boy?" Wale questioned, as he stepped next to Jaylen, who was standing near the entryway.

Jaylen grinned, before clasping hands with him. "Nothing, man. I thought you was bullshitting when you said that you was coming through."

Wale touched the tip of his nose. "Nah, I wouldn't bullshit you like that."

Jaylen nodded, knowing exactly why Wale had really come over. Keyasia was there, and Amir was known to visit. It wasn't hard to do the math, but that wasn't his business. He'd met Wale years back, after dating a cousin of his, and they had remained cool well after he and the cousin were done. Wale was cool in his eyes, therefore he was as welcome as anyone else in the house. Still, he didn't know if that was going to work in Key's favor, and definitely not Amir's.

"That's what' up," Jaylen commented. "If you drinking, then help yourself, man. We got plenty to go around."

Wale nodded, but it was obvious that he'd mentally checked out of the conversation, as he watched Keyasia.

She was sitting on the pool table, with her back to him. She was engrossed in a seemingly intimate conversation with Amir, as there were only inches of space between them. Amir was smiling from ear to ear, as she ran her mouth.

Jahrein, and Kevin paused the moment they'd realized that Wale had entered the room. They'd both witnessed him and Amir exchange blows, and were now bracing themselves for what was bound to be round two.

Wasting no time, Wale swaggered over to them, posting up directly in front of Keyasia, with his arms folded. Immediately, Keyasia's smile vanished.

"What's up, Keyasia? Don't let me interrupt you. It looked like you was in the middle of a funny joke, since everybody's all laughs, and shit."

She squinted. "Baby, what are you doing here?"

"I told you that Jaylen was my boy."

"Oh, okay. So, you came to check on me?" she asked with a slight slur.

"Yeah, you can say that." He nodded, cautiously inspecting her. "But how many drinks have you had, though?" his eyes shifted to Amir, who hadn't bothered to give her any physical space, despite the fact that he was standing there. "My nigga, can you give us some breathing room?"

Amir scowled. "Shit, I'm good right here, nigga. Make me move."

Keyasia whipped her head around, and glared at him. "Amir. Really?"

"Really, what? Fuck this nigga. Ion have no respect for him. Who the fuck is he supposed to be?"

"See…okay," she sighed, easing off the pool table. "Baby, let's step over here." She grabbed Wale's hand, hopping to pull him away from Amir. He wouldn't budge, though.

"Bitch ass nigga, I'm somebody you don't wanna see. On God, I'll rock your hoe ass to sleep. I already told you to stay away from my bitch. You think this a fuckin' game!" Wale roared. He was about look past Amir Sr. coming to him, wanting to squash the beef between him and his son. Due to Wale's relationship with Amir Sr. he'd vowed to let the tiff between Amir Jr. and himself go, under the condition that he'd respect that Keyasia was done with him, and keep his distance. However, Amir had apparently forgotten about their truce the minute he laid eyes on Key.

"You act like she's your fuckin' property!" Amir belted. "I been knowing her, before anybody knew you existed. So, you or no other nigga can control my interactions with her. I had her first, and I really don't give a fuck what nigga is laying claim to her today. I aint respecting nothing that came after me."

"Get yo bitch ass back!" Wale seethed, shoving Amir, sending him crashing into the wall.

Reacting, Amir charged at him, but Jah caught him in the nick of time. "Nah, man, chill out!"

Whatever tipsiness Keyasia had been experiencing wore off instantly. Swiftly, she stood in front of Wale. "Corinthian, don't do this. It's not that serious."

"Keyasia, get the fuck outta my face," he seethed, before looking past her. "Let his ass go, Jah. That nigga been asking for me to knock him out!"

Jaylen shook his head. "Amir, man, chill out."

Amir frowned. "Chill out?! The fuck you telling me to chill out for? Talk to his hoe ass. Why the fuck is he here, anyway?"

Jaylen furrowed his brows. "Nigga, you tripping. I know this man, just like I know you. And even if I didn't know him, he's with my cousin, so he'd still be welcome. If I fuck with her, the fuck I look like telling her that she can't bring her nigga around? You tripping. I'm a grown ass man, and can't no other nigga dictate who I'm cool with."

"Yeah, Amir, you tripping," Jah added.

"Baby, please let's go," Keyasia pleaded with Wale.

He nodded. "You know what, I'm gone burn, because this aint my house, and I'ma respect your shit, Jaylen. I'll catch your bitch ass in the streets, Amir." He glowered down at her. "Let's fuckin' go."

Keyasia hesitated. "I'll meet you at home, because I have to bring Josairah back to her car first."

"Man," he drawled. "I really aint trying to hear that shit. You leaving right muthafuckin' now." He bucked his eyes.

"Listen to his hoe ass nigga," Amir chattered, looking at Kevin. "You cool with him handling your sister like that?"

Frustrated, Jah stroked his waves. "Key, I got Josairah. I'll take her to her car. You can go ahead."

After grabbing her keys and phone off the pool table, Keyasia stomped out of the room. Wale tugged at his sagging jeans, as he followed closely behind her. Amir was fuming, as he was forced to see Key leave with another man. Angrily, he glared at his boys.

"Yall niggas switching sides on me, huh? I'm supposed to be your boy, yet you niggas is riding with him!"

"Man, go'on with that bullshit." Jaylen waved him off.

Kevin shook his head. "Amir, you on one tonight."

"What the fuck is you saying?" Amir spat.

"I'm saying that you are tripping. You my boy, and all, but that's my sister. You fucked up, and she moved to the next man. That's on your body. So, now, you wanna go off on us, because we aint backing you up. Like my sister can't kick it with her own people, because we don't wanna piss you off. That shit aint gon fly. Whether you like it or not, she's with that man, so he will come around. Really, you out of line for trying to make people choose between the two. Cause I aint on yours or Wale's side. I'm with my sister, because she's family, regardless. So, don't put yourself against her, because I swear you'll lose every time, fucking with me."

******

"Corinthian, do you hear me talking to you?"

Wale said nothing, as they made their way into the townhouse. Keyasia was determined to get him to understand that she was not trying to disrespect him. On the drive there, she'd had time to think, while she trailed his Lambo. Ever since they'd decided to put the past behind them, things between them had been smooth sailing. She'd been the happiest she'd ever been in young life, and she couldn't have this situation catapult them right back into a space they'd vowed to leave behind.

"Baby." She grabbed his hand, halting him. "Listen to me. I'm trying to explain to you that I wasn't doing anything…"

"Stop, Keyasia," he cut her off. "Ion wanna hear that bullshit."

"But it's not bullshit. I'm telling you that I don't give a damn about Amir. I don't know why he continued to stand there once you walked over."

"Oh, you know why," he contended.

"I don't," she denied.

Wale sucked his teeth. "That nigga stood there, because he feels like you're still his. Him backing up would mean that he's respecting the fact that you got a nigga. And we both know that he don't. He was standing there, because he wants you."

"But what does that have to do with me, Corinthian?" she whined.

"Why would you go somewhere if you know your ex will be there?'"

She frowned. "I mean, I don't know what you want from me. I wasn't at one of Amir's family member's houses, hoping that he wasn't there. I was at my cousin's. I can't help that Amir has a long-standing relationship with my family. Hell, he comes to my parent's house. So, tell me how I'm supposed to avoid him. Why won't you trust me?"

He breathed, "I do trust you. It's him I don't trust."

"But what does that have to do with me?"

"I'm saying, if I was him, and you was with another nigga…I wouldn't let yall be in peace. On God. I'd do everything in my power to tear that shit up. I wouldn't give a fuck about respecting shit, so I can't help but think he'd do the same," he admitted. "But you right. You can't always avoid being around that man. And honestly, I'm not mad at you."

She gradually smiled. "That's all I want. I can't let this turn into what happened last time."

"It won't." he shook his head. "I wouldn't let that dumb ass shit shake us. Really, nothing should be able to do that."

She nodded. "But you still don't give me the benefit of the doubt, because if you did you wouldn't have come. You need to know that you don't have to keep a watchful eye on me like that. On my life, I wouldn't do anything to jeopardize our relationship."

"I hear you, and I'm not gonna bullshit you. I'll probably always be a little uneasy about you being around him. I'll probably always make my way around whenever you're in his presence. I'm not gonna lie, but that don't mean that I'm tripping with you, either. That just means that if he's there, then know that I'm coming too. Then we'll see how much conversation he'll have for *us*."

She tittered. "I guess I have to accept that."

"You might as well. You aint got a choice," he grinned.

"That's okay." She wrapped her arms around his neck, kissing his lips.

He gripped her ass with both hands, easing her skirt up. "We gone be alright, though." He pecked her lips. "As long as we talk shit out, and don't allow nobody to come between us, it'll be us against the world."

Aggressively, she reached into his jeans, and grabbed his hard-on. "I know." She whipped his dick out, and commenced to stroking him. Lowering down into a squat, she jerked him off with both hands. Flicking her tongue, she licked the tip of his dick. "The way that I love you...aint nobody changing that," she proclaimed, before taking him into her mouth.

"Oh, fuck." His eyes involuntarily closed, as his head fell back.

Rocking her head back and forth, she sucked him up rapidly. It wasn't long before his knees became weak. "Wait." He eased himself out of her mouth. "Fuck that. Stand up."

Obediently, she did as she was told. Spotting a chair, he dragged it over, before yanking his jeans to the floor, and sitting down. "I want you to ride this dick, until you cum." He stroked himself.

"Okay," she motioned towards him.

"Nah, man. Take off them clothes. I wanna see it all."

"Okay," she giggled, as she stripped down to nothing. She posed in front of him. "Like this?"

"Hell, yeah," he breathed. "Like that."

"Or like this?" she twirled around, and made her ass clap.

"Uh, come do that on my dick."

"Okay." She sat on his lap, easing onto his fat head. "But you got it wrong. This is *my* dick." She sat completely down on him. Leaning forward, she placed both palms on the floor, and began working her hips.

Nicole Jackson

Wale gripped her hips, as she fucked him upside down. "Got damn this pussy good. You doing acrobats and shit." He slapped her ass.

Keyasia was popping her pussy on his stick, becoming so wet that they could both hear it. The position may have been awkward, but it was directly stimulating her clit. She rolled her hips hurriedly, as her butt cheeks wobbled.

"Damn," he grunted, as their skin clapped. "You better slow down, before I drop a load in you," he warned.

Seemingly encouraging him to bust, she picked up the pace. "Do what you do, then," she panted.

"Ahhhh," he growled, as released inside of her. "Shit."

Keyasia kicked into third gear, refusing to give up, as she continued to ride his dick. "Uh," she moaned, enjoying every second.

Wale grinned. "You be knowing what you doing. Always trying to put the pussy on me. That's where I fucked up. Letting you fuck on the first night," he laughed. "After one night, a nigga was in love."

Chapter 32

Keyasia lied casually on the couch, sick to her stomach. She was clutching a pack of saltine crackers, as her phone sat on her face. "So, how's the baby?"

"Girl, laying here sleep. It's sad. Even when he's sleep he looks just like his raggedy ass daddy," Josairah responded.

Keyasia tittered. "Bitch, aint nothing raggedy about my damn cousin."

"Whatever," Josairah breathed. "Huh?" she spoke to someone in the background. "This is Keyasia. No, I'm not talking to him. Jah, I told you that I wasn't talking to him," she explained.

Key rolled her eyes. Ever since Josairah had given birth to her son, things had changed rapidly. It was now a known fact that Jahrein was her son's father, their parents all knew the truth, and Meeko did as well. So now, Josairah and Jah were parenting together, and slowly falling back into some form of a relationship, although they were denying it. However, it was evident, as he questioned Josairah, completely interrupting her conversation.

"Tell that nigga I don't have a dick over here. With his jealous ass," Keyasia instigated.

"Hello," Jah spoke into the phone.

"Yeah."

"Aye, Key, she's gonna call you back."

"Really, Jah? How are you just gonna interrupt us?"

Silence.

"Hello?" Key uttered, before removing the phone from her face, discovering he'd hung up. "I know that muthafucka didn't," she grumbled to herself, as the front door popped open.

"It's hotter than fuckin' fish grease out there, main," Wale mumbled, as he stepped into the house, followed by Meeko, and Craven.

"Hell, yeah," Craven agreed. "Huh?" he spoke into his cell. "No, I was talking to Wale. We just made it to his house. Yeah, Keyasia in here. Man, she don't wanna talk to you. Quit playing with me. Where you going?"

Meeko hadn't said a word, as he wore a solemn expression on his face.

Key sat up on the couch. "That must be Jazel."

Craven nodded, as he sat on the recliner. "I'm serious, man. You aint high, are you? Jazel, stop playing with me, man."

Keyasia smiled, listening to Craven worry about every move Jazel made. It was funny how he'd do him, but try to keep her under his thumb. Well, actually, after Key thought about it, Craven had been rather chill lately, primarily spending time with Jazel, leaving little to no time for any other chick. Then when he wasn't with her, he'd have her on the phone, but Key found it odd that most of time he'd question her about getting high.

"You can call her all you want. That hoe is still gonna do her," Meeko grumbled, as he stood near the couches.

Keyasia glanced up at him. "You wanna sit down?" she asked him.

He frowned, looking at her like she had shit on her face. "Nah, I'm good."

"Here." Wale approached her, handing her the tacos from the Jack-in-the-Box she'd requested, along with a black bag from the store.

"Thank you," she grinned, quickly removing one of the tacos from its wrapping.

Wale then flopped down onto the couch, sitting next to her. He glanced up, realizing that Meeko was just standing there. "Nigga, are you gonna sit down, or what?"

Meeko paused for a second, seemingly glaring at Keyasia. "Yeah." He sat at the far end of the sectional.

Keyasia frowned. "What the hell is wrong with him?"

Wale stroked his goatee. "I don't know. That nigga been tripping, lately. Ever since your friend told him that her baby aint his, he's been acting like he's mad at the world."

"Oh," Key bit into her taco. "Okay."

He cut his eyes at her. "Them hoes are good, huh?"

"Yep," she happily chewed.

"It's crazy how you didn't like 'em, then you liked them, then you didn't, and now you like 'em again."

"Yeah, that is crazy, but what are you trying to say?"

He glared at her.

"What?" she lifted both brows.

"Look in the bag, Keyasia."

After biting another piece of taco, she opened the black bag, realizing that there was a pregnancy test inside along with the apple juice she'd asked for. "Really, Corinthian?"

"Really Corinthian what? Go take it."

"Why?"

He stared at her.

She rolled her eyes, although she knew why. Her period was late, she was having morning sickness, and she was eating anything that didn't eat her. Truthfully, she was surprised that it had taken him this long to catch on. Hell, she was nearly three months along, but had officially known for about a month. After aborting two of his kids, talking about pregnancy with him made her clam up, therefore she'd been patiently waiting on him to notice on his own.

"How long have you been feeling like this?" she asked, as she absently fiddled with the box.

"Honestly," he tucked his lips into his mouth. "For almost three months. I was waiting on you to say something, but I'm done with playing with you. Even my grandma asked me yesterday how far along you was, talking about you showing." He leaned over, whispering. "You don't think I notice how round your belly is when you're riding my dick?"

She scratched her head, as she shrugged. "I don't know. Is that why you've been falling asleep, palming it?"

"What you think?"

"I was just waiting for your birthday. It was gonna be your gift."

"What?" he narrowed his eyes.

"I was gonna tell you on your birthday, as a gift," she reiterated.

"Tell me what?"

"That we're having a baby," she giggled.

He lifted his chin. "Why you sitting here playing with me, Keyasia?"

"You think I'm playing? Boy, please." She grabbed her phone, and scrolled through a few things. "Look." She displayed a photo of a t-shirt that read: *I aint buying Corinthian a gift. His ass better be glad with this baby. The fuck?*

He fell over with laughter. "Get the fuck outta here. Where the fuck was you going with that damn shirt? And then you got my real name on it. You really are crazy, man."

"What's so funny? I'm wearing it at your birthday party. What you thought?"

"Stop playing with me, man. If you pregnant, then let me see the paperwork," he grinned from ear to ear.

"Okay." She eased off the couch, and lifted one of the cushions. Feeling around, she was able to locate her pictures. "See." She pulled out several ultrasounds.

Craven stuck his neck out, being nosy. "Well, I'll be damned."

"Let me see." Wale practically snatched the ultrasounds out of her hand. "This shit crazy." He thumbed through the photos.

Keyasia studied him, and swore that his eyes were a little misty. "Bae…"

"What's up?" he glanced at her.

"You about to cry?"

Craven howled with laughter. "Ole friendly ass nigga!"

Wale tucked his lips into his mouth, as he reclined into the couch. "Fuck you, nigga."

Keyasia snickered. "Give me the pictures. I'ma put them up." She held out her hand.

"Watch out, man. I got them." He pulled the ultrasounds back.

Key was tickled. "So, I can't have my stuff back?"

"Nah." He shook his head. "And why the fuck would you go to the doctor, without telling me?"

"You were out of town, when I went."

He frowned. "Don't do that shit no more, Keyasia."

"Shit, she probably had that other nigga go with her," Meeko spoke up. "You see how her and her friend get down."

Keyasia's head snapped around. "What?"

Meeko smirked. "Don't trip. I was just bullshitting with you."

"Nigga, who the fuck is you playing with, though?" Wale sat up. "What her friend did to you aint got nothing to do with her. So, you better watch your fuckin' mouth, cause I take off on disrespectful muthafuckas. Family or not, nigga."

"I know your pussy whipped ass gone take up for her," Meeko seethed. "The fuck you cool with a bitch, after she basically helped her friend run game on a nigga? The bitch was fuckin' with her cousin, and you mean to tell me that she didn't know?"

"Whoa, whoa, who the fuck are you referring to as a bitch?" Keyasia snapped. "And don't be mad at me, because my friend was preoccupied with some real nigga dick. Your fuckin' weak ass wanted that baby to be yours so bad that you was ignoring facts. She fucked you once, never told you when she was due, and never gave you any of that pregnant pussy. Shit, the only muthafucka you need to be mad at is ya daddy for releasing such a dumb muthafucka from his balls. Ya mammy should've swallowed your lame ass."

Meeko shot to his feet. "You need to check this bitch, Wale!"

Casually, Wale stood up. He tapped the bridge of his nose, before going berserk. Meeko was defenseless, as Wale's fist plowed into his mouth. "Who the fuck is you talking to?!" he raged, gripping Meeko by the rim of his shirt. Viciously, he repeatedly hammered into his face, as he drove him up against the wall.

Keyasia was shocked at how violent he was with his own cousin. He was throwing haymakers, as Meeko leaked blood all over the floor. Both Craven and Keyasia stood back, refusing to interfere, as Meeko got the daylights beat out of him. Delivering the final lethal blow, Meeko hit the floor with a loud thud.

"Awww," Meeko released, with his mouth wide open, crawling to feet, while blood spilled from his mouth.

Snatching his pistol from the small of his back, Wale held the gun at his side. "You got something else you wanna get off your chest, dog? Let me know."

Meeko staggered a bit, attempting to catch his bearings.

"Craven, take his bitch ass home, man," Wale ordered.

"Shit, that fuck nigga aint finna get in my car with all that blood on him," Craven quipped.

Meeko grimaced. "Bitch ass nigga, don't make me pull yo hoe card, ole follow the leader ass nigga."

"Shit, nigga, pull my hoe card. I wanna hear this."

"It aint hard. Tell them how yo weak ass is going home to a fucking sherm head. You act like you really on yo shit, when you really hustling backwards. As soon as you hit a lick that bitch at home goes on a binge, smoking all the wet and snorting all the powder she can find."

"Fuck you!" Craven belted, before charging at Meeko, piecing him up, and knocking him to the floor.

Once again Meeko crawled to his feet. "Fuck the both of you niggas. Yall some weak ass fools for these hoes yall lay with. And I wear them bitches gon be yall downfall. Just wait and see."

"Nigga, take your bitch ass on, before I kill you!" Craven blurted.

"Fuck yall! I mean that shit!" Meeko lashed, before storming out of the house.

Both Wale and Craven were fuming, as Keyasia stepped over to lock the door, before twirling to face them. She hated seeing her boo upset like that. "Well, as I quote

Becky, 'He can rest assured that he's off my Christmas list.'"

Wale cracked a smile. "You play too fuckin' much."

"I know, but the baby doesn't like to hear daddy upset." She rubbed her belly.

He stepped to her, placing his hand over hers. "The baby, huh? I still can't believe this shit."

She gazed up into his eyes. "Is it what you wanted?"

He nodded, before gently kissing her lips. "More than anything in this world."

She giggled. "Well, damn. The baby gets more love than me, huh?"

"Nah, without you I never would have wanted this. It had to be with you. Nobody else would do."

******

"Toot that ass up," Wale gritted, as he gripped her waist. "Don't run from the dick now."

Keyasia clawed at the satin sheets, uselessly, as he drove deeply into her. He was showing no mercy, as he delivered long strokes. Due to the news of her pregnancy, he would only use baby-safe positions, and doggy-style was his absolute favorite. He loved powerfully plowing into her, serving her every inch he had to offer.

"Baby, it's too biiiiiig," she whined, as she felt his balls slap against her ass.

"Take it," he commanded, slapping her ass.

"I'm trying," she gritted her teeth, as she bounced her cheeks.

Multitasking, Wale grabbed the remote to the TV, increasing the volume, after seeing something about a pharmacy burglary flash across the screen. Still, he eased in and out of Key, as she arched her back.

"Reporting live from northwest Houston outside of a pharmacy that has just been burglarized. Owners claim that thieves stole thousands upon dollars' worth of medicine, depleting their entire inventory of prescription drugs, including Xanax, and codeine which are both popular drugs sold on the streets. Surveillance cameras were able to capture four suspects wearing ski masks entering the building…"

Wale stopped stroking, as he recognized Meeko's Polo hoodie on one of the assailants. "Aint this about a bitch?" he spewed, as he pulled out of Keyasia.

"What?" she immediately sat up.

"Man," he drawled, as he grabbed his cell. "That bitch ass Meeko just hit our lick!"

Keyasia glanced at the TV. "That is that Polo jacket he was wearing the other day."

"Hell, yeah. And that's the job we've been working on for weeks. We was supposed to hit that bitch tomorrow, and he knew it. I mean, we did all the leg work, while he just sat back. And now his bitch ass is eating off of our work. Then we had the pharmacist in on it, so he's expecting a cut, and I'm willing to bet that he aint gon believe that we wasn't in on this shit."

"That's crazy." Keyasia shook her head.

"That nigga better hope that I get my money back from his ass. Because I swear I'll blast his ass. I mean, I'll let him live, but he'll definitely lose a limb. I aint finna play about my money." Wale called out on his cell.

"Nigga, I was just about to call you," Big Block answered. "Your fuckin' lil' cousin just pulled a hoe ass stunt."

"I know. I just saw the shit on the news."

"You'd think he'd be smart enough not to wear that fuckin' hoodie that we all recognize."

"Exactly. But I got something for his ass. Meet me at his house in about a hour. We going in, regardless if he there or not."

"For sho'. I'll be there with my fuckin' crowbar."

Wale smiled. "Already. You know what it is, nigga."

Keyasia sat shaking her head, realizing that they were going to have a serious talk. Enough was enough. He needed to begin thinking of something else to put all his energy into. That whole burglary hustle was getting old. Quick.

******

"Fuck this nigga. He aint playing fair, and I aint either," Big Block spat, as he threw several pairs of Meeko's Jordan's into a trash bag.

"Shit, fuck it." Wale shrugged. "Take all his shit. Let him start over. Build his own hustle from the ground up to buy new shit." He loaded all the pills Meeko had stashed into another trash bag.

For an hour, they'd been there, going back and forth to Big Block's Escalade, loading anything of real value out of Meeko's condo. Being petty, Big Block had taken all of Meeko's designer shoes and clothes, although he couldn't fit the clothes. More than likely, he'd give it all to a few of his nephews, who'd gladly accept the clothes, especially since half of the clothing still had the price tags attached.

"It seems like them niggas never had a chance to divide this shit up. It's too much shit here for them to have sold any. My guess is they didn't even have a real buyer lined up for all this, yet," Wale assumed.

"Probably not," Big Block grumbled, as he stuffed Meeko's platinum chains into a bag. "But that's their bad."

"True," Wale agreed. "But that nigga is lucky that I don't have time to sit here, and wait for his bitch ass to walk through the door. Cause I still got a bullet with his name on it."

Big Block cut his eyes at him. "So, you'd really shoot your cousin?"

"Yeah." Wale shrugged. "Just in the leg or something. Nothing too major."

"Get the fuck out of here," Big Block chuckled, as he threw the trash bag over his shoulder.

"Nigga, I'm serious," Wale laughed, as he dragged the last bag out of the condo, before pulling the door closed behind them.

Together they traveled back to the truck, tossed the bags inside, before casually pulling out of the lot. They knew that Meeko would be sick once he discovered that he'd been hit, and they were both hoping he'd bring the static, because they were more than ready to put a foot in his ass.

Chapter 33

"Uh, can you be still?"

Keyasia bit into her Jack-in-the-Box taco, while her beautician, Shan, tried her best to work around it. "I'm trying," she answered with a mouth filled with food.

"Damn, when are you not feeding your face?" Jazel questioned, as she sat next to Key in Big Tasha's chair.

"Fuck you," Keyasia stuck her tongue out.

"Let her eat. The baby must be hungry," Tam added, as she sat in an empty chair, waiting to get her hair done by Shan next.

Jazel rolled her eyes. "Bitch, please. The baby is hungry my ass. This hoe done let Wale fill her head up with that bullshit. He feed her ass all day, trying to put some weight on her. She gon fuck around, and get big as a house."

"Bitch, in your dreams. And even if I did, I bet Corinthian would still love every inch of my fat ass."

"Yeah, cause you put some blood is his spaghetti," Jazel tittered. "The way he be sniffing after you just aint natural."

Tam smiled. "Oh, hush, Jazel. I remember you and Craven being the same way at first."

"Yeah, until reality set in," she grumbled.

Key lifted a brow. "What reality?"

Jazel pursed her lips. "Just stuff. Niggas change after you lose a couple of their babies. After the third miscarriage, his ass started fucking around…and I went back to getting fucked up," she confessed.

Keyasia swallowed, feeling guilty. She'd killed her babies, while Jazel struggled to hold one. Now Meeko's little outburst all made sense. Fertility issues was probably driving Jazel to get high, and causing problems between her and Craven. "Girl, you don't really believe that having miscarriages made Craven cheat, do you?"

"No, it didn't," Tam spoke up. "If anything it was her disappearing for days, driving him crazy. I've watched that boy search this city high and low for her. Jazel would be the one tripping, saying that he's gonna leave her, after she'd lose a baby. His ass was never going anywhere. It be all in her head, but they supposedly got their shit together. I keep telling her that I know a specialist that can probably help her carry a baby full term."

A tear slipped from Jazel's eye, and she quickly wiped it away. "Tam, aint nobody worried about no damn baby."

"Girl, please," Tam pursed her lips. "Tell that lie to somebody else. But I'm serious, I've done some research, because I really want you to hold this one."

"Wait, wait," Keyasia halted them. "What do you mean about hold this one? Jazel is pregnant?"

"Yeah," Tam revealed. "That's why Craven's been keeping her so close. He's scared that she's gonna get fucked up, while she's carrying."

"Ooh," Key's jaw dropped. "That's crazy. How far along are you, Jazel?"

"Four months," Jazel wiped her eyes again.

"Well, why didn't you say something?"

"Because. I'm tired of having to announce it, only to lose it a little while later. I get tired of people coming up to me, asking where my baby at. That shit irks me, so I didn't do all that this time. I wasn't even worried about it. Craven was the one who had to go buy the test, and shit. He knew before me, and is being all optimistic even though this is our sixth damn pregnancy. He keeps saying that he got a good feeling about this one, and I'm just like whatever. He be getting on my nerves, wanting to be under a bitch all day, and know where I'm at twenty-four seven. I swear I be wanting to cuss his ass out. He's being all friendly, and in love now, but all that shit gone change when this baby falls out of my ass like all the rest," she became choked up. "Hold up, Tasha." She stood up. "I gotta pee, right quick." She hurried to the back of the beauty shop.

Big Tasha shook her head. "That's my girl, I be rooting for her, but I swear she's her own worst enemy. I aint gon lie, a lot of people don't know what Craven be going through with her. And no matter what that nigga stays on solid ground. Never leaving her side, but she can't see it."

"True," Tam agreed.

"Well, she's been there for him too. Let's not forget," Shan added. "I remember how she would be in them streets, stealing, helping him set niggas up. Anything for him to get on his feet. That bitch even took one of his cases. I mean, he didn't want her to, but she did it. So, like I said, that loyalty shit goes both ways with them, and if she's going through something, then his ass needs to ride it out. She would."

"Also true," Tam commented.

Nicole Jackson

Keyasia simply nodded, not having anything to say. Everything uttered was news to her, and she didn't feel that it was her place to speak on the situation.

"We done all been through it with these niggas of ours," Tam continued. "I know me and Big Block have had our moments. Shit, we still do."

"I know, right," Keyasia co-signed.

Before Tam could say another word, her cell went off. "Hello," she answered the phone. "Wait, wait, slow down. Say that again," she urged. "They shot Big Block?!" she sprung to her feet. "When?! Where?!" she shouted. "I'm on my way up there." She ended the call.

Keyasia sat at the edge of her seat. "What happened?"

Tam held her mouth with her hand, while her face turned beet red, and tears streamed down her face. "Some…some niggas from Greenspoint just shot him. They was claiming he stole their pills."

"That's fucked up." Keyasia stood up. "Let's go see if he's alright."

"Yeah, you and Jazel go with her," Shan urged. "We'll be right here, praying for him."

******

Keyasia sat watching Wale intently, as he paced back and forth. They'd just left the hospital, where Big Block was clinging to life. He'd been shot three times; one bullet puncturing his lungs. With all the damage his body had sustained the doctors weren't sure if he'd live past the next few days.

Nicole Jackson

"What you saying, nigga?!" he shouted into his phone. "I don't give a fuck! That nigga go too. From this day forth, Meeko aint no cousin of mine."

Keyasia slid her tongue across her teeth, as she processed everything that had happened. Meeko was now public enemy number one, as he'd weaseled his self onto everyone's shit list from Wale to Little Jah. Just a few weeks prior, he'd shown up to a family's function where Key had foolishly brought Josairah, thinking that Meeko wouldn't be present. He'd approached Josairah aggressively, and Little Jah stepped in, in the nick of time. Meeko was floored, after his cousins idly stood back, while Little Jahrein whupped his ass. And now there was talk that Meeko was associated with the guys from Greenspoint who'd gunned Big Block down. Supposedly, Meeko had been running with the dudes, and they'd helped him break into the pharmacy, which was why they'd approached Big Block over their stolen pills. The altercation quickly escalated, leading to Big Block getting shot, right outside of a barber shop in Greenspoint.

The world was truly small, because those Greenspoint dudes were allegedly the same ones who'd attempted to rob Taraj. Apparently, Meeko had been running with the dudes, hitting licks with them. Therefore, when Wale and Big Block had broken into Meeko's condo, they'd taken from those cats, as well. Of course, Wale didn't care about their perspective, because it was his work they were eating from. Clearly, there was no honor amongst thieves, as Meeko allowed the almighty dollar push him to turn his back on the very men he'd hustled with for years.

Key thought about what he wanted to say to Wale, when she noticed that Josairah was calling. "Hello," she answered the phone.

"Hey," Josairah sighed into the phone.

"You're on your way to school, trick?" Keyasia questioned.

Josairah gripped the steering wheel of her car. "Yep. What are you doing up this early? You took the semester off to deal with getting fat, remember?"

"Bitch, stop playing with me."

Josairah giggled. "Uh huh, aint no fun when the rabbit got the gun, huh? Your ass over there trying to hide a belly, but think I'm crazy."

"I don't know why you keep saying that. I'm not hiding anything, and it damn sure aint no belly over here. But anyway, what's up with you and ole boy from school?" Keyasia asked, knowing that Josairah and Little Jah were on bad terms, although she was sure that they'd end up together again. It was evident at this point that they were in love, but Key figured that it was something they'd have to realize on their own.

"Oh, Gary is cool. Every day he brings me lunch, and walks me to my car after my last class. We've gone on a few dates, and he keeps me laughing…and he has a big black dick," she grumbled.

Keyasia gasped. "Josairah, no! You fucked him?"

"Yeah, a few times," she admitted easily.

"Girl, girl, girl. Sometimes I wonder if the light is on upstairs with you. I really thought you was on a little get-back, playing with Jah's teammate. But you really fucked the nigga. This shit will not end well, and you're asking for tsunami bullshit to come your way," Key preached. She'd encouraged Josairah, who was now attending local TSU, to put something on her cousin's mind in the form of another guy, but definitely didn't mean for her to grab someone so close to Little Jah. That was asking for trouble.

"How is that? I'm single. You think Jah walks around campus, avoiding certain broads because of what I'll feel?"

Keyasia grabbed her forehead, realizing that her girl was cutting up in her absence at school. "Jah-Jah, you're missing the point. We're talking about someone he has to deal directly with. They're on the same fuckin' team, and this will cause major conflict. There's no way around it. And I swear you're lucky that I don't have a nigga on that team, because I'd have to beat your ass. You could fuck up everything. Its way too many niggas out here for you fuck that close to Jah. He's gonna lose his shit when he finds out. Watch."

"Fuck him," Josairah spat bitterly.

Keyasia tittered. "Bitch, you really are evil. You did this shit on purpose, didn't you?"

"So, what if I did? He wanted to play with me, and now I'ma play with him. Have his ass crying," she scoffed.

"I don't know, Josairah. I think you might be playing with fire right now. Keeping it real, he's been calling asking me if I know who you're dealing with. Like on some he's gonna turn up up on you, and beat your ass type shit."

"What? I wish he would."

"Yeah, I told him that he better not do anything stupid, but he didn't seem to be hearing me. Hell, I think he's gonna roll up on your ass today."

"Shit, let him run up if he wants to."

Nicole Jackson

"Whatever. And I think he'd actually lay hands on you, if he caught you with the Gary dude. I really think you need to chill. Cause you know damn well that you don't want that boy."

"Key, I hear you, but I'm not ending anything to appease Jah. He can be in his feelings, just like I was, while he had me walking around looking stupid. Had me thinking these hoes were all hating, when he was really fucking them. I bet everybody had a really good laugh at me."

"Aye, everybody plays the fool sometimes, right?"

"Anyway, it was something else I meant to tell you."

"What's that?"

"Why did I run into Meeko at Jhyshun's daycare?" Josairah referred to her son.

"What?" Keyasia gasped. "What the fuck was he doing there?"

"He claimed he was dropping off his little cousin."

"Oh, okay," Key drawled, looking up at Wale, who now fully engrossed into her conversation. "That must be where he's hiding out at."

"Hiding out?"

"Yeah. That nigga can't come back to the hood. Him and some Greenspoint nigga been out here stepping on everybody's toes, and Wale is ready to kill his ass."

"Kill him? For what?"

"Well, you remember Big Block?"

"Yeah."

"Well, he was shot, and might not make it. And there's been speculation that Meeko's pussy ass had this bitch ass nigga named Bleed do it. And he's supposed to be one of the dudes that shot Taraj, and killed Trell."

"Wow," Josairah's jaw dropped. Trell used to hustle for her daddy, and had been cool. Personally, she didn't know him well, because he never really came to their house much, but he'd been around for years, and her daddy was deeply impacted by his death.

"Yeah, so, you need to watch that nigga. He's been on some other shit, lately. And Wale told me that before they fell out that Meeko would always talk about taking Jhyshun from you…by hook or crook. Like he's really convinced himself that your baby is his, telling people that his baby mama just be tripping, not letting him see his son."

"See, he's off his fucking rocker. That's exactly what he was saying a few minutes ago. Asking for a DNA test, and I told him anything to get him out of my face."

Keyasia shook her head. "Well, with the moves he's been making I wouldn't chance anything with him. You might have to remove Jhyshun from that daycare. And you know that if Jah, your daddy, or Raven knew they'd tell you to do it today."

"I know. Fuck," Josairah vented, knowing that all this drama was self-inflicted, and could have been avoided, had she done the right thing from the beginning. "This is definitely my bad karma," she sighed. "Oh, what a fuckin' tangled web we weave, when we practice to deceive."

Key giggled, "Hey, you said it. But I'm serious, Josairah. Don't trust Meeko, and take his threats seriously."

"I hear you, girl. This will be Jhyshun's last day at that daycare. I promise."

"Good, because this will be the one time that I'll tell my cousin on your ass. I'm not playing," Key warned.

"Bitch, I got you. Damn."

"Alright, then. Now take ya ass to school, and get some A's," Key laughed, before ending the call.

"Meeko's bitch ass showed up to that baby's daycare?" Wale questioned, as he sat down on the bed next to her.

"Yeah," Key sighed. "His ass better not pull nothing with my little cousin, because that would definitely be signing a death sentence."

Wale stroked his goatee. "I hear you."

She stared at him, wondering what he was thinking, until her cell rang again. Lifting the phone, she saw that her mama was video calling her. "Hey, mama," she answered.

Raquel smiled, as she studied her oldest child's face. "What's up? Your face is looking mighty plump."

Keyasia diverted her eyes to the wall. It had been weeks since she'd been to her parents' home, and was purposely avoiding them, as her belly became harder to conceal. For some reason, she'd been procrastinating on telling her mama and daddy about her pregnancy, but she knew that she was running short on lies, and would be forced to tell the truth soon. "Mama, don't start."

"Don't tell me not to start. I haven't seen you in person in God knows when. That nigga aint the only one who loves you. Tell him that he has to share you," Raquel griped.

Wale grabbed Keyasia's wrist, aiming the camera at his face. "Ms. Raquel, I swear that's Keyasia." He raised his right hand to the man. "I'm not keeping her from going to see yall. That's her running."

Raquel frowned. "Well, what is she running for? We already know her ass took this semester off. So, what is it? And why is her face all fat?"

Wale smirked. "You gotta ask her that. If I say anything she'll beat me like I'm a red headed step child."

Keyasia popped the back of his head. "You talk too much. Nobody asked you to say all that."

Wale playfully winced. "You see what I mean?"

"Yeah, I see what time it is with her ass," Raquel mumbled. "Wale, do me a favor, baby."

"What's that?"

"Bring her over here today. Please."

He nodded. "I will."

Keyasia angrily glared at him.

"Okay, baby, I'll see yall later." Raquel hung up.

"What the fuck?!" Keyasia blurted out, as she bucked her eyes. "Why did you agree to that?"

He shrugged. "What you wanted me to say, Keyasia? That's your mama. Fuck, you already got people thinking that I'm holding you hostage over here."

"You and this baby do have my heart held hostage." She kissed his lips.

He smiled. "Stop bullshitting me, man. You know what I mean. So, be a woman about it, and tell your people the truth. I really believe your T-lady already knows. She probably just want you to keep it real."

She exhaled. "I know they'll be disappointed."

"Maybe they will be, but we can't live our lives for them, right?"

She slowly lowered her eyes, as he wrapped his arms around her. "Right."

******

"Ooh, mama, Keyasia is here, and she's fat!" Kevia announced, as she raced through the living room.

Keyasia held her head in embarrassment. "Why did I have to be born into this loud mouth family?" she groaned.

"Naw, don't be hiding in the hallway. Bring that ass in here!" Roz, Keyasia's grandma shouted.

Wale narrowed his eyes, as he stood behind her. "Who's that in there talking?"

Key continued to hold her head. "My granny. She's young enough to be my mama, and loves to talk shit."

He grinned. "Well, come on." He grabbed her hand, leading her into the living room.

Roz sat up in the couch. "Well, I'll be damned. That belly is bigger than I thought it was. She's at least four or five months."

Wale attempted to stifle a chuckle, as Keyasia's grandmother called her out. The lady was utterly beautiful with her milk chocolate complexion mixed with honey colored eyes, and long coal black hair. She looked like a voluptuous, dark, Native American, who wasn't a day over thirty.

Raquel carefully regarded her daughter. "Yeah, she's at least four months."

Keyasia twisted over to the couch, wearing overall blue jean shorts, and a baby tee, leaving no room for speculation. Her baby bump was evident. "Do yall have to be so loud?" she asked, as she sat down.

Raquel frowned. "You're lucky that I'm not going upside your head. Why would you hide this from us?"

Roz glanced up at Wale. "Baby, you can sit down."

Tugging at his slightly sagging jeans, he sat beside Keyasia.

"Mama, I was coming to tell you. I was just waiting for the right time," Key responded.

"When was that gonna be?" Roz quizzed. "When you went into labor?"

Key scratched her head. "I don't know."

"Well, I don't know what Raquel be over here saying, but she nor your daddy can judge. Her hot ass had you during her first year of middle school. So, I say you did damn good. You got a few years of college under ya belt, and you're grown," Roz offered.

Raquel cut her eyes at her mother. "Really, mama?"

Roz bucked her eyes. "Really mama what? You and Kevin's ass didn't give a damn about my feelings. Fucking all in my damn house. Hiding pregnancies and shit. Don't get me started."

Keyasia giggled. "Granny tell her. She likes to forget about all that."

"Oh, I won't let her forget. Trust me. Sometimes I still have the urge to punch Kevin's ass in the head. He was a sneaky muthafucka, even way back then. He knew what he was doing, making all them damn babies. Shit, it would probably be ten of yall if his ass hadn't gone to prison for all that time."

"Roz, we still young, baby. We can still shoot for that tenth mark. I know you're down to baby-sit." Kevin winked, as he stepped into the room.

Keyasia's heart skipped a beat, bracing herself for her daddy. He was the one she'd really been afraid to tell. Wearing a muscle shirt, and basketball shorts, Kevin looked like a ripe twenty-year-old boy, but had sternness of a man twice his age.

"What's up, nigga?" Kevin greeted Wale, as they clasped hands.

"Chilling, big homie," Wale replied.

Kevin hovered over his daughter. "Where you been hiding, Keyasia?"

She glanced up at him. "Nowhere, daddy."

He grimaced. "What's going on with your stomach? You swallowed a watermelon?"

Keyasia shamefully covered her eyes. "No, daddy."

Kevin grabbed her hand, removing it from her face. "Then what is it?"

"I'm having a baby," she confessed.

"A baby? From the looks of it, you've been carrying this baby for quite a while, so why are we the last to know?"

"Because," Key whined. "I thought that you'd be mad at me."

"And you think we're over here sleeping with Mickey, and all them other muthafuckas from Disney Land too? Like this is some type of fantasy land. Baby girl, me and your mama aint lame. We know that you're grown, and obviously having sex. So, when you choose to reproduce is out of our control, and we definitely can't judge you. Shit, you even refuse our financial help now, which means that we aint got a damn thing to say."

Wale nodded, because that was all his doing. He'd been adamant about Keyasia refusing to allow her parents to pay any of her bills, because that was now their responsibility, and he took that seriously. Besides, one man couldn't demand that another stays out of his business, while the other is helping to provide for the woman he lays down with. Key had no choice in the matter, and had to cut those financial strings from her parents.

Keyasia nodded. "I guess that I didn't want to disappoint yall, either."

Raquel sighed. "Well, I guess we did something right, for you to even feel that you owe us that much. But feeling like that can be bad for us, because I don't want you feeling like you can't come to us. Regardless of what it is, and I need you to really understand this while you're pregnant with this baby." Raquel placed a palm on her daughter's stomach. "Oh my God, this is real." She covered her mouth, as her vision became blurry. "I'ma be a young ass grandma. The baby is gonna be confused, questioning which one us actually had it."

Key giggled. "Mama, you play too much."

"Ahhh," Raquel screeched.

"What?" Everyone asked simultaneously.

"That little critter just kicked!"

Wale grinned, remembering how he'd reacted similarly when he'd first felt his baby kick.

"Look at that nigga over there grinning from ear to ear. Just like Kevin's sneaky ass. You dropped that seed on purpose, huh, baby?" Roz questioned, now calling Wale out.

Wale licked his lips. "Huh? What you say?"

"Yeah, act like you didn't hear me, baby. Deny it. But thank you for giving her daddy some karma. He deserves it."

Kevin sighed heavily. "Roz, you still stuck in the past. Keyasia is twenty years old now. You act like I knocked Quel up last week. I done married her and everything."

"Whatever." Roz waved him off. "Sometimes I still have flashbacks. Your ass was all in my nightmares. I swear I would wake up and check Quel's room in the middle of the night to make sure that your ass wasn't in there with her."

Wale laughed heartily, loving their family's interactions.

Kevin glanced at him. "Say, man, let me holler at you for a second."

Nicole Jackson

Wale hopped up, and followed Kevin out of the living room. Together they stepped into the game room. Kevin sat on the pool table, and folded his arms.

"My daughter must be crazy about you to be walking around with your child inside of her."

Wale slid his tongue across his teeth. "The feeling is definitely mutual."

Kevin nodded. "So, you in love?"

Wale stared directly into his eyes. "I am."

Kevin smirked. "I can't front. That shit feels weird, because she'll always be my little girl, you feel me?"

"I feel you."

"Look, I know that yall had a little shakiness at one point, and I really don't know what that was all about. Something tells me that Keyasia may not have been completely innocent in any of that, either. I know my daughter can be a handful, so I'm not going to run you down about that. It's in the past. But this baby business…changes the entire game. Like, I gotta deal with you to a certain extent, regardless. So, imagine where my head is at, after just receiving word that your boy was shot. As a father, I can't help but feel concern for my daughter's safety."

"I completely understand where you're coming from. That's not for Keyasia, and I don't plan on her being affected by it, but I would be lying if I said that I can guarantee anything. Aint nothing promised in the streets, but I can promise you that I'd lay down and die for your daughter, and my child. Shit, honestly, I think my own cousin had something to do with my boy getting popped, and he will be dealt with accordingly. And if there's ever a time where I feel like it's getting too hot for Keyasia, I'd put some distance between us myself. You have my word."

"I hear you, man. I just hope that you're sincere with this shit, and as a man I'ma hold you to your word."

They shook hands, right before Keyasia ran outside. "Corinthian, your fuckin' cousin has lost his rabid ass mind!"

Kevin frowned. "So, you cussing in front of me now, Keyasia?"

"I'm sorry daddy, but I'm so mad, right now," she apologized, as her chest heaved up and down.

"What's wrong?" Wale quizzed.

"Meeko," she breathed. "He just kidnapped my cousin's son. He took Jhyshun."

Chapter 34

Keyasia rested her head on Wale's chest, as her mind wouldn't stop wondering. It had been hours, since Raven had called Raquel, yelling hysterically. She told her sister how Meeko had shown up to Jhyshun's daycare, and basically strong-armed Josairah, before taking her baby. And now there was a massive manhunt for him, as Big Jahrein had rallied the troops, ready to go to war over his grandchild.

Immediately, Wale felt out of place, as his family member had violated in such a way, and he was surrounded by people who loved baby Jhyshun. Still, he placed himself in their shoes, and offered any information he could. The problem was that no one knew where Meeko was currently laying his head, and was scrambling to figure it out.

So now, both Keyasia and Wale were in deep thought. Wale couldn't believe that his cousin was stoop so low, and do something so stupid. Either the laws were going to put his ass under the jail, or he was going to die. It was a no-win situation, and he hated that Meeko was taking his mama through those sort of changes. It was crazy to watch someone he'd known forever take dive off the cliff like that.

"This is weird," Key whispered.

"What's that?" Wale inquired.

"We're laying in my bed. I never thought my daddy would go for some shit like this."

"I'm guessing he wouldn't have under normal circumstances."

"Yeah," she breathed. They'd stayed behind, while her parents, and grandmother left to comfort and help

Raven, Little Jahrein, and Josairah. Key was supposedly holding down the fort, until her parents returned, but had gotten sleepy, and decided to take a nap. "Probably not."

Before their conversation could go any further, Key's cell rang. Picking up the phone, she saw that it was Josairah calling. Nervously, she picked up. "Hello."

"Key, this shit is crazy. He shot Jalero," Josairah wasted no time.

"What?" Key sat up in bed. "Who shot Jalero?" she asked, referring to Big Jahrein's younger brother. Although, they were just related through marriage, Jalero had always treated her like family in every sense of the word.

"Meeko's crazy ass!" Josairah shouted through the phone.

"Nooooo, is he okay?" Keyasia sniveled.

"I…I…think he'll be alright."

"Wow, I can't believe this. Well, did the police at least catch Meeko's ass?"

"No, he's…he's dead." She whispered, "Jah had to do it."

Keyasia was momentarily speechless, as she caught the look on Wale's face. He'd clearly heard the entire conversation, and had just learned his cousin's fate.

"That's crazy, man. I know this is gonna fuck with my cousin, man," Keyasia sighed, knowing that Little Jah was no murderer, and killing someone would probably weigh heavy on his conscience. "Is the baby okay, though?"

"Yes," Josairah sniffed. "The baby's fine, but I got a lot going on, right now. The police are everywhere, and we need to see about Lero. I was just calling to let you know what's going on."

"Okay. Call me when you find out what hospital Jalero's at. I'll come up there tomorrow."

"I will," Josairah agreed, before hanging up.

Keyasia clutched her phone, as she eyed Wale.

"What? Why are you looking at me like that?" he queried.

"Look, I'ma just come right out and say it. My cousin had to shoot Meeko, and I know that you had your own beef with Meeko, but he's your family. So, if you feel like you gotta avenge your people's death or any shit like that, let me know. Because you got me fucked up, if you think that I'd be alright with you doing anything to my cousin."

Wale frowned. "Keyasia, have lost your damn mind? The fuck are you talking about?"

"I'm saying, I know how people can be over their family. We can fight amongst each other until we're blue in the face, but let somebody else try us. So, I'm letting you know that my cousin don't go."

His scowl deepened. "Keyasia, I'ma say this shit once, okay. Did I have love for my cousin, despite the fact that he'd fucked me over? Yeah. But I got love for Big Block too, and I wasn't about to uphold Meeko. So, whatever came his way was on him, and I was still leaning towards putting him out of his misery myself. Then after what he did to your people, I knew what was next. It's understandable, and I'd do the exact same if I was in your cousin's shoes. But beyond all that shit, me, you, and this baby are family. Yall are my main concern. Really my only concern, and I would never put you in a fucked up position by going at your cousin like that. Because where would that leave us? This aint no temporary thing. We in this shit for life, and nobody is coming between it. Nobody. So, it's fucked up that my kinfolk had to go out like that. I wish he'd made better decisions, but that aint got shit to do with us. And fuck anybody who'd try to make it our problem."

"Okay, okay," she huffed, as she straddled him, forcing him to lie on his back. "I got you." She kissed his lips. "If they got a problem, then fuck 'em." She grinded into him. "Now, relieve some of my stress, and fuck *me*."

******

"Is that the same hoe Craven was fucking in the backroom one morning?" Keyasia scrunched her face, as she watched Craven stroll over with some unknown chick, and a little girl.

Wale gripped the bridge of his nose. "Shit, I guess so."

They were sitting at a table in the elegant Steak 48 restaurant, having dinner, after a tumultuous week. Meeko had just been buried, Jalero had just been released from the hospital, and Big Block's condition had drastically improved. But now here Craven was, bringing the dramatics. Apparently, he'd called himself leaving Jazel, and was now attempting to bring some other broad around Keyasia. Wale thought his boy knew better.

"What's up, boi?" Craven questioned, as he clasped hands with Wale.

"Nothing, main," Wale answered, as Craven's guests sat at the table with them.

"Hello." The girl waved.

"What's up?" Wale spoke, while all Keyasia offered was an eye roll.

Craven sat down. "Aye, this is my friend Elle, and her daughter Lele."

Keyasia casted her eyes down, gazing at the little girl. "Hi, sweetie. You must get your cuteness from your daddy."

Wale attempted to stifle a laugh, knowing that was the same shit Jazel would do to any other chick he'd try to bring around.

Craven's little friend arrogantly flung her hair over her shoulder. "She looks like the both of us. I hope that the little bundle of joy you're holding has better luck, though. It would be gorgeous if it looked like its daddy."

Keyasia arched a brow, as to say *Bitch*.

Craven tittered. "Yall chill out, man. We came here to eat good, and relax, so retract those claws."

"Whatever," Keyasia snapped.

"Bae, it's all good. I'm chilling," Elle claimed, as she stroked her long flowing weave.

Keyasia quietly assessed the chick. She was fair skinned, with green eyes, which were obviously fake. She had so many bundles of her hair in her head, it was a wonder of how she was holding her head up straight. Narrowing her eyes, Key was now certain that the girl was the same bitch who was riding Craven one morning, back at the townhouse. "Ole freaked out ass," she murmured.

She then studied the little girl, who seemed disconnected with reality, as she gazed out into space. The little girl was pretty, but had the saddest eyes Key had ever seen on a person that size. "Are you hungry, little one?" she questioned.

Elle rolled her eyes. "She's good. She'll just eat off my plate."

Wale frowned. "I think she's big enough to have her own food. Damn, aint she like six or seven?"

Craven nodded. "Yeah, she can have her own food. What you wanna eat, Lele?"

Lele hesitated, as she peeked at her mama. "I'll eat with my mama."

Keyasia quickly took stock of the small bruises on the little girl's arms. She then shifted her eyes to Elle, questioning what the woman was doing to her little girl.

"Why do you keep staring at those people?" Wale whispered into her ear.

"Cause something is off about this hoe. I just can't put my finger on it," Keyasia replied, hardly whispering.

Gripping her chair, Wale scooted her closer. "You don't like her, because she aint Jazel."

Key shrugged. "That too. Craven is out of line for bringing this girl here."

Elle wrapped her around arm Craven's, assuming Keyasia was talking about her. "Bae, are we still going to Double Tree after this?"

Craven glanced at her. "What about your daughter? I thought you said that you didn't have a baby-sitter for tonight?"

"Yes, and no," Elle responded. "Push comes to shove, my cousin can always keep her. He does all the time."

Lele's expression quickly changed. "Mama, noooo," she whined. "I wanna stay with you."

Elle gritted. "Girl, shut up. You gon fucking stay wherever I tell your ass to stay."

Wale shook his head, as he spoke into Key's ear. "You better not ever force my baby to stay with somebody, after they react like this little girl just did."

"Boy, please. What I look like?" Key piped.

"You better know." He pecked her cheek, causing her to blush.

"So, how's Meeko's mama been handling his death, man?" Craven questioned.

Wale sighed. "Shit, taking it hard. Kaydoa and Black Reign are over there, right now."

"That's fucked up." Craven shook his head. "I'm still trying to wrap my head around what that nigga was thinking."

"Shit, your guess is as good as mine. He'd completely lost it, even killing the little chick he was living with. That nigga had to be going through something. Maybe he was smoking sherms with them niggas he was running with."

"Had to be," Craven concurred, as his cell buzzed, grabbing his attention.

The waiter stepped to the table, taking everyone's order, while Craven remained engrossed into his phone.

Promiscuous Girl: Keyasia and Wale

"Uhhhh," Elle loudly groaned, as Craven sat, texting. "Can't that wait? You've been texting her all day."

Craven blatantly ignored her, as his fingers moved rapidly.

Elle glanced up at Wale. "Have you ever seen a man so concerned about his ex?"

Wale glanced at Keyasia. "You getting dessert too?"

"I guess nobody wants to talk about that," Elle mumbled.

Keyasia giggled, "You mad or nah?"

Elle rolled her eyes.

"Damn, my stomach hurts," Wale winced, clutching his abs. "I'll be right back." He stood up, before darting to the bathroom.

Keyasia tittered. "Those sympathy pains are a muthafucka."

Craven glanced up with a smirk on his face. "Tell me about it."

Elle cleared her throat. "Well, me and Lele are about to go use the little girls' room," she announced, as she scooted back from the table. "Come on," she grabbed her daughter's hand, and they headed towards the restrooms.

Keyasia wasted no time. "Craven, what the fuck are you doing here with that basic ass scallywag? I bet the bitch is in the men's bathroom as we speak, trying to suck Corinthian's dick."

Craven shrugged. "I wouldn't doubt it."

Nicole Jackson

"So, what is she doing here? I mean, I know that you used to fuck around, but you've been on some chill shit. Why are you doing my girl like this?"

"Man," he drawled, as he shook his head. "Shit aint that simple, Key. You don't understand."

"Well, make me understand, Craven."

He gulped. "She was fucking up. I thought we was good. This is the furthest any pregnancy has ever made it. We just found out that we're having a little boy. So, I'm happy as fuck, right? I'm running through the house, and accidentally knocked over one of her purses, spilling everything across the floor. Anyway, I go to pick everything up, and find a fuckin' baggie of powder. Then I fuckin' lost it. I couldn't believe that she'd jeopardize our child, after we struggled so hard to get him. I came this close to beating her ass, while she's carrying my baby." He demonstrated, putting two fingers together. "So, I dipped."

Keyasia lifted both brows. "That's fucked up, and I know you're disappointed in her."

"Like a muthafucka."

"But I thought you loved her."

He grimaced. "I do, man. More than you'd ever know."

"Then act like it."

"What you saying? I been there every step of the way…"

"No, listen," she cut him off. "Of all the times you've had to save her from herself, this time is the most crucial. I don't know, maybe she's scared that this pregnancy will end up like all the rest, so she's self-destructing. It could be a number of things, but what I do know is that it makes no sense that you'd walk away at a time like this. She's vulnerable. Hell, your baby's vulnerable, and they both need you. Don't have her stressing over you, because that'll only help her lose the baby. Go be there for her…all the way. And if she can't shake those drugs, then get her some help. Being there for her when she falls short doesn't make you weak, Craven. I don't know if you never speak on her problem, because you feel ashamed or what, but there shouldn't be a soul out here that could make you turn on the woman you love."

Silently, he nodded, as he blankly stared down at the table.

"Say, man, let's go. Some shit just came up," Wale chided, as he stepped up to the table.

"What's wrong?" Keyasia stood up.

"I'll tell you about it," he promised, as he tossed a few bills onto the table. "Grab the food when they bring it. I already told them to fix our shit to go. I'll be in the car."

"Okay," Key agreed, as she watched her man stomp off.

"What's wrong with that nigga?" Craven questioned, lifting his head.

Key shrugged.

A few seconds later, Elle ambled back to the table, with a sneaky smirk on her face. "Where did Wale go?" she probed, as her daughter slowly tracked up to the table, grabbing a seat.

"Why are you so worried about it?" Keyasia snarled. "He is definitely none of your concern. I got that on lock. Trust."

Elle leered. "If you say so."

Keyasia glowered down at her. "Girl, don't get cute. Fuck around and get your ass beat."

Craven shook his head. "Key, chill out. Do I need to call Wale back in here?"

"Here's the food the gentleman asked to take out," The waiter interjected.

"Oh, thank you," Key offered a fake laugh, before grabbing the bag. "I can't wait to dig into the lobster, and crab cakes." She cut her eyes at Elle. "See you around, slut."

Craven shook his head for the umpteenth time, as Keyasia sashayed out of the restaurant.

Skipping across the lot, Key stepped to the Ferrari, and eased in. "Here." She placed the food in Wale's lap. "Now tell me why you ran out of there."

He sighed. "I didn't run out of nowhere. I just can't believe that Craven would be dumb enough to have a hoe like that around on a personal level. She's fuckin' trash."

Keyasia bit the inside of her jaw. "What did she do?"

"Man," Wale licked his lips. "That hoe left her daughter in the hall by herself, while she followed me into the men's restroom. That bitch begged to suck my dick. I cussed her ass out, but the bitch wasn't hearing me. It's something about that hoe. I saw the devil in her eyes."

Keyasia shook her head. "I knew it, I knew it. Craven needs to get rid of her, and I definitely don't like the fact that he brought her to the townhouse, before."

"Yeah, I feel you, but I wish that bitch would. My Nina don't discriminate."

"And these hands don't either."

Wale glared at her.

"What?"

"Don't play with me, man. You better not *think* about fighting, right now. My baby is more important than any scandalous hoe, so chill out. Be cool."

Keyasia slid her tongue across her teeth. "I will," she grumbled. "As long as I don't see her ass again."

Chapter 35

"Have you ever loved somebody so much it makes you cry? Have you ever needed something so bad that you can't...sleep at night? Have you ever tried to find the words, but they don't come out right? Have you ever..." Old school Brandy pumped from the Benz's speakers.

Keyasia gazed out of the window, enjoying a rare winter day in Houston. It was cold outside, but her heart had never been warmer. She and Wale had just left the doctor's office, where they'd learned that they were having a little girl. Joy filled her heart, as she saw a 3D image of her child, resembling both mother and father, making it real for them both.

Gazing down at his hand, clutching hers, she smiled. Newly etched across the back of his hand was her name. It amazed her to think of how far they'd come. There were definitely some nights where she didn't know if they'd make it beyond sunrise, but now there they were. Together. And genuinely happy. Nothing in life felt better, as she found inner peace within his arms.

"Damn, it's a bunch of muthafuckas here," Wale mumbled, as he pulled up to Big Block's home. After being hospitalized for the past few months, he'd been released, and now everyone was coming over to welcome him home.

"I see," Keyasia sighed.

"Stay right there," he commanded, as he exited the car, and scurried over to her side, opening the door for her. "Come on." He grabbed her hands, assisting her out of the car.

"Corinthian, you really act like I'm a baby. Can I do anything on my own?"

"Nope." He zipped up her jacket for her.

"Aww, Zaddy really loves me," she cooed, before sensually kissing his lips.

"Alright," he pulled away from the kiss. "Let's go in the house, man, before you catch a cold."

"There you go with that shit." She rolled her eyes, as she allowed him to guide her into his boy's home.

"'Bout time, nigga," Big Block cheesed from the couch, glad to see his friend.

"What's up, boi?" Wale asked, as he sauntered over to the couch, and they clasped hands.

"Hey yall." Keyasia waved, before Jazel practically rushed her.

"Friiiiiiiiiiiiend!" Jazel screamed, wrapping her arms around Key, letting their bulging bellies rub together. Playfully, she rained kisses all over Key's face. "You missed me, baby?"

Wale furrowed his brows. "Say, Jazel go'on with that funny shit, man. Aint nothing poppin'."

"Whatever." Jazel gave Wale the finger. "Key, let me talk to you, right quick." She pulled her into the hallway.

"What's up?" Keyasia questioned with concern.

Jazel stood, as her chest heaved up and down. "I…I just wanna thank you. Nobody has ever done anything like that for me." Her eyes filled with tears. "Craven told me about the talk yall had. He told me when he came back to meee," she sobbed. "And I really appreciate that." Jazel hugged her tightly. "Thank youuuuu."

Keyasia soothingly rubbed her back. "No problem, girl. It's no more than I know you would've done for me."

Jazel nodded. "I would've done the same, and just know that from this day forth…you're my fuckin' sister. I'm here for anything you need, and I mean that."

"Aww, that's sweet, Jazel. But on the real, all I need from you right now is to deliver a healthy little boy."

"We just made it out of the danger zone. So, even if the baby came today, he'd live. I mean, he'd spend an extensive time in NICU, but the survival rate is ninety percent at this point within the pregnancy," she explained, after getting thoroughly educated on high-risk pregnancies, and premature babies. "And I know that you probably don't care, but I swear on my mama that I never got high, after finding out that I was pregnant. I don't even remember when I bought that coke, and honestly forgot that it was in my purse, until Craven found it."

Keyasia nodded. "I believe you, but what are you gonna do after the baby comes? Are you planning on getting high sometimes?"

Jazel shook her head. "After this last hiccup between me and Craven, I'm done with all that shit. I had never seen him so mad before, and I really thought that he was done with my ass. Especially with how mature he was handling things. He was still there for me, but wouldn't come home. I really thought that I'd lost him," she sniveled.

"Girl please," Key pursed her lips. "That nigga was looking so lost without you. His ass was coming back, regardless. I probably just helped him to see the light a little sooner."

Jazel grinned, glad to hear that she wasn't the only one looking crazy during their break-up. "But bitch, who is that Elle hoe?"

"Girl." Key rolled her eyes. "Some scruffy hoe Craven brought around. Bitch was trying to issue that stale ass pussy out like government cheese."

"Well, that bitch is gonna make me pistol whip her ass."

"Why? What happened?"

"The bitch won't leave Craven alone. She's been blowing all three of his phones up, and today she started threatening him, telling him that he better be careful out in these streets, because she know several niggas looking for a come-up. I told Craven that he needed to pay that bitch a visit, before the shit get out of hand. He claims that he don't know where the bitch lives, because he would always pick her up from a public spot."

Keyasia sucked her teeth. "That bitter Betty is probably all talk, but I would keep an eye out, in case she did lose her mind."

"Exactly," Jazel agreed. "But if she keeps calling, she won't have to worry about Craven. Because I'll find her ass, and fuck her up."

Key giggled. "Bitch, what are you gonna do with that round ass belly."

Jazel snaked her neck. "The fuck you mean?" she bucked her eyes. "That hoe don't know me. I'm resourceful. I'm taking a bitch down. By any means necessary."

"Whatever," Keyasia tittered.

"You think it's a game. I aint gon play with her. I'll mace her ass. I aint playing."

Key shook her head. "And what's crazy is that you mean every syllable. Yeah, if that hoe knows what's best for her, she'll forget all about Craven's ass."

******

"Slow down," Wale breathed.

"I can't," Keyasia panted, as she hopped up and down on his dick.

He gripped her hips, as they were in the tub, sloshing water all over the floor. Her knees were hitting her breasts, as she swayed her hips, fucking him rapidly.

"Umm," she moaned, as her head fell back, allowing her hair to dip into the water.

Leaning his head forward, he took a nipple into his mouth. Soon she was bucking her hips, as he smashed into her, matching her aggression.

"Uhh!" she screeched, as she could feel it in her toes. "Fuck me! Fuck me!"

"Fuck that," he growled, as he lifted her off his dick, and onto his shoulders. Swirling his head around, he licked every nook and cranny.

"Ahhh!" Key screamed, as an orgasm took her by surprise, causing her to dip all her hair into the water.

Enjoying driving her crazy, he zoned in on her clit. Unlike so many other times, she didn't run. The baby had her sex-drive at an all-time high, as she rolled with the punches, welcoming the unspeakable pleasure.

Nicole Jackson

"Wait, wait," she halted him, as she crawled to the foot of the tub to drain the water.

She then crawled backwards onto him, putting her pussy back in his face. As soon as he worked his tongue between her second lips, she took his hard-on into her mouth, while upside down.

It took a second for Wale to catch his bearings, but he had to stop her. "Hell nah. What are you doing, Keyasia? You gon kill my baby like this. She probably can't breathe with you upside down."

She giggled, while his dick was still stuffed in her mouth.

"Aww fuck," he vented, as his head involuntarily fell back. "Keyasia, I'm not pl…pl…playing. Shiiiiit," he sputtered, as he skeeted into her mouth.

"Umm," she moaned, finally lifting her head. Gradually, she crawled in an upright position, before sitting of the ledge of the tub. "That was sweet." She licked her lips.

Wale stared at her in astonishment. "You's a fuckin' super freak, man."

"So." She shrugged. "You want me to stop?"

He scratched his head, before cracking a huge smile. "Hell nah."

"That's what I thought," she snickered, before reaching over to grab her ringing cell. "What's up, bitch?" she answered the phone.

"Uh, so, you don't know nobody no more, huh?" Taraj questioned.

"What are you talking about, girl?"

"You know what I mean. You don't hang out no more, and I can barely get you to answer the phone. Tell that Corinthian that he has to share you. Damn."

"Bae, you hear this hoe?" Keyasia glanced at Wale.

"Yeah, I hear her. Ask her why is she hating."

"Tell that nigga that aint nobody hating. We need to go somewhere," Taraj insisted.

"Where you think you going, man?" Keyasia clearly heard Taz in the background.

"Nowhere far, baby. Just a short girls' day out," Taraj explained.

Keyasia giggled. "Uh huh, look at her, talking all that shit, but that nigga aint having it."

"Whatever, bitch," Taraj jeered. "But for real, let's at least grab something to eat today."

Keyasia thought about it. "You know what? Today would be a perfect day for me, you, Josairah, and my girl Jazel to get together. I've been dying for yall to really hang with her. She's cool as hell."

Wale scratched the back of his head. "More like crazier than a muthafucka," he grumbled. "Nobody wanna meet her loony ass."

"That sounds like a plan. Where do you wanna go?" Taraj enquired.

"Since it's still early, let's meet at the Breakfast Klub."

"Okay. I'll be there by ten."

"Cool. See you there, girl." Key hung up the phone.

Wale eyed her.

"What?" she lifted both brows.

"I don't remember you asking me if you could go anywhere."

She burst into laughter. "You're funny." She straddled him. "Now come on. Fuck me again. I gotta go."

He licked his lips, as he allowed her to hop on his instant boner. Rolling her hips, she looked into his eyes. "I gotta make sure that I give you something to hold you over."

He held on tight for the ride. "Got damn. You definitely know how to do that."

******

"So, what's been up with you?" Keyasia asked Josairah, as she, Taraj, and Jazel all sat in the Breakfast Klub having brunch.

Josairah sighed heavily. "Girl, stressing."

"Why?" Taraj spoke up. "Don't tell me that Little Jah is still on that bullshit, after everything that has happened."

Josairah twirled a few strands of her hair around her finger. "I mean, he's not dealing with other girls. Trust me. I practically held Jhyrah upside down for information. I think it has something to do with the whole Meeko ordeal, and he's having trouble adjusting. So now he has me and the baby in a big ass house, but he's still at his mama's."

Keyasia smirked. "You need to go over there, and have a talk with Raven. I bet she's over there babying his ass. Tell her to pop her titty out of that boy's mouth so that he can go home, and help you with his son. I know how she is. She's probably at home right now, telling him that she'll be Jhyshun's daddy, until he feels like it," she jested.

Josairah laughed. "Bitch, that's exactly what she's doing, but he won't let her take over like that. I know he's going through something, but I'm giving his ass a few more weeks, and then I'm turning up on his ass. He's coming to stay with us, or I'll drag his ass to the house. Shit, I called myself trying to move back home to my parents' and he damn near fought me. So, it's about to be a two-way street. Fuck he think this is."

Jazel smiled, as she listened to everyone with their different set of issues. It was actually refreshing to be in the company of Key's friends. They were so different from the friends she'd had over the years. Outside of Black Reign, and her brothers' women, she didn't trust most chicks, but these girls didn't strike her as the catty type, which allowed her to put her guard down.

"Girl, I know how you feel, because Taz is just starting to really smile again. He's worried sick about his daughter, but nobody seems to know where his baby mama took her," Taraj added.

"And that's fucked up," Keyasia acknowledged. "I couldn't imagine not knowing where my baby is."

"True," Jazel agreed, rubbing her belly. "After seeing my brothers go through it with these worrisome ass hoes, I'm glad that Craven's ass aint got no kids out there. Shit, it's bad enough that I have to deal with the crazy stalkers who don't know how to let go."

"Is that Elle bitch still calling?" Keyasia wanted to know.

"Girl, she's sending all types of shit. One minute she's threatening him, then the next the hoe is sending naked pictures. I'm this close to posting her photos on in the internet, and blasting her ass."

"Hell, let me see her picture. I'll do it now," Key volunteered.

"Let me see," Jazel mumbled, as she scrolled through her phone. "Here." She handed Key the phone.

"Ewe, ole nasty hoe," Key cringed.

"I wanna see," Taraj uttered, as she leaned over, peeking at the screen of the cell. "Aint this about a bitch?!"

"What?" everyone asked simultaneously.

"That's fuckin' Lani!"

"Who?" Jazel frowned.

"This bitch in the picture. This is Lani. Taz's BM." Taraj pointed.

"Get the fuck outta here." Keyasia's jaw dropped. "So, you mean to tell me that Taz's little girl was sitting across from me, and I didn't know?"

"You saw Lyra?" Taraj lifted a brow.

Keyasia gasped. "Bitch, now it makes since. Elle must be short for Lani, and that's why she was calling her daughter Lele. That must be her little nick name."

"Wait a minute," Jazel interjected. "Key, I thought you said that her BD's BM had something to do with her getting shot?"

Taraj nodded. "She did. Them niggas were in her car, and she disappeared right after that. She didn't even go to her own cousin's funeral."

"Shit," Jazel hissed. "Let me see my phone. I need to call Craven."

Right then, Keyasia's cell vibrated on the table. "Corinthian's calling now," she announced, before picking up. "Hello."

"Say, where yall at?" Wale asked hurriedly.

"At the Breakfast Klub. Why?"

"Man," he drawled. "Try not to panic her, but get Jazel to come up here to Ben Taub hospital. Them niggas shot Craven."

Keyasia's eyes landed on Jazel, as she wore a look of concern.

"What?" she questioned, about to go into full panic mode.

Keyasia took a deep breath. "We gotta go."

*****

"Jazel, calm down, girl. I'll be alright, but I'ma fuck you up if you go into labor. I'm for real," Craven stressed, as he lied in the hospital's bed.

"How can you tell me to calm down, when there's a fuckin' hole in your shoulder," Jazel cried.

"Cause I'm still here. No matter how this shit looks, I'm right here with you."

Wale sat back, fuming. For the past few months, his team had been taking hit after hit, and he was ready to go on a killing spree. His leg was shaking, as he anticipated putting in work. "Main, I promise I'm laying them niggas down. Then you say they didn't bother wearing ski masks? They out here not giving a fuck, calling us out."

Nicole Jackson

Keyasia sat at the back of the room, palming her forehead. Craven had been robbed for his chain, and Escalade. This whole street shit was becoming a never-ending thing with Wale, and she was quickly becoming weary. Meeko was dead, Big Block had to use a cane for now, and now Craven was lying in a hospital bed with a bullet wound. Where would it end?

"Keyasia," Taraj called out, sticking her head in the room. "Come here for a second."

Wale cut his eyes at her. "Don't leave out of this hospital, Keyasia."

She sucked her teeth, as she scooted out of the chair. "I won't." Wobbling to the door, she stepped into the hall with Taraj. "What's up?"

"Taz is here. He wants to talk to Corinthian and his cousin."

Keyasia glanced behind Taraj and noticed Taz sitting next to Josairah. "Okay. Let me give them the heads up," she offered, before re-entering the room. "Corinthian, umm, Taz is outside. I guess he wants to talk about that Lani chick."

"Shit, tell that nigga to come in," Craven spoke up.

"Yeah," Wale stroked his goatee. "We definitely need to holler at him."

"Okay," she breathed, before stepping back into the hallway. "Taz, come on." She waved him over.

Hastily, Taz hopped up, and followed her into the room. "What's up?" he spoke.

"'Sup?" both Wale and Craven replied.

Taz licked his lips. "My girl was telling me that she thinks Lani got her cousins to rob you."

Craven slowly nodded. "They was telling me about that too."

Taz reached into his pocket, and pulled out his cell. Scrolling through his phone, he located a photo. "Is this the little girl she had with her?" he brandished a picture of his daughter.

Wale extended his neck out. "Hell, yeah. That's the little girl she had with her."

"Yep. That's her daughter, and the last time I saw her, she beat the hell out of the little girl, claiming that she was walking around pissy," Craven added.

Taz swallowed hard. "And you don't know where they live?"

"Nah, man." Craven shook his head. "I would pick that hoe up from a corner store. She would always say that she lived with her antie, and the lady didn't like it when niggas came to pick her up. But I'm willing to bet that she don't live too far from that store, because all the niggas outside knew her."

"Yeah?" Taz narrowed his eyes. "Where was this?"

"In Northwood Manor," Craven revealed. "And I believe her cousins live there too, because a bunch of niggas would be in the background, and she'd always get her little girl to stay with one of them, even though lil' mama didn't seem to like it."

Taz frowned up. "That bitch haven't learned her lesson after…man, I gotta go get my daughter," he grumbled to himself. "Say," he looked from Wale to Craven. "I'm riding out there tonight. I happen to know for a fact that her cousins shot my boy, and my gal. Their bitch asses been bragging about it. So, I'ma find all of them, and Lani can get it too. I mean, Taraj just told me what happened, and I was trying to see if anybody wanted to put in some work."

"Shit, I know for a fact that it was that bitch who sent them niggas at me. One of them had the nerve to tell me that Elle said what's up," Craven admitted.

"Fuck it. I'm down," Wale spoke up.

"Corinthian," Keyasia blurted.

He frowned. "Corinthian what? This shit aint up for debate, Keyasia."

"I'm going too," Jazel volunteered.

Craven scowled. "Man, Jazel, sit your ass down somewhere. You aint going no fuckin' where. On my mama. With this hole in my shoulder and all, I'll drag your ass back in here."

"See," Keyasia's voice cracked. "This the bullshit I be talking about." she stormed out of the room.

"There she go," Wale muttered. "Let me talk to this girl, right quick." He eased out of his chair, before leaving the room. Stepping out into the hall, he found Keyasia leaning against the wall with her arms folded, crying, and pouting all at the same time. "What's the problem, Keyasia?"

"Leave me alone," she snapped, as the tears rolled down her cheeks.

"So, you aint gon talk to me?" he inquired, closing the gap between them.

"No," she sulked.

Lowering his head, he kissed her. "I love you. And that's why I gotta go. You know that bitch knows where we live. I can't let it rock like that."

She whimpered. "But what if something happens to you?"

"Keyasia, I'm a man. Ten toes down, you hear me? I'ma be alright. You just hang tight, until I come back. Okay?"

She sniffed. "Okay."

"Good."

"But I swear that I'ma kill you if you don't make it back to me."

He smiled. "Promise?"

Chapter 36

"Say, man, you look like you could use a couple of dollars."

Benny's palms became sweaty, as he thought about getting his hands on some cash. He'd been standing on the corner all day, begging, and wiping down people's tires. Still, all he had was a few measly dollars. Hell, he could really use a hit on the pipe, right then. "What you say?" he asked, inching closer to the late model Lexus.

The man in the driver's seat waved a crisp hundred-dollar bill. "I said it looks like you could use a couple of dollars."

Benny smiled, revealing his rotten teeth. "Hell yeah."

"Okay." The man pulled the money back. "Well, I need some information first."

"And what's that?"

"You know where Bleed and Lani stay?"

"Bleed? That lowdown muthafucka? Hell yeah, I know where he stay. They stay on Ribstone in the fifth house to the left. It's a red car parked outside."

"Appreciate you," the driver smiled, as he forked over the bill.

"No, problem. Shit, I would've told you for free. Them niggas aint no good. Bleed's bitch ass stole money out of my bucket last week."

The driver shook his head, as he pulled off the block.

Taz grimaced. "And this bitch got my daughter around that hoe ass nigga."

Wale gripped the steering wheel. "Yeah, you need to get your baby from her. She be on some other shit, and I know that I wouldn't want my child with a broad like her. Craven said that the bitch was trying to bring the little girl to the hotel with them. Talking about she can sleep on the couch, while they fuck."

"Sounds like bad business to me," Danny Boy sneered, from the backseat, as he cocked his gun.

"I told Taz not to fuck with the hoe," Jarell snorted, as he gazed out of the window.

Slowly, Wale crept through the neighborhood, until he arrived at the home the bum on the corner had described. Being that it was well after two in the morning, the street was quiet, and there was no apparent movement going on in the house.

"Look, I'm about to walk to the backyard, and let yall know what's good. I say we kick in the backdoor, and just go for what we know," Danny Boy suggested.

"Shit, sounds like a plan to me," Jarell agreed.

Taz rubbed his hands together. "But yall can't go in there on no reckless shit. Lyra could be in there."

"And how do yall even know if this is the right house?" Wale questioned.

Taz squinted. "That's her Lexus parked next to the red Ford Focus. Oh, we got the right house."

"Alright, well, I'ma run through the backyard first." Danny Boy hopped out of the backseat. After carefully surveying his surroundings, he jogged into the yard, and around the old brick home.

Everyone else sat waiting, while gripping their pistols. Shortly after, Danny Boy waved from the side of the house, signaling them to join him. They then collectively placed on their ski masks, and gloves, before all at once, springing out of the car, and tipping to the side of the home.

"Aye," Danny Boy whispered. "At the count of three, me, Taz, and Wale need to kick this fucking door down."

Everyone nodded, before gathering together, ramming their feet into the wooden door. On the first try the door gave in, tumbling to the floor. Luckily, there was loud music playing throughout the house, as they all entered the home. Splitting up, they searched the house with their weapons drawn.

Upon entering the living room, Danny Boy found one dude peacefully sleeping on the couch. Without hesitation, he placed his gun to the man's skull. The silencer minimized the noise, as he pulled the trigger.

"Bitch ass nigga," he gritted, as he left the room, in search of his next victim.

Both Taz and Wale had canvassed relatively every room in the home with the exception of the last bedroom they were currently standing outside of. Since the music was coming from this particular room the assumption was that someone was inside.

"I'm going in," Wale announced, before pushing the door open, and tipping inside. Catching a glimpse of activity in the bed, he halted. For a second he stood in shock. "What the fuck?"

Taz stepped into the room right behind him.

Feeling someone's presence, Bleed scrambled out of the bed, stark naked. "Didn't I tell you to knock, nigga?" he frowned when he noticed two dark figures standing there. "What the fuck is this?" he questioned with a rock hard dick, and loud alcohol reeking from his pores.

The person who was in the bed with him immediately sat up, attempting to drag the cover over her little naked body.

Taz's hand shook. "Ly…Lyra, is that you?"

"Daddy?" she jumped out of the bed.

Wale grimaced, as he swung, slamming his gun into Bleed's head. He delivered one blow after another, until Bleed dropped to the floor.

"I'ma kill this muthafucka!" Taz spewed, as he joined Wale, stomping Bleed as he withered on the floor.

Jarell and Danny Boy raced into the room. "What the fuck is you niggas doing?" Danny Boy wanted to know. "Kill his ass, and let's go."

"This…this bitch ass nigga was back here raping his little girl, man," Wale revealed.

"What the fuck?" Jarell uttered, as he saw Lyra stand there motionless, watching them stomp Bleed.

Danny Boy shook his head, as he blindly felt around the room, until he located a shirt. "Here, lil' mama." He pulled the men's shirt over Lyra's head. "We're gonna go to the car, and wait on your daddy, okay?"

"Kay," Lyra whispered, as Danny Boy lifted her off the floor. Leaving everyone else behind, he headed back to the car.

Taz had seemingly blacked out, as he stomped Bleed mercilessly, staining his clothes with his blood. "Say, my nigga, we gotta go." Wale grabbed him. "Put him out of his misery, and let's go."

Stoically, he aimed his pistol at Bleed's dick, and pulled the trigger. Bleed howled in pain, as he clutched the area where his penis once was.

"Bitch, shut up," Taz growled, before aiming the gun between his eyes. "I hope you burn in hell," he spewed, before pulling the trigger.

Bleed's limp body fell back, as all three men stood over him. Wale was truly disgusted by what he'd just witnessed, and felt that death wasn't good enough for Bleed.

For good measure Wale delivered one final kick. "Bitch ass, child molesting, pervert. This was one time I wish that I could've pulled that trigger. We ought to find ya mama, and kill her ass for bringing your bastard ass into this world. No lie."

******

Keyasia sleepily gazed at the alarm clock that read 5 a.m. Her eyes slowly lowered, as she felt him wrap his arms around her. She breathed easier, as he nuzzled his nose into the crook of her neck.

"I'm tired as hell," Wale whispered.

She gently rubbed his arm. "Did yall find her?"

He hesitated. In the past, he'd never had pillow talk with a woman when it came to his dirty deeds, but he recognized that Keyasia wasn't any of those other women. "Nah, we didn't find that bitch, but we found her cousins."

She slowly nodded. "I don't know if that's good or bad."

"Yeah." Was all he could say.

"What about Taz's daughter? Was she there?"

"Man," he drawled.

"What? What happened?" she pressed.

"We found her," he confessed. "But the shit I saw…man. My heart goes out to that little girl."

She gulped. "What happened?"

"Lani's cousin…he was in the bed with the little girl. Naked. The little girl was naked. And his dick was hard."

Keyasia grabbed her mouth, as she cried. "You're lying, Corinthian."

"Shit, I wish I was. That's how we found her, Keyasia."

"But that little girl…is like six years old."

He sighed, "Exactly."

"What's wrong with him? Why would he do that to her? That little girl has already been through enough." She shook her head. "Lord, I hope that Taraj and Taz can help her through this, because stuff like that can alter a person forever."

He shook his head. "It's all fucked up, and I could tell that ole boy wanted to break down. The little girl was telling him how that nigga be making her suck his dick. The shit is crazy."

"Wow," Keyasia gasped. "That's one sick muthafucka."

"That's what I said."

"That poor little girl. And what type of mother leaves her child with men like that? I knew something was off about that little girl's behavior."

"Somebody should cut that hoe's pussy off," Wale snarled. "That shit had me thinking about our little girl, and I'm telling you now, Keyasia. Ion care what's going on. You better not ever leave my daughter with random people. If it aint your immediate family, then aint shit popping. Shit, sometimes you gotta watch them muthafuckas too."

"Trust me, you don't have to worry," she promised. "My mama would kill me, anyway. She has already stressed that point on more than one occasion. Talking about the baby can't go to my daddy's granny's house," she giggled.

"Well, what she got against your granny?" Wale asked curiously.

"Nothing, but she doesn't clean her house."

Wale chuckled. "Well, that'll do it."

"Won't it?" Keyasia continued to snicker.

"But, baby, for real. We gotta get some sleep, but before we go, let's do a silent prayer for Taz's little girl."

Intertwining her fingers with his, as they rested upon her protruding belly, she smiled. Corinthian may have been a lot of things, but his heart was pure. "Okay, bae, let's do exactly that."

Nicole Jackson

Chapter 37

"So, what's been going on with you, and your precious *Corinthian*?"

Keyasia laughed from the passenger's seat of the Benz, as she glanced at her aunt. "You love being funny."

"I'm serious," Raven claimed, as she focused on the road. "We all know that nigga got you gone. We have to make appointments just to see you these days."

"It is not like that," Key denied. "All yall are busy, and then look up every blue moon, and realize that I haven't visited. But that's when yall should hop into one of those million cars you have, and come see me, for once."

"Okay, you got me there. I guess I am used to you coming by the house. Me and Quel are gonna have to start driving to yall 's place sometimes."

"Pretty much." Key batted her lashes.

"Whatever," Raven smiled. "So, has Wale been staying out of trouble? He haven't killed anybody lately, has he?"

Key cut her eyes. "What would make you ask that?"

"Well, damn," Raven bucked her eyes. "I was only playing, but I'ma leave that alone. Ole boy is still heavy out there in them streets, I see."

"I don't know about that," she claimed, as she absently gazed out of the window. Truth was, she was on edge. Wale had been running the streets more often, swearing that he needed to get his money up. He was more paranoid, as he found himself hustling with new faces, and she was about to drive herself crazy, worrying about him.

Then there was still the lingering threat of Lani. From what the streets were saying, the cousins she'd run with, and hit licks with were dead, but she was alive and kicking. Luckily, for her, she'd been with one of her dips when Taz and Wale ran up in her house, which was how her life was spared. Still, she knew exactly who killed her people, but her own trouble with the law was preventing her from speaking on it. Therefore, she'd left things as they were, forgetting about her child, while Taz continuously combed the streets, searching for her.

With all her issues, Key had begun to think about her own career path, which was non-existent at the time. A year ago she was doing videos, club appearances, while juggling school full-time. And now she'd been reduced to staying at home, waiting on her man to come in from doing illegal activity. She'd seen enough to know that if they didn't find a better way they'd surely sink. Wale's hustle only provided two outs; death or jail, and she wasn't about to sit back and accept either option. Therefore, she'd gone to lunch with her aunt, and they sat discussing her career options. Raven told her that there were still several people interested in working with her, ranging from a few small acting gigs to some major club appearances. It was all awaiting her the moment she had the baby.

Key knew that Wale was dead set against her little Instagram modeling career, but it provided disposable income, and could relieve some financial strain off him. The last thing she wanted was to bring a baby into a hostile environment, or spend most of her time worrying about child's father's safety. So, she was determined to get off her ass, and figure out a way to take care of her family.

"Key, why is your door wide open?" Raven asked, as she pulled into the townhouse's driveway.

Nicole Jackson

Keyasia narrowed her eyes, knowing that their door being ajar was highly unusual. "I don't know. Let me call Corinthian." She whipped out her cell.

"What's up, Keyasia?" Wale answered the phone immediately.

"Bae, where are you?"

"Right up the street. Why? You back at home already?"

Keyasia's heart dropped down to her stomach. "So, you're not in the house, and you didn't leave the door wide open?"

"Hell nah!" he shouted. "Why? Is the door open?"

"Y…yeah," she stuttered.

Raven shook her head, as she began texting on her phone.

"I'm on my way. Don't go in there, until I get there. You hear me, Keyasia?"

"I hear you."

"Shit, we aint scared around here," Raven spat, as she reached underneath her seat. As she pulled her hand out, Key realized that she was gripping a silver gun. "I'm licensed, and certified to shoot me a muthafucka."

Keyasia offered a weak smile, attempting to display a calm demeanor, but she was see-through. Raven saw the fear stamped all over her face. She nearly jumped out of her skin, when Wale pulled up behind them. With his gun already drawn, he jogged up to their townhouse, and dashed inside.

Raven shook her head. "Yall young muthafuckas love living life on the edge, but that shit is bad for your health. You'll learn one day."

Keyasia grabbed her forehead, feeling emotional. She'd grown up seeing too much, therefore she'd lost her innocence a while ago. She wasn't naive. Therefore, she knew that Wale couldn't continue on like this. Something had to give.

She exhaled, after not realizing that she was holding her breath. Wale had stepped out onto the porch, telling her that the coast was clear. She grimaced, as she eased out of the car. Slowly, she wobbled up to him.

"Is everything alright?"

He silently shook his head, as those green eyes darkened.

She sucked her teeth, as she stepped around him. Standing in the doorway, she peered around the living room, seeing that it was trashed. All the furniture had been ripped to shreds, and the walls were spray painted, reading: *You went to my house and now I been to yours.*

Keyasia curled her lips. "I know that bitch Lani did this."

"More than likely," Wale stated calmly. "That hoe really don't know who she's playing with, though."

"This shit is crazy."

Raven eased out of the car, and leaned against the side, while talking on her phone.

Wale licked his lips. "I guess we can go to the hideaway for a few, until we find somewhere else to move to."

Holding her back, Keyasia sat on a step, leading up to the porch. "Yeah, I guess so." Their baby kicked at that very moment, reminding her of all they had at stake.

For a few minutes, they both said nothing, as they thought. Their heads lifted, when they heard tires burning rubber on the pavement. Key's heart sank to her toes when she noticed her daddy's BMW, pulling into the driveway.

"Shit," she hissed, knowing this wasn't about to end well.

Quickly, both Raquel and Kevin hopped out of the car. Raquel was dressed in a business suit, indicating that she'd been working, while Kevin wore Versace from his head to his feet. Still, they both looked to be ready for war.

"What's going on?" Kevin questioned, as they approached them. "Raven told us that somebody broke into yall's house."

Wale nodded. "Somebody did."

Raquel frowned. "Why did it happen, Wale?"

Wale shrugged. "It was some chick who was dealing with my cousin."

"Lani, right?" Raquel lifted both brows, letting him know that she knew exactly what was going on. "The same chick that Taz is looking for, correct?"

Dragging his palm over his mouth, Wale nodded.

Raquel shook her head. "I know that little bitch bleeds like the rest of us, but this can't be taken lightly. She obviously knows where yall live, and who knows who she'll send this way next? This shit has gotten out of hand, and I know her cousins were killed the other day, so I'm assuming that's why yall haven't attempted to dial up the police."

Keyasia and Wale's silence was considered an admission of guilt.

"Look, enough is enough. Keyasia, I need you to get up, hop in your Rover, and follow us home. You're not staying around this bullshit another night," Kevin seethed.

"But daddy," Keyasia whined, looking up at her father with the saddest eyes. "I can't leave Corinthian like that."

Wale gazed down at her. "Keyasia, I'm a grown man. I'll be alright. Go with your people."

She vehemently waved her head. "I don't care what you say, Corinthian. I'm not leaving you, and that's all there is to it."

Raquel sighed. "Keyasia, baby, I understand that you love him, but you have to think about your baby. It's a lot going on, right now, and there's no telling what that girl has figured out. We can't chance you having a run-in with her. Definitely not in your current state. Come to the house. Let the streets cool off, baby. Please."

"Mama, I am grown. I am not some little girl, dealing with a little boy, who's about to run because things are getting real. Yall can't protect me from life, and as much you love me, he loves me too. And I can't swear that I love a man, but walk away, because he has drama in his life. I decided to be with him, which means I have to accept the good with the bad. Ride it out. So, I'm not going anywhere."

Wale stood back not saying a word, because he was appreciative of her not allowing them to sway her so easily.

Promiscuous Girl: Keyasia and Wale

If the roles were reversed, he positively wouldn't leave her, either.

"Keyasia, I don't give a fuck about what you talking about," Kevin fumed. "This aint a fuckin' joke. Fucking with that girl, people have died, and that's not something I'ma take lightly. Now the bitch has come to where yall rest yall's head at. Been through all your shit, and I won't feel right, until you're at home, where I know that I can protect you. The shit is non-negotiable. You coming!"

Raquel grabbed his shoulder. "Kevin, calm down. Let's try talking to her sensibly. There's no need to cause a scene."

Ignoring his wife, Kevin glared at Wale. "So, you aint gon be a man of your word? You told me that you'd leave my daughter alone, before putting her in harm's way. So, what do you call this shit?"

"Big homie, no disrespect, but she's my family. That's my baby she's carrying, and you expect me to just walk away?" Wale frowned.

"And nigga that's *my* baby carrying your baby! Be real. What would you do if your daughter was caught up in bullshit? Would you idly sit back, and hope that she survives, or would you step in, and do what you gotta do for yours?"

Wale squared his shoulders. "I'ma do whatever I gotta do for mine."

"Exactly." Kevin nodded, as his nostrils flared. "So, I'm asking you, man to man, to do the right thing, here."

Wale clenched his jaw, as he looked down at her. "Keyasia, go with your people, man."

Nicole Jackson

Promiscuous Girl: Keyasia and Wale

Feeling infuriated, Key leaped off the step. Within the blink of an eye, she was on the porch, and in his face. "How are you gonna listen to them?!" she screamed.

"Calm down," he urged.

"Don't tell me to fuckin' calm down!" she belted, as angry tears ushered down her face. "I don't know why you'd stand there, and agree to this bullshit! I'm not going nowhere!" She clucked him in the head.

"Keyasia," Raquel attempted to grab her hand.

Key jerked away. "Don't touch me," she cried, as she gripped Wale's shirt. "What's wrong with you? You don't love me?"

He gazed into her eyes. "Yeah, I love you."

"Then tell them I aint I going!" she shook him.

Raven stepped over to the porch. "Quel, this aint working. Yall are getting her all worked up, and that's not good for her or the baby. Maybe yall need to think of a better resolution."

Wrapping his arms around her, Wale attempted to hold Keyasia still. "Alright, man, calm down. Your body is hot. Stop all that crying." He wiped her tears away.

Kevin huffed out in frustration. It was painfully clear that his daughter wasn't going anywhere without that nigga.

Raquel closed her eyes, as she thought years back. She'd loved Kevin beyond reason, and there wasn't a person walking the earth who could change that. There was no talking her down, then and now. She'd been a fool, thinking that her child would be any different. They loved hard. To a fault, really.

Nicole Jackson

"Kevin," she whispered.

"Huh?" he furrowed his brows.

"Let's get the both of them to come to the house. That's the only way she'll come, and I can't sleep at night, unless my child is safe under the same roof, right now."

Kevin exhaled, realizing that she was right.

"I'm not going," Key carried on, refusing to let up.

Kevin cleared his throat. "Wale."

Wale glanced up, while still holding an irate Keyasia.

"Why don't the both of yall come to the house, until this shit blows over, man?"

Wale paused, truly not expecting that. "I…I don't know."

"Please, baby," Keyasia blubbered. "Don't make me go without you. We need you."

Feeling her body tremble, and the look of devastation written on her face was too much for him. In good conscience, he couldn't add to her worries. Therefore, he had no choice. He took a deep breath, before caving in. "Alright, Keyasia. I'll go."

******

It was one in the morning, and Wale was sitting poolside, puffing on a blunt, attempting to clear his mind. Life was funny as hell. He'd been on his own since his mid-teens, and after confessing his love to a broad, he was now under her parents' roof. Love was clearly a powerful force, because two years back no one could've paid him to make a move such as this.

After getting Keyasia worked up the way that she was, they decided to take her to the emergency room earlier, where the doctor diagnosed her with high blood pressure. Therefore, everyone had vowed to keep her stress down to a minimum, which was why Wale was out in Katy, instead of combing the streets for Lani.

Once she'd fallen asleep, he made his way outside. There was so much on his mind, and he was frustrated, because he couldn't deal with his problems in a manner he was used to. He now had to think about how his actions with effect Keyasia and their child, which had him in uncharted waters. For the first time in years, he was considering walking away from the game.

Never in life had he experienced a love like he had with Keyasia. It was empowering, and urged him to be a better man. However, it was also downright terrifying. For so many years he'd been getting money the fast way, and it provided a very comfortable lifestyle, but he'd spend it as soon as he'd get it. It wasn't to say that he didn't have a stash, but five hundred racks was virtually nothing, when he could spend upwards to thirty grand in one month.

In his eyes, there simply wasn't enough cash flow to walk away, right now. So, his mind was working overtime, thinking of a way that he could have it all. The money and his family. Then there was the impending threat of Lani pulling another stunt, but frankly, Wale had dealt with bigger fish, and wasn't the least bit concerned. The way he was feeling…he could break the bitch's neck with his bare hands. Yet, he also fully understood Keyasia's parents' concerns. What parent in their right mind would be comfortable with their child getting mixed up in murders and home invasions?

"I gotta get my shit together," he mumbled to himself, as he blew smoke into the night's air.

Nicole Jackson

"Yeah you do," a voice agreed, startling him.

Wale's head snapped around, realizing that Kevin was standing behind him. "Damn, I didn't hear you come out here."

Kevin smirked. "You wasn't supposed to. Been the predator far too long to ever become the prey."

Wale nodded. "I feel that."

"Hell yeah," Kevin breathed, as he grabbed a chair, and copped a seat. "Usually, I'm the one out here, smoking."

Wale extended his arm, offering him the blunt. Civilly, he accepted, taking a few drags off the exotic marijuana. Blowing smoke through his nostrils, he focused on Wale's face. "Keyasia...she's crazy about you, man. I've never seen my daughter act like that. Reminds me of her mama back in the day," he leered.

Wale bobbed his head. "Big homie, I'm crazy about *her*. So, it's a two-way street."

Kevin narrowed his eyes. "You love my daughter, nigga?"

Wale gulped. "With everything in me."

Kevin reclined in his seat, as he rubbed his chin. "I hear you, but I'm not gonna lie to you. A part of me was hoping that this thing with you and her was a phase."

"Damn," Wale grunted. "Tell a nigga how you really feel."

"That's no disrespect to you, man. I fuck with you. You know that, but as men we always want our daughters with men better than us. So, the last thing I wanted was for her to run out and get a wilder version of myself."

"I understand that. Even more so since I'll have a daughter in a few."

"Yeah, you'll see how it is when the baby gets here. For sure," Kevin commented. "And I'ma tell you this. Although, I see a lot of myself in you, I also recognize that you're smarter. Shit, you've been doing your thing. Bigger than a lot of other niggas have, who've mastered the same hustle. And just think what you could do, man, if you channeled all that ingenuity into something legal. You have an intelligent girl on your side, and there aint nothing wrong with you allowing her to pitch in. If yall are truly in this together, then yall should make a way together. A way that aint putting her or your baby in constant danger."

Wale rubbed his hands together. "I can't argue with anything you just said."

"I hope not, man, and honestly, I learned a lot today myself. I see that my daughter is grown, and has really made her own family. That makes you a part of *this* family, so I want you to know that I aint the enemy. I'm not trying to break you and her up. I respect what yall have, because that's all I wanted when me and Quel was coming up. Still, I won't sit here, and bullshit you. I'm gonna push you, and you know why?"

"Why?" Wale furrowed his brows.

"Because that's what Keyasia deserves. She needs your hundred and ten percent, and as her father I can't see her getting anything less."

Wale nodded, as he listened intently. "I feel you. I really feel you, and on my life that's exactly what she'll get."

Chapter 38

"Keyasia, quit playing with me, man. What are you doing on Homestead?" Wale pressed.

Key giggled, as she facetimed him. She'd left the house merely two hours earlier, and he was already hounding her, demanding that she come back. "Corinthian, keep your drawls on. I'm hanging with Jazel and Taraj. We're riding with her sister-in-law, and she stopped to visit her cousin here in Swiss Village."

"Swiss Village?! Is you serious? That apartment complex be on the news every other night."

She glanced around, as she stood on the sidewalk. "And I know every other person over here. Chill out."

"Girl, hang up on his ass. Nobody says a damn thing when he hangs in the jungle for hours, waving his pistol around," Jazel pushed, leaning her head into the camera's view.

He snorted, "Jazel, you need to mind your business. I'm about to call Craven, anyway. I bet he don't know your ass is over there, neither."

She hooded her eyes. "I knew you looked like a damn snitch. Keep talking and I'ma buy Keyasia a soda. We both know you'd die if she drunk something bad for that baby."

Keyasia tittered. "Bitch, you play too much."

Wale squinted, as he tried to see what Jazel was doing, as she was now behind Keyasia. "What…what the hell do Jazel have back there?"

Keyasia glanced over her shoulder. "Oh, her brother gave her his pit-bull."

"What the fuck is she gonna do with that dog? It's bigger than her ass."

"Piru, sit," a chick with the hugest booty Wale had ever seen commanded. The dog obediently did as he was told.

"Who is that?" Wale squawked.

Keyasia glanced back, and laughed. "Oh, you see all that ass, huh? Well, that's Aaron. Jazel's sister-in-law."

He sucked his teeth. "Main, aint nobody looking at that girl's ass," he lied.

"Whatever," she smiled.

"I know my eyes aint playing tricks on me," Taraj blurted.

Key whipped her head around. "What happened?"

Taraj pointed. "Aint that Lani's bitch ass across the parking lot?"

Key squinted. "Hell, yeah. That's that hoe."

"Say, Keyasia, you chill out. I'm finna come through there. Don't you do a muthafuckin' thing. You hear me?" Wale hopped up, scrambling to find his keys.

Keyasia wasn't listening to a word he said, as she and her friends jogged through the lot.

"Keyasia!" he shouted to no avail.

"All you bitches wanna run up on me?!" Lani yelled, balling her fists. "What's up? You mad because I sat on our babies' daddy's dick? Did he tell you how I fucked the shit out of him?"

"Bitch, he told me that you tried to hop on him while he was sleep. He said that pussy is open like the seven seas," Taraj rebutted.

"Yeah, just like ya mammy's!"

"Oh, you don't know me, because that bitch go too! Yeah, what's up now, bitch?!" Taraj shouted, before charging at Lani.

The dog began barking, as Jazel swung.

"Nah, nah!" Aaron yelled, pulling Jazel back. "You're carrying that baby. Let sis handle this." she handed her the dog's leash. Aaron then proceeded to grip Lani's weave, yanking her to the ground.

"Get that hoe!" Keyasia gritted, as Taraj and Aaron stomped her.

"Fuck all you bitches!" Lani taunted through a bloody mouth.

"Fuck me, bitch?! Fuck me, bitch?" Taraj went berserk, kicking Lani's head repeatedly. "I should kill this hoe!"

Jazel hatefully spat in her hair. "I hope this hoe die."

The dog growled.

Jazel glanced down at the dog, as an idea came to her. "Hey, yall back up. I'm finna unleash this dog on her ass."

Immediately, Aaron and Taraj retreated, as Jazel released the pit.

"Bite her, Piru," Jazel instructed, before the dog viciously bit into Lani's flesh.

"Ooooooowwww!" she howled in pain. "Help meeeeee! Somebody please!"

"Shut up, hoe," Taraj spewed, kicking Lani, while Piru continued his attack.

"Keyasia, that's enough. Yall need to burn off, before the laws get there. They're taking her to jail the minute they run her name, anyway. Leave!" Wale demanded.

Seemingly, Keyasia came to her senses. "Jazel, get the dog, and let's go."

Jazel nodded. "Piru! Stop!"

Being well-trained, Piru followed her orders, and released a bleeding Lani.

"Fuck her," Aaron spat. "Let's go, yall."

Collectively, the women ran back to Aaron's Escalade, and hopped inside along with the dog. Aaron then calmly drove out of the lot, while Lani was still lying on the pavement. A few older women had come to her aid, and appeared to be calling the paramedics.

Wale was considerably calmer, as he thought about damage control. "Keyasia, tell ole girl to call her cousin, and get her to stand around to see what happens to Lani. If the police roll up, make sure that they find out exactly who she is. Then her word won't mean shit. That bitch is wanted for armed robbery, fraud, and accessory to murder."

Keyasia nodded, before glancing up, realizing that Aaron was already on the phone, doing just that.

"Trust me, we aint got nothing to worry about. Kimmy knows everybody over there, and that bitch is solid. She's so down with the scheme that she'll give the laws a whole statement, giving the names of hoes she have beef with," Jazel spoke up.

Aaron nodded. "That's what she's doing, right now. The police are there, and she's telling a whole slew of lies. And then she say that nobody is defending Lani, because half the girls outside have issues with her," she reported, as her cousin gave her a play by play. "Ooh, shit. They're putting her in handcuffs, and the bitch is crying."

"Good," Keyasia mumbled.

"That aint good enough. I wish that I could go back and put a bullet in that bitch's head," Taraj seethed, as she thought about all the pain Lani had caused in her life.

"No bullshit," Jazel co-signed. "The police better keep her ass, otherwise I promise that I got something hot for her ass. Aint no place in the city safe for that bitch."

******

"I don't get why you won't let me drive," Keyasia pouted.

"Cause I keep telling you. You act like this is a fuckin' race car. I'ma fuck around and sell it," Wale chided.

"Yeah, yeah," she rolled her eyes.

He shook his head, as he focused on the road. "I don't know what's been up with you, lately. You and Jazel act like yall run some type of pregnant broad's mafia. Running up on bitches, attacking them with dogs, and shit. Almost had me lose my religion on your ass. Out there tripping with my fuckin' baby. I don't know what be going on in that head of yours. It's like the further the pregnancy gets the more you lose your mind."

"Corinthian, miss me with that. Aint nothing crazy about me. We couldn't pass up on that opportunity. At least I didn't fight the bitch myself. Lord knows that I wanted to."

"And if you would have I would've fucked you up, right after."

"Yeah, right," she smirked. "Fuck me up, and risk hurting Corian? Picture that." She knew that he'd never do any such thing, especially if it would agitate their daughter.

He shook his head, knowing she had him. "Whatever."

Seconds later, they pulled up to Trace's home. Wale had known him for years, through Kaydoa, and they'd often put in work together. He'd swung by that day to discuss a possible play that Trace was orchestrating. Of course, Keyasia was none the wiser, as he'd told her that they were there for a mere social call.

Together they exited the Ferrari, and tracked up the driveway. Before they reached the door, Monkey swung it open. "Well, if aint the Money Team. Nah, nah, yall the Pretty Team. Big Ballin' Team," she joked.

Keyasia playfully rolled her eyes. "Monkey, your ass always gotta have jokes."

"I know," Monkey grinned, revealing the gold on her front teeth.

Key had known Monkey for years, because they were both from Fifth Ward. Monkey was a tad older, a little funny looking, but had a superb figure, and was cool as hell.

"Pretty eyes," Monkey referred to Wale. "They're all waiting on you in the back."

Wale nodded, as he and Keyasia stepped into the house.

"Key, too bad you can you can't have none of these drinks, girl," Monkey taunted, as Wale strolled past the living room.

Keyasia glanced around the room, and noticed that there were a handful of women sitting on the couch, each sipping on a cocktail. "Hello," she spoke to everyone.

"Bitch, don't be shy. Have a seat," Monkey urged.

Key nodded, as her mental wheels began spinning. The women and men being in two different rooms definitely smelled like a low key meeting to her. She couldn't keep her composure, as she thought about going off. The dust hadn't even settled from the Lani situation, and he was toying with the idea of putting himself back out there.

The women cackling around her was like inaudible noise, as she thought of a way to figure out what Wale was up to. Her feet were bouncing all over the place, as she became anxious.

"Keyasia, what's wrong? If you need to use the bathroom, its right up the hall," Monkey offered.

"Okay," she sighed, as she slowly scooted off the couch. "Right up the hall, you say?"

"Yeah." Monkey nodded.

Key wobbled through the hall, right past the bathroom. Following the voices, she found herself near the den. Quietly, she leaned against the wall, listening.

"So, are you down, man?" Trace questioned. "I mean, when you look at it, it's a no-brainer. We're talking millions here."

"I don't know," Wale hesitated.

"See, man, I told you that nigga wouldn't be with it," some dude voiced. Keyasia couldn't determine who he was.

"What is there not to know?" Trace pressed.

"Well, for one, you say it's a inside insurance job, but you claim that we need pistols. Since when do you need a gun to break into a building? Nigga, that's the difference between a two to five, and a ten to twenty. What I do has high payoffs with minimum risks. Jail sentences are light for burglary, Trace. We know this. This shit you proposing sounds riskier than a muthafucka, and that's not something I want to jump headfirst into," Wale explained.

"Trace, you said that he was in for sure. If that nigga aint trying to eat, then something aint right. You got me rethinking shit," the same unknown dude commented.

"Look, the guns are for show. They'll be guards there, but they're in on it. It's politics. The owners want the job to look legit."

"Shit still don't sound right to me."

"Man," Trace stressed. "Wale, my nigga, you gon leave me hanging like this?"

"Trace, why you trying to make this personal, when we discussing business? Don't try to pull that guilt trip bullshit on me. We all came into this world by ourselves, and that's how we'll leave this bitch. So, I'ma do what's best for me and mine. And right now I don't know if I want to do this. But I'll be in touch," Wale uttered, before sauntering out of the room.

Keyasia gasped, as he bumped right into her within the corridor. He frowned, but didn't say a word, as he pulled her hand. Speedily, he guided her through the house.

"Yall gone already?" Monkey probed, as they stepped to the front door.

"Yeah, she aint feeling too good," Wale spoke up, pulling the door open.

"Okay, well, feel better, girl," Monkey called out, as they exited the door.

"What was you doing in that hallway, Keyasia?" he quizzed, as they dropped down into the Ferrari.

"I was looking for the bathroom."

He shook his head, as he backed out of the driveway. "Don't lie to me."

She absently gazed out of the window. "I know you're not going to work with them, right?"

He clenched his teeth, as his temples thumped. "Keyasia, I probably would have had to kill one of them niggas if they'd caught you listening, thinking that I'm on some snake shit."

"Fuck them," she spat, whipping her head around. "I don't give a fuck about any of 'em. I heard yall talk about guns, and I know that's not your M.O."

He grimaced. "Keyasia, what I do out here in these streets is not for us to discuss."

"So, what you do doesn't affect me, right?" she bucked her eyes.

"I'm done with this conversation," he grumbled.

"Oh, you don't want to talk about that, huh? You can tell me what I need to do, and how I should I do it, but I can't tell you shit? Yeah, okay. Duly noted."

"You tripping."

"Tripping?!" she snapped. "Nah, I aint tripping. I'm getting tired of this bullshit is what I am. We've been through all this drama. You acted like I was the worst person on earth for choosing not to have those babies. You said that you wanted me to have faith in you, and now look at us. I'm having your child. I put my fuckin fears aside, and you aint man enough to do the same."

His scowl deepened. "I'm not man enough for what? What are you talking about?"

"You aint man enough to do what every other man has to do. You refuse to get your shit together, and find a legal way to make your bread. And if you think that I'ma be running up and down the road to see you when your ass goes to jail…you got me fucked up!"

He nodded. "I hear you. Go ahead. Speak that real shit. Let the truth come out. When I go to jail you aint fuckin with me, huh? Not *if* but *when*. Okay, I got you."

"You know that's not what I fuckin' meant. Quit trying to twist my words. I was just saying…"

"You was just saying how you feel," he cut her off. "No need to try and clean that shit up. You down, but you aint *down* like that."

"Corinthian, that is not what I'm saying. I just want you to understand that the things you do has no good endings. It's really time for a change. I'm tired of losing sleep, worrying about you. I'm tired of all this gun totting, constantly looking over your shoulder bullshit!" she raged.

"Alright, I got you. It's all good, and understood. I'm on my own."

As Key felt a spike in her blood pressure, she knew that she had to let it go. "You know what? That's your fuckin' life. So, if you wanna throw it all away…that's on you. I'm done with the shit," she spewed. "I got my own fuckin' problems."

******

For five days, there'd been an awkward silence between them. Both were still pretty heated about their argument in the car, but that was merely the tip of the iceberg. The bigger question was what did the future have instore for them?

At this point Keyasia knew that she had to put her child first, and protect her from any and everything, including her own parents if need be. Her child deserved to grow up in a loving, but also safe environment, and she was praying that Wale shared this vision.

Wale found himself at a crossroads. The streets were calling, but it was no longer just about him. His actions could have detrimental effects of the people he loved, but that didn't change what he'd be potentially giving up by passing up this current lick. According to Trace, this next job could be his last, if he played his cards right. Yes, the risks were higher, but so was the payoff. Then what Keyasia hadn't considered was that the lick could offer an out for him. A cool million or two would provide a comfy cushion, and allow investment wiggle room, without putting everything else at stake. That alone could open so many possibilities for them.

Nicole Jackson

Keyasia felt out of whack with her and Wale at odds, as it silently drove her crazy. There it was, barely eleven o'clock, and they were lying in her bed in her room, purposely ignoring each other. Thinking that even if it meant that she had to apologize first, she was going to put their beef to bed once and for all.

"Corinthian?" she hovered her head over his.

He lied with his eyes open, seemingly seeing right past her. "Oh, I didn't know if you still remembered my name."

"How could I forget it?" she whispered.

He swallowed. "What do you want, Keyasia?"

Slowly, she crawled over, straddling him. "I've been thinking about that day in the car."

His gaze remained trained on the ceiling, as he didn't bother responding to her statement.

"I...I didn't mean what I said. I was upset, emotional, and frustrated. But I need you to know that no matter what happens...I'ma be right here. It doesn't matter how much we argue, or if I wholeheartedly disagree with your actions, I'm riding. So, if some shit should ever go down, and the judge hits you with fifty, then I'll be doing that fifty right along with you. Because you are a part of me." She placed his hand on her belly. "You're a part of us, and I'd never turn my back on you. I put that on everything I love."

Wale stroked her stomach without uttering a word.

"You hear me, baby?" she rolled her hips, causing him to harden underneath her.

Still, he said nothing.

"Corinthian," she breathed, as she grabbed his stiffness, removing it out of his boxers. Like second nature, his hands lifted her nightie above her ass. Slightly lifting, she was able to glide down onto his dick.

"Uhh," he grunted against his will.

"Corinthian, do you hear me?" she rocked her hips.

He gripped her hips. "Aw shit," his mouth fell open, as she popped her back.

Swirling her hips, she lifted her nightie above her head. Her swollen melons bounced, as she relentlessly rode his dick. "Umm," she moaned, as he gripped a boob. "Corinthian," she purred. "I love you sooo much, and I'm down to riiiiide."

"Got damn," he jawed, as she was fucking the shit out of him.

Grabbing his hands, she intertwined their fingers. "You hear me Corinthian?"

"Fuck," he bit his bottom lip. "I hear you."

"Tell me you love me," she begged.

"I love you," he admitted.

"Promise that you'll always be here for me, and Corian."

"I'll always be here for you and my daughter."

"You'll never leave us?"

"On my life, I'll never leave yall."

"Promise meee," she threw her head back, as her movements grew wild.

"I promise," he huffed, as his back stiffened.

"Oooouuuu," her body trembled, as she released all over him.

"Come here." He pulled her face down, before sloppily kissing her.

Gradually, she rolled off his dick, and lied beside him. They were both breathing hard, as she dozed off. It wasn't long before she was lightly snoring. After a lovely fuck session her sleep was pleasant, until she could feel Corian all in her back. Wincing from the uncomfortableness, she opened her eyes.

Key frowned, as she noticed that Wale had fully redressed, wearing all black, including his usual *work* hoodie. Immediately, she sat up in bed. "What are you doing?"

He knelt down, tying his shoes. "I'ma make a quick run."

"A quick run? Dressed like that, Corinthian? Really?"

"Come on, Keyasia. Don't start," he groaned.

"Don't start what?" she inquired, easing out of bed. Glancing around, she spotted her nightie. Hurriedly, she pulled it over her head.

He eyed her. "Keyasia, what are you doing, man? Go lay down."

"No, you lay down!" she yelled. "Where are you going, Corinthian?"

"You know where I'm going," he gritted.

"You got me fucked up!" she belted.

Promiscuous Girl: Keyasia and Wale

"Lower your voice," he clenched his teeth.

"Why? You don't want nobody to know that you're about to go break the law? Huh? Is that it?"

"Man," he stressed, as he attempted to stomp around her.

Jumping in front of him, she pressed her body up against the door. "Move Corinthian! You aint going nowhere!" she aggressively shoved his chest.

His jaw twitched, while his phone buzzed in his pocket, and he ran short on patience. "Keyasia move!" he exploded.

"Key," Raquel said from the other side of the door, as she twisted the doorknob. "What's going on in there? Open the door."

"Nothing mama," Keyasia responded in a trembling voice.

"Nothing my ass. Open this damn door!"

"You see what you did?" she cried, before reluctantly easing off the door.

Wale pulled the door open, and was greeted by Raquel and Kevin's scowling faces. "What's going on in here?" Raquel questioned.

Wale shook his head. "That's you daughter in here, tripping."

Kevin frowned, and pulled Quel to the side, allowing Wale to step out of the room.

Keyasia then came barreling out of the room, charging at him. "You aint fucking going nowhere!" she pummeled his back.

"Ay, ay, ay," Kevin corralled her, pulling her back, as Wale jogged downstairs. "The fuck is wrong with you, girl?"

"Daddy, let me go," she huffed, clearly out of breath.

"No, daddy can't let you go. Keep your hands off that man, because if he was putting his hands on you, I'd be ready to grab my pistol."

"Okay, okay," she attempted to seem calm. "I hear you, daddy. You...you can let me go."

The second Kevin released her, she jotted downstairs.

Raquel shook her head. "My child has lost her damn mind."

"Her ass is gonna fuck around and give me my first grey hair," Kevin vented, before descending the stairs. Once again, he found his daughter preventing Wale from exiting out of a door.

"Keyasia, let me go. I'll be back, girl." Wale struggled to pry her hands off him.

"You aint going nowhere! I told you that." She dug her nails into his arm.

"Key, stop this shit," Kevin commanded, yanking her back.

Wale then proceeded to the garage, where he grabbed a black tool bag. After grabbing his trappings, he hit a button, opening the garage's door. Before he could step fully outside, Keyasia was meeting him in the driveway.

"Corinthian, come in the house," she demanded.

Raquel stood beside her. "Keyasia, let him go. You come in this house."

Wale marched towards his car, and she sprinted in front of him again. "Corinthian, please," she sobbed, snot dripping from her nose. "Don't go. I got a bad feeling about this. Just stay here with me and the baby. I'm begging you."

"Keyasia, man, I'ma be right back. Let me go so that I can come back," he pleaded, as she held onto his hoodie.

"Nooooo. Stay with meeeee," she boohooed.

"Let him go, girl." Kevin stepped in, prying her hands off him.

Wale adjusted his now crooked hoodie, as he stepped to his Audi.

"Corinthian! You gon leave us? You really gon leave us?!" she screamed. "Wale, you don't hear me talking to you?"

Wale opened his backdoor, and tossed the bag inside.

"Bitch ass nigga, you don't hear me?! Huh? You fuckin' liar! You just told me that you'd never leave us! That's what you said, but you're a fucking liar!"

He paused, as his phone did a jig in his pocket. "I'm not lying, Keyasia. I'll be right back."

"Lies! You fuckin' liar! Put that on a bible! I bet you can't, because there is no guarantees! But I tell you what. Right now. Here today. You gotta choose. It's either me and Corian, or them fuckin' streets. You can't have us all. Choose!" she roared.

He placed his hands in prayer position. "Keyasia, chill, baby. I'll be right back."

"Fuck that!" she spewed. "Choose you fuckin' coward!"

"I'll be right back." He grabbed his door handle.

Her chest heaved up and down, as he slid into the car.

"I'll be right back," he reiterated.

"Fuck you!" she lashed. "If you leave, don't ever fuckin' come back! We don't need you!"

"I'll be right back." He closed the car's door, and pulled away from the curb.

"I hate yoouuuuu," she howled, as she watched him drive down the street.

Raquel held her head, as Kevin grabbed Key. "Let's go in the house, baby girl. You've done enough clowning. If he wanna go, then let him go. Fuck it."

"Daddy, why did you let him leave?"

Kevin didn't know what else to say.

Keyasia's lips quivered, as she whimpered. Slowly, she tracked back up to the garage. Spotting a chair, she grabbed it, and flopped down.

"Key, come on. Let's go in the house, baby," Raquel insisted.

Wiping a tear, she shook her head. "Give me a minute, mama. I'm sorry for disrespecting yall's house, but I need moment alone."

Nicole Jackson

Raquel lifted her head, locking eyes with Kevin. He gave her a slight head nod. Reluctantly, she twisted back into her home, giving her daughter some space, with Kevin trailing right behind her.

After driving through the neighborhood, Wale reached the exit gate. His phone was continuously buzzing, and he finally decided to pick up. "Yeah?"

"Say, nigga, where you at?" Trace wasted no time.

"I'm on the way, why, what's up?"

"Shit, we already at the spot. Hold up," Trace turned his attention to something in the background. "Nigga, use the sledge hammer. Not the crowbar. Did you remember to grab the wire cutters?"

Wale had to remove the phone from his face for a second, and stare at it. "Is this nigga really hitting a lick, with me on the phone, while he's on his personal fucking line?"

"Hello," Trace spoke into the phone. "Yeah, as soon as we leave this bitch, I'm falling off in V-Live, making it rain on some hoes. You know how we do. Win big. Spend big. Then do it all again."

Wale had heard his boys say this a few times, but never had it sounded so stupid to him. They were putting their freedom on the line to live the highlife that was equipped with mountains of worry and strife. What a thoughtless, selfish, redundant way to live?

Keyasia's face popped into his head. He could see her streaming tears vividly, and it fucked him up. He said that he'd never cause her that type of pain again, yet there they were. He just couldn't get right.

"Say, how long will it be, before you pull up?" Trace wanted to know.

Wale closed his eyes, as he tried to gather his thoughts. He considered his girl. His baby. His responsibilities as a man. Fuck it. He had to do what he had to do, no matter who didn't agree with it. It was what it was. "Give me thirty minutes, man. I'll be there."

******

Keyasia sat in the chair, in the garage, sending him angry, long, and drawn out, text messages. She had to cuss his ass out. She'd completely submitted to his will, giving him everything he'd asked of her, but he couldn't give the one thing she requested. The one thing she needed from him.

"I can't stand his bitch ass," she sniveled with tears still in her throat. "All this talk of loving me. That nigga don't love nobody but himself. Chasing fucking money. That shit comes, and goes. I would be happy broke as fuck, in a one room shack, with me, him, and Corian, and would be just fine. But no. His stupid ass can't see that."

"He can't see what? And who's stupid, girl?" Wale questioned, emerging from the dark, startling the hell out of her.

"What the fuck?" she gasped, holding her chest.

He smiled, as he dropped his tool bag near her feet. "You was so busy talking that shit that you never saw me coming."

"What…what are you doing here?"

He stroked his goatee. "I could've sworn that this is where you strong armed me into staying."

"Fuck you," she sneered.

"Watch your mouth," he playfully poked her temple. "And what the fuck is you doing here, outside by yourself? It's late as fuck."

She sucked her teeth. "Boy, bye. We're in a gated community, and aint nobody thinking about my ass."

"Well, that's a lie right there. *I'm* thinking about your ass…all the time. Even when I don't want to."

"Tuh." She snaked her neck. "Well, what happened to you going to *work?*"

He smirked. "Dealing with your crazy ass is all the *work* I can handle right now."

She tried her hardest to conceal the blushing, but it was useless. He had her. "So, you brought your raggedy ass back to us?"

He knelt over, kissing her lips. "I never left. Couldn't get beyond the gate. Your annoying ass voice was stuck in my head. Choose Corinthian. Choose," he mimicked her.

She smiled from ear to ear. "It comes a time where you have to listen to me. I listen to you."

He pulled her to her feet, and into his arms. "Believe me. I listen to you. Fuck. I aint got a choice. Ole loud ass. Corinthian, you's a bitch ass nigga," he mocked.

She tittered. "Well, at least you know that I say it with love."

Nicole Jackson

The Epilogue

"Kevia, why are you over there, bothering those people?" Raquel yelled from the hallway.

Kevia glanced up at her mama with her thumb in her mouth. "Mama, I'm rubbing my fat sister's feet. I know you gon let me."

Keyasia's head shot up as she was leaning on Wale's shoulder. "Fat? Kevia, really?"

She giggled. "Sister, you know that I'm only playing. You're not fat. More like pleasantly plump."

"Now see." Key yanked her feet out of her sister's grasp. "I'm not about to play with you, little girl."

"Who's playing? I was trying to do my brother, Wale, a favor. I know he's tired of scratching your wide back, and rubbing your crusty feet every other hour."

"Mama!" Keyasia shouted. "Please come get your daughter."

Wale chuckled heartily. "Kevia is my lil' homie. She holds no punches. Serving you a dose of your own medicine."

"Fuck you," she grumbled, as Kevia hopped off the couch, running off to disturb someone else's peace.

"Oh shit, let me catch the news," Wale chattered, lifting the remote.

Key cut her eyes at him, finding it odd that he watched the news religiously, especially after he'd hit a lick. There were a few times where they'd sat watching TV, knowing that they were seeing him on the screen in his *work* clothes.

After he turned to channel thirteen's news, their jaws dropped. "Say," he mouthed.

Keyasia shook her head. "That's a damn shame. Look at your boy. Trace didn't have to take that mugshot with his mouth wide open like that."

"What the fuck happened?" Wale asked aloud, as the news switched to another story. As if on cue, his cell rung. "Hello," he answered.

"Nigga, was you watching the news?" Craven cut straight to the point.

"I caught the tail end."

"So, you saw our boy, Trace, huh?"

"Hell, yeah. But I didn't catch what happened."

"Shit, they're saying that it was a sting operation, and Trace's ass fell for the okeydokey. Some detectives had him believing that they were the owners of a jewelry store, and then they entrapped his ass, telling him to bring pistols. His dumb ass is going down for robbery, nigga."

Wale was floored. "Man, get the fuck outta here. Did they catch everybody?"

"Hell yeah. Shit, they even shot one of them niggas, claiming he was aiming a gun at them. I was tripping out, because I know that you was considering rolling with them. Then Big Block called and told me that you sat this one out."

"Hell yeah, but I aint gon lie, I was about to go. I got dressed, hopped in the car, the whole nine."

"So, what happened?"

"Keyasia. Her ass got to going crazy, telling me that something bad was gonna happen, and I needed to choose either her or the streets."

"No bullshit?"

"Yep."

"That's some deep shit, but I know you're glad you listened, nigga. Her crazy ass is good for something. She got your stubborn ass to stay out the way."

"Fuck you," he chuckled.

"No, but seriously. Key, that's my dog. She be looking out for your ass. Be getting you to sit down when nobody else can. She's good for you, man. Do right by her."

"Get the fuck outta here. Where the fuck is all this talk, coming from?"

"I'm saying, I feel like it's time for a change. I got a healthy baby due any day now. My gal has been keeping her nose clean, chilling. And I just got other shit that I wanna focus on. You feel me?"

"Yeah, I definitely feel you," Wale admitted.

"Real. But say, I'ma let you go. Jazel over here, smuggling soda in my fuckin' house, and I'ma end up hurting her ass," he said loudly, making sure that she heard him.

"Nigga, fuck you!" she shouted in the background. "You aint my daddy, and I'ma drink all the soda I want."

"Girl, you got me fucked up!" Craven belted, ending the call.

Keyasia giggled, having heard the entire phone conversation.

"What's so funny?" he poked her side.

"You and your throwed off ass cousin."

"Oh, okay, says the woman who don't mind causing scenes everywhere she goes. Always running her mouth, thinking she can whup everybody and their mamas. Jumping ships. Coming to the club with one nigga, and leaving with another."

"Shit, and says the nigga who low key likes when I cause scenes over him. He wanna carry a gun every place he goes, and swears he's the hardest nigga around. Then he goes to the club, pull other niggas' dates. Even if it's his boy's, and then let's the broad sit on his face on the first night."

He laughed. "You always gotta call a nigga out. Shit, I should've made your ass wait a little while. I went in, eating pussy, and shit, but still ended up in love after one night. On some sucker shit."

She grinned. "Don't feel bad. My ass was in love too. Hell, I had to be. Aint no way in hell I'd let another nigga fuck me outside on a damn picnic table. Damn ants was all in my ass crack."

"I know one thing. I better not catch yall nasty asses fucking in my backyard!" Raquel yelled, clearly eavesdropping.

They beheld at each other, smiling. With all the things Wale had done in life, he never thought he'd find himself on some girl's parents' couch, while her mama sneakily listened to their conversation. And he definitely never thought he'd feel like there was no other place on earth he'd rather be. After experiencing enough for two men, he'd found all he needed within Key.